PRAISE FOR *A HEART LIKE HOME*

"*A Heart Like Home* tells the story of two children deeply traumatized by abuse and loss, and the emotionally closed-off woman who takes them in. An adoptive parent herself, Nolfi writes with flawless empathy and understanding about the ugliness of family violence but, more importantly, about the healing power of love and belonging. A perfect book club read."

—Kerry Anne King, bestselling author of *Whisper Me This* and *A Borrowed Life*

"In *A Heart Like Home*, Christine Nolfi delivers a masterful plot brimming with family secrets, suspense, and tough choices for its engaging, believable characters. Perfect for book clubs, it will appeal to the reader who enjoys emotionally satisfying, top-tier women's fiction."

—Julianne MacLean, bestselling author of *These Tangled Vines* and *A Storm of Infinite Beauty*

"Nolfi engages readers with her signature depth and wisdom in this emotional story of becoming family even when the odds are stacked up against you. A book that will stay with readers long after the last page, and a family who reminds us of what it means to be truly connected. This is Nolfi at her very best. *A Heart Like Home* is poignant and unputdownable."

—Rochelle B. Weinstein, bestselling author of *What You Do To Me*

A Heart Like Home

A NOVEL

ALSO BY CHRISTINE NOLFI

A Brighter Flame

The Passing Storm

The Road She Left Behind

The Sweet Lake Series

Sweet Lake

The Comfort of Secrets

The Season of Silver Linings

The Liberty Series

Second Chance Grill (Book 1)

Treasure Me (Book 2)

The Impossible Wish (Book 3)

Four Wishes (Book 4)

The Tree of Everlasting Knowledge (Book 5)

The Dream You Make

Heavenscribe: Part One

Heavenscribe: Part Two

Heavenscribe: Part Three

A Heart Like Home

A NOVEL

CHRISTINE NOLFI

LAKE UNION
PUBLISHING

Published by Lake Union Publishing, Seattle

www.apub.com

Amazon, the Amazon logo, and Lake Union are trademarks of Amazon.com, Inc., or its affiliates.

ISBN-13: 9781662514074 (paperback)
ISBN-13: 9781662514067 (digital)

Cover design by Amanda Kain
Cover image: ©Lynn Whitt / Arcangel; © oksanka007 / Shutterstock

Printed in the United States of America

For Maxwell, Liam, and Alice,
the newest branches of our family tree

Chapter 1

BELLA

Spring 1982

Lights of red and blue flashed through the living room curtains and leaped onto the ceiling. Bella's heart jumped. The lights raced across the expanse toward the cobwebs fluttering down in the corners like swatches of old lace.

Her brother lay beside her on the floor with his eyes shut. Henry breathed softly, his cheek pressed against a Luke Skywalker action figure. His fingers curled around the blanket they'd carried downstairs after Pa went out. Sitting up, Bella watched the pulsing lights reveal dark spots on the living room ceiling. A spiderweb shimmered by the front door.

The sound of grown-ups talking drifted in from the front yard. The muffled voices prodded Bella to her feet. She pricked her ears, but the thread of conversation was impossible to untangle. Why were people outside? This late at night, only a dog barking or an owl hooting ever broke the silence.

Henry's eyelashes fluttered. Still, he slept on.

Needing to investigate, Bella crawled across the couch, an item of furniture she normally avoided since their move to Chardon. She didn't like the house. The furniture smelled bad. Green mold climbed the sides of the bathtub. The windows rattled in strong winds. Whenever she and Henry slept in the bedroom they shared upstairs, something scurried inside the walls. Mice or rats, or something larger, Henry believed, like the racoons they often spotted beneath the trees out back when the sun dipped low, burning the sky crimson.

Bella drew back the curtain to peer out. The breath froze in her throat. In the gravel driveway, a tall policeman listened closely to an old lady in a fluffy green robe. Wrinkles crisscrossed the lady's pale skin. Talking fast, she gestured toward the house. When she finished, she walked across the street. She disappeared inside a blue house with white shutters.

The officer strode to the curb.

A car eased to a stop. A Black lady got out.

Fear needled Bella's tummy. She was seven years old—two years younger than Henry, but no baby. She was old enough to spot trouble, and she knew better than to answer the door. She never disobeyed Pa's rules for weekend nights: Stay inside, out of sight. Don't make a ruckus someone might hear. *Since they'd moved in, Pa had avoided the neighbors. He didn't like anyone sticking their nose in his business.*

Scrambling off the couch, she knelt beside her brother. "Henry, wake up!"

He rolled over, away from her. "Go away. I'm tired."

"There are people outside."

"It's just the racoons. They won't hurt you."

"No, it's grown-ups. There's a policeman."

The announcement pulled Henry's eyes open. He was on his feet in an instant.

He swung his gaze across the room, taking in the lights strobing across the ceiling and the lamp they'd turned on before falling asleep. "We're hiding. Now." He flicked off the lamp.

"Where?"

"In the kitchen." Grabbing her hand, he tugged her forward.

"Wait!" Bella pulled free. "I have to get my treasure."

She'd left the heart-shaped tin in the center of the blanket. Once used for chocolates on some long-ago holiday, the container held Bella's most cherished possessions. Since Mama's death, the candy tin was the lifeline keeping her afloat. She rarely let it out of her sight.

Henry flapped his arms. "Just leave it!"

The command went ignored. Scooping it up, she raced back to him.

The kitchen floated in darkness. Only the faint moonbeam arcing across the floor gave a sense of direction. Sprinting toward it, Henry banged open the cupboard beneath the sink. The empty space exhaled the damp odor of rot mixed with a sharp chemical smell. Bella's eyes watered.

She pinched her nose shut. "Don't make me go in there." She stepped back. "Please, Henry."

"Stop acting like a baby."

"The cupboard smells. Can't we hide upstairs?"

"There's no time. Get in!"

Relenting, Bella dropped to her knees. She crawled inside. Her brother came next, scooting backward on his butt. Drawing his legs up to his chest, he reached for the cupboard door. It snapped shut, making them both jump. They sat shoulder to shoulder, panting.

The air stretched tight in the house.

A light rap sounded on the front door. When no answer came, a series of knocks followed, harder this time.

"Chardon PD." A man's voice—calm, strong. "Please answer the door."

Bella squeezed her eyes shut. Would the policeman find their hiding place? A sensation like falling plummeted through her as she imagined Pa's reaction when he learned they'd disobeyed. They'd catch hell. Bella knew to accept the punishments when they came, never making a peep. But Mama's death had changed Henry's behavior in upsetting ways. Lately he was prone to fighting back, battling with Pa for long minutes.

The doorbell sang out, one, two, three times. Then a rattling commenced. Would they break in? The answer became clear when the front door burst open. Bella sank her head onto Henry's shoulder.

"Hello? Children, it's all right. Where are you?"

A woman's voice. Young, like Mama's, before she was laid out in a box. "Don't be afraid. You can come out. We're here to help you."

Inside the cupboard's muddy darkness, Bella ran trembling fingers across her treasure chest. She traced a path around the curved edge, willing the object to calm her.

She considered opening the tin to retrieve the picture. The edges of the photograph were soft from handling. The image on its glossy surface gave Bella comfort pure as Mama's arms whenever she'd rocked her to sleep. Nothing held more goodness than a picture of a mama with her child.

In the living room, something crashed to the floor. She began to whimper, and Henry squeezed her hand. If she took out the photo and made a wish, could she make them both disappear? She'd take them to a happy place where no one could find them.

The notion fled from her thoughts. Heavy footsteps clunked around the living room.

"It's cold in here." The woman.

"The heat's not on in the house."

"The temps are in the fifties tonight. The heat should be on."

"A man who leaves his kids alone doesn't worry about keeping the place warm. According to the neighbor, he goes out a lot. Especially on weekends." Silence. Then: "Imani, why don't you check the kitchen? I'll take the second floor."

"All right."

The kitchen light snapped on. In tandem, Bella and Henry inched their toes away from the yellow glow seeping beneath the cupboard door. A failed effort. It took the lady—Imani—no time at all to find them.

She opened the cupboard, then surprised Bella by taking a step back.

"If we're playing hide-and-seek, you both win." She leaned against the counter, smiling. "My name is Imani Weiss. Who are you?"

Bella whispered her name, adding, "My brother is Henry."

"It's nice to meet you."

A savory aroma flooded Bella's nose. She couldn't resist leaning forward. Craning her neck, she nearly toppled from the cupboard. Imani hid something behind her back.

Food. It smelled delicious.

Imani bent down for a better view, her ebony hair spilling past her shoulders in tight, pretty curls. She came no closer.

"Are you ready to come out? You don't look too comfortable in there."

Henry pressed his face to his knees, refusing to acknowledge her.

She regarded Bella. "Are you hungry?" Her gaze fleetingly landed on the candy tin clutched to Bella's chest. "I brought you a treat. I hope you like it."

With a flourish, Imani drew the bag out from behind her back. She rustled it open. The meaty aroma grew tantalizingly thick in the air. Bella's stomach rumbled. Henry's did, too, but he kept his face stubbornly pressed to his knees. Before Pa had gone out tonight, he'd left a can of spaghetti on the kitchen table with a bag of chips. They'd finished the meal hours ago.

From the bag, Imani withdrew two cheeseburgers and two milkshakes. Turning away, she set the food out on the counter, along with napkins and straws.

Hunger prodded Bella from their hiding place. She'd let Henry eat most of the spaghetti and chips earlier; he was bigger and needed more food to keep going. Now her tummy burned with anticipation. Quiet as a mouse, she darted around Imani, took a cheeseburger, and hurried to the kitchen table. She wanted the milkshake, too, but she didn't have enough hands. Seating herself, she slid her treasure onto her lap.

Unable to resist, she bit into the burger. The cheesy goodness melted in her mouth.

She dared a glance. "You shouldn't be here," she whispered. "Pa will get mad."

"Where is your father?"

Bella lowered her gaze to her treasure. She knew better than to tell on Pa. Would Imani get angry if she didn't answer?

"It's all right, Bella. You can talk to me."

Imani placed a milkshake before her. She didn't look angry. She watched Bella tear the wrapper from the straw and begin drinking the chocolate shake. Above their heads, a thumping bounded down the hallway. The policeman, checking the bedrooms.

"*Does your father usually leave you and Henry alone on Friday nights?*" Imani seated herself at the table. "*The nice woman across the street says he does.*"

From the cabinet, Henry said, "*Stop asking her about Pa. You're scaring her.*"

"*Then why don't you come out and talk to me?*"

"*I don't want to.*"

"*Oh, c'mon. You're a big boy. There's a juicy burger and a chocolate shake waiting for you. Why not eat while we chat?*"

There was no telling what lured Henry out—the promise of a meal or the dare Imani set forth. Henry was *a big boy. He prided himself on the fact.*

Glowering, he crawled out of the cabinet. He took the food, then sat on the floor by the stove.

Imani swiveled in her chair to regard him. "*Where's your father, Henry?*"

"*Pa goes out on weekends.*"

"*To drink?*"

"*He likes to get lucky.*"

"*He gambles?*"

"*No, stupid. He's getting lucky with a chick. You know, at a bar.*" Henry smirked when disapproval flashed through Imani's gaze. "*Pa will sleep somewhere else tonight.*"

"*Does he usually go out on Friday nights?*"

With relish Henry bit into the burger. "*Are you done with the dumb questions?*" He tossed the wrapper aside.

"*Not quite.*" Imani smiled thinly. "*Do you know which bar he's at?*"

"*Pa keeps his business private.*"

"*Where's your mother?*"

"*She died.*"

Sadness rippled across Imani's face. "*What happened to your knee?*" She studied Henry, who was slurping down the milkshake in record time.

Cheeks flushing, he glared at her. Beneath the torn fabric of his jeans, a dark bloodstain formed a circle. The result of his latest fight with Pa.

"We'll have a doctor check you out. At the hospital," she said. "Do you understand? I'm taking you and your sister to stay somewhere safe until we get everything sorted out."

Setting the milkshake aside, Henry tucked his hands beneath his armpits. He arranged his features in a weak imitation of Pa's whenever his face took on thunder. Would the policeman haul him from the house kicking and screaming? What if he refused to go? Bella decided that Imani, with her kind eyes and soft smile, knew tricks to get Henry to agree. She wouldn't hurt him.

Bella hopped off the chair. She wanted Henry to stop looking like a mule.

She began rocking her treasure like a baby she'd lull to sleep. Was her wish coming true? Would Imani take them to a happy place? They'd get more burgers tonight and a big breakfast tomorrow. Eggs and bacon and pancakes piled high in tasty stacks, swimming in a river of golden syrup.

A temptation she quickly suppressed. Leave and they would catch hell once Pa found them missing.

The prospect shivered dread through Bella. When her legs started turning to jelly, Imani—her dark eyes filling now with compassion—came around the table and hugged her close. Bella gratefully sank against her.

The policeman entered the kitchen. Assessing the situation, he nodded with satisfaction. "Ready to go?"

"Just about," Imani told him.

"I found these." He held out two pairs of mud-spattered tennis shoes, one white, one pink.

Bella quickly put hers on.

Chapter 2

NOVA

The dream never changed.

The harsh glare of sunlight filtered through the trees. An empty road swept past cornfields rising in the distance. The mobile home sat near the edge of a forest, the site chosen to avoid prying eyes. Nova shivered with fear in the still, dank space.

The predator was inside the cramped dwelling, but she didn't have the ability to protect herself. The dream had peeled back the years, returning her to childhood with no hope of prevailing against the wolf.

Beneath thick fur, muscles girded the animal's back and hindquarters. They rippled menacingly with each step forward. Through the greasy windows, light slatted across its flattened ears. Slowly, the wolf advanced down the narrow hall, forcing Nova to retreat on unsteady feet. Boxing her in.

Dry mouthed, she reached the entry to the bedroom, where a tall stack of cartons blocked the only means of escape. Was she strong enough to push them out of the way? Make them tumble, and she could sprint to the bed and hide underneath. A child's solution. She'd make herself invisible until the danger passed.

The wolf lowered its head, as if goading her. Nova didn't dare look away. She pressed her back against the cartons and pushed hard. A growl rose from the wolf's throat. She pushed again, but the cartons refused to budge.

The wolf bared its teeth. Death whispered across her lips.

Nova cried out.

With effort she struggled out of the nightmare. Clawed her way past the forbidding images that were so familiar, they were tattooed on her brain. Her pulse beat erratically. Sitting up, she threw off the blanket.

Perspiration slicked down the fiery lengths of her red hair. Swiping a lock from her eyes, Nova made herself focus on the comforting domain of her bedroom, the oak dresser gleaming from a recent dusting, the jungle of plants by the windows reaching thick leaves toward the morning light. Her attention lingered on the photographs of her parents and of the family of her brother, Peter, that formed a pretty triangle on the wall beside the dresser. Love for them crested inside her, an impenetrable shield guarding her against the darkness.

No matter the roadblocks life threw at her, her family never let her down. They were Nova's greatest cheerleaders and steadfast protectors. Out of habit, she sifted through happy memories she'd shared with them. Savored them until the last traces of the wolf melted from her thoughts.

It was a secret embarrassment, how the nightmare still frightened her. How it still managed to invade her sleep after so many years. She was a woman now. Being unable to banish the wolf seemed like a failure.

Because it's not just a dream.

Dread trundled up from her gut.

There's more to it.

With distaste she examined the thought. Poked around the edges like she'd done countless times before. *Every* time she dreamed of the wolf. Normally, she didn't subscribe to superstition. Life was easier to navigate when she grounded herself in common sense. Dreams weren't supposed to *mean* anything. Yet the theory refused her attempts to dislodge it.

The wolf holds a warning. She'd never avoid the peril until she understood what it symbolized.

Nova went into the kitchen and plugged in the coffeepot. *Just let it go.* If the nightmare held an omen of misfortune, what were the odds of deciphering the meaning? In the past she'd tried repeatedly and failed.

A busy Saturday lay ahead. A million tasks awaited her, all of which she planned to tackle. Countdown weekend, with only hours to go. On Monday, she'd begin the most important job of her career.

The phone rang.

"Nova?"

"The one and only," she chirped with false cheer.

"I'm sorry to call this early," Imani said. "I hope I didn't wake you."

Nova glanced at the clock: 7:40 on the dot. Earlier than Imani normally called.

"Is everything all right?"

"Not really. I'm at the office."

The remark slowed Nova's movements. Opening the cupboard, she reached for a coffee mug. Imani was a social worker at Geauga County's Job & Family Services. She rarely worked on weekends.

"Nova, there's been an emergency. I hate to ask . . . can you stop by? I'd rather discuss this in person."

"What? Now?"

"I know it's a lot to ask."

"I'm not awake yet." Nova plucked at the oversize jersey she'd slept in. "I'm not dressed."

"Throw on some jeans and drive over. Please. I'm really in a bind."

Nova hesitated by the desk in the corner of the kitchen, which served as her makeshift office. She'd carved out space for business tasks, with shelves above the desk to hold landscaping books and other supplies. The plans for the Holly estate sat amid a stack of sketchbooks. Notepads crammed full of checklists competed for space with reference books on landscape architecture.

The installation would pay big and take weeks to complete. The design still required a few last-minute changes. She also needed to reread the rental agreement for the backhoe and other heavy equipment, and double-check the orders for plant stock. Dropping by Job & Family Services promised to put her behind schedule before the day officially began.

"Nova? Are you there?"

"Hang tight," she heard herself say. "I'll see you in twenty."

~

Nova steered her Dodge Ramcharger truck into the nearly empty lot before the social agency. Indecision led her into the building. If there was an emergency Imani needed to discuss, it meant only one thing.

In the world of foster care, Nova was an outlier. Twenty-eight, single, and self-employed, she didn't fit the typical background of married couples providing homes for children separated from their parents.

She understood the grim facts better than most. Adults who'd spent time in foster care during childhood were disproportionately represented in prison and homeless populations. They suffered higher incidents of substance abuse and mental illness, especially depression. Prior to 1960, the US Children's Bureau didn't even track the number of children in each state's system. Improvements had been made since then, but many counties lacked adequate funding. Nova felt this was especially troubling for parents desiring to reunite with their children. Many needed intensive drug treatment or counseling services that weren't often available.

Despite Nova's outlier status, she'd made a name for herself by successfully providing short-term care for teenagers. Some of the teens were fairly easy to handle; a few were argumentative or prone to ignore house rules and therefore difficult to place. She took them in anyway. In fact, the first teenager she'd fostered—the huge and soft-spoken Bear

Nowak—began working at her small landscaping firm after aging out of the system.

Inside the lobby, an unfamiliar girl in an REO Speedwagon T-shirt sat behind the reception bay. Nova smiled in greeting.

"I'm Nova Doubeck, here to see Imani Weiss."

The girl barely looked up as Nova signed in. Lanky, sleep-deprived, with dark patches beneath her eyes, she was probably in college, earning credit toward a social services degree and pulling a double on the weekend. A real sacrifice, given the weather. After months of unrelenting snowfall, northeast Ohio basked in the warmest spring in recent memory.

The lobby spun off in two directions. At a fast clip, Nova headed down the corridor to the left. Battling her reservations, she wondered whether the case involved a runaway. Or was a foster home needed for an adolescent with abusive parents? In her experience, the child in question rarely posed the problem. Alcoholism, drug addiction, or just plain indifference—many of the adults whose children landed in foster care were poorly equipped for the demands of parenting.

Inside the cubbyhole office near the end of the corridor, Imani riffled through paperwork. Folders rose in disorganized stacks on her desk. Two metal chairs pressed against the wall by the filing cabinet. The spider plant Nova had given to Imani on her twenty-ninth birthday hung limply by the window.

People were often puzzling, their motives incomprehensible. Plants were quite the opposite. Nova found comfort in the natural world. Plants never hid a secret agenda. They flourished once their simple needs were met. Food, light, water: give each in the proper amount, during the proper season, and the fussiest orchid thrived. Not that the spider plant fell in the "fussy" category. She'd purposely gifted a plant easy to grow.

She fingered a yellowing leaf. "Water, Imani. A plant won't survive without it."

"No lectures. I'm on my way to a five-alarm headache." Imani rubbed her temples. "Why didn't you give me a girly present, like bath salts? Some of us weren't born with a green thumb."

"The plant brightens up your office. It's dreary in here."

"Like I need another chore."

"C'mon. It's not much of an add-on. You juggle work, marriage, and parenting just fine. How *is* Miss Sunshine?"

Last week Imani's daughter, Maya, had taken a spill off her bike, fracturing her ankle. The accident would leave most children with a case of the blues. Not Maya. A veritable chatterbox, she enjoyed regaling the other first graders in her class with descriptions of the race to the hospital and the X-rays taken. Maya was proud of the crutches she'd decorated with rainbow stickers and glitter. The glitter shed a trail of purple sparkles whenever she hobbled past.

"My daughter's sunshiny behavior is long gone. She's cranky this morning."

"Why the change?"

"She's upset because I can't stop her ankle from itching. Like I have the power to make it go away." With agitated movements, Imani began swiveling in her chair. "She was complaining so much while I was getting ready for work, I thought she'd demand I break the cast. She's convinced ants are running around inside."

"The itching comes with the healing. It means the bone is mending."

"Not according to Maya. She's sure ants have invaded." Imani paused in her swiveling to shake her head. "Kids. They get the craziest ideas. Hopefully the cast will come off before I lose my mind. As it is, I'm nearing the edge."

Nova chuckled. "When the cast *does* come off, let's take Miss Sunshine out to celebrate. I'll spring for the pizza." Nothing delighted Maya like a double-cheese pie.

"Thanks. I'll take you up on it."

Letting the subject go, Nova tugged a dead leaf from the spider plant. "Where's the watering can?" It had been part of the birthday present, along with plant food and the macramé hanger.

Imani rummaged beneath her desk. She found the watering can and handed it over. She looked worried. Granted, an emergency foster placement was serious. The parent or parents might require a variety of services, including counseling or rehab, before they were reunited with their child. Yet Nova sensed this case upset her friend more than most.

The conclusion made her uneasy as she walked to the water fountain. Common sense warned she couldn't take on a foster child this week, or anytime soon. The job at the Holly estate would consume all her energies. Much as she hated letting Imani down, she couldn't afford the distraction of a teenager living with her at this critical juncture.

The sensible option? Decline to help—a first. In the past, whenever Imani came up short on an emergency home, Nova had readily pitched in.

When she returned to the office, Imani said, "I know the timing is bad." As Nova began watering the plant, Imani cast her a look of entreaty. "You've gone over and above to land the Holly job. You've worked hard for this chance. Once you impress Charlotte Holly with your gorgeous designs, her big brother will put Green Harmony in line to snag the best landscaping work in Geauga County."

Jonathon Holly's company, JH Builders, was remodeling the north wing of the Colonial Revival–style mansion with only months to spare before his sister's autumn wedding. Nova had been stunned and thrilled when Charlotte chose Green Harmony to overhaul the decades-old landscape.

"Everything I do must be first-rate." Nova set the watering can aside. "There's no room for error on a job this large. I'll be crazy-busy in the coming weeks."

"I get it. I do. You're my closest friend, and I know you've put everything on the line to land this job. I want you to succeed." Imani lifted her palms skyward. "If I weren't desperate, I wouldn't have called you."

"There isn't another home available?"

"Not one."

Nova fetched one of the chairs beside the filing cabinet, then sat down. "What about the Davises?" Longtime foster parents Jackie and Bill Davis often took in emergency cases.

"They're not available. I've also called the other families on the list." Imani sighed. "I hate pressuring you. But there's no one else. If you can't take the kids, I'm out of good options."

Kids.

The self-doubt Nova wore like a second skin made her shift uneasily on the chair. Dealing with one teenager on short notice was hard enough. But two? The second spare bedroom in her small bungalow was a mess. All the odds and ends dumped in there would have to be moved. Clothing, books, boxes of Green Harmony paperwork—how long would it take to clean? Yet another task to handle during an already hectic weekend.

"There must be someone else." Resisting, she exhaled a frustrated breath. "Can you check Summit or Portage Counties? See if either has an opening?" Cuyahoga County was out of the question. Foster homes in the densely populated Cleveland suburbs were always in short supply.

"What do you think I've been doing? I've been putting in calls since last night. Portage doesn't have any homes available. There *is* an opening at a group home in Akron. Normally they take kids aged twelve and up. Bella and Henry are considerably younger." Imani hesitated for a perilous beat. "Since this is an emergency, the supervisor will make an exception. If you're not on board, I'll have no choice but to send the kids there."

"How old are they?"

"Bella Croy is seven years old. Her brother, Henry, is nine."

Too young for placement in a group home. There'd be less supervision by the adults in charge compared to a placement in a foster home. *And more chance of older kids bullying them.*

"I've only taken in teenagers," Nova pointed out.

"By choice," Imani volleyed back. "Your foster certification covers children of all ages. You know that."

"Yeah, but I can't manage little kids. I don't have the skill set."

"Sure, you do. You're a pro with Miss Sunshine." Despite the gravity of the situation, Imani smiled. "If you ask my daughter, Maya will choose you over me or her father. You're sporty, and a more interesting cook. You can even give Bella and Henry their own rooms. There's no chance of that in a group home."

Nova felt herself softening. Yet the thought of handling young kids while working the Holly job was daunting. An added burden during the most important juncture of her career.

I can't walk away from this. It's the right thing to do. Shunting young kids off to a group setting didn't appeal.

Whatever the specifics of their past, they'd already been traumatized. No child removed from a parent's custody and thrust into the childcare system handled the change without anger, confusion, or tears.

"Okay, I'm in," she said, praying she wasn't getting in over her head. "Give me the background."

"It's still sketchy. I'll have more info once the PD locates Mr. Croy. His wife is deceased. Assuming the PD finds him soon, he'll appear in court this afternoon."

"He's missing?"

"Best guess, Egan Croy spent last night with a woman. Hopefully he'll show up at his house sometime this morning. I'm under the impression he usually leaves his children unsupervised on weekend nights. However, we *were* able to get the basics from Bella and Henry. Their mother died several months ago, in Columbus. A traffic accident, which the PD verified. The family recently moved to Chardon."

"Why the move? A job? Family?"

"We don't know yet."

"How long have they been here?"

"About a month, according to the woman who called in the report Friday night. She lives across the street from the Croys. I've checked all the elementary schools—Bella and Henry aren't enrolled anywhere. They've been out of school too long."

Irritation skimmed through Nova. Children from troubled homes rarely excelled in school. A long absence put them at risk of repeating a grade.

"When will you bring them to my place?"

"Does tomorrow at five o'clock work?"

She nodded, grateful for the time to prepare. "Where are they now?"

"At Geauga Hospital still running through tests. The pediatrician on call is keeping them another night. Henry has a cut on his knee, probably from a fall—the staff is checking for fractures to make sure they don't miss anything." Sorrow drifted through Imani's dark eyes. "Nova, they're both exhausted, malnourished . . . They've clearly been through a lot."

Nova's heart clenched. *Too much for any child.*

She made a mental note to run through the grocery store. In the past, she'd won over teenagers in her care by plying them with delicious meals. What comfort foods might young Bella and Henry enjoy? She settled on a menu Imani's daughter frequently requested whenever Nova babysat her. Assuming she plowed through the Green Harmony to-do list fast enough, tonight she'd make homemade banana pudding. Tomorrow, after sprucing up the house, she'd pull together roasted honey chicken and rice before the children arrived.

Chapter 3

Nova

In the smaller guest bedroom, green folders fanned out across the bed. Nova's mother surveyed them with a mix of dismay and amusement.

Tall and big-boned, with her sandy-blonde hair fading quickly to white, Helen Doubeck was the epitome of sensible. She rarely dressed up, preferring casual pants and the comfortable, low-heeled shoes that had served her well in her previous life as a nurse. Although nursing had made her impervious to shock, she *did* possess a sharp sense of humor. Helen cackled at any slapstick comedy. Still fit and hale in her sixties, she took daily walks on Chardon's picturesque streets during all but the snowiest winter days.

Nova adored her.

"What do we have here?" Picking up a folder, Helen peered inside. "Green Harmony's 1980 tax return. Please tell me it won't stay on this bed permanently."

Nova plucked the folder from her fingertips. "Where else would I put it? My kitchen workspace is bursting at the seams."

"After the children leave, why not move your office in here?" Helen knew the present situation—Nova taking in two foster kids—fell outside her normal preference. "You'll still have the larger guest bedroom whenever you take in a teenager. This room is perfect for your office."

"Maybe someday, once I'm confident self-employment isn't a pipe dream. It's only been three years. Not long enough to assume Green Harmony is a sure thing."

"It *is* a sure thing. Weren't you awarded the bid on the Holly estate? With all those firms in the running, Charlotte Holly chose you."

"It doesn't make sense," Nova said. "For starters, it's strange for Charlotte to even care *which* landscaping firm was awarded the contract. From what I've heard through the grapevine, her brother picked all the other subcontractors without her—masons, roofers, even the company hired to paint the interior once the remodel is done."

"I'm sure she's too busy to conduct every interview. Doesn't she run Holly's Mill?"

The historic mill and restaurant located on Holly's Bluff was a major tourist attraction. The mill had been in operation since 1891; the attached restaurant first opened during the Roaring Twenties.

"She handles the marketing. Her fiancé is the GM." Nova couldn't recall his name. Bill or Brian, maybe. Charlotte had introduced them soon after Nova was awarded the contract, when she'd dined at the restaurant. "I'm sure she likes my designs, and my bid probably came in the lowest. But with only two employees, it'll take me ten times longer to finish than one of the bigger firms."

"Stop overthinking this. Hold your head high and do a great job for Charlotte. What does it matter *why* she picked you?"

"With her wealth, she doesn't need the inconvenience. She can pick any firm she likes. Which makes me feel like there's an ulterior motive for hiring me." The suspicion had been eating at Nova for days. "If there *is* another reason why I landed the job, I can't figure it out."

Her mother grunted. "I'll tell you Charlotte's ulterior motive. She's giving another woman a leg up in the business world." She picked up the remaining files on the bed. "There isn't another landscaping firm in Geauga County owned by a woman. If I were in her shoes, I'd do the same thing."

The explanation slightly mollified Nova. "You think so?" She didn't like feeling undeserving of the work.

"Of course I do. Your business is doing well. Charlotte will help you go even further." Her mother dropped the files into her waiting hands. "On a related topic, you need to purchase a filing cabinet. No self-respecting entrepreneur gets far without keen organizational skills. If there's no room in the house, your father and I will help you clear a space in the garage."

They would also, Nova mused, offer to buy the filing cabinet. Despite their frugal lifestyle, Helen and Finch Doubeck never stinted on gifts for their son and daughter. Or their grandchildren—Nova's brother, Peter, and his wife, Jen, had recently welcomed the arrival of their second child. Helen had been purchasing gifts for baby William since March.

It was Sunday morning. This afternoon her parents were driving to Cincinnati for an extended stay to meet their new grandson. The trip was weeks in the planning, and Nova felt guilty about sending up an SOS last night. Without her mother's help, she'd never get the house ready in time. Imani planned to arrive near suppertime with Bella and Henry Croy.

In short order, the guest bedrooms were cleaned. Helen mopped the kitchen floor while Nova ran the vacuum through the house. As she put the honey chicken in the oven and made a salad for tonight's dinner, Helen pulled fresh sheets from the dryer. Once she made the beds, they dusted the living room together.

When they finished, her mother followed Nova into her bedroom. The bed, normally made with military precision, resembled a battle scene. The comforter sloped off one side. All the pillows were on the floor, dislodged while Nova had thrashed in her sleep. Embarrassed, she began scooping them up.

Her mother pursed her lips. "Bad dreams?" Walking to the opposite side, she fished the blanket out from beneath the comforter.

"Same old, same old." Nova tossed the last pillow onto the bed, then smoothed the comforter into place.

"That's strange. It's been a long time since you've had the nightmare."

Not true. She'd dreamed of the wolf two nights in a row. In the past, the nightmare had come infrequently. Was this the start of a trend? Nova hoped not.

"I'm sure it's just the pressure," she said. "The Holly job combined with a foster placement I wasn't expecting. I'm a little frazzled. It's nothing I can't manage."

"The children are in elementary school?"

"First and third grade." When she'd called her mother last night, she'd shared only the basics. Two kids, much younger than the teenagers she usually fostered. A boy and a girl.

"How long will you have them?"

"A few weeks at least. The family recently moved to Chardon. Imani still hasn't sorted out the details."

Helen approached, her brow furrowing. "Should I postpone my trip?" She gently smoothed Nova's hair. "You'll need help with the children, especially after school. Your father can go to Cincinnati without me. I'll drive down later this month to meet William."

"Mom, no. You've been looking forward to the trip. Besides, Imani has after school covered. One of the babysitters cleared by social services has agreed to pick up the kids from Longfellow Elementary. Kelly Whitehall—she'll watch them until I get home from work. It'll be fine."

"Are you sure?"

"Absolutely."

Helen rested her palms on Nova's shoulders. "If you change your mind, call me. I'm just a few hours away."

"How long *are* you and Dad staying with Peter and Jen?"

"It's up in the air. A week, maybe longer. Jen is still recovering from the C-section. I'm sure she's looking forward to the help." Helen fell silent for a moment. Then she appraised Nova with a smile forming on her lips. "You *do* know there's a difference between caring for a teenager and young children, right?"

Nova wasn't sure *what* to expect. Teenagers were usually moody or withdrawn, at least at the beginning. After a week or two, they generally became more trusting. Were young children much different? She couldn't hazard a guess.

"Should I run you through the basics?" Helen asked.

"Sure."

"Expect some acting out. Temper tantrums, refusing to eat—that sort of thing. And figure out every possible hiding place in your house. There's nothing more unnerving than being unable to locate a traumatized child who's decided to duck out of sight."

As a nurse, Helen had seen it all. *She's seen it all, and then some with me.*

According to family lore, Nova's first year in the Doubeck household rattled even Helen's steely nerves. Refusing to eat dinner with the family, then pillaging the kitchen past midnight for food. She howled if Finch or her brother came anywhere near her. Once, her brother foolishly threw himself across the couch after school while she watched cartoons. She hurled a building block at his head, giving Peter a serious goose egg. For a month afterward, he wore his football helmet whenever they occupied the same room.

Drawing herself from the reverie, Nova sighed. It dawned on her that she should've requested her mother's advice on childhood behavior the moment she agreed to take the kids.

"Anything else I should know?"

Helen patted her cheek. "Hide your breakables. Those tantrums can be quite . . . explosive."

～

At five o'clock, the crunch of car wheels on gravel drew Nova to the front porch.

Imani's gold Chevy Impala coasted into the driveway. In the back seat, Bella sat alone, pressing her hands to the window. Wide-eyed with messy brown hair, she appeared more frightened than curious. The car slowed, and she sank out of sight.

In the passenger seat, the boy—Henry—glued his gaze to the car's dashboard, with the expression of a fighter. He seemed none too pleased about the current situation. He looked furious, in fact, as the Chevy eased to a stop.

The trouble began immediately.

Henry shot out of the car and rocketed across the front yard. The jailbreak took Imani by surprise. Cutting the engine, she threw open the driver's-side door. She leaped out and promptly slipped on the gravel. She went down with a shriek.

Nova vaulted from the porch. Henry was fast, but he wasn't getting away. Not on her watch.

The boy never saw her coming. Charging from behind, she scooped him up. Without breaking stride, Nova slung him over her shoulder like a sack of mulch.

Henry pounded her back. "Put me down! I mean it!"

With his legs flailing, she risked getting a black eye. She pinned them. "It's nice to meet you, Henry. Are you always this exciting?"

"Let me go!"

"Not until you settle down." Pivoting, she marched toward the house. "Keep me posted, okay?"

In the driveway, Imani limped to the hood of the Chevy. There was a nice tear in the knee of her trendy balloon pants. She paused to dig a chunk of gravel from her thick curls. She tossed it aside.

With a gasp, she spied the car's back door hanging open.

"Where's Bella?" She spun around in a desperate circle.

Henry yanked Nova's hair. "Put. Me. *Down.*"

Shushing him, she glanced at Imani. "Hobble around the side of the car, Imani." Henry pulled her hair again. She failed to swat his hand away. "Check the back seat. Maybe she's hiding." *I'll join her if Henry doesn't stop pulling my hair.*

"She's not here!"

Nova climbed the porch steps with the grace of a drunk unsure of her balance. Granted, it didn't take much effort to carry Henry. His squirming, however, was a major hassle. He didn't weigh much—an alley cat had more meat on its frame. She scanned the street, east then west, searching for the missing Bella. How far could the child run in three seconds flat? Several houses down, Mr. Gibbons wheeled his lawn mower into his garage. At a house farther up, a boy washed his banana-yellow Mustang. There was no one else in sight.

"I don't see her, Imani. Go find her."

"I'm on it. Take care of Henry." Imani jumped back into the Impala.

At the front door, Nova steered Henry to his feet. She held him loosely by the wrist.

"Ground rules," she said. "No running away."

He eyed her warily. "Like you can stop me."

"You bet I can."

"Best of luck, asshole."

Nice mouth, kid. "Fine. Have it your way—I'll sleep on the living room couch if that's what it takes. I get that you don't want to be here, but I'm not the enemy."

"Take me back to Pa."

A slight quaver rimmed the demand. Pity for the boy darted through Nova. Did he miss his father? Or was he frightened he'd get in trouble if he *didn't* return? Children from abusive homes often harbored complicated emotions and unreasonable loyalties. Winning Henry over would take effort.

She tried another tactic. "Do you like chicken? With buttered rice on the side? Oh, and I made banana pudding. Do you like bananas?"

The remark caught him off-guard. Or the aroma of roasting chicken wafting from the house did. Either way, Henry's eyes brightened.

"Chicken's good," he conceded.

"There's whipped cream for the pudding."

"How much pudding can I have?"

"As much as you want. *After* finishing dinner, including your salad."

"Salad's okay." Easing from her grasp, Henry took in the porch with its matching rocking chairs. Turning toward the front door, he licked his lips. "When do we eat?"

The kid had an interesting face. His nose was large, a dominant feature. His eyes were an intense, deep green. He needed a haircut. That, or she could volunteer to braid his nearly shoulder-length hair.

She led him inside. "I suppose you can eat now. We'll feed Bella when she comes in."

"Okay."

A bees' nest of anxiety hummed through her as they entered the kitchen. Was she really destined for a night of crappy sleep on the couch? Giving up her comfy bed and overabundance of pillows wasn't her first choice.

Count on it.

Each new foster placement came with some excitement. Playing the role of prison guard, however, exceeded the norm. What other tricks were hidden up the boy's sleeve?

And I never got around to hiding my breakables.

He waited in the center of the kitchen while she dug silverware from the drawer. Pulling down three plates, she rattled them into a stack. At least he didn't seem prepared to run for the exits now. Would a week of tasty meals put her in his good graces?

Clinging to the possibility, Nova pivoted toward the table. She gasped. Forks and knives clattered across the floor.

The commotion woke Bella, who was dozing at the table. She lifted her head with a start.

Henry gaped at her. "Bella, how'd you get in here?"

"Imani fell down and Nova started chasing you . . . so I came inside. So what?"

"You're sneaky."

"I am not." She stifled a yawn. "*You're* silly for trying to run away."
Like her brother, she was small for her age. Slender with pale, nearly
translucent skin. Add a pair of wings, and Bella could pass for a pixie.
Beneath her long, wispy brown hair, her eyes flitted over the cutlery
scattered across the floor. She rested her hands on the red object in her
lap. A heart-shaped candy box. It was old, the lid scratched.

Her gaze alighted on Nova.

Wonder broke across her features. "Your hair is red. My favorite!"

"I'm glad you like it."

Bella cocked her head like a bird. "Can I touch it?"

A strange request, but she saw no harm in indulging it. Approaching,
Nova leaned forward. "Go right ahead." The long tresses swayed before
the child.

Bella poked tentative fingers into the heavy mass. The tiny crease
between her brows melted away. Smoothing her fingers down the length,
she appeared captivated by the bold color. Redheads were admittedly
rare, but was it possible she'd never *seen* one before? It seemed unlikely.

Amused, Nova bent closer. A mistake.

A few tendrils were promptly yanked out.

She yelped. Pain sizzled across her scalp. Henry laughed.

Nova straightened with as much poise as she could muster. What
other bad behavior hid behind the girl's angelic face? She recalled the
day when Imani's daughter, mired in a *four*-nado tantrum, bit Imani on
the neck like a mini vampire. She'd merely been carrying Maya to bed.
For days, Imani concealed the welt with fashionable scarves.

Bella wound the stolen tendrils around her finger. Intent on her task,
she was oblivious to the Nova's slack-jawed surprise and the humor lighting her brother's face. When she finished, she spotted the loaf of bread on
the counter. Hopping down from her chair, she skipped across the room.
She removed the bag's twist tie and secured it around the ring of hair.

Bella returned to her chair. She pulled the lid off her candy tin to
slip the hair inside. Like a souvenir. Baffled, Nova rubbed her stinging
scalp. The child returned the tin to her lap.

"Don't be mad at my brother," she said, as if only *his* behavior were out of bounds. "He didn't mean to run away."

Henry plopped onto a chair beside her. "Don't stick up for me, Bella. I can take care of myself."

"I'm not angry." Nova collected the silverware and dumped it in the sink. "I'm sure you're both a little out of sorts. There's nothing to worry about. I'm glad you're staying with me."

"The food at the hospital was yucky." Bella sniffed the air with approval. "Your house smells tasty."

"Do you like chicken?"

"Everyone likes chicken. It's even better than hamburgers."

"What else do you like?"

Henry shrugged. "What else *is* there besides chicken and burgers?" Clearly his knowledge of good cuisine was sadly limited.

"There are lots of great dishes." Nova eased the roasting pan from the oven. "We'll try some new ones this week."

By the time Imani stumbled into the kitchen, her lipstick smeared and her knee peeking out of the tear in her pants, Bella and Henry were finishing their second helping of chicken and rice. Their salad bowls sat empty. They'd also guzzled down tall glasses of milk and now eyed the banana pudding Nova had placed on the table. Conversation during the meal had been nonexistent. *Who cares?* The children were settling in.

The happy situation reduced the frantic air buzzing around Imani.

She set down a large bag that presumably held the children's clothes. Taking a seat, she regarded Nova with relief. "How did you find Bella? I drove around the block twice before giving up. I thought we'd have to call the PD."

"Bella came right inside. I found her in the kitchen." Nova winked at the girl, drawing a smile.

"She was here the whole time?"

"She's not a runner, like her brother."

Henry speared the last of his chicken. "I came back, didn't I?"

"Only because I thwarted your escape," Nova pointed out.

"What does 'thwart' mean?"

"It means I stopped you. But it wasn't easy—you really know how to run. You're faster than the wind."

The compliment eased the boy's surly expression. "You're fast for a girl. Strong too." Admiration colored the remark. "Do you lift weights or something?"

She scooped out a helping of banana pudding for him. "I get a workout with shrubs, mostly. I own a landscaping company. It's called Green Harmony." When the boy stared at her with confusion, she added, "Sometimes people want to change the plants around their house or have trees put in. I come and do the work. I have two very strong men on my staff. It's too much heavy lifting for me to handle alone."

Bella dug into the bowl of pudding that appeared before her. "Do you get to plant flowers?" she asked.

"All the time. It's one of my favorite tasks."

"Can I help?"

"Not while I'm working. Why don't we plant flowers around my yard? The beds are ready for summer annuals. I'll pick some up soon."

Bella nodded with satisfaction. "I like it here." She noticed the bag Imani had deposited beside the table. "Did you bring us a surprise?"

"I went shopping for you and your brother before I picked you up at the hospital." Imani withdrew a sweet blouse with green piping and matching green pants. "I thought you'd like to start school this week in new outfits. There are several for each of you. And new pajamas, book bags, and school supplies."

Henry pushed his dessert away. "Why do we have to go to school? When we left Columbus, Pa said we won't go back until fall. It's May. Summer break is almost here."

A challenge, and Nova decided it was time to take charge. From her experience fostering teenagers, she knew a stable, predictable environment gave children a sense of safety. Henry might resist the idea, but he needed the consistency of a normal routine.

"School doesn't end until June in this town," she told him. "You've already missed a chunk of the school year. It'll take time to catch up, but don't worry. I'll help you in the evenings, after dinner. In the meantime, would you like to see your bedroom?"

"Am I sleeping with Bella?"

"Not unless you want to."

"I want my own room." He started toward the hallway. "Where is it?"

"Take the blue room," Nova said. "Bella will sleep in the yellow one." The blue guest room was larger; she knew he'd prefer the extra space as the older child. "You and your sister will share the bathroom in the hallway. First door, on the right."

Scraping back her chair, Bella hurried to his side. "Can we watch TV for an hour if we get ready for bed fast?"

"You both need a shower first," Imani put in. "Can you manage, or do you need help?"

Henry rolled his eyes. "We're not babies." Taking the bag, he nudged his sister forward. "You go first."

After the children showered, brushed their teeth, and changed into pajamas in record time, they flung themselves across the couch to watch *The Incredible Hulk*. A series of Star Wars action figures sat beside them on the couch. Throughout the popular TV show, Bella kept her precious candy tin securely held in her lap.

Leading Imani back to the kitchen, Nova lowered her voice. "What's inside Bella's old candy tin? I'm guessing it's not chocolate."

"A little girl's trinkets, I suppose. I didn't feel comfortable asking."

"Well, she's added some of my hair to her trinkets. She pulled it right out." Nova tapped her scalp. "She wound the hair into a ring and tossed it inside."

"You're joking."

"Who jokes about being attacked, even by a pixie? I sure didn't expect her to pull out my hair. Do you think she's also a biter?"

Imani laughed. "Stay on her good side and you won't find out."

"It was strange how she plucked my hair out. No warning, nothing. Like it was a trophy or something."

"Well, your hair *is* gorgeous." Imani picked up the spoon beside Nova's dinner plate. She dipped it into the banana pudding, sampling the dessert. "Maybe you'll get lucky, and she'll let you peek inside her treasure chest."

"I doubt it. She's like a terrier, the way she guards her candy tin." Nova began clearing the table, hesitated. "Should I make you a plate?"

"Don't bother. Uri has dinner waiting for me." Imani's husband, Uri Weiss, was a surgeon at the Cleveland Clinic. His talents in the kitchen far exceeded his wife's. In Imani's perfect world, Uri would cook all their meals. "He's already fed Maya. He promised to keep a plate warm for me."

Nova lowered her voice. "Any word on Egan Croy?"

"He turned up Saturday and has appeared before Judge Cassidy. He's been informed that Bella and Henry will remain in foster case until we complete an investigation. Abandonment is a serious charge. I'm under the impression that, since moving to Chardon, he's often left the children unattended." Imani hesitated a beat, then added, "There's also the matter of the bruises."

"What bruises?"

"The ones on the children. There are several on Bella that are easy to miss, and much more on Henry's shoulders and back. The doctors found them during the hospital exam. It certainly resembles abuse."

Distress rippled through Nova. "You aren't sure?" she asked.

"I need proof. Bella and Henry won't talk about their father. Getting them to reveal anything bad will be difficult."

"They're probably frightened of him. What about the woman who called 911 on Friday night? Have you talked to her?"

"I'll interview her this week. She may be able to provide evidence of physical abuse." Imani cleared her throat, her expression grave. "Whether she can or not, I've decided to withhold your name from Mr. Croy. Bella and Henry understand. I explained on the drive here.

Once they begin supervised visits with their father, they're not to mention you."

The decision was startling.

During her past forays into foster care, Nova had worked directly with parents whose children were in her care. She'd attended meetings with them at J&FS and cheered them on as they completed treatment programs, worked on parenting coursework, or enrolled in anger management classes. A family in crisis was *still* a family, with reunification the primary goal. She'd never been involved in a case where the parent's behavior was potentially so problematic that Imani felt it prudent to withhold Nova's identity.

The charges against Egan Croy *were* serious. Abandonment, and possibly abuse. Was he at risk of losing custody of his children?

Severing parental rights was a last resort that Job & Family Services would consider only after a thorough investigation. The process involved court appearances and documentation of claims. This wasn't a typical foster case, with an adolescent staying with Nova for several weeks. Bella and Henry might remain with her for months.

Was she up to the task?

On a steadying breath, she finished clearing the table.

Chapter 4

NOVA

Nova happily stowed the last of her supplies in the back of her truck. At this rate, she'd drop the kids off at Longfellow Elementary and arrive at the Holly job thirty minutes early. She'd have ample time to discuss the day's projects with her two employees before the heavy equipment she'd rented was delivered to the estate. She'd also impress Jonathon Holly by appearing at his meeting with all the trades well ahead of schedule.

With satisfaction, Nova sprinted back toward the house. On the couch she'd only slept in fits and starts, but she felt energized. At least she hadn't dreamed of the wolf for a third night in a row. Adding to the winning streak, her young charges had woken up just fine, drawn to the kitchen by the aroma of frying bacon and fragrant apple pancakes. Rising before her alarm went off to prepare a cooked breakfast wouldn't become habit, at least not during the workweek. But she'd wanted to kick off their first day together on a positive note.

The forecast called for temps in the low seventies, with no chance of rain. Perfect weather to remove old and overgrown shrubs. She planned to start with the juniper bushes forming a drooping, spindly wall in the back of the Holly estate.

As she climbed the steps to the front porch, Bella poked her head out the front door. The trepidation in her eyes punctured Nova's high spirits.

Bella plucked at her new book bag's pink straps. "Henry changed his mind. He's not going to school."

"Wait. What?" Brushing past her, Nova halted by the couch. Not two minutes ago, she'd left Henry lacing up his new tennis shoes. "Where is he?"

"I'm not supposed to tell you."

"I need to know. Tell me, please."

"I can't. I promised Henry to keep my trap shut."

"Your *trap*? That isn't nice language, sweetie. You mean Henry wants you to keep a secret."

"Right."

"Be his loyal sidekick some other time, okay? Just not this morning." *So much for arriving to work early.* "There's no time for a scavenger hunt. Tell me where he's hiding."

Bella looked away. Ratting out her brother clearly wasn't her first choice.

"Please, kiddo. At least give me a hint."

Weighing the bedeviling request, Bella tapped her foot. She tipped her head toward the hallway.

Sure enough, the guest bathroom door was locked.

Nova rapped lightly. "It's time to leave, Henry."

"Go away."

"I can't do that. It's my responsibility to get you to school. Don't you want to make new friends? It'll be fun."

Bella wiggled the book bag from her shoulders and placed it on the floor. Slipping past Nova, she pressed her cheek to the door. "Don't be scared, Henry. I'm sure the kids at our new school are nice."

"I'm not scared. Go. *Away.*"

Nova heaved out a sigh. "I don't believe this." She put ice in her tone. "Henry—last chance. Unlock the door. If you don't, I'm coming in anyway."

"Try it, and you'll be sorry. I'm not kidding around."

The taunt put her feet in motion. She marched to the owner's suite, past the bed, and into her private bathroom. Rummaging through a drawer, she found a bobby pin. Releasing the bathroom door's push-button lock would be a cakewalk. If Henry thought he'd won this round, he was sorely mistaken.

Returning, she knelt to work the lock. Bella's delicate brows climbed her forehead.

"Don't break in." She rested a dainty palm on Nova's shoulder. "Henry will make you pay. And I mean *bad*."

How? By grabbing his toothbrush and challenging me to a duel? "Trust me," she assured Bella. "I can handle this."

"Don't go in! He'll come out when he's ready."

And wait here for hours? She refused to imagine Jonathon's reaction once she strolled onto the worksite whenever hunger or boredom evicted Henry from his self-imposed prison. Who risked losing a good job on the first day?

"I have to get to work," she told Bella. "Your brother's already put me behind schedule."

Jiggling the bobby pin, Nova felt the lock release. As it did, she heard the pounding of feet retreating from the door. The water roared on in the bathroom. Not the faucet—the pounding echo came from the shower.

Bella took a nervous step back. Nova clenched her teeth. Did Henry believe he'd evade capture by taking a shower? *Guess again, Mr. Troublemaker.*

She pushed open the door.

A hard stream of water slammed into her chest. The pummeling torrent nearly took her off her feet. The icy water lifted abruptly, nailing her in the face. Raising her palms to fend off the assault, she stared in wonder.

On the bathtub's rim, Henry perched like an acrobat. Arms raised, he aimed the showerhead like a Gatling gun to slow her every step forward. The resourceful boy narrowed the stream to a pinpoint, increasing the force of his unlikely weapon. Within seconds he soaked Nova to her skin. He also soaked his own shirt when he leaped down and tried to zip past her.

Slipping and sliding, she managed to grab hold of his waist. The growl he released echoed across the walls.

Together they tumbled to the floor. They tussled, with the much-larger Nova quickly gaining the advantage. Once Henry was effectively pinned, his sister—apparently well versed in his antics—calmly stepped over them. Bath towels, hand towels, and two slightly damp washcloths sailed through the air. They landed with soft thuds on the wet floor.

Grabbing a bath towel, Nova managed to heave the squirming boy to his feet. She half dragged, half carried Henry to his bedroom. The fire went out of his fury when she sat him on the bed. Or his sister's loving ministrations did: racing into the room with a towel, Bella promptly dried his face.

The sweet way she murmured encouragement put a lump in Nova's throat. During her own childhood, whenever she'd acted out, her brother, Peter, had offered similar tenderness.

Nova pulled a clean shirt from the dresser. "Henry, where's your book bag?"

"I dunno."

Bella piped up. "It's in the living room."

"Good. I'm in no mood to hunt for it." Nova pivoted toward the bed, spattering droplets of water across the floor. Henry needed only a dry shirt, but she'd have to change from top to bottom. Her hair and T-shirt were sopping wet. Her soggy jeans squeaked when she moved.

Her irritation melted away as the helpful Bella peeled her brother's shirt up his narrow rib cage. Last night the children had readied for bed without assistance; now the extent of the boy's malnutrition was apparent. There wasn't an ounce of fat on his body—Henry's ribs were too easy to count.

Arms raised, he waited listlessly. Bella tugged the shirt over his head. Nova's breath caught in her throat.

Bluish and yellow bruises formed a grisly pattern across Henry's shoulders. Heartache seized Nova. More bruises trailed down his back, darker in color and more recent. They looked painful. These weren't the typical injuries from a child's roughhousing. Someone had struck the boy repeatedly.

"Henry, who did this to you?" Stunned, she knelt before him. "Your father?"

His lower lip quivered. "It doesn't matter."

"Talk to me. I can't help unless you do."

Taking the dry shirt, he shrugged it on. "I don't want your help."

"Why not?"

"I don't belong to you. Bella doesn't either."

A feeling of helplessness swamped her. Did he believe the abuse was acceptable? Given the circumstances, he might assume most parents mistreated their children. Past experience forms our beliefs. For a child schooled in abuse, it was impossible to imagine a life where nurturing and love were commonplace.

"Henry, grown-ups aren't supposed to hurt children—ever. Whatever happened to you in the past, it stops now. You're safe with me."

"What about when you get mad?"

"Grown-ups get mad just like kids do. It doesn't mean they should lash out. Responsible grown-ups don't. *I* don't."

When his unreadable gaze lifted, she reached out to touch his damp, overlong hair. To demonstrate that not all grown-ups were harsh and unfeeling, or meant to be feared.

He leaned out of reach.

"I'll get my tennis shoes." He rose. "They're somewhere in the living room."

Bella hurried after him. "I'll help you look."

While the children collected their belongings, Nova hurried to her bedroom to change into dry clothes. She reappeared to find them seated together in the living room. With her emotions in flux, she ushered them from the house. She drove the five blocks to the elementary school with tears collecting on her lashes. First period was already in session. They walked to the office, and Nova signed them in.

The principal took charge, escorting the kids to their classrooms. Head lowered, Henry trudged forward without a backward glance. Bella turned around to wave goodbye.

An out-of-body sensation overtook Nova as she walked across the parking lot. Once, long ago, she'd relied on the reaction to shut down her emotions. To turn them off, like a spigot gone dry. It seemed Henry relied on the same coping mechanism to build a wall around his heart. Climbing into the truck, she imagined him before they'd met. Had abuse destroyed Henry's ability to trust? She'd been no different at his age. If not for Helen's gentle guidance, she never would've healed her emotional wounds.

But she didn't have her mother's training in mending ailing bodies. She didn't know how to restore a broken spirit. What if she failed to give Henry the comfort he needed?

Doubt rolled through Nova. Too quickly, her emotions broke to the surface.

On a sob, she lowered her head to the steering wheel.

Chapter 5

NOVA

Nova tapped the truck's horn, drawing Bear's attention. He stopped pacing behind the vehicles packed end-to-end in the Hollys' long driveway. Her heart sank. She'd obviously missed the meeting.

The moment she cut the engine, he pulled open the driver-side door. "Jeez, Nova. Where've you been?"

"Don't ask, buddy." She'd tell the sweet-natured youth about her new foster kids another time. Not now. The discussion might start her crying again.

"You're forty minutes late. You're never late."

"Tell me about it."

She glanced nervously toward the mansion. Men were streaming inside to begin the teardown in the north wing.

"Nova, what's wrong with your face? It's all puffy." Bear noticed the growing patches of dampness on her shoulders. "Did you just get out of the shower? You forgot to blow-dry your hair."

"Actually, I decided to leave it wet," she quipped, "to lure every mosquito in a ten-mile radius. It's what I do for fun."

Bear did a double take. "You're joking, right?" At twenty-two, he was still impressively gullible.

"Yes, I'm joking. It's a toss-up what I hate more—poison ivy or mosquitoes. The twin plagues of our trade. Now, stop grilling me. I've had a strange morning. Hopefully the rest of the day will be less weird." She ducked her head into the back of her truck, then filled his arms with rakes, shovels, and a canvas bag of hand tools. Slinging a larger canvas tote over her shoulder, she looked around for her older employee. "Where's Leroy?"

"Out back. You weren't here, so he signed for the heavy equipment. He's moving the backhoe into place."

"What about the boss? Where's he?"

Bear's massive shoulders lifted to his ears. "If we're lucky, he's working off steam inside the mansion. Someone ought to give him a sledgehammer. Tearing down walls might improve his mood."

"He's that mad?" *I'll bet I'm the reason.*

A suspicion quickly confirmed when Bear nodded. "Oh yeah," he said. "At the end of the meeting, he grilled Leroy about where you were."

"What did Leroy tell him? It's not like he knew where I was."

"Don't ask me. I ducked out." Bear rubbed his arms as if banishing a chill. "Do you think Jonathon gets pissed off a lot?"

"Doubtful. He didn't say much when I interviewed for the job. Charlotte did most of the talking, but he seemed friendly enough." Of course, he'd probably assumed Green Harmony had zero chance of landing the job and had been indulging her. "I hear Jonathon expects top-notch results from his crews, but he's evenhanded. Fair."

"I sure hope you're right."

Pivoting away from the truck, she pocketed the keys. "Did he really give Leroy a hard time because I'm late?"

"Jonathon read him the riot act in about ten different languages. It's okay with me if I never see his temper again." At over six feet in height and heavyset, Bear reminded her of an elephant spooked by a confrontation with a hungry lion.

Jonathon Holly was the lion. Hopefully he wouldn't eat *her* alive.

A foolish wish, she quickly discovered. When she neared the sweep of stairs rising into the mansion, Jonathon pushed through the crowd to corner her. The tradesmen entering the house quickened their pace.

"Doubeck! Mind explaining why you're showing up"—he glanced at his watch—"forty-three minutes late?"

Like her quivering assistant, Jonathon was a tall man. Unlike Bear, he radiated confidence and palpable irritation as he led her onto the lawn for privacy. Arms crossed, he waited for an explanation.

"It won't happen again," she rapped out. "But if it's all the same to you, I'd rather not go into it."

Suspicion bloomed in his eyes. "Why not?"

"Because it's private."

"Let me guess." He took a gander at her wet hair. "Were you taking a long shower and forgot to check the time?"

"No! I was delayed due to a serious matter."

"Like what? Is someone in your family grievously ill?"

She glared at him. Baiting her wasn't a great way to kick off a professional relationship.

An issue plainly not top of mind with her new employer.

"A parent is sick, and you stopped to pick up meds? Or your husband is under the weather?" His brows lowered. "I'm asking a reasonable question. Tell me why you're waltzing in late on your first day."

"She's not married," Bear volunteered. "Nova hardly has a life."

The personal info dump wasn't helpful. *Get Bear out of here.* Let him stay, and they *would* lose the job.

She pointed toward the back of the mansion. "Go," she commanded. "Find Leroy. I'll be there in a minute."

"Are you sure? I'll stay if you need me to—"

"Go!"

With confusion Bear glanced at the last of the men hurrying inside. Then he stared at his feet, clearly unsure whether he should put them in motion. He deserved points for loyalty. Bad timing, but still.

At last, he lumbered off.

Jonathon pinned her with a hard stare. "Ground rules." For emphasis, he leaned closer. "Take long showers on the weekend. Have back-to-back spa days for all I care. Just not on my dime. I expect you on the job, on time, no exceptions."

"Stop giving me the third degree. I wasn't showering." A defense, she realized, that was impossible to believe.

"Then why is your hair wet?"

Grief pierced her as she recalled the shocking bruises on Henry. The air of dejection surrounding him as the principal led him to class. Mention her foster kids or why Henry had barricaded himself inside the bathroom, and she was afraid she'd start crying. Not a great look in front of a client.

"Listen, I won't be late again. I swear." She brushed a soggy clump of hair from her face. "Can we leave it at that?"

"You'll be on time from here on out?"

"Scout's honor." The tears burning her eyes made her suddenly angry. "Are we done here?"

"Only if we're clear."

"Like crystal," she snapped. "You run a tight ship. You won't tolerate anyone showing up late. I get it. Are you finished threatening me with dismissal?"

Jonathon fell back on his heels. The hesitation flickering across his features came as a surprise.

"I didn't threaten to fire you."

"You could've fooled me."

"Are you always this combative?" He looked genuinely baffled. "Most guys would just apologize to the boss."

"I'm not a guy, but I catch your drift." He thought *she* was being combative? He was overreacting big-time.

Just apologize and get it over with.

The words lodged in her throat. On the back of her neck, the hairs stood at attention. Everyone else was inside, leaving them alone to hash this out. Or were they?

Nova sensed someone nearby, observing the argument. Looking past Jonathon, she scanned the wide lawn. It was empty. So were the stairs leading into the house.

Her heart thumped painfully when her attention landed on a man standing in the deep shade of an oak tree near the mansion's entryway. A carpenter, with a toolbelt slung across his hips. Middle-aged, handsome, he appeared delighted by their altercation. You got all types on a jobsite, and the way he regarded Nova—his lips quirking with derision, his eyes taking in her flushed complexion—jolted her into a defensive stance. The man was enjoying watching the boss take her down a notch.

Stepping around Jonathon, she shouted, "Hey, pal! Why don't you stop eavesdropping and get moving? This is a private conversation."

The man glowered at her. Alarm snuffed out the reaction when Jonathon swung around.

"The show's over," he growled. He stepped before Nova, effectively shielding her. "Get to work. Now."

Moving past them, the carpenter ascended the stairs to the mansion. The door slammed shut behind him.

The sound seemed to shift the ground beneath Jonathon. He blinked rapidly, as if he were waking up.

Flustered, he rubbed his jaw. His attention skipped across the lawn and then the house, landing everywhere but on Nova. It occurred to her that he was attempting to form an apology of his own.

Beating him to it, she blurted, "I'm sorry about showing up late. Every job matters. This one more than most." Their gazes tangled, and an unwanted pleasure dove through her. He had nice eyes, a deep Pacific blue. Unable to look away, she added, "You're making changes to the house that's been in your family since the 1800s. I get the headaches involved in the remodel of a century home. I promise my team will do a great job with the landscaping . . ."

She was still babbling when a bee landed on her head. Jonathon shooed it away, bringing her ramble to a halt. Or the mirth in his eyes did.

Tamping it down, he asked, "Do you want a towel? You can't work with your hair sopping wet. You'll draw every bug in Geauga County."

Nova was about to agree, *yes, thank you,* when Jonathon lifted a heavy lock of hair from her shoulder, his attention drawn to the rich color. The gesture—sudden, intimate—heightened her senses.

He's not the only one breaking the rules. She caught herself leaning closer to breathe in his tangy aftershave. Mortified, she looked away.

Jonathon took a clumsy step back. "Annie's in the kitchen." He gestured toward the house. "She's the cook. She'll get you a towel."

Nova bobbed her head. "That would be great."

"Turn left when you get inside. The kitchen's past the dining room."

"Got it."

Jonathon started off. Hesitating, he turned back around. "Do you need a blow dryer?" he asked, retracing his steps. He grinned suddenly, giving her the impression that he didn't want to leave. "I can find one for you."

"No, a towel is fine," she assured him. "Thanks."

With a nod, he walked away.

Chapter 6

Nova

During the following days, Nova struggled to balance parenting duties alongside work at the Holly mansion.

On Tuesday, Bear hit a pipe with the compact excavator she'd rented. The Depression-era water line wasn't listed on the plans. It took hours of hand-digging to discover the pipe led to an old well no longer in use on the property.

Wednesday brought other surprises. Nova arrived to discover the demo work inside the house blocked access to the area where she meant to install Charlotte's cutting garden—three massive dumpsters were parked on the spot. She and her crew spent that day, and Thursday, dodging men hauling debris from the house.

The carpenter who'd gleefully observed her argument with Jonathon added to the stress. She'd embarrassed the man by calling him out for eavesdropping. Whenever their paths crossed on the busy jobsite, he threw icy glances. Sometimes he watched her crew from the large slate patio hugging the back of the house.

His interest caught the disapproving notice of Leroy and Bear. She told them to avoid the guy. Everything about the carpenter spelled trouble.

A different type of stress marked her exchanges with Jonathon. Pretending they weren't interested in each other made their conversations awkward, stilted. They were doing their best to avoid each other.

Life at home was no better.

Henry remained moody and combative—with her, with Imani, and even with Kelly, the cheerful babysitter whose patience with foster kids had earned her star status at Job & Family Services. Getting him off to school each morning became a chore, forcing Nova to rise earlier than normal. Bella remained more agreeable, but loud sounds unnerved her. The roar of a neighbor's lawn mower or the vacuum whirring made her vanish. Given her talent for hiding from perceived danger, it took long minutes to find her in the back of a bedroom closet or huddling behind the living room couch.

By late afternoon on Thursday, when Kelly dropped the kids off, Nova felt sleep-deprived and edgy. Opening the fridge, she searched for a simple dinner option. An elaborate meal was out of the question.

Placing her book bag on the table, Bella joined her at the fridge. "What's for dinner, Nova?"

"Do you mind grilled cheese sandwiches and carrot sticks?"

"I like grilled cheese. Mama used to make it a lot."

It was the first time Bella had mentioned her late mother. An opening. Nova quickly seized it.

"You liked your mama's cooking?"

Bella daintily balanced on one foot. "Oh yes. She'd let me help too." A whisper of distress crossed her features as she came closer. "I liked making food with Mama."

"I'll bet you were a great helper." Nova caressed the girl's soft brow. "You still are."

"I am."

Talking about her mother surely pained Bella. *It's a good sign.* Encourage her to open up, and Bella might begin to trust her.

"What else did your mama cook?"

"Lots of burgers. Macaroni and cheese too. Fish sticks, sometimes, if Pa let her. I like fish sticks, but he didn't let her buy them too much."

"He doesn't like fish?"

Henry strolled into the room and dropped his book bag on the floor. "Pa's cheap." He wandered to the desk in the corner of the kitchen, where Nova kept her makeshift office. "Most of the time, Pa did the shopping. He told Mom she spent too much on food. It cut into his good-time money."

Nova pulled a stick of butter from the fridge. "Good-time money?" she asked, certain she knew where Henry was going with this.

"You know—to go out on weekends." From the desk, he picked up a Green Harmony brochure. "A man needs his recreation. He can't let his wife and rug rats tie him down *all* the time."

The comment stung Nova with irritation. Henry often spouted similar nonsense picked up from his father. No doubt Egan Croy viewed women as inferior and children no better.

"Marriage isn't a chore," she told Henry. "We should cherish the people closest to us. For a grown-up like your dad, that includes your children. I'm grateful to have my parents and big brother. Who wants to go through life without people who really love you? They always have your back."

"Is that why you have so many photos of your family?" He waved the brochure to encompass the kitchen wall nearest the door. The space was filled with a collage of framed pics of her parents and Peter's family. "You've got even more hanging in the living room. I've never seen so many photos in one house."

"Having them around reminds me that I'm not alone. It's good to feel like you belong. Don't you agree?"

"I suppose." Henry paused, considering. "What's *your* dad like?"

"He's sweet. Great with advice. He's a retired mechanical engineer." She took a package of American cheese from the fridge and handed it to Bella. "You'll meet my parents soon. I'd bring you over this weekend, but they're out of town."

"Does your dad party-hearty on weekends?"

"My parents don't party much at their ages. They're both retired. They *do* enjoy going out to dinner with friends."

Bella said, "Pa has lots of friends. He never shared them with Mama. It's nice to have friends."

Henry smirked. "Yeah, Pa keeps lots of *lady* friends." He tossed the brochure back down on the desk. "Mom didn't like it, Bella. She just kept her trap shut so Pa wouldn't get angry."

The remark stirred Nova's mothering instincts. No wonder the kids were underweight. To Egan, cash spent womanizing took precedence over feeding his children. Pity for their late mother followed. She couldn't imagine living with a husband who cheated. Glory Croy had deserved a better life for herself and her children.

Bella fetched the loaf of bread and placed it by the stove. "When do we have to see Pa?" she asked.

Have to, not *When can we see Pa?* Plainly she wasn't looking forward to the visit.

"Not until Saturday." Nova reached for a skillet. "You'll see him for an hour at Job & Family Services."

"What's that?"

"The place where Imani works. It's a big building. There's a playroom inside where kids can meet with their parents."

"Will you stay with us while we see Pa?"

The hope rimming the query slowed Nova's movements. In cases where a parent agreed to release a child to social services, they were normally given the foster parent's name and address. They often worked together with the goal of reunification in mind. During Nova's previous experiences fostering teenagers, she'd attended meetings with those parents at Job & Family Services. Not the visitation hours, though. They were supervised by a social worker on staff.

This case bore no resemblance to past experience. The Croy children had been removed from Egan's custody without his consent. Whether he'd eventually regain custody was still up in the air. Given everything

Nova had discovered about his appalling behavior, she was glad Imani had chosen to withhold her name.

"I can't go with you on Saturday. I wish I could." She ruffled Bella's hair. "Didn't Imani explain this to you?"

"She did," Henry put in. "Bella, don't you remember? Imani told us last weekend, in the car. When she brought us to Nova's house."

"What did she tell us? I don't remember."

"We're not supposed to talk about Nova with Pa. He doesn't know where we're staying."

"We can't tell him we're at Nova's house?"

"It's a secret. That's why she can't go with us."

Bella's face fell. "Okay." Her worried gaze found Nova. "Will Imani be there?"

"She'll stay with you the whole time. It's called a supervised visit. Your father won't visit alone with you and Henry, at least for now." When Bella nodded, clearly relieved, Nova turned on the stove. Dropping butter into the pan, she said, "Why don't we get started on your homework while we eat? If we hurry, you can watch TV for an hour before bedtime."

As they finished the meal, the sun dipped low on the horizon. Above it, a thin band of darkening clouds drifted across the sky. Readying the children for bed, Nova hoped the spring storm wouldn't arrive until they were asleep. Given Bella's fear of loud noises, the crack of thunder would send her scurrying for cover—under a bed or in a closet. And Henry looked for any excuse to delay bedtime.

After Nova tucked them in, they fell asleep within minutes. From the hallway linen closet, she fetched a blanket for another night on the couch. Since Monday, Henry's disenchantment with school hadn't led to more outright rebellion. Even so, she wasn't confident he'd given up on the idea of running away.

She'd just unfolded the blanket when Imani stepped inside the small foyer. "The door was unlocked," she said by way of greeting. She grinned as Nova smoothed the blanket out. "Still concerned about a midnight jailbreak?"

"Henry seems like he's settling in, but I'm taking no chances. At least he's going to school without too much arguing."

"How's Bella?"

"Easier than her brother. Clingy at times, then distant. She likes it here."

"Have you solved the mystery of the candy tin?"

"Not yet. At some point, she might let me see what's inside. I kid you not, she goes nowhere without the tin. I've tried talking her out of dragging it to school, but she's a tough customer." Nova spied the bottle of Merlot dangling from Imani's fingers. "You're a lifesaver. I could use a glass."

They sat in the wicker rocking chairs on Nova's front porch. The sun conspired with the clouds to ripple bands of reddish light across the sky. The wind kicked up, sending a draft of warm air across the yard. They sipped their wine in comfortable silence.

Breaking it, Imani said, "This morning I interviewed the woman living across the street from Egan Croy. She wasn't much help. If he's been physically abusing his children, he's done so out of sight of the neighbors. She *did* verify he's left the children alone most weekend nights since moving in."

"What about Egan? Have you met with him yet?"

Imani took a contemplative sip of her wine. "The meeting was scheduled for tomorrow afternoon," she said with irritation. "Yesterday Egan called J&FS to reschedule."

Nova wondered what he was like. A man with a penchant for illicit affairs was probably a smooth talker. Persuasive.

"What *is* his line of work?" She guessed sales.

"I'm not sure. I had a conflict, so Tim went in this morning to meet with Egan. He only gave me the highlights."

Tim Kenner was still learning the ropes of social work. A newlywed with a baby on the way, he'd joined J&FS last year. Nova had met him only once.

She asked, "How did the meeting go?"

"According to Tim, Egan Croy is . . . likable. Friendly. He insists the bruises we found on Henry are the result of roughhousing. Climbing trees, running around outside, that sort of thing. He claimed no knowledge of Bella's bruises, which appears to make sense because she didn't have many. He repeatedly assured Tim that he'd never mistreated his children."

Anger sparked in Nova. "And Tim believed him? C'mon, Imani. I've seen the bruises on Henry. They aren't from playing outside. He's been hurt repeatedly. Bella still won't let me help at bath time, but you know what the doctors found at the hospital. She has several bruises on her back."

"I know."

"What about leaving the kids unsupervised? Did Tim bring it up?" A bitter laugh escaped her. "If he did, I can't wait to hear Egan's excuse. Since he's such a likable guy."

"Of course Tim brought it up. He's under the impression Egan is behaving erratically due to his wife's recent death. Some people don't handle grief well, Nova. Most people, in my experience. It's no excuse for leaving children unattended, but it *is* a reasonable explanation."

Nova recalled her conversation with the children before dinner. "Imani, this isn't a one-off. Ask Henry. He'll tell you Egan has been partying most weekends for a long time now. He's using his wife's death as an excuse."

"That may be. However, Tim suggested grief counseling and Egan readily agreed. We have a course starting at the agency next week. Mostly older folks who've lost their spouses sign up, but that doesn't mean the coursework won't benefit Egan too."

"Why am I getting the feeling you'll reunite him with Bella and Henry? All he has to do is attend a few classes, and the kids are back with him." A sense of foreboding crept into Nova's blood. "He's abusive. His kids are malnourished. You know he leaves them unattended on weekends. He's not fit to parent."

Imani regarded her with reproach. Apparently, she planned to keep an open mind. A necessity for any social worker.

"Don't judge Egan too harshly," she said. "People change. I see it all the time. When I've given up all hope—when I'm convinced they've lost the ability to love their children—they somehow pull it all together. Haven't we both seen our share of miracles?"

Doubt lowered Nova's elbows to her knees. She recalled the day she'd taken in Bear when he was seventeen. The shock of seeing his arms bloodied from fending off his father's blows. Like so many out-of-control parents, Bear's father had also grown up in an abusive household. No one expected him to seek therapy. He sought out a psychologist, paying out of pocket for the sessions.

By the end of counseling, he was a changed man.

"I want to keep an open mind," Nova admitted. "It's not easy. This isn't like Bear or the other teenagers I've helped. They were nearing adulthood, old enough to bounce back. It's different with Bella and Henry. They're so young."

"Adoption brings its own set of problems. Especially for older kids. Henry is almost ten."

One of the reasons, no doubt, why Imani leaned toward reunification. "Even so, I can't help feeling Bella and Henry need a fresh start."

"Nova, I get it. But I can't shout 'fire' without proof. Not when factoring in the death of a man's wife. It matters, whether you think so or not."

"What *will* you do?"

Setting down her glass, Imani rose. She leaned against the railing. A gust of wind shook the trees. Clouds heavy with rain stole the last traces of light from the sky.

From over her shoulder, she appraised Nova with a mix of frustration and compassion. A familiar expression, a spark that lit fond memories from Nova's childhood. How the confident Imani drew her out in fourth grade, striking up their friendship with Oreo cookies and easy chatter. How she tempered Nova's dislike of strangers by dragging her to Girl Scouts and, later, convincing her to join the theater group in high school. Imani's father, now gone, had been a local school psychologist. His career had influenced his daughter's choice to dedicate her life to social work.

Nova's personal story had also left a profound mark. The horror of it, and the salvation. The proof it gave of renewal, of a child's astonishing capacity to heal. On balance those lessons, shared in whispered voices during their teenage years, gave Imani the final push. During their second year at Kent State, she declared her major.

A choice that seemed to hover between them now.

Imani gave a rueful smile. "Promise me something." Affection softened her features, but her voice held a warning. "I'm serious, Nova."

"Anything." She joined her at the railing.

"Don't forget the big lessons you learned when you took the foster-adopt coursework."

"I won't."

"Keep some emotional distance. I know it's not easy. A foster parent is a support system—a stand-in family, not a permanent one. Promise you won't fall in love with Bella and Henry."

The pledge was difficult to make. "I won't," Nova said, uncertain if she knew her own heart.

"You're sure? That's not the vibe I'm picking up."

"It *is* loads easier with teenagers. Striking up a friendship with a kid who'll return to his family once things settle down."

"Teens aren't defenseless. Most will make peace with the past and move on."

A weight of confusion settled on Nova. "Maybe I wasn't prepared to see the bruises on Henry," she admitted. "To see proof of how badly an adult can mistreat a small child. It got to me, Imani. Really tore me apart."

Surveying the clouds, Imani leaned into her, shoulder to shoulder. The sisterly gesture harkened back to their childhood, when they'd sat pressed together in the school lunchroom. The familiar comfort boosted Nova's sagging spirits.

"Do you understand *why* Henry's bruises got to you? They're an echo of everything you've suppressed."

"Probably."

"They are, Nova. I wish I'd had the sense to recognize all the similarities right from the start. It's stupid, how much I missed."

"You didn't miss anything. On any given day, you're juggling a dozen case files. More, probably. No one expects you to memorize every detail about every child put in your care."

"I should, though. It's part of the job." Imani studied her, a summing look. "Are you angry with me? I put you in a tough situation. I didn't give you the chance to back out."

"Stop it, okay? I *want* to help Bella and Henry. If it means dealing with my own past, it's time. I can't put it off forever."

"You're not entirely in the dark," Imani reminded her. "Your dad gave you the basics. When we were kids. Remember? It was right after we finished fourth grade."

Nova recalled that hot summer day. Her parents had taken them and Peter swimming at Headlands Beach. They returned home sunburned and famished, trooping sand across the kitchen in a beeline to the fridge. Helen ordered them out, suggesting Finch keep the kids entertained while she pulled dinner together.

Nova's brother helped her dad set up the Monopoly game. They were about to begin playing when Imani noticed a photo album tucked deep on a shelf in the living room. Inside were a trove of Peter's baby and toddler photos. She asked Finch why there weren't any pictures of Nova. Was it because Nova didn't become part of their family until she was older? When he didn't answer immediately, she pelted him with questions. Why didn't they have Nova when she was a baby? Where did she come from, anyway?

At the time, Nova hadn't processed the adoption in any meaningful way. She'd likened it to any number of common traits, like Peter's hazel eyes or Imani's brown skin. Nova had red hair and green eyes and an extra trait, *adoption*.

With much throat clearing, Finch stumbled through an explanation. He told them Nova's birth parents were an older couple who'd been together for many years, although they'd never married. He didn't know much about the man, since he wasn't listed on Nova's birth certificate. Nor did he know why the couple didn't pass along photos from her early childhood when she became a ward of the state. Finch added that they'd loved Nova very much, but poor health made it impossible for them to raise her.

A simple explanation with no follow-up, Nova mused. Not then, at least. In the following years, she became adept at dodging a more thorough explanation. She'd never wanted to learn more.

Out of habit, she traced the scars hidden above her wrist. Were they from a stove or a cigarette? Thankfully they weren't noticeable. She assumed her father's description, *poor health*, was code for *mental health issues*. Which might explain the abuse she felt sure her biological father had committed and which, later, made her wary of men. But the proof lay dormant in Nova's memories. She remembered nothing from her former life.

Only the nightmare of the wolf remained.

Drawing from the reverie, she regarded Imani. "That summer was the only time the topic ever came up," she said. "Not that I blame my parents. Every time they tried to broach the subject, I shut them down. I didn't want the details of my early life. Is that gutless, or what?"

"It's normal. Not everyone who's adopted wants to revisit the past. Stop beating yourself up."

A lump formed in Nova's throat. She swallowed it down.

"I'm scared," she admitted.

"I would be, too, in your situation. Facing the past means remembering things you've blocked out. Dredging up the worst moments of your childhood. It takes courage. For what it's worth, I believe you *will* face those memories, whether you do so now or sometime in the future."

Nova doubted she had the courage. Which probably explained why, growing up, she'd been in awe of children born into relatively normal lives. They walked an unbroken path to maturity, oblivious to the complications on the road others trod. If you didn't know where your life began—*who* you were, from the very beginning—how could you understand anything about yourself?

"I've always felt it's better to keep the past buried," she said, falling back on the flimsy logic she preferred to prop herself up. "What does it matter now, anyway? I have a good life."

"That's true, but those blocked memories *do* have an impact. You're too guarded. You'd fight to the death for the people you love, but you don't let many people get close. Look how infrequently you date. Whenever a man shows too much interest, you dump him. You're scared of commitment."

"Let's not analyze why I'm lousy at relationships." She thought of Jonathon, and the sudden attraction that had sparked between them. Oddly, the thought proved comforting. She sensed he was also wary of intimacy. He wouldn't ask her out.

One less thing to worry about.

Imani stretched her back. "I have a friend at the Ohio Department of Job & Family Services in Columbus," she said, changing the subject. "I'll ask her to check into Egan Croy, see if his family was ever in contact with the agency. It may take some time to get an answer—Columbus is perpetually understaffed. It's a big ask to have her dig through old files in hopes of unearthing something."

"What about our PD? Can they help?"

"They've already checked. Egan doesn't have any priors, not even a traffic citation. I'm pinning my hopes on Columbus. My friend might turn something up. If she does, it will help me decide the best course of action."

"Meaning you *are* still considering severing Egan's parental rights?"

"I won't make the final decision, Nova. It's up to the court. But yes. It's still a possibility."

Chapter 7

Nova

Lightning flashed across the sky. Soon after, the boom of thunder accompanied Nova into the kitchen. She placed the wineglasses in the sink.

Outside the window, rain pummeled the patio and the flower beds she'd prepared for summer annuals. Gazing absently at the quickening storm, she mulled over the conversation with Imani. Was Egan Croy at risk of losing custody? Much as she wanted to reserve judgment, even the loss of his wife didn't exonerate him. Was his bad behavior the result of grief? She wanted to believe he possessed the capacity to change, but her feelings were mixed at best.

The final decision wouldn't rest with her. The matter hinged on whether there was a case file on the Croy family at the main branch of the Ohio Department of Job & Family Services. Barring that, Imani needed confirmation from Bella or Henry of mistreatment by their father. It seemed clear she wouldn't sever parental rights otherwise. For children so young, Nova doubted they'd readily confirm the abuse that, to her mind, was patently obvious.

I need to gain their trust. Dousing the kitchen lights, she wandered back to the living room. *If they'll talk to me, it'll give Imani the proof she needs.*

Henry was a tough customer. Getting on his good side was an uphill battle at best. Bella was more easygoing. She liked Nova. However, she was much younger than her brother. She might lack the ability to put voice to past abuse.

Whether the court ruled against Egan Croy or not, the case promised to drag out. The judge might not rule until summer, or next autumn.

Which brought Nova to the crux of the problem. How to care for the children long-term without becoming emotionally invested? Even the best-case scenario—delivering them safely to new adoptive parents—pricked her with sadness. She liked coming home at night and listening to Bella and Henry share the high points of their day. Their young, animated voices revived some of Nova's warmest memories from her own childhood. Despite the extra work and Henry's less-than-friendly attitude, she enjoyed having them around.

A jungle of plants was arranged before the living room's large picture window. Outside, the wind blew a limb across the yard. Rain drummed on the roof. Pausing by the couch, Nova caught herself grinning. On a night this stormy, what were the odds of Henry sneaking out of the house?

Exactly zero.

After folding the blanket on the couch, she returned it to the linen closet. There was no harm in sleeping comfortably tonight in her queen-size bed.

A quick peek into Henry's room confirmed he was fast asleep. Near the doorway to Bella's room, Nova stopped in surprise. Light spilled from her own room at the end of the hallway. She went to investigate.

The overhead light and all three lamps were ablaze. The drapes were pulled shut, muffling the howls of the wind. Nova liked to sleep with lots of pillows, six in all. They formed two fluffy stacks on the bed. Between the protective walls, Bella sat rigidly upright, nervously fondling the candy tin in her lap. In her palm, she cupped the ring of hair yanked from Nova's head earlier in the week.

Amused, Nova approached. "Nice move, with the pillows. Do they block out the noise from the storm?"

"A little." Bella tucked the ring of hair back into the tin.

"Are you scared?"

Her long-lashed gaze lowered. She nodded.

"Here's an idea. Let's get you tucked back into your bed. I'll stay until you fall asleep. It'll be sort of like a slumber party."

Her eyes lifted. "What's that?"

"When you have a friend sleep over. I'm sure you'll have lots of slumber parties with girlfriends when you're older. It's fun."

Anticipation lit Bella's face. "Can we make popcorn?"

Chuckling, Nova tugged off her tennis shoes. "No, but I'll make popcorn for you tomorrow if you'd like."

"You won't leave until I'm asleep? You promise?"

Nova made an X over her chest. "Cross my heart," she said, helping her out of the bed. Bella made for the door, then spun around on her heel.

"My treasure!" Racing back, she retrieved the candy tin from beneath one of the pillows.

As Nova tucked the child into her own bed, she resisted the urge to touch the cherished object. Scratches and dents marred the metal surface. The object reminded her of the sturdy candy tins her father had given her mother on holidays when she'd been around Bella's age. These days, whenever Finch bought Helen chocolates, the sweets arrived in a cardboard box. It seemed likely Bella's treasure was manufactured in the 1960s or earlier. She wondered if the late Glory Croy had picked it up at a garage sale.

Intrigued, she asked, "What do you keep inside your treasure chest?"

Bella slid the tin beneath her pillow before lowering her head. "My best happy." In the murky darkness, she studied Nova closely. "I keep my best magic inside too."

A child's cryptic response, difficult to interpret. Were photos of Bella's late mother hidden inside?

She was about to ask to view the contents when thunder boomed across the room. The windows rattled. Bella nearly jumped out of her skin.

"It's okay." Nova sat down on the side of the bed. "The thunder won't hurt you."

"Why is it so loud?"

"When hot and cold air run into each other, they make lots of noise."

"Mama used to say the angels were bowling in heaven."

Nova smiled. "My parents used to tell me the same thing."

"Did you believe them?"

"Of course."

"When will the storm end?"

"Soon. The angels can't bowl all night. They have to get back to their other duties, like guarding small children." Leaning back against the headboard, she steered Bella into her arms. "Go to sleep, sweetie. I'll keep you safe."

Bella nestled against her side, tucking her head against Nova's breast as if they had snuggled close a thousand times before. On impulse Nova dipped her head into the wispy hair crowning Bella's head. The soft strands tickled her nose; her skin carried a sweet scent that reminded Nova of freshly mown grass.

Rain drummed harder against the roof. Lightning shot flashes of white across the floor and then was gone. Shadows danced across the ceiling. Nova followed them as a sweet heaviness built inside her, a bright warmth spreading through her chest. With sudden clarity she identified the emotion.

Affection.

She cared about Bella, more than was sensible. *She needs me. Henry does too.* There were people in Nova's life who loved her—Imani, her parents, even Bear—but when had she last felt *needed?*

She closed her eyes, weary from the long day. To ensure she didn't nod off, she began mentally reviewing her to-do list at the Holly estate. After Tuesday's debacle, when they'd lost hours on the job after hitting the old water line, she needed to double-check with Jonathon if any other ancient wells were situated near the house. If he wasn't sure, she'd have to check with the county. There might be plans on file from the 1930s and earlier. Unlikely, but anything was possible.

The rain was lessening to a steady patter when Bella spoke again.

"Nova?"

"Hmm?"

"Where did Mama go?"

The heartbreaking query opened her eyes. The shadows on the ceiling were thicker now, a rolling, impregnable wave. In vain Nova searched them for consoling words. None existed. What comfort could she provide a child whose mother had been torn from her life?

"Your mama is with the angels," she said.

"Will she ever come back?"

She smoothed a hand down Bella's side, tucking her tight against her ribs. "She can't, baby girl. I wish she could. Don't worry. She's always nearby, watching out for you and Henry. She loves you very much."

Bella rubbed her eyes. "I want Mama to come back." Her cheeks grew damp with the tears she quietly wept. "I miss her."

"I know you do."

Snuggling closer, Bella continued to cry. Her small body shuddered with the force of her sorrow. Once the last tears were spent, Nova smoothed the hair from her face.

"Nova?"

"Yes?"

"Do you believe in heaven?"

She pressed a kiss to Bella's forehead. "At times like this I do."

Chapter 8

BELLA

On Saturday morning, Bella pretended to eat breakfast. Her tummy hurt, and so she pushed the blueberry pancakes around her plate and only made teeny bites in the sausage links. She hid chunks of melon in her napkin. When the phone rang and Nova left the room, she slid her plate toward her brother. Henry gobbled down the last of her meal.

Grabbing her treasure chest, she went outside.

Bella climbed atop the picnic table. Beneath the maple tree's curtain of leaves, birds hopped from branch to branch, chirping in a wild chorus. Wings fluttered through the air as they took turns perching on the bird feeder dangling from a limb.

Nothing compared to Nova's backyard. Beside the path of shiny white stones through the green grass, the sun threw sparkles across the birdbath's clear water. The white fence boxing in the yard looked new. Bright cardinals, tiny sparrows, and fat mourning doves perched in a row like fidgety old ladies. Near the back of the property, ceramic gnomes hid beneath the oak tree. The gardening shed opposite the tree resembled a miniature house with its skinny door and small windows.

The garden's serenity usually made Bella happy. It didn't today. Angry bees zipped around inside her tummy. Even the pretty birdsong couldn't make them go away.

More than anything, she wanted to stay here with Nova. She wanted Henry to go to the place where Imani worked and leave her behind. He didn't mind seeing Pa this morning.

If she asked nicely, would Nova let her stay home? They'd buy flowers at a gardening store, then spend the day planting them. Bella didn't know how to plant flowers—before Mama went to heaven, Pa never let her buy even a pot of those orange flowers at the supermarket.

Pulling off the lid of her treasure, she took out the magic picture. She traced a finger around the two faces, captivated by the love weaving between. She kept moving her finger in tiny circles until the bees in her tummy flew away.

Closing her eyes, she whispered, "Please make Nova let me stay home." She repeated the words over and over, wishing with all her might.

The screen door creaked open. Henry sauntered over with his mouth tipped into a frown. Bella still wasn't used to his changed appearance. Last night after dinner, Nova had taken them to a big shopping mall for ice cream. Afterward, they stopped into a beauty salon. A lady with laughing blue eyes gave Henry his first haircut in months. With his hair now barely skimming his ears, he looked older.

Nearing the picnic table, he noticed what she was holding. "There's no magic in your picture. Mama only told you nonsense to make you feel better. You were always getting scared."

Injured, Bella pressed the photograph to her heart. "Mama never lied to me. Mamas always tell the truth. It's the rule."

"People lie all the time, Bella. Especially to kids. They think we're stupid or something."

"I'm not stupid."

"You are if you believe in wishes." Henry thumped on his chest. "I'm the one telling you the truth. There's no such thing as magic. All those storybooks Mama read to you, and the dumb stuff she said to make you feel better—it was just pretend. Like on Halloween. Kids dress up and pretend to be someone else."

"My magic picture is different."

Henry snickered. "Nova's got a mushy side like most chicks," he said, glancing toward the house. "Why not show her the picture? Maybe she'll believe you. You can dress up like fairy princesses and make wishes together."

"Stop being mean."

"Stop acting like a baby, and I will."

Hurt by the taunts, Bella tucked the photo back into her treasure chest. She put it beside the ringlet of Nova's hair and pressed the lid shut. There was no winning an argument with her brother. Henry didn't believe in anything but the unreliability of grown-ups. That, and the hard sting of Pa's anger.

He sat on the picnic table beside her. "You only love that photo because Mama did too." He flicked an impatient finger against the side of her treasure. "It was one of her favorites."

"Mama didn't have favorites. She told me any picture of a mama and her child is special."

"Why not wish on a photo of me with Mama? Or one of you and her? You don't even know the people in that picture. They were gone before you were ever born."

Eyes lowered, Bella slid the box away from his curious hands. Henry believed she kept family pictures in her treasure box alongside her other special things. He assumed she kept a whole stack of them.

There weren't any.

On the day of Mama's funeral, when they came home and Henry stomped off to his room, Pa threw them all away. Pa usually only drank when he went out, but that afternoon, he finished half a bottle of liquor. He'd been angry at Mama for leaving him with two rug rats to raise. His words. The photo album of Bella and Henry as babies, the packets of photos Mama had kept in kitchen and bedroom drawers—Pa dumped them all in the garbage. Only the magic photo had escaped his wrath.

Nova came out of the house.

"Kids, Imani is here." She noticed their hunched shoulders and gloomy expressions. "Is everything all right? Oh, Bella—it'll be fine. Don't worry."

When she opened her arms, Bella scrambled off the picnic table.

She hugged Nova tight. "Do I have to go?"

"You do, sweetie. But everything will be fine." Nova kissed the top of her head. "After you see your father, Imani will take you out for lunch."

"I want you to go with us."

"I can't, sweetie. This morning I have a meeting at the Holly estate. I'll see you this afternoon when you get home."

With a sigh, Bella nodded. She pretended she couldn't feel the bees zipping back into her tummy because she didn't want to make Nova sad. She already felt sad enough for both of them.

Letting her go, Nova reached for Henry. When he marched past, disappointment spread across her face. He'd stopped threatening to run away, but he still wouldn't let her get anywhere near him.

From over his shoulder, he said, "C'mon, Bella. Pa is waiting for us."

Voices echoed through the building where Imani worked. Old people were seated in one room, listening to a lady with a thin, eager face. In another, more crowded room, couples chatted loudly as they filed into line before a long table. The scent of coffee wafted past, and Bella glimpsed a small cafeteria, where a man stood before a vending machine. After the clink of change, something dropped into his waiting hand.

At the end of the hallway, Imani led them into a big room. Child-size tables and chairs were scattered about, with bigger chairs for grown-ups nearby. Bella spotted a couch at each end of the room, the cushions lumpy and the armrests frayed from use. At a bookcase near the windows looking out on the parking lot, stacks of picture books, toys, and board games competed for space.

Pa strode forward. He wore a nice shirt and the spicy cologne he used on weekends. His eyes were crinkly and warm as he paused before Imani.

"I'm sorry about rescheduling with your associate Tim Kenner." Pa held out his hand. "I've been looking forward to meeting you."

Imani shook his hand. "It's not a problem. I had a scheduling conflict. Tim was happy to step in." Her chin lifted a wary inch. The way she acted reminded Bella of Mama, whenever she'd tiptoed around Pa's emotions.

"Mr. Kenner mentioned you're one of his favorite colleagues. He said you're an expert at helping families in crisis. The best social worker on staff."

At the sugar in his voice, she folded her arms. "Oh, I don't know about that. Every case is different. It's a learning curve, really. A week doesn't pass when I don't encounter a situation I haven't seen before."

"I appreciate everything you're doing for my family. Losing my wife . . . me and the kids have been through a rough patch. We're grateful you're helping us out."

Bella and Henry exchanged a look. Bella almost heard her brother's thoughts.

You see? Grown-ups lie all the time.

Imani said, "I'm sorry for your loss, Mr. Croy."

"Please—call me Egan." Pa's smile widened to show lots of teeth. "The way Tim sang your praises, I assumed we were assigned to someone my age. You're a lot younger than I expected. Pretty too. You look like a model. I guess people tell you that all the time."

"Actually, they don't. But thank you."

They shared a few more pleasantries before Imani walked to the couch at the far end of the room. From her briefcase she removed papers and a pen. Looking up, she sent Bella a reassuring smile.

The silent interchange put a hard gleam in Pa's eyes.

He flicked at Henry's bangs. "You look different. Who cut your hair?"

"A lady in Mentor. We went to a big mall last night. It was cool."

"Do you like your foster home?"

Imani cleared her throat. "Egan, please remember the rules. The children can't discuss their current living arrangements. I'm sure Tim Kenner explained this to you."

The gentle reprimand deepened the lines around Pa's mouth. "Sorry. I forgot." Turning away, he led the children to the opposite end of the room.

"You've still got that candy tin your mama picked up at Goodwill?" he asked Bella. "It's old and rusty. You ought to throw it out."

Henry mimicked the annoyance on Pa's face. "It's stupid, how she drags it around everywhere." He looked happy to help Pa take aim at her. It kept him safe from criticism, at least for now.

Pa noticed Imani, watching the exchange. Sweetening his tone, he said, "Here's a promise. After I get you kids back, I'll buy you some real toys. Whatever you'd like. We'll go on a shopping spree, like it's Christmas."

Henry bit at his lower lip. "When are you getting us back?"

"Soon, I hope. I'll keep you posted."

"Will you get me a Star Wars fighter plane? Like the one Luke Skywalker flew when he fought the Death Star? Jason at school has one."

"If that's what you want, boy."

"You bet it is!"

Henry took the lead, talking about the toys Pa would never buy. They walked toward the bookcase with Bella trailing behind. Her feet itched with the desire to race across the room. She'd gladly spend the rest of the hour with Imani. A prickly energy coiled around Pa like a wasp's nest buzzing with danger.

Imani returned to the papers in her lap. Henry shuffled through the games on the bookshelf like he meant to pick one to play. As the minutes wound out, she began reading in earnest. Her pen scratched across the pages.

Bella knew Henry was up to no good when he put his back to Imani to shield his movements. Quick as lightning, he pulled a Green Harmony brochure from his pocket. Her eyes widened when he thrust it into Pa's hand.

There was a photo of Nova on the cover.

Pointing to it, Henry whispered, "She's the lady we're staying with."

A protest formed on Bella's lips. Henry knew the rule. They weren't supposed to talk about Nova. It wasn't allowed. They were supposed to keep her name a secret.

Pa gripped her shoulder. A warning, and she clamped her mouth shut.

He winked at Henry. "Good boy." *Pocketing the brochure, he chuckled softly.* "I'll be damned. The chick you're staying with? I know her."

Chapter 9

Nova

Checking her watch, Nova brought her truck to a halt at the end of the Holly estate's long, winding driveway. She'd left the house too early, right after Imani picked the children up for their supervised visit with their father. She wasn't due to meet with Charlotte for another ten minutes.

The faultless blue sky and pleasing temperatures invited her from the truck, and she left the engine running as she eased herself out to take in the bright spring day. In the distance, sunlight glowed on the Colonial Revival–style mansion built by Charlotte's great-grandfather in 1894. The proud edifice nestled in the valley behind the historic mill at Holly's Bluff. From her vantage point, she spied a row of cars before the attached restaurant, glinting in the sunlight like colorful beads. The mill wouldn't open until nine o'clock and the restaurant an hour later, but the staff managed by Charlotte and her fiancé were already on site.

Leaning against the hood of the truck, Nova let her thoughts wend back to Bella. She'd been nervous this morning. Picking at her breakfast, then sneaking outside with her treasure clutched in her hands. Clearly she would've been happy to skip the visit with Egan. Was Henry equally nervous? Given his standoffish behavior, it was harder to assess his true feelings. If time spent with Egan proved too stressful for the kids, Nova reassured herself that Imani would intervene. Cut the visit short, if needed.

An equally pressing concern weighed on Nova. The instant connection she shared with Bella—and her fierce desire to protect her—echoed her own forgotten past. Bella was seven; Nova had been a year younger when her world fell apart. They'd both endured abuse at the hands of their fathers.

Nova didn't need the proof of specific memories to hold this conviction—she'd harbored a fear of men from the very beginning. It took years before she began to trust her adoptive father. On jobsites, her antennae went up around certain men, the ones who talked down to women and seemed predisposed to mistreat their wives and girlfriends. In fact, she'd consciously chosen to foster teenage boys to help allay the fear, tackling the problem at its source by helping them learn constructive ways to manage their anger.

Even Bear, who'd grown into a sweet, softhearted man, might have turned out differently without her influence. When she'd first taken him in, Bear had punched a hole in her guest bedroom wall after a particularly difficult visit with his father. Henry was no different. While there were exceptions to every rule, he displayed all the classic signs that often marked the behavior of abused boys: lashing out at others, allowing anger to rule his emotions. Girls, on the other hand, usually internalized their suffering. They hid from the world, and themselves. They suffered in silence.

Bella did. At the same age, Nova had too. Were there other similarities—echoes from the past capable of unearthing Nova's buried memories? Anxiety carried her back to the truck.

Unable to dispel it, she parked before the Holly mansion and promptly strode around the side of the house. There were still a few minutes to kill, and nothing settled her emotions like being outdoors on a beautiful day. The lawn flowed in a river of green all the way to the forest. The view was partially obscured by the wrought iron tables sprinkled across the large patio and the cantilever umbrellas shielding a row of teak chaise longues near the low stone wall encasing the outdoor space.

She didn't yet have all the details, but Charlotte had mentioned she'd like to add a gazebo to the project. Reaching the center of the lawn, she began visualizing where best to place the structure in the generous sea of grass.

"Nova!" With a cheery wave, Charlotte bounced down the patio steps. "I saw your truck out front," she said, joining her. "Thanks for coming on short notice. I hope it wasn't inconvenient, dragging you out here on the weekend. I was afraid I'd never find time to go over this with you on Monday. I leave for work early."

That made sense, since she never appeared on the jobsite. "It's no problem," Nova assured her. She was more than happy to take on the extra work. "Why don't you tell me about your new inspiration?"

"Well, I love to throw parties. I always have. The house is big, of course, and there's tons of room inside, but the more I mulled it over, I started thinking outside the box—I mean, look at all this space! It seems a waste not to put it to use, at least in the warm-weather months. So, I thought, why not add a gazebo? It'll become the focal point when I have parties outside."

It was impossible not to enjoy Charlotte's buoyant personality, and Nova followed behind like an obedient dog as the Holly's Mill director of marketing led her out toward the woods. Frowning, Charlotte retraced her steps. She was still chattering about the parties she'd host when they again neared the patio.

Charlotte swiveled around in a semicircle. "I thought I'd decided the best spot for the gazebo," she murmured, more to herself than to Nova. "Now I'm confused."

"This is too close to the patio."

"You're sure?"

"Unless you're talking about a small structure."

"No! I want something big."

"Big enough to seat . . . ?"

Charlotte pursed her lips. "Twenty people? Does that sound enormous?" She beamed. "Brent and I have *a lot* of friends."

"Then the gazebo will need some distance from the house. I suggest placing it over there." Nova gestured to a spot in the center of the lawn.

"What about electricity?"

On your budget? Not a problem.

"Oh, that's simple. Jonathon can have an electrician run the lines beside the path I'll build from the patio to the gazebo."

"Perfect!" Charlotte started off toward the area. "We'll need a wide path. Not gravel—it's a killer on high heels. How should we lay it out?"

Nova was about to follow, and suggest a design for the path—curving, feminine, like the other landscape features she'd designed—when goose bumps rose on her arms. A glass door swished open, and a woman appeared on the patio. Older, with perfectly coiffed, silvery-blonde hair—Denise Holly.

They'd never met, and what happened next left Nova baffled. Denise was about to take a sip from the mug she held when her eyes lifted. Her attention flew to Nova, and she released a soft gasp. Out of shock? Or wonder? Unable to decipher the reaction, Nova was taking a startled step back when Denise's grip loosened on the handle of the mug. A stream of coffee spilled on the ground.

Twenty paces off, Charlotte cut off her latest ramble. She turned around.

"Mom!" Bustling forward, she left Nova marooned on the lawn. "I thought you'd gone out."

Denise wiped the distress from her features. Fingering the thin gold necklace at her throat, she came down the patio steps, her silk blouse fluttering on her slender frame. Nova caught the stiffness in her gait. A hesitancy, as if she'd stumbled into an awkward situation.

"I don't play tennis at the club until this afternoon." Denise's voice, soft, lilting, put a smile on her daughter's face. "I'm sure I told you."

"I don't remember. Well, I'm glad you're here. I have so much to tell you!" Charlotte did a double take. "Mother, you look absolutely green. Did you eat something that didn't agree with you?"

"Not yet."

"Very funny. You know how I worry. Honestly, you look . . . seasick."

"I slept poorly last night. Par for the course at my age."

"Are you coming down with something?"

Her daughter's concern seemed to provide Denise with much-needed ballast. Smiling, she said, "If you're concerned about my welfare, stop fluffing off the preparations for your bridal shower. You flit from one thing to the next like a butterfly." She allowed her gaze to rest on Nova. "I wasn't aware you had company this morning. What's going on?"

"We're discussing my new idea. I've already run it by Nova. Do you care if I add a gazebo to the plans? We'll put it right . . . there." Charlotte pointed down the lawn. "Jonathon promised his crews will build it once they finish inside the house. But only if I have your go-ahead. Do I, Mother? Say yes. The gazebo won't cost much."

"Charlotte, we've already added the Jacuzzi tub in your new bathroom to the original plans. I also agreed to let you put in a cutting garden and redo every inch of landscaping around the house. Isn't that enough?"

"This is the last big ask, promise. We'll use the gazebo for summer bashes. Set up a band inside, with our big, beautiful lawn for the dance floor. You know how much I love to throw parties."

Nova managed to wipe the smile from her face. It took no effort to imagine the effervescent Charlotte blasting Fleetwood Mac and The Go-Go's across the grounds while a hundred of her closest friends danced until dawn. Luckily for the Hollys, there were no neighbors living nearby to complain about the noise.

"We're already over budget." There was no missing the affection in Denise's eyes as she studied her daughter. "What's the price of your latest whim?"

Charlotte inspected her flawlessly polished nails. "I don't know the precise cost. It's not expensive, though. Ask Jonathon. He promised to stop by this morning."

"He's coming over? Why didn't you mention it?"

"I told you last night. After I called him." When Denise folded her arms in clear disagreement, Charlotte quickly added, "It must've slipped my mind. Well, it's water under the bridge." She flashed a winning smile. "Will you at least keep an open mind about adding the gazebo?"

Jonathon appeared on the patio, sparing Denise from answering. He murmured a greeting to Nova, standing quietly to the side, before jumping into the debate.

He regarded his mother. "Has Charlotte brought you up to speed?" he asked. "Don't blame me. She doesn't need my help dreaming up crazy ideas to drain your checkbook."

"My ideas aren't crazy," Charlotte protested. "They're inspired. We'll surround the gazebo with azaleas and rhododendrons, and maybe some flowering cherry trees. It will look elegant."

"Except on the nights when you host a *bash*," Denise remarked. "Then my property will resemble a frat party."

Jonathon rocked back on his heels. "Don't invite the potheads when you throw parties, sis. Especially your old college pals. They couldn't walk the straight and narrow if you kept them on a leash."

"Shut up!" Charlotte attempted a look of displeasure, but her eyes danced.

Nova's pulse thumped out of rhythm when Denise's probing gaze found her again. "What's your opinion, Nova? Will a gazebo in the center of my four-acre backyard look elegant, or ridiculous?" When she grimaced, clearly unsure about weighing in, Denise changed tack, adding, "It's nice to meet you, by the way. I'd hoped to meet last week, when my son's crews descended on my house like a swarm of locusts. I didn't see you in the crush."

"*Our* house," Charlotte put in. "We're co-owners now." Pulling Nova close, she whispered, "Best. Wedding gift. Ever."

Jonathon glanced at his mother. "You didn't meet Nova on the first day because she came late." Grinning, he kept his attention fastened on her, seeming to relish how he'd left her tongue-tied. "Don't bother asking why. She won't go into it."

"Oh. All right. I won't then."

"She was an hour late, in fact."

"That's unfortunate."

"Yeah, I thought so too," Jonathon agreed, clearly intent on teasing her. Or flirting. Nova's breath hitched. *Flirting, definitely.* The realization scattered a dizzy sort of delight through her blood.

Covering it, she shot him a look of annoyance. "I wasn't an hour late," she countered. "More like forty-five minutes."

His grin widened. "Which is still late, any way you cut it."

"It couldn't be helped."

He folded his arms, enjoying himself at her expense. "I'm curious about the reason, and why your hair was sopping wet when you *did* finally show up. But I'm getting over it. Some mysteries aren't meant to be solved."

The good-natured teasing put spots of color on Nova's cheeks. Or his roving appraisal did. *It's the way he's drinking me in, definitely.* She didn't appreciate the way he was making her go weak at the knees in front of his family. Denise watched him with ill-concealed surprise. Charlotte appeared giddy at the sight of her normally dignified brother flirting so openly.

Charlotte laughed. "Should we leave the two of you alone to hash this out?" She hugged Nova. "Don't let Jonathon get to you. He's only teasing because he thinks you're special."

"She is," Jonathon agreed, his expression devilish, "but I still wish she'd let us in on the mystery."

"There's no mystery." Nova jumped when she realized she'd spoken. "It was just . . . one of those mornings when nothing goes right."

She left the comment dangling. During the ensuing hush, all thought fled her mind for several humiliating seconds. Coming to a decision, she raked a hand through her hair.

She plunged forward. "I was delayed because one of my foster kids refused to go to school. Henry locked himself in the bathroom. When I got inside, he was standing on the rim of the bathtub aiming the showerhead at me like a high-powered water gun."

Denise pressed a hand to her throat. "Good heavens," she murmured.

"He nailed me, and good." Nova chuckled. "Drenched me from head to toe."

"How unpleasant for you."

"Oh, it wasn't too bad," she said, needing to dispel the concern on Denise's face. "When kids act out, you just deal with it. I did have to get Henry changed into dry clothes—school was already in session by the time I drove the kids to Longfellow Elementary. There wasn't time to go back home to dry my hair."

The disclosure sobered Jonathon. No doubt he now regretted teasing her. Denise's eyes shone with admiration and Charlotte appeared amused. It didn't take much to amuse Charlotte.

"How many foster children do you have?" Denise asked gently. "If you don't mind me asking."

Nova shared the basic details. Summing up, she added, "There were no other homes available, so I agreed to foster Bella and Henry without an end date. I might have them all summer, maybe longer."

"How many young children have you fostered?"

"This is my first time. The learning curve is steep. Usually, I take in teenagers for short-term care. A few weeks, maybe a month."

Jonathon asked, "How long have you been doing this?"

"Oh, about four years now. Sometimes I go several months without a placement. It's hard work."

"But you're not married." He blanched. "Sorry. None of my business. What I meant is, it's a big load to take on solo."

"The rewards are worth it."

"I'm sure you're good at it."

Warmed by the compliment, Nova glanced at him. "To be honest, I wasn't prepared for Bella and Henry." She felt the blush on her cheeks deepening, but she couldn't draw her attention away, to sever the strong current passing between them. "There are lots of tough calls when you're dealing with young kids. Figuring out how to make them feel safe without getting emotionally involved. What to discuss, and what topics to dodge. Like walking on a tightrope."

Jonathon opened his mouth, apparently to proffer another compliment. He looked away, plainly silenced in the face of compassion. It was another surprise in a morning rife with them. She'd never before seen him at a loss for words.

Rescuing him, Denise said, "I'm sure your parents are very proud of you. Your mother especially. She's such a lovely woman. Please give Helen my regards."

Nova cocked her head. "You know her?"

"I did, years ago. Helen was the visiting nurse who cared for my husband during the last stages of cancer." A shadow of that former grief flickered across Denise's face. "Your mother was the perfect blend of sensitive and stern. If she wasn't holding my hand whenever I went to pieces, she'd tactfully remind me to get showered and dressed. Bossy and compassionate, depending on the need. The perfect combination for a nurse."

"She hasn't changed." Nova smiled.

"Is Helen still working?"

"She's retired now. She's with my dad in Cincinnati visiting my brother. Peter and his wife just had their second child. Dad is retired too." Nova cleared her throat. "I'm sorry for your loss, Mrs. Holly."

"Please, call me Denise."

"Thanks." Nova hesitated. "When did Mr. Holly pass?"

"Oh, it's been more than twenty years. Charlotte was only four. Jonathon was older, of course—twelve years old at the time. My son became the man of the house while still in middle school. A terrible burden. During those final, difficult months, your mother was a great comfort."

"I'm glad."

The galloping reverie was getting away from Denise. Her children were casting odd looks—Nova suspected she rarely broached the topic of their father's death. And she appeared about to add something else as she kept her attention trained on Nova, her expression now inked with regret, or worry. As if she feared she'd already said too much. Nova wasn't sure what to make of her changed behavior.

Then Denise reined herself in, steering the conversation onto a safer path. "Jonathon, how much will the gazebo set me back? Men, supplies, the works." While he drummed his fingers on his jeans, mentally tallying up the cost, she turned back to Nova. "I also need an estimate for the additional landscaping."

"Azaleas and cherry trees, to start," Charlotte put in. "Nova, can you suggest whatever else we'll need?"

"Of course."

"Don't forget the hardscaping," Jonathon told her. "You'll need to install a path from the patio to the gazebo."

Nova pulled a notepad from the pocket of her jeans. "No problem," she said.

Chapter 10

Nova

Nova smiled in greeting as Imani appeared in the kitchen. Letting go of Bella's hand, Imani glanced over her shoulder, no doubt to check that Henry wasn't trying another prison break. At the heavy thump of footfalls, she nodded with satisfaction.

Bella came forward. "Did you miss us?"

"Absolutely," Nova assured her. "I've been counting down the minutes until I'd see you again."

Bella made it halfway across the kitchen, skidded to a halt, and gasped. Her gaze flew to the flats of spring flowers arranged on the table.

"Do you like them?" Nova asked.

"They're the prettiest flowers in the world!"

"I think so too."

After leaving the Holly estate, she'd dropped by Garden Haven in Chesterland to purchase the annuals. Two flats of begonias, and a flat each of impatiens, snapdragons, marigolds, and petunias—the kaleidoscope of colors promised to make her yard a real standout. She'd also picked up child-size gardening tools, gloves, and pails. Two sets of each, in case the normally unsociable Henry decided to join them.

Giggling, Bella cupped a purple snapdragon. "Can we plant them together? Will you teach me how?"

"That's the plan. The beds around my house are ready to go. What do you say we spend tomorrow putting the flowers out?"

"Sure!"

Henry skirted around Imani to see what all the fuss was about. "How much did you spend on girly stuff?" He surveyed the flats with clear disapproval. "Flowers aren't cheap."

"Oh, they weren't too expensive."

"That's what chicks always say when they spend too much."

"My money, my choice."

"When will they die?"

Really? That's what you want to know? Nova tamped down her irritation. A child with a cheerier disposition might've asked, *How long will they live?* Not Henry. The cloud of discontent following him around was thicker than ever. For good reason. After spending an hour visiting his father, he was in full macho mode. Sure to counter any positive feedback with a surly retort.

"They'll continue to flower until September, at least," she told him. "October, if we don't have a hard frost. But sometimes it snows before Halloween."

"You spent a lot of dough on something that won't last."

Imani ruffled his hair. "Nova doesn't need your opinion." She noticed the Kmart bag on a chair. "What's this?"

Carrying the bag to the counter, Nova shook out the contents. "Stuff for the kids to play with. A basketball, beach balls—they were on sale, so I grabbed three—and a really cool ladder." With a flourish, she unrolled the sturdy rope ladder with its bright-red plastic rungs for easy climbing. "Henry, we can tie the ladder up on the oak tree at the back of the yard. Would you like that?"

He nearly smiled. Catching himself, he stuck his thumbs in the pockets of his jeans.

"Can we do it now?" he demanded, reverting to grumpy behavior.

"Why don't you and Bella take the basketball outside and play? Take the beach balls, too, if you don't mind blowing them up. We'll hang the ladder tonight, after dinner."

At the request, he grabbed the toys. "Bella, c'mon." He sprinted outside.

Bella, however, stayed rooted by the table. She rocked the candy tin like a baby in need of comfort. Nova exchanged a curious glance with Imani. Normally Bella followed Henry whenever he summoned her—their bond, unbreakable.

"I'm not playing with Henry today." She lifted her chin to a haughty angle. "Can I take the flowers outside? I'll pick where we'll plant them."

"Sure." Nova placed the flat of petunias in her hands. "Do you need help carrying them out?"

"No."

The child attempted to balance her treasure and the flowers. When the flat threatened to tip, Imani rushed forward.

She returned the flowers to the table. "Bella, you need both hands to carry the flats outside. I suggest you go to your room and put your treasure away. Hide it from Henry if you're afraid he'll look inside."

The suggestion furrowed Bella's delicate brows. Parting with her cherished keepsake, even for a short time, clearly didn't appeal.

"Or don't follow my advice. Makes no difference to me." Imani feigned a careless shrug. With a daughter Bella's age, her mastery of little-girl behavior was excellent. "Keep your treasure and leave the flowers inside. Nova will take them out later."

They traded sharp looks. In a huff, Bella stomped off to her bedroom.

Nova returned to dinner prep. "What's going on between the kids?" She placed a green pepper on the cutting board. "Why is Bella mad at Henry?"

"Got me. They were awfully quiet on the ride here. I thought they usually got along well."

"They do, for the most part. Not today, obviously."

"All kids have their moments."

"Bella isn't usually moody. Henry must've done something to upset her." Reconsidering, Nova thought back to the teenagers she'd fostered. "Or she's upset about seeing her father. In my experience, kids aren't always sweetness and light after supervised visitation."

Imani nodded in agreement. "I've seen some serious meltdowns, especially after that initial visit."

"She *was* nervous this morning. She wanted to stay with me." Nova began slicing the green pepper, aware that something didn't fit. "But I don't see why she'd funnel her angst at her brother. She doesn't, normally. She's totally devoted to him."

"Don't worry about it. Whatever's eating at her, she'll get over it. Even close siblings have disagreements. Look at you and Peter. Growing up, he was super protective of you, but he always gave you a hard time after you played a pickup game of basketball with him and his friends."

"Only because he was jealous of my perfect aim." Nova had never enrolled in sports in school, but she had killer eye-hand coordination. "Peter couldn't sink a basket if his life depended on it."

"That's true. Your big brother's a great guy, but he sucked at basketball. I don't know why he didn't give it up." Letting the topic go, Imani studied her with interest. "How was your meeting at the Holly estate?"

"I've landed more work, which is great. Charlotte wants to add a gazebo to the project. Jonathon's men will build it after they finish inside the house. They're a long way off completing the remodel, so I'll have ample time to come up with the landscape design."

"Why do you sound disappointed?"

"Not disappointed," she clarified. "I'm confused. I met Denise."

"I've run into her several times at charity events. Jonathon usually escorts her. She's a classy lady. Kind, smart—she donates to lots of charities." Imani frowned. "Didn't you get along with her?"

"No, that's not it. She was very gracious."

"Then what?"

"I started picking up the strangest vibes from her. I can't put my finger on it. I felt like there was something she wanted to tell me. Something she knew I wouldn't like."

"About the job?"

"No. It felt personal. Like she had a secret she wanted to share." Nova shook her head, irritated suddenly with her overactive imagination. She was reading too much into it. "My mother took care of Denise's husband when he was dying," she added. "Maybe she seemed unsettled because she doesn't like to talk about him. I got the impression his death is a taboo subject in their family."

Imani nodded. "That's understandable. Most people aren't comfortable discussing loved ones they've lost."

Bella returned with her pique still in force, pausing the conversation. She made repeated trips to carry the flats outside. Finally, the screen door slammed shut. A quick peek out the window confirmed she'd arranged the flats on the picnic table. Henry was sitting on the grass, blowing up the beach balls. Without giving him so much as a glance, Bella carefully lifted out each small carton of flowers. Steering a wide berth around her brother, she began arranging them in the garden beds.

Nova returned to her task. They were having roasted vegetables and chicken tacos for dinner tonight. Hopefully the children would enjoy their first introduction to Mexican cuisine.

Imani picked up stray flowers from the floor. "I still have to grocery shop this afternoon. What I'd give for a maid." Tossing them onto the table, she plopped into a chair. "I promised Maya we'd have lasagna tonight. Like I have the energy to whip up a lavish meal."

"Since when do you make lasagna?" Imani's talents in the kitchen were sadly limited. She'd been known to burn hamburgers and turn mashed potatoes into gooey mush.

"I'm trying to learn. The recipe looks easy enough."

A disaster in the making, but Nova kept the opinion to herself. "How's Maya?"

"Still complaining about the ants in her cast. But there's light at the end of the tunnel. The orthopedist plans to remove the cast soon. In another week or two."

"That's great news."

Tugging off her flats, Imani settled her feet on a chair. "Speaking of Maya, we bought her a new swing set. We let her pick it out last night. Would you like our old one? It's in great shape."

"I'm thrilled to take it off your hands. Thanks."

"If Bella and Henry are with you all summer, it'll help keep them occupied. Oh, I'm also looking into day camp options. The YMCA has a nice summer camp program."

Nova set the vegetables aside. Leaning against the counter, she took care to dampen the expectancy in her voice. "Should I expect to have the kids all summer?"

"If it's too big of a commitment—"

"It's not. I'm happy to keep them until the court makes a final decision. We have our ups and downs, but they're settling in. I'd hate to see them moved to another home."

Imani smiled with relief. "I wish I could give you an exact timeline," she said, rubbing her feet. "Some cases are harder to decide than others. Especially when a parent wants to maintain custody and seems willing to make behavioral changes."

"You believe Egan Croy falls into that category."

A statement, not a question, and Nova wondered at the disappointment she felt. Reunification was the primary goal. Adoption was a last resort, after every court-mandated intervention failed. Imani was merely doing her job, despite the suspicion of abuse. Regardless of the clear example of abandonment on weekend nights.

"I'm not sure what I believe," Imani said. "This morning, Egan seemed fully engaged with his children. He was friendly. Thanking me for helping his family, telling the kids he'd take them on a toy-buying spree once they were back together. He acts like a man hoping to keep his family intact."

"How were the kids?"

"Bella was standoffish. Not Henry. He has a strong bond with his father."

"I'm not sure that's a good thing. Some of the stuff Henry says . . . it's sexist, Imani. He's been tutored to believe men are superior. Egan's done a great job convincing him that women are brainless."

"It's not a crime for a man to fill his son's head with nonsense. Happens all the time."

"What about your friend in Columbus? Any word from her?" Nova suffered a small sting of guilt. There was nothing high-minded about praying a case file existed on Egan Croy, one sure to blacken Imani's opinion of him.

"Not yet. She has to dig through a mountain of files. Any casework from 1980 or earlier sits in dusty cartons in the basement of Ohio Job & Family Services. I don't envy her the task. She'll need a snow shovel. It might take weeks to dig through."

"Really? That long?"

Wiggling her toes, Imani sighed with exasperation. "What? You presumed she has years of case files at her fingertips? Girlfriend, you haven't seen paperwork overload until you've worked for a government agency. We do everything in triplicate. Then we forget where we've stashed the copies."

Nova grimaced. "My tax dollars at work."

"More like the *lack* of tax dollars. We're perpetually underfunded." From the table Imani picked up a snapdragon blossom. Absently she twirled it between her fingers. "You know, my husband is talking about buying one of those IBM personal computers."

"He's wasting his money. It won't do much more than let him play games."

"Well, Uri is convinced we *will* have all the data we want at our fingertips, someday. Once personal computers have enough memory to hold our stuff."

Nova gave an incredulous laugh. "If someone ever makes a computer able to hold all my crap, I'll do the happy dance."

Chapter 11

Nova

Sunday brought a remarkable development. Bella appeared for breakfast without the treasure chest she relied upon for emotional security.

She daintily ate her cheese omelet without mentioning the object that had been practically glued to her fingertips until now. She chatted nonstop with Nova about the flowers they planned to set out today without offering a clue.

Bella ignored her brother. The feat proved easy to accomplish. Henry—predictably sullen, his teeth unbrushed and his face unwashed—was busy wolfing down five pieces of toast and two omelets with cheese, ham, and every vegetable Nova had scoured from the fridge. He was pouring a second glass of milk when Bella padded to the dishwasher with her plate, then skipped off to get dressed. Nova assumed she'd reappear with her treasure in tow.

Bella returned with a smile. The keepsake was nowhere in sight.

Why had she unexpectedly shrugged off that attachment? Nova wondered if it was proof Bella felt safe in foster care. Or was the decision more pragmatic? Bringing the old candy tin outside while they dug in the dirt risked getting it dirty.

Nova settled on a more obvious reason—Bella had taken Imani's advice to heart.

Yesterday Imani *had* suggested she leave her treasure in her bedroom before carrying the summer annuals outside. Apparently the remark made a big impression on the little girl, who now slept in her own bedroom, with its many places to hide an object she valued above all else. Whether the tin was now stuffed inside Bella's closet or tucked beneath the mattress, Nova viewed the change as a positive development.

Gold-tipped clouds drifted across the sky. The light breeze carried the fragrance of lilacs blooming near the garden gate. Savoring the sweet air, Nova finished adding organic fertilizer to the garden bed by her small patio. The balmy temperatures promised an early summer. Lazy weekends swimming at Headlands Beach once the school year ended, and visits to the emerald necklace of Metroparks studding northeast Ohio.

Wielding a child-size gardening trowel, Bella began digging holes in the soft earth for each plant. They got into a rhythm. Each time she finished, Nova gestured like a game show host at the selection of flowers bobbing their colorful heads on the garden path.

Bella studied the flowers. She looked as fresh and bright as the sunlight spilling around them in glittering pools. A nutritious diet was adding fullness to her cheeks. Her blue eyes sparkled. One of Nova's old gardening hats listed to the side of her face. The small pink gardening gloves, purchased yesterday along with the child-size gardening tools, fit perfectly.

She pointed at a begonia. "That one."

Nova tipped the silver-leaved plant out of its container. "Here you go."

Bella lowered it into the ground, minding her new jeans, then patted the dirt back into place. Fingers poised beneath her lips, she blew the flower a kiss. She'd assured Nova that flowers grew faster if they knew they were loved.

The same was true of children.

Bella asked, "Which one do you like best?"

Nova surveyed their handiwork with satisfaction. In less than thirty minutes, they'd filled half of the flower bed. For a child, Bella possessed good focus. She'd quickly learned to dig each hole the proper depth and how to handle the fragile plants.

"I don't have a favorite." Nova brushed her palm across the top of an impatiens, delighting in the softness of the petals. "Every flower is beautiful in its own way. Some are very special. Take the lowly marigold. It's not the most glamorous flower, but lots of bugs don't like the smell, so they stay away. It's a big help to other plants, keeping them free of pests. And some flowers are edible, like nasturtium. You can toss them in a salad."

"You know a lot about plants."

"I love the natural world. Ever notice how trees sing to us?"

Bella wrinkled her nose. "Trees don't sing."

"Yes, they do. When they rustle their leaves. It sounds like music if you listen closely. Sweet and soothing on a warm spring day—or louder and more thrilling if a storm's coming. And flowers are really cool. They start blooming near the end of winter, beginning with the crocus. Daffodils come next. Then lots of other flowers come into bloom, like the ones we're planting today. They keep up the color parade clear into fall."

"A color parade—that sounds nice. Like there's a party outside and anyone can go."

"It *is* nice."

A cardinal rocketed past in a streak of crimson. Bella followed the bird's ascent as it flew into the yard next door.

"I like nature too." She began digging the next hole. "I like anything pretty."

"Do *you* have a favorite flower?"

"I can't pick only one. It would make the others sad."

"That's true," Nova said, playing along. "You don't want to hurt their feelings." Chuckling, she withdrew a rubber band from her pocket. She'd forgotten to tie up her hair before coming outside.

She lifted the long tresses from her neck. Bella watched intently, the hole she'd dug momentarily forgotten. Her interest morphed into rapt amazement when the last strands were collected up, revealing the crimson birthmark nestled beneath Nova's right ear.

The gardening trowel plunked to the ground. Bella's mouth dropped open. Pulling off the sun hat, she surged to her feet. She couldn't have looked more entranced if a unicorn magically appeared on the patio and began prancing about.

"There's a heart on your neck!" She scrambled closer to inspect the blemish. "Did angels put it there? When you were a baby . . . did they paint it on you?"

"Do angels paint birthmarks on babies?"

"Yes!"

"Then I suppose they did." The unusual birthmark, nearly the size of Nova's thumb, normally hid beneath the thick curtain of her hair. "Do you like it?"

"I do! Can I touch it?"

Leaning closer, Nova angled her neck. Bella traced curious fingers across the birthmark.

Drawing away, she frowned. "Why didn't the angels put a heart on *my* neck? It's so pretty."

"Sorry, kiddo. I'm no expert on angel behavior. Maybe they were too busy giving you those gorgeous blue eyes."

"I wish they'd remembered."

On the garden path, the row of tiny plants was beginning to wilt in the sunlight. If they weren't planted soon, they'd need a good soaking.

Nova gestured at them. "Should we get back to it? The flowers are waiting for you to decide where they'll grow."

"Okay."

They returned to work in a pleasurable silence. At the back of the yard, Henry sat in the oak tree, moping. Balling up leaves into hard little pellets and hurling them at any squirrel foolish enough to hop onto the tree limbs above him. The squirrels' furious chatter spiked the air whenever his aim got too close. Apparently, Henry wasn't yet bored with the cruel game.

The minute they'd ventured outside, he'd climbed the new rope ladder and kept to himself. Trouble was brewing between the siblings, but why? Nova resolved to get to the bottom of it.

When Bella sat back on her heels, she took the plunge.

"So . . . can I ask you something?" Nova lowered her voice to a whisper. An unnecessary precaution, with Henry out of earshot. "What's going on between you and your brother? You've hardly said two words to him since yesterday."

"Henry is bad." Bella finished planting a snapdragon. "I'm mad at him."

His penchant for less-than-stellar behavior wasn't exactly news. Henry left the toilet seat up. He flung clothes down wherever he happened to be skulking around in the house. He clomped mud through the living room despite constant requests to leave his shoes in the foyer. He seasoned mealtimes with roaring belches, turning Bella a nasty shade of green and stealing her appetite. Then he plowed through whatever food remained on her plate.

Lately his desire to make Nova equally nauseated was bearing fruit. The pop, pop, pop of farts did the trick.

The boy's transgressions were abundant and creative. Yet plainly a specific moment had annoyed Bella.

"What did Henry do to upset you?"

Pressing her lips together, Bella flicked specks of dirt from her gloves. She picked up a marigold plant.

"You can tell me." Nova donned a reassuring smile.

An arrow that missed its mark: Bella grabbed up her child-size trowel. "It's not allowed," she said, spearing the trowel into the ground and flinging dirt everywhere.

"Why not?"

"It's a secret."

"There's no crime in telling a good friend about your troubles. Aren't we friends?"

"Sometimes."

The grumpy admission took Nova aback. *Sometimes? What am I doing wrong the rest of the time?*

Flunking out with Henry was a fait accompli. He didn't like women in general and Nova in particular. Yet she'd assumed her easy camaraderie with Bella meant she'd earned gold stars all around. Securing friend status with a little girl was harder than anticipated.

"Are you worried I'll blab to Henry? I won't, I promise." She tapped Bella's chin, encouraging her to lift her eyes. "Can't you tell me what's up?"

"No." Bella huffed out a breath. "I'll get in trouble."

With her brother or her father? Nova frowned. *I'll place my bet on the latter.*

A man capable of abusing his children knew how to control them emotionally. Had Egan Croy warned the kids to never confide in their foster mother? Disappointment flooded Nova. She'd never get Bella to reveal instances of past abuse if she didn't trust her enough to discuss a simple disagreement with Henry.

Sensing defeat, she said, "If you change your mind, I'm here for you. Anything you want to talk about, I'm all ears. Day or night."

Bella threw a puzzled glance. "What's 'all ears' mean?" Sitting down on the garden path, she crossed her legs.

"That I'm happy to listen. I want to help, in any way I can . . . if you'll let me. Totally up to you."

"Can I ask *you* something?"

"Of course."

Doubt scudded through Bella's gaze. Fleeting, a momentary reaction. Out of habit, she reached into her lap. But she'd hidden the reliable lifeboat of her keepsake somewhere in the house.

At last, she regarded Nova. "When do we have to go back to Pa?"

The dismal *have to*, not *can we*. As if returning to Egan represented the worst possible outcome. Which seemed tragically accurate.

Selecting the right words proved difficult. "I wish I could give you a simple answer. The situation is pretty complicated. I'm not sure you *will* go back to your father. A decision hasn't been made yet."

"Who gets to pick?"

"A judge will decide. She's a very wise lady. The judge assigned to your case is named Tammy. After she gets a final report from Imani, she'll choose what's best for you and Henry. Probably not for another few months, though."

"It won't happen soon?"

"No, sweetie."

"I'll stay here with you?"

"Absolutely. You and Henry are settling in well at my place, and your father needs to take some classes."

"Pa's in school?"

"To learn how to be a better parent. In case Tammy decides you should return to him."

Dropping her gaze, Bella drew anxious squiggles in the dirt. "Why can't I pick for myself?"

Nova was struggling to form a comforting response when Henry materialized beside her. Yet another of his unnerving traits—the boy moved with uncommon stealth.

"Don't be stupid," he told his sister. "Kids aren't allowed to pick the important stuff."

Bella flinched. Her lower lip quivered.

"She's not stupid," Nova said. "I'd appreciate if you'd watch your mouth."

Henry smirked. "Don't tell me what to do. You're not the boss of me."

Another cocky remark picked up from his father? Nova felt her irritation rise. If Henry returned to Egan's custody, he'd earn his stripes as a bully before reaching high school.

The prospect compelled her to reason with him. "Henry, kids aren't helpless," she said. "The situation isn't completely out of your hands. You *can* help decide what's best for you, long-term."

Suspicion filled his eyes. "Yeah? How?"

Anxiety prickled Nova's skin. They were moving into uncharted territory. Knowing how much to discuss required a delicate touch. Err in how to explain the situation, and Henry was sure to rebuff her. Was she up to the task?

Vaulting past her reservations, she said, "Here's an example. Last year, I was the foster mom for a girl in high school."

"What's that got to do with me?"

"I'll explain if you'll listen."

Tapping his foot, Henry glared at her. *I'm listening.*

"The girl's mom kept getting fired from jobs. She lost her apartment after missing too much rent."

"She was too lazy to work?"

"That wasn't the reason—but everyone thought it was."

"Was she ugly? You couldn't pay me to work with an ugly chick. No way."

"Henry, you don't work." *Or listen well.* "Do you want to hear this or not?"

He rolled his eyes. "Go on," he said.

Bella, silent until now, jumped in. "The girl came to live with you because her mama didn't have a home?"

"Exactly. After living here for a few weeks, she trusted me enough to explain the situation. You see, her mother didn't feel good, but she refused to see a doctor. That's why she kept losing jobs."

Henry donned an expression of cynical maturity. "No health insurance, right?" To Bella, he said, "We didn't have it, either, until Mama got the job at the factory. That's why she made us go to a doctor last year."

"I remember." Scooping up the sun hat, Bella cradled it in her lap. "We had to get shots."

"Which sucked. Works for me if I never see another doctor." Henry landed his chilly regard on Nova. "What's your point?"

"After the girl told me her mother didn't have insurance, social services got the lady an appointment at a free clinic. Turns out, she had a problem easy to fix." A mouth riddled with cavities and a sinus infection requiring a month's course of antibiotics. Like many uninsured adults, the woman had gone years without proper healthcare. "After she felt better, she landed a new job and moved into a nice apartment. Her daughter came home to live with her. They've been doing great ever since."

"What's that got to do with me and Bella?"

"Henry, the girl trusted me with an important secret. If she'd never explained, social services couldn't have stepped in to help." Hesitating, Nova captured his wary gaze. "If there's a reason you're scared of your dad, talk to me. Your concerns *can* make a difference on where you'll live permanently."

"Like if we'll go back to Pa or live somewhere else?"

"That's right."

"I should tell you if I'm scared of Pa?"

"Are you?"

"Get real, Nova." Henry tilted his head back. "You want me to rat him out?"

The colloquialism reminded her of Jimmy Cagney and the old black-and-white flicks her parents watched. It sounded weird dropping from a kid's mouth. Another colorful phrase from Egan Croy's repertoire?

"I want you to trust me with the truth," she said. "Has your father hurt you in the past? If there's a reason you're scared about living with him again, don't keep it to yourself."

The air stretched tight. From the path, Henry picked up a stone. He tossed it from hand to hand.

"Forget it. You don't know anything about Pa. You don't know anything about *us*." He hurled the stone across the yard, striking the fence. "You're all grown up. You get to pick what you want. No one bosses you around."

"Henry, I *do* know."

"Yeah, sure." He thumped himself hard on the chest. "You're not a kid like me. You don't know what it's like to be scared all the time."

"Yes, I do. When I was younger than you, I had nightmares all the time. I never felt safe."

"Bullshit."

The oath loosened her control over her emotions. "Henry, I know all about fear," she blurted. "You think my life's great? I'm doing okay, but it took a long time. When I was six, I was put up for adoption."

"You were?" He looked nearly gleeful. "Your parents dumped you?"

The cruel remark scattered pain through her. She wanted to recall the words. The wound of her private misery ran deep. It wasn't meant to be shared—or mocked by a boy with his own share of wounds.

Now she *had* gone too far.

Chapter 12

Nova

At the heated exchange, Bella seemed to shrink into herself. She bowed her head, then pulled a thread loose from the rim of the sun hat. After it fluttered to the ground, she began picking nervously at a new thread. Left alone to her own devices, she'd disassemble the hat before calming down.

Nova held out her arms. "Bella, come here."

Tossing the sun hat aside, she scrambled into Nova's lap. The change of allegiance barely registered with Henry. Arms crossed, he kept his eyes trained on Nova. He seemed fully aware she'd given up the secret unwillingly.

"Why did your real parents get rid of you?" he demanded.

The query made Bella shudder. Did she fear a similar outcome? A mother dead, a father lacking parenting skills—did she believe children placed in foster care were stripped of worth? An easy enough conclusion to make when the people who'd brought her into the world were unable or unwilling to protect her.

Pressing her close, Nova met Henry's gaze.

"Parents don't get rid of kids, Henry. There are lots of reasons why a couple might be unable to care for their child." She punctuated the firm reply with gentle strokes across Bella's arms, signaling with each caress there was nothing to fear. "And let's get the terms straight. There's nothing 'unreal' about adoptive parents. They're lasting, permanent. The people who give birth to a child are called biological parents."

Henry struggled to process this new information. "Why did your . . . biological parents let you go?"

"They were an older couple with health problems."

"Like old-person old? With wrinkles and white hair?"

The clumsy reply seemed nearly comical, especially since it dovetailed with Nova's assumptions that a hard life had aged those people too fast. She'd never given Helen and Finch the chance to tell her the specifics. Which left her to concoct a private story to explain *why* her biological parents were unable to raise her. A couple in middle age, assuming conception was impossible and skipping birth control. The woman might have reached the second trimester before realizing she was pregnant. As for the wolf stalking Nova's dreams: perhaps the unmarried couple owned a large, fierce dog. She assumed they'd lived in a ratty trailer home, like the one in her nightmare.

"I don't know if they had white hair," she told him. "They *were* getting up in age. I'd guess they were in their fifties at the time of my adoption."

"They didn't keep you because they were sick?"

"I guess so. Maybe they had heart trouble or cancer. Something they battled for a long time. I've never asked my adoptive parents for the real deal. As far as I'm concerned, those people don't matter."

Henry eyed her with disbelief. "You don't care? *I'd* want to know everything."

She did care, deeply. But she didn't have the stomach for the truth. That her biological parents had been mentally unbalanced, or alcoholics. Why they'd physically abused her. Too much information might dredge up memories locked deep in her subconscious.

Those reasons weren't appropriate to discuss with a nine-year-old. "It's not important, Henry. My biological parents did the right thing.

They called social services. They knew I deserved a better home than they were able to provide."

Bella, toying with Nova's long hair, tugged lightly to get her attention. "Did they call Imani?" she asked.

"No, sweetie. Imani was a kid like me."

"How did you get new parents?"

"My mother Helen was a nurse. She was good friends with a doctor. After he moved to another county in Ohio, this doctor heard about a six-year-old girl coming up for adoption. He knew my parents were looking for a little girl to adopt. He called my mother, totally making her day. The rest is history."

Henry lost a trace of his bravado. "Your parents didn't want a boy?"

"They wanted a boy *and* a girl. They already had my older brother, Peter." She offered a reassuring smile. "It's pretty typical. Lots of couples want one of each."

"Like me and Bella."

"Which is how my parents looked at it—having a son and a daughter was the perfect combination. If they'd already had a daughter, they would've looked for a son."

The explanation mollified Henry. "Why didn't your parents have more babies on their own?"

"They tried but weren't successful."

"How come?"

"Well, sometimes a couple has trouble making a baby."

"Like they forget how to do it? Why don't they read a book or something?"

Nova stalled the grin creeping across her lips. Make light of Henry's innocence and he'd assume she was mocking him.

"It's not a matter of knowing *how* to make a baby," she explained with suitable gravity. "A man or a woman might have a health issue. Or the couple is getting older, which makes it difficult to make a baby on their own."

"Pa says a man has to watch his step. Chicks are always trying to hog-tie guys into marriage. That's what happened to him. Mama had me in the oven and made him get hitched." Henry shoved his fists into his jean pockets. He resembled a little man, wise to the ways of the world. "Ladies get knocked up if you look at them the wrong way."

Nova searched for a suitable reply. She came up empty.

Bella yanked on her hair.

"Will *I* have a baby?" Consternation raised her voice to a squeak. "Boys look at me all the time!"

"Relax, munchkin." Nova smiled. "You won't become a mama until you're all grown up. And only if you *want* to have a baby."

~

Will I ever catch a break?

With impatience Nova tapped her foot. Here she was, beginning a new week at the Holly estate with yet more problems. The compact excavator had started belching smoke soon after they'd put the big boy to use. The stench wasn't restricted to the back forty, where she worked with her small crew. A group of Jonathon's carpenters, setting up heavy tarps and sawhorses on the Hollys' ballroom-size patio, tossed dark looks as they waved away the stench.

Leroy hopped down from the excavator. Opening the machine's back panel, he fished around inside.

Scarecrow thin, with deep lines etching his forehead, Leroy smiled easily. When he did, he revealed gaps from two missing teeth. The teeth were lost during Leroy's homeless youth, when he'd used drugs. Now in his early forties, he'd been clean from heroin for nearly fifteen years. One of the fortunate few. Or doubly fortunate, in Nova's estimation, since he was Imani's cousin. She kept an eye out for him and often invited him over for Sunday dinner.

He raised his head from the engine. "I need to fiddle around in here," he announced.

Nova swabbed the perspiration from her brow. "Any idea what's wrong?"

"The air filter could be clogged. We might need a replacement."

Bear said, "I can drive into Chardon to pick one up."

Which would involve another delay. "When will you know for sure?" she asked Leroy.

"Not soon, if you keep staring. Makes a man nervous." He ducked his head back under the hood. "I'll get the excavator running a lot quicker without an audience."

"Right." She led Bear away.

From the patio, a cacophony of electric saws and pneumatic nail guns punctuated the air. The men were fast at work sawing through two-by-fours and building framework in tall sections. For Charlotte Holly's new owner's suite?

From what Nova had gleaned from Jonathon's crews, the demo work inside the mansion was nearly finished. The new remodel, beginning this week, would stretch into June. Or possibly July if Charlotte continued altering the architect's original design. She was so good natured, no one seemed to mind the constant changes. Every morning she breezed through the worksite complimenting the tradesmen en masse before hurrying off to Holly's Mill.

Nova yearned to sneak inside to see the remodel taking shape.

She checked her watch. "Fiore Wholesale should've delivered our first shipment of plant stock by now," she told Bear. "They're an hour late."

Bear frowned. "They promised we'd have the plants first thing today."

"They're usually reliable." Nova scrubbed her palms across her face. Bumper-to-bumper trucks and vans filled the Hollys' driveway. "Are you sure the delivery isn't sitting at the end of the driveway?"

Bear rolled his beefy shoulders. "You want me to check again? I've been out there three times already. The plumbers are off-loading a

Jacuzzi tub big enough to pass for a pool. There's no delivery for us, at least not yet."

"Then go inside. Ask the Hollys' cook if you can use the phone. Her name is Annie. Call Fiore and find out why they're late."

"Sure."

Avoiding the carpenters—who were still lobbing dark looks—Bear lumbered toward the side of the mansion.

Nova thought of something else. "Bear! Your boots are covered in mud. Take them off before you go inside."

He gave the thumbs-up.

There was a ton to accomplish but no way to get started. At least not until Leroy found the problem with the excavator. Frustrated, Nova raked a hand through her hair. Falling behind on her end made her feel like an amateur. Not a great look, especially after receiving the go-ahead last weekend to add the gazebo's landscaping to her jobs list.

Determined not to waste the morning, she crossed the back lawn. She paused at the section she'd chosen, where Jonathon would build the new gazebo. The twenty-by-twenty-foot structure required tall plants, and a walkway leading to the patio. She planned to create a curving design for the walkway. Matching the slate pavers to the stone of the decades-old patio might prove difficult. She made a mental note to pick up a variety of samples this week.

Strolling in a slow circle, she imagined Beauty of Moscow lilacs rimming the gazebo's foundation. One of the most fragrant lilacs available, they usually survived winter's coldest blasts. The addition of clematis vines creeping across the gazebo's latticework promised to keep the structure abloom throughout summer. Charlotte also wanted azaleas and rhododendron somewhere in the design; they'd look nice tucked between the taller lilacs. Nova wondered if she should add boxwood too. An evergreen necklace to draw the eye during the flowering shrubs' winter dormancy.

Mulling it over, she didn't see the man approach.

"Excuse me . . . miss?"

Nova looked up. Her stomach lurched.

The carpenter sauntered closer. Since the day he'd eavesdropped on her argument with Jonathon, she'd done her best to avoid him. Was he working with the crew on the patio? She hadn't noticed him among the men.

He seemed to sense her unease. He took a drag off his cigarette, exhaling a plume of smoke. The smile he offered didn't reach his eyes.

"I didn't mean to startle you," he said.

"It's all right." *Not even close.* She resisted the urge to walk away. Instinct warned a display of fear would put her at a disadvantage. "What do you want?"

The sharp reply stamped annoyance on his features. Dousing it, he paused before her with his smile blazing—a false, amiable veneer.

He cleared his throat. "I owe you an apology. When you and the boss were having it out, on our first day here, I shouldn't have stuck around."

"You got that right." She didn't like the way he canvassed her face with probing intensity. As if he knew better than to pose the questions taking root in his mind.

"Can't be easy for a woman on a jobsite. Not like there's many in the trades. Must get lonely."

"It's fine . . . most of the time."

"I'll bet you were embarrassed when Jonathon came down on you. Nothing worse than getting called on the mat by the boss. Probably doesn't happen to you much."

"It doesn't. I'm good at my job."

He took a last drag, then flicked the cigarette away. "That's not what I meant."

She sensed an insult beneath his oily sincerity. *Walk away.* There was something off-center about him, something combative beneath the practiced charm. It wasn't enough to get her feet moving.

"What *do* you mean?" she demanded.

He appeared delighted she'd risen for the bait. "Even a hard-ass like Jonathon can't enjoy giving hell to a foxy woman. A sexy girl like you gets to call all the shots." He stepped closer. His breath smelled of tobacco, and his eyes suddenly reminded her of a shark's. Cold and killing. "Men will do just about anything to get in a pretty babe's good graces. Hell, there isn't a man on this jobsite who isn't dying to ask you out."

Nova bristled. Where was he headed with this so-called apology? An offer to meet for beers tonight? He was nearly twice her age. Yet with his muscled build and good looks, he probably scored often with younger women.

"Are we done here?" His attempt to flirt put bile in her throat.

"I suppose."

"Good." She gave him a pointed look. "You can leave now."

The smile sank from his lips like the moon dipping beneath dark waters. For an instant, he appeared shocked by the blunt dismissal. When he found his voice, his words stung with venom.

"You're awfully full of yourself, aren't you?" A vein throbbed in his neck. "Pretty girl strutting around the place. Swinging your ass and making us all crazy. What do you want from me, chocolates?"

Nervous laughter burst from her throat. "No, I want you to get lost." He was too close, a physical threat. The danger should've dampened her anger. "Save the smooth talk for the next babe you pick up in a bar."

"I'm trying to make peace."

"Don't bother."

"You're really something, Nova." He leaned in, his fists clenched. "Where do you get off, acting like a bitch?"

"Hey!"

He was about to launch another insult when they both sensed a change in the air. On the patio, every last power tool had fallen silent.

While Leroy was too busy working on the excavator to notice the altercation, the tradesmen had drifted to the edge of the patio, their attention drawn to Nova and the furious carpenter.

Jonathon pushed through them.

With long strides he came across the grass. The muscles in his throat worked in an attempt to control his fury.

He clamped on to the carpenter's shoulder and swung him around. "What are you doing out here? You've got no business talking to Nova."

Stunned, the carpenter blinked rapidly, his gaze latching on to Jonathon.

"I asked you a question. Answer me."

He shrugged out of Jonathon's hold. "I was just apologizing to the lady."

"It looked like you were about to land a punch."

"I wasn't!"

Jonathon turned to her. "Is he telling the truth?"

"Not entirely." Nova swallowed down her panic. A delayed reaction, one she wished she'd felt before shooting off her mouth. "Let it go, Jonathon. It doesn't matter."

"Like hell it doesn't." With the advantage of height, he regarded the man with a look of pure rage. Yet he kept his tone even, saying, "I don't tolerate harassment. It's forbidden, period. You want to keep your job? Stay away from Nova."

"Yes, sir."

"If I so much as see you within ten feet of her, I'll fire you on the spot. Do you understand?"

"I do." Incredibly, the carpenter tipped his head at her. Like a perfect gentleman, taking his leave. "Ma'am. Have a good day."

He walked away. Within seconds the air filled with the roar of power tools.

The jarring noise startled Nova. Her nerves were already frayed, her legs weak. Another delayed reaction, and it dawned that she shouldn't have tangled with the man. What if he *had* taken a swing at her? Allowing her anger to override common sense was a foolish miscalculation. Even with a man putting the moves on her.

Especially because of his interest. Some men, once rebuffed by a woman, became dangerous.

A large boulder sat near the edge of the forest. Pivoting away, she made a beeline for it.

She plunked down on the rock's cool surface. Cupped her face in her hands. Then lowered them to her lap and took several deep breaths. The temperature was blessedly cooler by the forest. Calming birdsong filtered through the trees, and she did her best to focus on it.

A shadow fell across her—Jonathon's. She'd assumed he'd returned to the patio to supervise his men.

He rubbed his jaw, apparently searching for the right words.

Rescuing him, she said, "I'm fine. Don't let me keep you from your duties."

"Taking care of the people in my employ *is* one of my duties."

"I just need a moment to pull myself together." His close proximity ticked her pulse up a notch. "You don't have to stand watch. Seriously, I'm good. Just a little rattled."

"You've gone pale, and you look jumpy. Which falls in the category of more than a little rattled."

She glanced up at him peevishly. "I'm okay, Jonathon. This isn't my first jobsite. Doesn't happen often, but I've dealt with assholes before." His close study made her heart knock around. The predictable result of the attraction they were both lousy at hiding.

"Can I get you anything? A cup of coffee? Water?" His lips quirked into a grin. "A shot of whiskey? There's a bottle of Maker's Mark in the house."

She welcomed the attempt at humor. "At ten o'clock in the morning? It's a little early for shots."

"Depends on your viewpoint. It's five o'clock somewhere."

"Not on this continent."

"Now you're splitting hairs."

She gulped down more air. "My prerogative, totally," she tossed back, touched by his determination to stay.

"Want a paper bag? It'll help if you're hyperventilating."

"I'll keep you posted."

His grin widened. "If you're a fainter, though, you're on your own."

"You won't carry me to safety?"

"I'll roll you into the woods to save your pride. At least it'll keep the guys from teasing you. Men on jobsites get macho—they'll think you're a sissy."

Another joke, and the humor did something marvelous to his face, softening the hard planes of his jaw and high cheekbones. His eyes sparkled with warmth. Their deep-blue color, bordering on purple, shivered pleasure down her spine. The way Jonathon stood over her, taking care not to stand too close—yet close enough to shield her from the curious glances of the men on the patio—spoke volumes about his nature. It brought to mind his mother's remarks last weekend.

My son became the man of the house while still in middle school. A terrible burden . . .

Ditching the humor, Jonathon folded his arms. "Before I intervened, was Ethan harassing you? He's a new hire. Mostly keeps to himself. If he's going to be a problem, I'd appreciate a heads-up."

"He wasn't harassing me." Much as she disliked the carpenter, she didn't want him fired. What if a wife and kids relied on his paycheck? "He came over to apologize for eavesdropping on my argument with you."

"That's not how it looked from the patio. You were arguing."

"Because he followed up with a stab at flirting. I should've let it go." Embarrassed, she looked off toward the forest. "I shouldn't have been so . . . testy with him. Nothing's going right this morning. Bad luck on top of a rough weekend."

"With your foster kids?"

His curiosity moved her. He seemed genuinely interested, as if he understood just how much juggling the kids and work taxed her energies.

"It wasn't my finest moment," she told him. "They were asking difficult questions."

"About what?"

When she didn't immediately reply, Jonathon telegraphed his concern in a more obvious way: he sat down beside her.

The boulder scarcely held them both. Their thighs touched, sending a tangy kick of adrenaline through her bloodstream and the back of her throat. A reaction thankfully hidden as Jonathon brushed sawdust off his jeans, lending her time to compose a response. His nails were cut short, the cuticles rimmed with grime. Nicks and cuts marred the fleshy parts of his hands. Nova suspected he enjoyed the physical labor of the building trade more than the business end.

When he glanced at her, she said, "Bella and Henry wanted to know if they'll go back to their father. I'm supposed to avoid making judgments—it's not my job to decide what happens, long-term—but I'm failing miserably. From what I understand of their background, they'd do better with adoptive parents. Clean slate, new start. Which might happen if they trusted me."

"They don't?"

"Not enough to reveal if their father has been physically abusive. I totally fumbled the conversation. Started talking about my own childhood, as if it would help."

"Talking about yourself isn't a bad thing. Kids don't often see adults as vulnerable. I'll bet you made inroads. Capitalize on them later."

The sensible advice lifted her spirits. "I *am* connecting with Bella," she conceded. "She took to me from day one. Likes to follow me around the house, loves to help make dinner and plant flowers. She's the sort of kid it's hard not to fall in love with."

"I'm guessing it's a different story with her brother." When she blew out a breath, Jonathon looked at her directly. Their gazes tangled, and the now familiar energy sizzled and snapped between them. "How old is he?"

"Nine going on nineteen. Henry is determined to turn my house into a pigsty. You would *not* believe all the places he drops his dirty clothes. No room is sacred. I kid you not—yesterday, I found his stinky

T-shirt beneath the kitchen table. Like it's a major inconvenience to place dirty clothes in the laundry room."

"He sounds like fun." Jonathon grinned.

"Not even close," she said, with heat. "There's no getting on his good side. Believe me, I've tried. I put up a rope ladder in the backyard to let him hang out in the oak tree, but all he does is throw rocks at the squirrels."

Jonathon laughed. "So a BB gun is out of the question?"

"No way. Henry's already determined to clear all the wildlife from the area. The kid's got seriously good aim. And some of the comments that fall out of his mouth blow my mind."

"Like what?"

"He totally believes men rule the universe and women are the weaker sex in every way."

Jonathon bit back a laugh. "Wait. *Aren't* women the weaker sex? You had me fooled."

"Ha-ha."

Without thinking, she bumped him, shoulder to shoulder. Like she'd do when Imani teased her. The gesture tangled their gazes again, longer this time.

A quandary that seemed to please Jonathon. Without seeking permission, he brushed a strand of hair from her brow, taking his time, savoring the moment. "Do you want my two cents?" His fingers lightly traced across her cheek, making her shiver.

"Sure." She felt adrift when he lowered his hand.

"A nine-year-old boy is almost in puberty. Rebellion comes with the territory. Henry needs to build self-reliance and learn a strong work ethic. You'll help by giving him chores. Taking out the garbage, raking leaves, sweeping out the garage—and pay him something."

An obvious solution. Why hadn't she thought of it?

Rising, Jonathon added, "When you dole out the allowance, use small change. It'll look like he's earned more."

"That's a great idea. I'll start Henry on chores this week."

"Don't leave his sister out. Give her chores too. Something easier, since she's younger." Jonathon took a step back. "Let me know if it helps."

His interest in their welfare pleased her. "I will," she promised.

The interlude came to an end. Bear trudged across the grass.

"There's a problem," he told Nova. "Fiore can't make the delivery today. They want you to call tonight to reschedule."

Behind them, Leroy climbed onto the excavator. The engine growled, then fell silent. Smoke billowed across the lawn.

Nova's heart sank.

Jonathon arched a brow. "More problems?" When she winced, his expression cooled. "Get your act together, okay? Delays get expensive fast on a job this size. I need you to stick to the schedule."

Without awaiting a reply, he walked off.

Chapter 13

Nova

On Tuesday evening, Nova climbed out of her truck with every muscle on fire.

The missing delivery from Fiore Wholesale had arrived promptly that morning. The excavator was also back up and running after Leroy replaced the air filter and changed the oil. Working double time, Nova used the backhoe to ferry larger plants behind the Holly mansion while Bear moved the smaller, more delicate perennials in a wheelbarrow.

Given Jonathon's remark yesterday to avoid more delays, no one wished to fall any further behind.

While they worked, Leroy manned the excavator. He cleared the last of the undergrowth from the edge of the forest, where Nova planned to add flowering plum trees. The teardown inside the mansion was finished, and the three dumpsters blocking the area were gone. Leroy removed the old shrubs on the side of the house to make way for Charlotte's cutting garden.

Next up, they got started on the cutting garden, grading the soil and marking out the position for each plant. They used cypress planks to erect the raised beds in the center, to feature a variety of roses. At the outer perimeter, they bordered the area with forsythia. Next came fat hydrangeas clustered in each corner, and perennial flowers—purple lupine, white wood aster, wild geranium, and black-eyed Susan.

Once the sun dipped behind the house, Nova called it a day. Tomorrow they'd install the remaining perennials and the roses before moving on to the more intimidating task of renovating the overgrown landscape at the front of the house.

Nova pocketed her keys. Reaching her front porch, she tugged off her muddy boots and placed them by the door.

A rusty Buick pulled into the driveaway. Behind the wheel, a moon-faced blonde tapped the horn in greeting. Kelly, the babysitter.

From opposite sides of the car's back seat, Henry and Bella hopped out. A frosty silence accompanied them across the lawn.

Kelly rolled down the driver-side window. "Nova!" She stuck her head out. "Bella finished her homework. I couldn't get Henry motivated. He has math and a short essay to write for English class."

"Thanks, Kelly. I'll take care of it." Nova waved as she drove off.

At the bottom of the steps, Henry shoved his sister out of the way. With a yelp, Bella grabbed the handrail and righted herself. She glared as he raced inside, shouting, "I'll do homework later."

She gave Nova the once-over. "You're dirty. Your jeans are more brown than blue." She wrinkled her nose. "There are smudges all over your face. *Big* ones. Were you playing in the mud?"

"No one plays at work, sweetie. I spent hours putting in shrubs and flowers."

"Are the flowers nice?"

"They're spectacular. You'd approve."

Bella halted on the steps. "You smell bad."

"What can I say? I love digging in the dirt. BO is part of the trade-off."

"What's 'BO'?"

"Body odor. Sometimes folks stink from hard work!" Nova held open the door. "How was school? Did you meet any new girls at lunch?"

Unlike her antisocial brother, Bella was happily striking up friendships at Longfellow Elementary.

"I did! I made friends with Suzy—she moved to Chardon last year—and the funny girl with freckles. She even has freckles on her arms. She laughs like a hyena, but she's nice to everyone."

"What's the grand total now?"

Bella was inordinately proud of her social skills. "Let's see," she said, counting on her fingers. "Lori, Jasmine, Mary Margaret, Luisa, Tammy, Tara, Freckles, and . . . the girl who smells like peanut butter. I don't remember her name."

"Counting Peanut Butter, that's eight girls. Wow."

"I'm *very* popular."

"You are."

In the kitchen, Bella slipped the book bag off her shoulders. "Did you make any new friends at work?"

Ridiculously, the query set butterflies loose in Nova's stomach. She'd seen Jonathon only in passing today. A few fleeting moments, long enough for his smoldering glances to shiver across her skin. Each time they traded looks, Jonathon checked himself, turned away, and returned to whatever task demanded his attention. Hot and cold, that man. Plainly doing his best to keep a lid on his emotions.

Not that she blamed him. Jonathon wasn't the type to date a woman on one of his crews.

A minor issue, really, since there weren't many women in construction or landscaping. Even so, she was sure he'd worry about setting a bad example, especially given how he'd yelled at Ethan for just that. Besides, she had a strict rule about never mixing business with pleasure. On the occasions when she'd installed landscaping while construction took place, she'd turned down all offers.

Nova remembered her *other* rule: no dating while kids stayed at the house. With the teenagers she'd cared for in the past, there'd never been time. Most of them had participated in after-school sports or other activities, and they'd all struggled with high school academics. On weekend nights, she'd stuck around the house to ensure they returned home at a reasonable hour. A task impossible to accomplish if she'd been out herself.

Of course, Imani regarded the "no dating" rule as a flimsy excuse. She believed Nova feared letting any man get too close. Normally the theory, at least in part, was accurate. Nova preferred her boring, predictable life to the thrills—and the emotional risks—of romance.

Scratch that. I'd gladly take a chance with Jonathon.

"There's not much time to make friends at work," she told Bella. "I'm busy all the time. I do like Bear and Leroy, though."

"Are they good friends?"

"Sure. We get along great."

"Imani is your best friend, right?"

"Absolutely. We've been close since we were about your age."

Recognition broke across Bella's face. "I have *nine* friends." She puffed out her chest. "Imani counts too."

Dropping the subject, she walked into the mudroom to peer out the window. Nova joined her. In the yard's lengthening shadows, Henry gathered up twigs with single-minded focus.

At least he wasn't throwing stones at the squirrels.

"Question." She rested a hand on Bella's shoulder. "I'd like to start giving you and your brother an allowance. Do you think I can interest Henry in doing chores around the house if I pay him?"

"You'll have to give him lots of money. He doesn't like you much, Nova."

He doesn't like me at all. Henry's opinion of her lowered with each passing day. She was already in the pits.

"What do you think it'll take?"

Bella leaned closer to the window to ponder the dilemma. After a moment, she said, "At least ten."

"Dimes or quarters?" Nova hoped she didn't mean dollars. *I'll need a second job to keep Henry on the payroll.*

"Which is bigger?"

"Quarters. They're a lot bigger than dimes." She reconsidered. "But dimes are nice too."

"Henry will like the bigger ones more."

"Can I give him both? I don't want the dimes to feel bad."

Bella sighed. "That's true," she agreed. "You can give him both."

Having offered her wise counsel, Bella pressed her nose to the glass. Her curious gaze followed her brother across the yard on his scavenging mission. "How much will you pay me? I help out all the time *and* I like you. I should get more because I like you a lot."

Securing a child's affection with cash didn't fall within the realm of great parenting. *What the heck. The munchkin already likes me.*

"I guess I owe you back pay. Will fifty cents cover it?" Remembering Jonathon's suggestion about the lure of small change, she added, "I'll pay you with a quarter, two dimes, and a nickel."

The glimmer of avarice lit Bella's eyes. "What about pennies? Can I have those too?"

"No problem. I'll add ten pennies for a tip. You *are* a great helper."

Outside, Henry finished collecting twigs. He plucked several leaves from the maple tree shading the small patio and put them on the picnic table. Nova spied the beginnings of a building project. The twigs were set in a nice cone shape.

"What's he making?" she asked Bella.

"A teeny-tiny . . . what do you call a house where Indians live?"

"A tepee."

"He saw a boy making one at recess."

"You know, Imani is bringing over the swing set on Saturday. Where do you think we should set it up?"

"How about . . . there." Bella pointed to the section of lawn right behind the patio. When Nova smiled in agreement, she asked, "Will Imani bring her daughter?"

"Yes, Maya is coming too."

"I've never met anyone with a broken leg."

"Maya broke her ankle, not her leg. I'm sure she'll let you write your name on her cast. She'll even let you pick the color. She has a bunch of pens. She's already got about a million autographs." At the confusion in Bella's eyes, she added, "A cast is a hard, white covering to keep Maya's leg from moving around. She'll have it removed once the bones in her ankle heal."

"Does the cast hurt?"

"Not even a little. Maya has decorated hers with sparkles. It's pretty."

The conversation subsided as they looked back out the window. Henry had returned to scavenging. He noticed the neon-pink beach ball on the grass, Bella's favorite, and kicked it out of the way. Bella gasped.

Nova winced. Another kick, and the ball crashed against the fence. Thankfully he turned away to continue picking up sticks.

Nova glanced at Bella. "Do you want to go outside and play?"

Bella shook her head.

"You're still upset with Henry?"

She nodded.

It was futile to press. Sociable and sweet Bella possessed a stubborn streak a mile wide. She'd reveal the reason for her pique when she felt like it. Or not.

"Do me a favor." Nova walked back into the kitchen. "Will you set the table? I need to jump into the shower before we eat."

"I'm tired of setting the table, Nora. I always do it. Tell Henry it's his turn."

"Do you want to earn an allowance or not?" Ducking her head into the fridge, she withdrew a bowl of macaroni salad. "And my name isn't Nora."

"Yes, it is."

"Bella, you're being silly. You know my name." Grinning, Nova spelled it out.

With a grunt, Bella tugged down the zipper on her book bag. "No. It's N-O-R-A." She withdrew her lunch box and slapped it down on the table.

As Nova set the bowl on the counter, her amusement fled. Unease shivered down her spine. There was something unsettling about Bella's confident tone. She seemed genuinely put out, as if Nova's insistence represented a personal attack.

She walked to the sink, perplexed. "Stop it, okay?" Turning on the faucet, she washed her hands. "You know my name. It's Nova."

Bella frowned. "It *should* be Nora."

"Why, exactly?"

"You have the same heart on your neck." Bella pointed an accusing finger. "And I know how to spell. N-O-R-A."

The argument was nonsensical, but she strove for a reasonable tone. "Lots of people have birthmarks, sweetie."

Bella darted an angry glance. "Not hearts painted by angels." Turning away, she took her sweet time unlocking the clasps on her lunch box. "Yours is special, *Nora*."

In a huff, she carried her lunch box across the room. She stomped on the garbage can's pedal, whooshing it open. A crust of bread and a granola bar wrapper tumbled out of the lunch box.

Was Nora a classmate with a birthmark on her neck? Another new friend like Tara, Freckles, and Peanut Butter? Baffled, Nova opened the cupboard and took down three plates. Her curiosity vanished when she caught a whiff of her armpit.

"Listen, I'm desperate for a shower. I stink, and I'm shedding dirt everywhere." She wrenched open a drawer, jangling the silverware inside.

Brooking no argument, she handed over napkins and three forks. Red faced, Bella set her jaw. She looked like a balloon ready to pop. Their first real argument, although there was no logical explanation for the entire conversation.

"Do me this one favor, sweetie. I promise you don't have to set the table for the rest of the week."

When no reply was forthcoming, she turned away.

From the hallway, she listened to the child stomp across the kitchen. Silverware rattled onto the table.

"Whatever you say, *Nora*."

Chapter 14

Bella

Bella thumped the plates down.

An itchy sort of anger crawled across her skin. She tossed forks on napkins that she didn't bother folding into nice triangles. She banged down three glasses. The small juice glass clinked against Henry's plate; she gave herself and Nova tall plastic tumblers.

She was tired of Henry acting like Mr. Lazy Bones. He never set the table or emptied the dishwasher or folded clothes on laundry day. If Nova asked for help at dinnertime, he ran into the living room and turned on the TV. Mostly Bella was angry because he'd stolen the Green Harmony brochure and shown it to Pa.

Telling Pa they were staying at Nova's house scared her too. While they were driving to the place where Imani worked, she'd reminded them to keep Nova a secret. Henry had given his promise. Then he'd gone and done a very bad thing anyway.

Bella wasn't angry with Nova—she was hurt. It made no sense how she didn't remember Nora at all. Bella couldn't recall being a teeny-tiny baby, but she remembered lots of things now that she was a big girl. Which made it hard to imagine how Nova could forget Nora completely.

It was true, grown-ups forgot lots of things. They made spinach for dinner after you told them lots of times how much you hated slimy food. They *scribbled notes they stuck on the fridge, then forgot about them. Grown-ups wrote mountains of to-do lists but still didn't keep everything straight. Sometimes they came home smelling of booze and ladies' perfume and lied about the places they'd been.*

But Nova hated lies. She always told the truth.

Did she forget being Nora? Did grown-ups erase their memories like a blackboard at school? Bella nursed this awful possibility. She mulled it over like a sour grape stuck between her teeth. She loved the way Nova tucked her in at night with silly conversation. Her feet nearly floated off the floor when she came into a room and Nova's face lit up like fireworks in July. And to be fair, Bella forgot important things too. Lately she couldn't recall the sound of Mama's voice unless she tried with all her might.

Which left the crushing awareness she'd made a mistake. Nova and Nora weren't connected at all. No more than Bella was tied to Mary Margaret or the girl with the hyena's laugh. Both of those girls had light-brown hair the exact shade of Bella's.

Did angels paint lots of hearts on the necks of lots of baby girls? Was it more common than Bella had known? Confusion made her eyes sting, and she yearned for the comfort of the magic picture.

The shower pounded with rushing noise inside Nova's bathroom. Returning to the mudroom, Bella peeked out the window. Twigs sat in piles on the picnic table. With his head bent low, Henry started building a second tiny house. The breeze shivered through the maple tree above his head. The green and yellow beach balls rolled across the lawn.

The neon-pink beach ball was nowhere in sight. Bella pressed her palms to the glass and scanned the lawn. She considered going outside for a thorough search.

There wasn't time.

She hurried to the living room. Across from the couch, plants clustered before the picture window on tall stands and low pedestals. They hung from gold chains attached to the ceiling and sat on ceramic plates, right on the carpet. One of the pedestals—large, square-shaped, and made of dark wood—was hollow underneath. The lime-green plant on top, with its frilly, slender leaves, nearly hid its sturdy throne. The leaves tickled Bella's wrists as she lowered the plant to the floor.

Flipping the pedestal over, she wiggled the candy tin loose. And whispered a prayer.

"Magic picture, protect us. Tell the angels to keep us safe with Nova."

She wasn't sure if the angels were listening, but she was worried about how Henry's badness was growing by leaps and bounds. On the school days when she didn't hide good enough, and he found her on the playground, he teased her in front of the other kids. In the noisy corridor on the way to their classrooms, he stuck out his foot in hopes of tripping her. When school ended and they climbed into the back seat of the babysitter's car, he'd pinch Bella in secret places—on the ribs or the inside of her arm. But she never let him win because she never cried out.

Henry saved his worst behavior for home. He snuck into Bella's room in search of her treasure. Did he want to throw it away? The hateful act wouldn't make him feel better.

With a grunt, Bella worked off the lid. A musty odor wafted out, making her nose itch. She sorted through her special things, listening closely for the rustle of tissue paper. At last, her fingers brushed across the nearly translucent paper; she lifted out the carefully folded packet. Unwrapping it, she withdrew the magic picture of the little girl reaching up to hug her mama. The sight of so much love flowed comfort through Bella like a river of honey.

Flipping the photograph over, she read the familiar words that were written in a lady's pretty handwriting.

Me and Nora at Sil's house

March 28, 1959

Sighing with pleasure, Bella traced the date. Every child knows the most special day in the world, the one day marked by sweetness and celebration and the brightest of candles. She knew this too. On March 28, angels had flown down from heaven with a baby girl named Bella.

The year was wrong—1959. It didn't matter. On the day of Mama's funeral, Bella had rescued the photo from Pa's wrath. He threw out every last picture of Mama with her own babies, along with her clothes, shoes, nail polish, and most of her jewelry. He even threw out Mama's only bottle of perfume. He meant to clear out every last reminder of her, but the perfume bottle and her favorite necklace landed behind the kitchen garbage can.

Bella rescued them both—along with the photograph he'd missed while dumping out the dresser drawers in his bedroom. The photo had fluttered beneath the bed.

A talisman. A bit of magic to safeguard Bella from sadness.

With a quick kiss, she tucked the picture back into its bed of tissue. After she wedged her treasure box inside the pedestal, she placed the frilly plant on top.

From the corner of her eye, she caught a flash of pink outside. She rushed to the picture window. In yet another display of meanness, Henry had thrown her beach ball over the backyard fence.

The wind carried it across the lawn. It bounced down the sidewalk toward the house next door before veering toward the street. Bella shot out the front door. At the bottom of the steps, she fell, scraping her knee. The pain hardly registered. Jumping up, she ran across the grass.

She captured the beach ball a second before a green car flew past, kicking up air and whipping her hair into her face. She watched the car disappear with her heart thumping in her ears. The street grew silent. In the approaching dusk, lights flicked on inside the house across the street. Hugging the ball close, she sank against a tree.

An engine's familiar rattle lifted her head.

Gears shifted with a growl. Two houses down, the truck crawled forward, coming closer. Bella couldn't get her feet moving to run away from the threat. Pa's arm dangled out the window. Smoke trailed from his cigarette.

Noticing her, he glided the truck to a stop. The air froze in Bella's throat. Fear slithered all the way to her bones.

Pa leaned out the window. He pressed a finger to his lips. A warning. Don't tell anyone you saw me.

A trickle of urine seeped down Bella's leg. When she nodded, Pa smiled with satisfaction.

Then he drove away.

Chapter 15

Nova

Finch Doubeck pocketed a handful of galvanized bolts. He measured the length of the swing set's blue metal swing beam, then strolled around the banana-yellow and bright-green supports arranged in Nova's backyard. Morning sunlight glittered across the heavy chains and heaps of fasteners put to the side.

Finch was nearly bald, and tall like his wife. The retired engineer looked out on the world from behind round spectacles that made him resemble a starry-eyed professor. If Nova's mother was the epitome of sensible, her father brought a dash of silliness to their long, devoted marriage. A characteristic on full display for today's project.

On the patio, Helen caught her daughter grinning. "I should kill your father," she informed Nova.

Finch dropped his tape measure back into his tool belt. "I heard that."

"I should've killed him dead when we got home from Cincinnati," Helen added. "I would have if I'd known what he planned to have us wear today. Your father can't resist giving me prank gifts. Why didn't I throw this one out?"

Nova chuckled. "You look fun, Mom."

Helen plucked at the bib of her overalls. "I look ridiculous."

Across the bib's denim fabric, GRANDPA'S LITTLE HELPER was embroidered in thick silver thread. Finch had ordered the matching overalls last Christmas; the message on his pair read: I'M AN ENGINEER. SAVE TIME: ASSUME I'M NEVER WRONG.

Nova shrugged. "It could've been worse. The farmer duds came in lots of colors—I saw the catalog. Dad almost picked the red ones. You would've looked like matching Christmas elves."

"More like jolly red giants. Petite, we're not."

"Then thank your lucky stars he stuck with classic denim."

Finch unraveled a length of extension cord. "Are you two done yammering? I need some help." He plugged into the outlet by the back door.

"It's almost eight o'clock," Nova said, checking her watch. "I have to wake the kids and put a breakfast casserole in the oven." She planned to serve a buffet to feed a crowd.

"Well, make it quick. I can't put the swing set together without a second pair of hands."

"Isn't Uri helping you? He's coming over with Imani and Maya." Imani had promised as much. Less than an hour ago, she'd called when Nova's parents had arrived at the Weiss home to pick up the swing set. "I thought that was the plan."

"Not anymore. Uri has surgery this morning. Something about a traffic accident on East Ninth."

"This is the third Saturday in a row he's been called in for an emergency. I doubt Imani's thrilled."

Her father grunted. "She didn't look happy. They were supposed to take Maya to a movie later today. I guess that's off too." Plugging his drill into the extension cord, Finch glanced toward the house. "The boy staying with you—what's his age?"

"Henry? He's nine."

"Old enough. Roust him from bed."

"I don't know, Dad. Henry won't be interested unless there's hard, cold cash involved." In the last few days, he'd begun doing simple tasks around the house, like clearing the dinner table or taking out the garbage. But he'd spurned the concept of a weekly allowance, and pitched in only when Nova offered immediate payment. "Let me finish making breakfast. I'll help you."

Helen bristled. "What am I, chopped liver?" She pointed at the message on her overalls. "Your little helper is standing right here, Finch."

"No, thanks. You're grumpy this morning. Go inside and have some coffee. Don't come back out unless it improves your mood."

"You're maddening, Finch. Do you know that?" Even as Helen delivered the retort, affection for her husband put warmth in her eyes. "I'm grumpy because you insisted on rousting *me* from bed at the crack of dawn. Not to mention the Weisses. It's Saturday, for Pete's sake. Some people like to sleep in."

The screen door creaked open. Yawning, Henry padded across the patio. He looked nearly approachable in his rumpled pajamas, his features soft from sleep. Rubbing his eyes, he walked past Nova like she didn't exist. No greeting, nothing. She was Invisible Foster Mom. She wondered if that superhero came with a cape.

He gave Helen the once-over.

"Who are you?" he demanded, in the same tone in which an adult might say, *What gives you the right to break into my house?*

"I'm Nova's mother, Helen. You must be Henry."

"Who else would I be? I'm the only boy here."

"How rude." Helen huffed out a breath. "Are you always this unpleasant?"

He shrugged, taking the accusation in stride. "I'm starving. When's breakfast?"

"I suggest you ask your foster mother."

"She's not my mother. Foster, or any other kind."

Nova channeled a modicum of patience. After her adoption, whenever her parents had managed to draw her out of her shell, she'd been equally rude—and her mother had never failed to call her on it. Finch had been softer than the jelly doughnuts he'd plied her with when Helen wasn't looking. He'd let Nova get away with murder.

"We'll eat soon," she informed Henry.

The remark went unheard—her mother's overalls had captured his attention.

Eyes narrowing, Henry scanned the message. "That's dumb," he announced, taking a gander at Helen's impressive height and sturdy build. "'Little helper' . . . like Santa's little helper? Lady, elves don't come in your size. You'd squash Santa's reindeer."

"Thank you for pointing out the obvious." Helen scowled.

"You're welcome."

She nodded toward Finch. "My husband has a proposition for you."

"What's a 'proposition'?" Henry asked.

"A job," Nova clarified.

Sauntering over, Finch introduced himself. "I need someone to hold the supports while I put the swing set together," he told the boy. "It won't take long. What do you say, Henry? Are you game?"

"How much will you pay?"

"What's your going rate?"

Henry's bravado slipped. The concept of an hourly rate was beyond his comprehension. The kid barely managed basic addition and subtraction. And only if he counted up or down on his fingers.

Needing to protect his self-esteem, Nova stepped in.

She pulled a handful of change from her pocket. "I have five dimes," she announced, placing them in a tempting row on the picnic table. Henry studied the coins with ill-concealed lust. "Dad, what have you got? Any spare change?"

Finch didn't miss a beat, producing two quarters and a handful of pennies. "It's all yours, Henry, on one condition."

"Which is?"

"Add it all up."

When Henry balked, Finch eased himself down at the picnic table. "Come here, son. I'll help you. It won't take long. We'll build the swing set after you get dressed and eat."

While the counting lesson ensued, Nova and her mother went inside to finish making breakfast. Nova put the egg casserole in the oven, then began chopping up a fruit salad.

Manning the toaster, her mother cast a sidelong glance. "He's quite a handful," she said. "Why does the boy dislike you?"

"Oh, he's not singling me out for special torture. He's hard on his teachers, the babysitter, and everyone else of the female persuasion. Henry doesn't think much of women."

"When did his mother . . . what was her name?"

"Glory Croy."

Helen dropped slices of bread into the toaster. "When did she die?"

"It's only been a few months. A traffic accident on I-71 in Columbus. Glory was coming home from her job at a factory. The kids never talk about it."

"They might, eventually. Once they're past the shock." Helen shook her head with sympathy. "Her death certainly explains Henry's behavior. He's angry about losing his mother. Lashing out at other women is easier than dealing with the sorrow. Be patient with him."

"I'm doing my best. It's not easy."

"Is his sister also difficult?"

"Bella is a dream. Sweet, helpful—she has her ups and downs, but she never shuts me out. At least not completely." Nova placed a cantaloupe on the cutting board. Cutting it into bite-size chunks, she added, "I'm more concerned about the change in Bella's attitude toward her brother. She used to follow him around like a puppy dog. Now she barely gives him the time of day."

"She won't tell you why she's upset?"

"Not yet."

"You and Peter didn't always get along," Helen said of Nova's older brother. "Sometimes kids need to hash things out on their own."

Footfalls resounded from the hallway, drawing the conversation to a close. Bella skipped into the room in white shorts and a sweet eyelet blouse Nova had purchased from the sales rack at Higbee's Department Store. She'd pulled her hair into pigtails. Her face looked freshly washed.

"Morning!" She raced into Nova's arms.

Nova scooped her up for a kiss, swinging her in a circle. When she set her down, Bella approached Helen.

"Are you Nova's mama?" She smiled brightly. "I'm Bella."

"Yes, I'm Mrs. Doubeck. It's nice to meet you."

"Nova told us you and Mr. Doubeck went to Cincinnati to see her brother and his family. Did you take pictures of the new baby?"

"I certainly did. He's precious. I'll show you photos of Baby William later."

"I like babies. They're cuddly."

"I do too."

"Where's Henry?"

"Outside with Mr. Doubeck. Are you excited about the new swing set?"

"I'm more excited about making a new friend. Why isn't Maya here yet?" Thwarting a response, Bella gestured for Helen to lean closer. When she bent down, Bella whispered, "I already have *nine* friends. Maya will make *ten*. That's not even counting this summer. School ends soon, you know. I'll meet lots of girls at YMCA camp. Maybe some boys, too, but I don't like many boys."

"Why not?"

"They tell poop jokes in class and have burping contests in the lunchroom. Boys are icky."

"You may feel differently when you're older," Helen said, plainly charmed by the child. "A kind prince might sweep you off your feet."

"I don't think so. Not unless he brushes his teeth and doesn't pinch girls."

"You should insist your kind prince also floss. It's an important part of dental hygiene."

"*I* floss." Bella clicked her pearly whites for Helen's inspection. "I floss every day."

"Good for you."

"Henry won't, though. Even when Nova asks him."

"Why am I *not* surprised?"

Tiring of the subject, Bella began hopping up and down. "When is Maya coming? I want to see her cast."

Nova flipped open a carton of strawberries. "Relax, sweetie. She'll be here any minute."

"I can't wait to meet her."

"I know."

"Imani won't forget to bring her, will she?"

"She won't forget, sweetie."

The doorbell rang.

"I'll get it!" Bella dashed from the room.

The front door banged against the wall. From the porch, Bella's voice sang out. Maya joined in. The zesty excitement of little-girl chatter commenced. It was anyone's guess how long it would take Imani to herd them into the house.

Nova tumbled strawberries into a colander. Turning on the faucet, she caught her mother's pointed regard.

"What?"

Helen arched a brow. "Is it a good idea to call Bella 'sweetie'?"

"It's just a word, Mom."

"You're treading a dangerous path, using endearments with a foster child."

"You're overreacting."

"In your dreams." Helen drew herself up to full height. Yet she also managed to convey a healthy dose of compassion when she added, "I suggest you reconsider how much affection to lavish on Bella. She isn't your daughter. Your relationship with her *will* end."

Nova set the fruit salad aside. "I don't want it to end," she admitted.

"It will, though. The months spent with her . . . they're nothing more than a stolen season. She'll return to her father or transfer to an adoptive home. Whatever the outcome, you're doing her a disservice by encouraging her to become too attached."

The unexpected censure pierced Nova. She reminded herself that her mother never offered criticism without good reason. A practical woman, she shared her wisdom only to heal. It didn't help that her advice dovetailed too closely with Imani's concerns.

Promise you won't fall in love with Bella and Henry.

Nova's shoulders sagged. "How am I supposed to keep Bella at arm's length?" She'd already begun to love her. It had taken no effort at all. "You've seen for yourself. She's irresistible."

Approaching, her mother sighed. "Yes, she is. For a child who's been through too many difficulties, she's managed to keep her spirit intact. It's remarkable." She took Nova's hands, squeezed gently. "You do understand my concern. You're *my* child, Nova. I don't want you hurt. You've done a fine job helping teenagers short-term. The rules change with younger children."

"It's easier to feel a mother's love?"

"Yes, it is. Frankly, I wish Imani hadn't put you in this predicament."

"Don't blame her. She was in a bind. There wasn't another foster home available."

The ready defense put a sparkle in Helen's eyes. "You know I love Imani. If she'd never taken you under her wing, you would've gone through school with no one but Peter looking out for you. But it's worth considering what your feelings for Bella truly mean. It's time, Nova. I can't help but wonder if you crave a child of your own."

"Are you lobbying for more grandkids, Mom? Just because it's raining babies in Peter's world doesn't mean I'm ready for marriage."

"I'm not lobbying." She smoothed Nova's hair behind her shoulders. "I can tell you this. A young woman who uses her spare time fostering kids has strong maternal instincts. You'll be a fine mother someday. Assuming you get out of your own way and find a good man.

He's out there, you know. Why not put your reservations aside, and start dating again?"

"I'm busy. I don't have the time."

"A convenient excuse."

In the living room, laughter rang out. Imani walked into the kitchen.

Taking stock of Helen's poise and Nova's damp eyes, she asked, "What did I miss?"

Chapter 16

NOVA

Bella made her tenth friend at breakfast.

Maya, who'd inherited her mother's long legs and people skills, showered her with attention. Which of the My Little Pony toys did Bella like best? (Cotton Candy.) Did she have a charm necklace? (No.) Did she like the Fashion Wheel game? (Bella, unfamiliar with the game, was eager to learn how to play.)

With her cast shedding purple sparkles like fairy dust, Maya hobbled on her crutches to the buffet set out on the kitchen counter. She announced they would share a plate. While she heaped egg casserole on the plate and slathered jelly on two slices of toast, Bella scooped fruit salad into a bowl. Maya complimented her pigtails. She invited Bella to write on her cast in any color she'd like. She decided Bella's cornflower-blue eyes were the prettiest she'd ever seen.

Nova carried three cups of coffee to the table. Her mother and Imani were already seated. Finch, after waiting for Henry to dress, made two plates and carried them outside. At the picnic table, Henry shoveled food into his mouth while sorting through the coins he'd amassed.

Nova set the cups down. The lightning-quick friendship between the girls was heartening. With summer approaching, it would be easy to set up play dates.

"Do you want to sit with us?" she asked them.

Maya handed the plate to her eager companion. "Can we eat on the front porch?" She patted the backpack dangling from her shoulder. "I brought coloring books and crayons. We'll make pictures after we're done."

"Stay in the yard, okay?"

"We will," the girls said as one voice.

Imani surveyed the trail of glitter left in her daughter's wake. "Nova, I'll clean up the mess after I finish your fabulous casserole."

"Don't worry about it. I'm thrilled you brought Maya over. She's totally made Bella's day."

"The feeling is mutual. Let's get them together again soon."

"That would be great."

Imani took another bite. "Please don't give me this recipe." She closed her eyes with an expression of pure bliss. "Sausage, cheese, a hint of bacon . . ."

"I may have gone overboard with the cheddar cheese. Henry loves it. The kid has a serious dairy obsession. Milk, ice cream, cheese of any variety. He can never get enough. I *have* noticed he's easier to manage when he's in a food coma."

"Whatever works."

Her mother cast a knowing glance. "Henry struggles with math, doesn't he? When your father asked his going rate to help with the swing set, you were keen to bail him out."

"All his academics are a struggle. We have daily battles over homework. Henry *does* like earning his own money, and we count out the coins together. Not that I can take credit—Jonathon came up with the idea of paying him to help out. He gave me great advice on how it would help Henry build self-reliance."

A shimmery hush overtook the room. Together, Helen and Imani studied her with the full-blooded interest of hungry cats encircling a mouse.

Imani pounced first. "You discuss the kids with Jonathon Holly? Sounds cozy. What other personal info do you share with that tall, sexy drink of water?"

"It's not like that, Imani."

"Oh, really? Then why are you blushing?"

"Stop it! There's nothing going on. Jonathon asked about the kids. So I told him about my troubles with Henry . . ." Nova let the words dangle. The denial wasn't believable, even to her own ears. "All right, you win. It *is* like that. We've been throwing enough sparks to start a fire."

"I'm not surprised."

"You're not?"

Imani rolled her eyes. "Nova, sometimes you're totally clueless. Completely lacking the observational skills to know when a man has the hots for you. Strike that. You're *always* clueless when it comes to the mating dance. We should get you a primer." She grinned, adding, "You've been on Jonathon Holly's radar for a long time. You're just too dumb to know it."

"You're crazy," Nova sputtered. "We've only recently met."

"Guess again, dimwit. He first laid eyes on you around the time we graduated from Kent State."

"No way. If I'd bumped into Jonathon back then, I'd remember."

"Not so. Mostly because of those observational skills you've never developed. It's pathetic. You should've picked him up on *your* radar immediately. He put out enough signals to stop maritime traffic on the Atlantic."

Dumbfounded, Nova sank her elbows onto the table. "What are you talking about?" Imani didn't normally invent tall tales, but there was a first time for everything.

"For your information, we ran into him at a bar in Mentor-on-the-Lake. Well, we didn't run into him exactly. Jonathon was at a table with Charlotte and some of her friends—playing chaperone, from the looks of it. The minute you walked into the place, his eyes were glued to you. Like you were the sun, and he'd gladly go blind just for the chance to stare at you."

Helen made a small sound of approval. "How romantic," she murmured.

Imani smirked. "Sorta-kinda, Mrs. D." Her grin widened. "He spent a whole lotta time staring at Nova's ass."

"Well, men will be men."

"Especially during mating season. Which basically describes all bars in Mentor at the boozy height of summer."

Helen giggled like a girl. She never giggled, and certainly not like a girl. Nova felt her jaw loosen. It was an odd look for her substantial, normally serious mother.

"Imani, you *are* bad," Helen said.

"Hey, I wasn't the one checking your daughter out. Jonathon put down his beer and started smoothing his hair back—I'm sure he was gearing up to waltz on over and sweep Nova off her feet. Sadly, a frizzy blonde in mile-high heels picked up his scent. She had her claws in him so fast, he couldn't get away. The poor guy was still staring at Nova when the blonde dragged him off to the dance floor."

"How unfortunate."

"Especially for Nova. She's dated some real duds since then."

Helen sighed. "She has."

"Stop it—both of you." With faltering dignity, Nova straightened too quickly and nearly fell off her chair. She blamed the shock whipping through her. "Imani, are you sure about this?" she demanded, and a small trill of excitement shot through her.

"Yes, I'm sure."

"Why didn't you tell me sooner?"

"Like, when you started the Holly job?"

Her mother, eagerly watching the interplay, held up her hand. "I can answer that," she said. "Nova, sweetheart, you were nervous about taking the job. I lost track of how many times you considered backing out. If you'd known Jonathon was interested, you would've turned down the work."

Imani snorted. "And fled into the nearest hidey-hole."

"Yeah, I would've." Nova blew out a breath. "I have absolutely no memory of seeing Jonathon in a bar. Why can't I remember?"

"Because you didn't notice him," Imani said, "or the gazillion other guys checking you out. You were in one of your take-me-to-the-nunnery phases with absolutely *no* interest in dating. You went through those phases a lot. Come to think of it, you still do." Imani tipped up her chin. "But enough about your squandered youth. From the sounds of it, Jonathon is willing to give you a second chance. How long have you been trading hot glances on the jobsite?"

"Since day one. But we have no plans for taking it further. None, nada."

"That's a pity," her mother said. "I'm sure he's a good man. He was certainly a responsible boy. I met Jonathon when I nursed his dad. Such a serious child. He was a big help to his mother and little sister."

"I know, Mom."

"You do?"

"Denise told us, last weekend. Me, Jonathon, and Charlotte. We were discussing the gazebo Charlotte has added to the project. Oh, Denise said to tell you hello."

"How sweet. Please give her my best."

Her eyes dancing, Imani pushed her plate away. "Sounds like the Holly women are in your corner, Nova. Better get ready. Jonathon may leave roses on your backhoe."

"Ha-ha."

"He's a builder, you're into landscaping—think of how much fun you'll have getting dirty together."

"Will you stop? It doesn't matter if he noticed me in a bar years ago. He's a client, meaning he's my boss for the time being. He wouldn't feel right asking me out."

"What's stopping you from taking the initiative? Ask him out."

"She's right," Helen put in. "Why not ask him to meet for dinner? Or drinks. There's a new martini bar in Chagrin Falls. What have you got to lose?"

My self-esteem if he shoots me down. In none of her infrequent and thoroughly unfulfilling relationships had Nova ever taken the initiative. How *did* a woman ignite the flames of romance? She wasn't sure. Her talent lay in dousing them if a man got too serious.

She shifted uncomfortably in her chair. "I'm not putting the moves on my boss. I don't have the nerve."

"*Temporary* boss." Imani balled up her napkin. "You'll finish the Holly job soon." Taking aim, she threw the napkin at Nova's head.

Nova batted it away. "Not true. I'm back at the Holly estate sometime in June. I'm working up the landscape design for Charlotte's new gazebo. I'm not sure when I'll finish the job."

"Ah. I see. Jonathon is doing his best to keep you around. Why not let him lure you into his web?" Leaning close, Imani lowered her voice. "Remind me, Nova. When was the last time you got down and dirty with a man? No—don't tell me. It'll only make me cry." Catching herself, she glanced at Helen. "Sorry, Mrs. D. This is probably more girl talk than you'd like to hear."

"Don't let me stop you." Collecting up their plates, Helen set them in the sink. "I should check if Finch needs help with the swing set." On her way to the mudroom door, she winked at Nova. "Listen to her. You need a little spice in your life. If Jonathon is the one to supply it, I'm thrilled."

Imani raised her arms in triumph. "Exactly!"

Chapter 17

NOVA

An air of possibility carried Nova outside.

Strolling past the picnic table, she picked up a wrench. She tossed a screwdriver to Imani. Together they helped Finch and Henry finish building the swing set. As they worked, Nova mulled over the encouragement she'd received at breakfast, and the news that Jonathon had once noticed her at a Mentor bar. Not only noticed her: if Imani's account were accurate, he would've approached and struck up a conversation if some blonde hadn't pounced before he got the chance.

Contrary to the resistance she'd posed, the idea of dating him excited her. She liked him. If Nova were honest with herself—*which is better than deluding myself*—she'd never felt so drawn to a man. So restless to see him, so flustered when he smiled or held her gaze too long.

Did it matter who made the first move? Women asked men out all the time. There was nothing wrong with letting a guy know you were interested.

A disturbing thought intruded. If she rallied the courage to approach Jonathon, what if he begged off with a lame excuse? She'd heard through the grapevine that he was divorced. What if he'd already found someone else?

What if he laughs in my face?

They heaved the swing set into place with Helen shouting encouragement. Stepping back, Nova pushed away her doubts. *I'm overreacting. Jonathon won't embarrass me.* An invitation to dinner might not appeal. If so, he'd decline gracefully.

Of course, dealing with a rejection while working at the Holly estate posed its own set of problems. The awkwardness of being around Jonathon after making her feelings known. Walking by him on the jobsite while feeling three feet tall. Or—God forbid—the workers cluing in to her feelings. Teasing her with dirty jokes and laughing behind her back.

Nightmare scenarios, all.

In silent turmoil, Nova helped her father attach the swing set's chains and bright plastic seats. She caught her thumb on a bolt and winced. She came to a decision with the dart of pain hardly registering. Assuming she mustered the will to approach Jonathon—a big *if*—she'd wait until the last day on the job. If he shot her down, no problem. She'd avoid crossing his path for the rest of her natural-born life.

No pain, no gain . . . but no humiliation either.

Little-girl chatter carried around the side of the house. The garden gate creaked in complaint as it was pushed open. Spotting the finished swing set, Bella squealed with delight. She pulled the gate wider to allow Maya to ease through on her crutches. They both took seats on the swing set.

Only Bella kicked off. Swinging high, she filled the air with laughter. Imani nodded at the cut on Nova's thumb. "Need a bandage?"

"It's okay." Nova wiped the blood away. "Just a scratch."

"Not to change the subject, but . . . what did you decide?"

"About what?"

"Jonathon. You're going for it, aren't you?"

Am I? Nova visualized jumping from a plane . . . without a parachute.

"There's lust in your eyes," Imani said. "Stop fantasizing about him. If you don't, I'm dunking you in a cold shower." Leaning closer, she whispered, "Let's shop for a red silk dress. Something tight enough to show off all your curves."

"A red dress on a redhead. Sounds like too much of a good thing."

"Fine. We'll buy a slinky black dress. You'll make Jonathon senseless with desire on your very first date."

"Imani, get a grip. I'm not ready to buy that kind of dress. Not yet anyway."

"Your stubborn streak drives me crazy."

"And you're pushy." Nova poked her in the ribs, drawing a cackle. "It drives me insane."

"Be fair. If I didn't give you the occasional push, you'd spend your days standing in place. You'd ossify." With a grin, Imani rocked back on her heels. "Who convinced you to open Green Harmony? You didn't believe you could make a go of it."

"That's true."

"You're welcome." Dropping the subject, she gestured toward the garden gate. "Let's take a walk. Your parents will watch the kids."

Sudden tension worked its way across Imani's features. The change put Nova on alert. Whatever she planned to discuss, the topic involved Egan Croy or his children. Or the three of them, if for some unforeseen reason Job & Family Services was moving quickly to reunite the family.

Her stomach clenching, Nova looked past Bella—still swinging with peals of laughter—to Henry. He sat alone in the oak tree, taking aim at the squirrels chattering above his head. Despite the challenge of gaining his trust, Nova wasn't prepared to lose him. She prided herself on her ability to make positive changes in the life of every child she'd fostered. But she'd failed with Henry. She yearned for more time to break through his distrust.

She followed Imani through the garden gate. Across the street, a group of children played hide-and-seek, racing from one house to the next to dive for cover behind shrubs and parked cars. The rich scent of lilacs perfumed the air.

Unable to quell her nerves, she pulled Imani to a halt. "You don't have to let me down easy," she said. "Are you reuniting the kids with their father? That's it, right?"

"Take a deep breath, Nova. You're upset."

"Just tell me."

"This isn't about reinstating Egan's custody. Actually, I'm leaning in the opposite direction. *Leaning*, Nova. I can't recommend the court sever parental rights unless I'm certain it's in the children's best interest."

"But you *are* leaning toward adoption." It was inappropriate and selfish, yet she couldn't stop from relishing a surge of relief. "I'm sorry, Imani. From where I'm standing, Egan Croy doesn't deserve another chance. The faster he's out of the picture, the better for Henry and Bella. Especially for Henry—he's already nine years old."

They both knew the score. Siblings were hard enough to place. Most couples preferred to adopt a baby. Some families settled for a toddler; others at least considered adopting a child closer to school-age. For children above the age of eight, the odds of locating a forever home became difficult. Too many of those kids spent the remainder of their childhood bouncing from one foster home to the next. Worse still, many teenagers landed in group settings with little one-on-one parenting. Aging out of the foster care system led many into delinquent or criminal behavior.

"I understand what's at stake, Nova. I don't want this dragged out any more than you do." Imani resumed walking. "I'm meeting with Bruce next week to discuss the Croys. There's been a development."

Bruce Oblanski was the executive director of Geauga County Job & Family Services. He was affable, smart, and dedicated, and he had nearly twenty years' experience in social work. Imani wouldn't request a face-to-face without good reason.

"What sort of development?" Nova asked.

"I've heard from Jean, my friend in Columbus. She's turned up a case file from 1979. A short interaction between a social worker at the

Columbus agency who's now retired and Egan's late wife, Glory. At the time, Henry was in kindergarten."

"His teacher contacted the agency?" Many cases of suspected abuse went unreported until a caring teacher noticed the telltale signs in the classroom.

Imani nodded. "She'd known since early in the school year that he often came in hungry. She'd bring in food—egg sandwiches, granola bars, fruit—whatever she had on hand to ensure he didn't fall asleep in class. One day in early spring, she found bruises on his arms."

Sorrow rolled through Nova. She mustered the courage to breathe it in. "What happened after she called Job & Family Services?"

"The social worker, Paulina, reached out to Glory, who agreed to discuss the matter at home. The Croys lived in an apartment in Franklinton. Not the best area in town, and it was obvious the Croys were struggling. Glory blamed Henry's bruises on a fall at the playground."

"Sounds like the same story Egan used this time. When you took the kids into custody, he said the bruises were from roughhousing."

"He did. However, in the report filed by Paulina, she determined Glory also exhibited signs of abuse. A dark welt on her neck. Bruises on her left arm. She also noted Glory was left-handed."

Nova understood the implication. *Glory received the bruises while shielding herself from blows.* "Where was Bella?" she made herself ask.

"Asleep. The apartment was a one-bedroom. Paulina saw her in a crib in the living room. From outward appearances, Bella seemed fine."

"What about Egan?"

"He was out of town." A maple tree's limb draped over the sidewalk. Slowing her pace, Imani ducked underneath. "He was here, Nova. In Geauga County, attending a family funeral."

The news brought Nova to a standstill. "Egan has family in Geauga County?"

"He did in 1979," Imani said, pulling her forward. They resumed walking. "A parent, an aunt, maybe a sibling. Your guess is as good as mine."

"Forget about guessing. We need hard proof."

"I *have* checked. The phone book, real estate records—there's no one by the name of Croy living in the county. I even dropped by the library in hopes the surname meant something to the reference librarian."

"And did it?"

"Indirectly. The librarian recalled a man named Dale Croy who'd lived in the area during the 1950s. A big guy—he towered over most people. Heavy drinker, too, from what she remembered. Most weekends Dale made the rounds at the local bars, where he got into a lot of fights. Married, didn't belong to any of the churches. He lived somewhere on Chardon's outskirts. The librarian thought he had children but wasn't sure."

"If Dale Croy lived here in the 1950s, he might be Egan's father."

"Apparently."

"How did he earn a living?"

"As a handyman. One of the best in the county, a wizard with all things mechanical. And you'll love this." Imani reconsidered. "Or it'll give you the shivers."

"What? Don't keep me in suspense."

"In the 1950s, Dale Croy worked at Holly's Mill."

The disclosure sent a chill down Nova's spine as she quietly ticked off dates. Jonathon's father died in 1960, the same year as her adoption by Helen and Finch. During the early fifties, Oliver Holly had been fit and hale, managing the historic mill and restaurant beside his wife.

Denise might remember Dale Croy, and know if Egan is his son.

"Imani, should I talk to Denise Holly? It's been decades, but anything's possible. She might remember a hard-drinking employee."

"Don't bother. Dale's possible relation to Egan, while fascinating, is immaterial. At least with regards to Henry and Bella. What *does* matter is the report from 1979. It gives Jean a starting point. If Egan mistreated Henry during the onset of his school years, other teachers may have submitted similar reports."

They neared the stop sign at the top of Nova's street. A teen with a high-top fade and a frizzy beard bicycled past. Turning around, they started back toward the house.

Nova asked, "Will Jean look through the 1980 files next?"

"That's the plan. If nothing turns up, she'll move on to '81. She can't get back to digging right away, however."

"What's the holdup?" With a groan, Nova answered her own question. "Don't tell me. Jean can't locate all the files."

"She'll find them, Nova. After reading the '79 report, she's motivated. Jean doesn't have her hands on them yet, but that isn't the setback." Imani hesitated. "She has a bigger problem to sort out. A woman in South Carolina sold her toddler to an adoptive couple. She changed her mind and wants her son back. She filed a complaint with her local PD."

"No way. It's *legal* to sell your child in South Carolina?"

"They don't have enough regulations on the books. Thanks to the woman's complaint, state legislators are now revisiting the issue. I doubt it'll be legal much longer."

Nova kicked a stone off the sidewalk. "Let me guess. A couple in Ohio paid the woman for her toddler."

"One of Jean's clients. She completed the home study without knowledge of their plan. She has to review the case before flying down to South Carolina."

"When's the court date?"

"Next week. She'll continue digging for us once she's back."

Chapter 18

Nova

Shafts of rosy light glimmered above the trees.

Nova was thankful for the early start. The babysitter was at the house getting the kids ready for school. Kelly would drop them off at Longfellow Elementary.

As she drove, Nova sorted through her mental checklist. The installation of nine flowering plum trees behind the Holly mansion. A walk-through at two o'clock with Charlotte to ensure the completed job met with her approval. A last check of the proposed hardscaping and landscape design for the gazebo, which Jonathon's crews planned to build next month after completing the mansion's renovations. Jonathon didn't have an exact timeline for Nova. It didn't matter. With June fast approaching, work was plentiful. She'd already lined up several jobs to keep her small crew busy until they returned to the Holly estate.

In the last week, there'd been other positive developments. With the school year nearly over, the kids brought home less homework. This kept battles with Henry to a minimum. Supervised visits with their father still left the kids moody and withdrawn, but they bounced back faster than before. The kids were looking forward to summer camp.

Best of all, Imani's friend in Columbus was back from South Carolina. Last night she'd called Imani with a promise to continue searching for case files on the Croy family.

The road inclined steadily higher. The mill came into view, the golden oak structure glowing brightly in the early-morning light. The three-story mill sat atop massive slabs of sandstone; matching stone walls encased the two-story waterwheel, which drew its energy from the Chagrin River.

On impulse, Nova pulled into the empty parking lot. The river's burbling waters drew her from the truck. The tantalizing aroma of freshly baked bread wafted from the restaurant next door, opening soon for the breakfast crowd. The mill didn't open for shoppers eager to purchase the regionally famous baking mixes and flours until ten o'clock. Tours of the historic mill began at noon, twice a week.

Little had changed at Holly's Mill since the mysterious Dale Croy worked here in the 1950s. *Was* the man Egan's father? It seemed a distinct possibility. Egan's possible connection to Geauga County scraped against Nova's emotions like a pebble caught in her shoe. She hated how much it bothered her.

Walking around the side of the mill, she appraised the huge waterwheel, still silent, waiting to be put in motion by the employees arriving soon. If Egan had grown up here, had he also worked at Holly's Mill?

For days, Nova had toyed with the idea of asking Denise Holly. While she might not recall Dale Croy, she could surely get her hands on the information. Any enterprise listed on the National Register of Historic Places kept voluminous records. It was a safe bet Holly's Mill had records on every employee dating back to the first miller in 1891.

But she hadn't approached Denise for fear of what she might reveal.

Dig any deeper, and Nova feared she might turn up relatives still living nearby. What if a distant aunt or cousin asked to adopt Bella and Henry if their father lost custody? Abuse ran through some families like a virus, and when Nova combined what she'd already learned about Dale Croy with Egan's past maltreatment of the kids, it seemed too big a risk to place them with a relative. Which left her with the conclusion that the less she knew, the better.

"Nova. What are you doing here?"

She swung around. Jonathon ambled toward her.

"I'm getting an early start. Last day and all." She noticed the glossy white bag he carried. The pastry inside smelled divine.

When she licked her lips, Jonathon smiled. "Cherry Danish—just baked. I'm happy to share." He opened the bag and tore the pastry in half. "Is everything okay? You look stressed."

She accepted the sweet. "I'm always stressed before a walk-through," she said, brushing aside her concerns regarding the Croy family.

"Stop worrying. Charlotte will be pleased."

"I hope so."

"Count on it. You do great work, Nova. I don't mind telling you, I wasn't on board when my sister chose Green Harmony. I didn't believe you could handle a job of this size." Taking a bite of the pastry, he held her gaze too long. His eyes were soft as they canvassed her face. "I'm glad you proved me wrong."

"Me too." Unable to look away, Nova drank him in.

"I'll let you know in a week or two when you can get started on the next phase."

"No problem. I have other jobs set up."

"There's a development going up in Chesterland—not one of mine, but I know the firm. Good people. Several of the homeowners still haven't picked a landscaping company. Are you looking to add to your summer schedule?"

"Sure."

"I'll give your name to the builder."

"Thanks."

Jonathon glanced toward the parking lot, then back at her. He plainly needed to go. Yet he prolonged the conversation, saying, "I'd like to work with you again. Maybe in the fall? A six-home development in Burton. There are a few headaches to solve with the zoning committee, but I should close on the property soon. It's enough work to keep you busy for a month."

"I'd like that," she said, delighted. He wanted to see her again. Professionally, but it still meant something. He didn't want their relationship to end.

I don't either.

Emboldened, she searched for the right words. How did a woman ask a man out?

By taking the plunge. Jonathon likes me. He won't shoot me down.

"Great." He started back toward the parking lot. From over his shoulder, he said, "I'll give you the details in June when you're back at the estate."

"Jonathon—"

"Yeah?" He turned back around.

Nova's pulse skittered. "Do you want to meet sometime?" she said in a rush. "Dinner, drinks—do you have plans next weekend?"

Surprise registered on his face. He rolled back on his heels. An apology rose on his features, telegraphing her error.

"I'm sorry," he said, too fast. "The development in Burton, the zoning issues—I have to meet with my attorney to hammer out a solution. Miss the deadline and the deal falls through. And I won't wrap up my sister's remodel until late June. I'm buried."

"It's fine." She felt naked. Humiliated. "Just thought I'd ask."

"Thanks for understanding."

"No problem." Summoning her emotional reserves, she managed a careless shrug.

Chapter 19

NOVA

Leroy and Bear heaved the last stone pavers into place. Wiping his brow, Leroy glanced at Nova. "Are we looking good?" he asked.

"It's perfect," Nova said, pleased with the final effect.

They'd run into several problems installing the ornamental pond behind Kitty and George D'Ambrosio's stately Colonial in Chardon. The couple's initial plan put the water feature too close to the house. Nova had pointed out a better site farther away, near the southern end of their large, rectangular patio. The D'Ambrosios—attorneys with a thriving law practice on Chardon Square—fluffed off the suggestion, insisting she build the pond to their original specifications.

Knowing better than to argue with clients, Nova and her crew dug out a ten-foot span near the northern corner of the house, where it was hidden by a mature maple tree. The D'Ambrosios quickly saw their error and apologized. Afterward, they followed Nova's suggestions to the letter. The pond was moved to the site she'd suggested, which lent perfect viewing from the living room.

Within minutes of work resuming, the excited couple decided to increase the pond's size. The decision sent Nova scrambling to order more pavers, and a larger air pump and liner.

A minor inconvenience in the grand scheme of things. The couple was paying handsomely for the project. Between their new water feature and smaller landscaping jobs Nova had secured, there was little time to nurse embarrassing thoughts about Jonathon.

She still wasn't sure how she'd completely misread the situation. Jonathon's long, lingering glances. The uninvited moments of intimacy, when he brushed the hair from her eyes or sat too close. He'd displayed the signals of attraction. Even so, only a fool asked a client out.

Was Jonathon currently in a relationship? Or was he put off by women who took the sexual lead? Perhaps his past divorce had left him raw, and he wasn't ready to date.

Any of the theories would explain his fast retreat.

Whatever the reason, Nova continued to mentally chastise herself for a major faux pas. She dreaded seeing him again. She envied women capable of hiding their feelings around men they liked.

The second week of June was nearly over. Jonathon still hadn't called with a date for her to landscape the gazebo. In more pitiful moments, Nova prayed Charlotte had once again changed her mind. Remove the gazebo from the design plan, and she'd gladly avoid setting foot on the Holly estate ever again. She'd take her private humiliation to the grave.

Bear ambled onto the D'Ambrosios' patio. "What's next?"

Nova flipped open the cooler she'd brought. "Let's install the pin oak. It's our largest design element and will anchor everything else." She tossed him a thermos of water. "We'll put in the foundation shrubs afterward."

"We'll get started while you map out the rest of the color."

"Already done." She nodded toward her truck. "I picked up five rosebushes this morning. We'll use them for accent once we've installed the coneflowers, daylilies, and butterfly bushes."

Joining them, Leroy dug a Tab from the cooler. "You left the roses in your truck? It's eighty degrees, Nova."

"Sorry. I forgot to unload them. Blame the sleep deprivation. It's making me forgetful." She turned away. "I'll get them."

The men followed.

Bear said, "Did the kids see their father yesterday?" In the last month, Bear and Leroy had become well versed in the problems with her current charges.

"Yeah, and I'm running on fumes." She handed over the plants. Thankfully the roses displayed no sign of leaf wilt. "For reasons I don't understand, the kids revert back to hostilities after each visit. My house becomes a war zone. Egan must be pitting them against each other in some way. Imani's sidekick hasn't noticed anything wrong during the visits. But he *is* a newbie. He's missing something."

Leroy frowned. "I thought those kids were Imani's clients."

"They are, but Tim—the new guy—is helping out. She's wrapping up two adoptions this month. When she's not available, Tim handles the supervised visits." The change bothered Nova, but she understood the demands on Imani's schedule.

Leroy carried the last container of roses to the lawn. "Have the kids told you why they aren't getting along?"

"I wish. If I bring it up, Bella immediately changes the subject. She launches into a discussion of whatever project she's currently doing at summer camp. At the moment, she's building a dollhouse from Popsicle sticks."

"What about Henry?"

"He's worse. Broach the subject of why Bella's angry with him, and he walks away. Whatever he's done to ruffle her feathers, it's major."

Bear guzzled down the thermos of water. When he'd finished, he said, "What about offering Henry cash if he'll tell you what's going on? The kid likes earning money. Tell him you'll give him a buck if he'll spill. Promise you won't punish him for whatever he's done to get on his sister's bad side."

Nova regarded him with disbelief. "You want me to *bribe* a nine-year-old? Great thinking, Bear."

He shrugged, flustered by the mild censure. "It's just an idea."

"A crazy one."

"It's not crazy," Leroy put in. "You're already paying him every time he lifts a finger. Seems to me you're already on a slippery slope. Trying to buy his love and all."

Not his love, Nova mused. She held no illusions. Henry made it perfectly clear how much he disliked her. *At least he doesn't outright hate me.* Getting him to semi-accept her attempts at parenting was enough.

"Leroy, the boy's had enough bad influences in his life. Don't ask me to add to the list. I'm not teaching Henry that grown-ups might pay for the truth. No way."

The conversation subsided. Imani's car pulled into the driveaway. She got out. With a wave, the men went back to work.

Imani wore typical attire for a day in court, a conservative blue suit and matching pumps. She came forward slowly, as if walking into a battering wind.

"What's happened?" Nova asked. She never made unexpected visits during the workday.

"Let's not talk here."

"Where, then?"

"I picked up lunch after my hearing." Imani nodded toward the car. "Salads with grilled salmon and iced tea. I thought we'd eat in Chardon Square."

Grilled salmon—Nova's favorite. And it was barely eleven o'clock. Whatever Imani planned to discuss, it couldn't wait.

Nova promised the men she'd return in an hour. Chardon Square was only a few blocks away; they parked near the library. Past the large gazebo in the center of the manicured green, they found an empty picnic table.

Plainly stalling, Imani slowly removed the salads from the paper bag. She fished out two bottles of iced tea with faint worry lines deepening on her brow. After a long moment, she found her voice.

"I'm not sure where to start. None of it is good." She poked at her salad. "The files Jean has unearthed, the details the original social worker recalled from her interview with Egan's late wife in '79—and

I'm upset with Tim. After his first interview with Egan, he dropped the ball. One of those amateur moves you never want to make."

The testy remark came as a surprise. Imani never criticized Tim. If anything, she went overboard heaping praise on her mentee.

"How did Tim drop the ball?"

"He forgot to update the file with Egan's current employer. A small error, normally. Not this time." Leaning across the table, she briefly clasped Nova's hands. The gesture, meant to reassure, frightened Nova more than the tension scuttling across Imani's features. "Egan moved to Chardon for a position as an assistant manager at a hardware store in Chesterland. Something better came along, so he quit."

"When did he switch jobs?"

Imani faltered. She unwrapped a straw, her hands shaking as she lowered it into her bottle of iced tea.

At last, she said, "After we took Henry and Bella into custody."

"Did he notify Job & Family Services?" The rules for a parent with children in state care were explicit.

"He did. Egan provided the name and address of his new employer."

"In person or over the phone?" With a start, Nova became aware that *she* was now stalling. Delaying Imani from confirming the suspicion forming in her mind.

"One of our intake coordinators took the call. She verified his new employment, and even checked the location where Egan currently works. She left the information on Tim's desk weeks ago. He found the note last night—it's been buried on his desk all this time." Imani took a hasty sip of her iced tea. She looked up, her gaze brimming with apology. "Nova, it's JH Builders."

"Egan works for Jonathon?" A frisson of anxiety dove through her.

"He's a carpenter on the crew remodeling the Holly mansion. He was hired on the spot, on the day work commenced at the estate. Apparently, Jonathon needed to hire extra men at the last minute. The intake coordinator spoke with someone in Jonathon's office . . ."

Imani rattled on, the words unable to penetrate Nova's rapidly moving thoughts. Had Egan taken the job because he'd worked for Holly's Mill in the past? Most people were creatures of habit, and it certainly made sense. Then she recalled her first day working at the estate, when she noticed the carpenter eavesdropping on her argument with Jonathon. Middle-aged, attractive. Plainly delighted by the altercation. And later: The ruse of proffering an apology, how Nova had sensed an undercurrent to the interaction, an agenda. Even the attempt to flirt now seemed a ploy. Had he planned to ply her with booze at a local bar to loosen her tongue? It seemed an efficient way to ferret out information on his children.

Nova's blood ran cold. Egan Croy had wanted to take her out to prove she was unfit to provide foster care—and lobby social services to return Henry and Bella to his custody.

Drawing from the reverie, she thought of something else. "Ethan," she whispered.

"What?" Imani studied her with confusion. "Who's Ethan?"

"Jonathon got the name wrong. He said Ethan, but he meant Egan." Nova's mind whirled. "A carpenter on the site was hassling me. We got into an argument . . . Jonathon broke it up. He asked me to inform him if *Ethan* bothered me again. The guy was a new employee. With such a big crew, Jonathon botched the name. He was talking about Egan Croy." Chilled by the certainty of her conclusion, she added, "I'm sure of it. Somehow, Egan knows I have his kids. Someone on the jobsite mentioned I'm a foster mom. He put two and two together."

"Bear," Imani guessed. "He likes telling everyone how you fostered him in high school and hired him after graduation. It's not much of a stretch to assume Egan overheard the remark. He asked for details about you."

"And Bear told him I'm currently fostering kids named Bella and Henry."

"It makes sense."

The savory aroma of grilled salmon wafted from the containers Imani had set out on the picnic table. Nova's stomach rumbled. Physical labor put extreme demands on the human body. Even with her emotions in flux, she couldn't skip lunch. There was too much left to do this afternoon before she finished landscaping at the D'Ambrosios' house. After unwrapping a plastic fork, she began eating in earnest.

Imani, less inclined to join her, lowered her chin on her knuckles. "You can't go back to the Holly estate." She flashed a warning look. "I mean it, Nova. Bow out on the final landscaping. Tell Jonathon something came up."

"I can't. The Hollys are influential, and Jonathon's mentioned he'd like to work with me again." A situation Nova planned to avoid, even if she *did* hope for referrals. "It'll hurt my reputation to leave before finishing the job. Jonathon has contacts all over the county. I *need* those contacts, and the work they'll bring."

"Tell him the truth. For your safety, your name has been withheld from the parent of the children you are presently fostering. Mention that social services has been apprised of Egan Croy's employment by JH Builders, and you feel it's in your best interest to decline further work."

Taking a bite of salmon, Nova chewed thoughtfully. "I appreciate your concern, but it's unnecessary." She dug back into her salad.

"I'm not having you get into it with Egan Croy *again*."

"I won't," she promised between mouthfuls, "but I wouldn't have any problem handling him if I did. I work jobsites all the time. I know how to deal with guys like Egan."

"That's exactly what I'm worried about"—Imani pointed an accusing finger—"that look on your face. If he so much as looks at you the wrong way, you'll be reading him the riot act."

"It's time someone put him in his place."

"Nova—"

She held up a hand, stopping the protest. "I don't go back until *after* the remodel wraps up."

"Why am I *not* reassured? What if some of the carpenters are still completing finish work? You've said it yourself—Charlotte Holly has changed the design plan a dozen times. Egan may still be working there—and will probably try to hang back anyway so he can see you again. I don't want you crossing paths with him."

"It won't be an issue. Jonathon can't indulge his sister's whims forever. He will have moved his crews to Burton for a six-house project. Construction begins soon. Everyone will have to have cleared off the site for a job that big—including Egan."

"Fine. But if anything changes—"

"Relax. Nothing will change. Jonathon has my back too."

Nova polished off the last of her salad. She dropped the carton into the bag. Whether from anger or the need for more calories, she found herself eyeing Imani's forgotten salad.

She took a sip of her iced tea. "Can we move on now? I'd like to hear what Jean found in Columbus."

"Finish eating, first." Imani pushed her salad forward. "The stuff we've already covered is the easy part. The rest will be difficult to hear."

Chapter 20

NOVA

Nova dutifully finished her meal.

Silently she assured herself: nothing she had yet to learn would unravel her. She resolved to hold fast to the composure she'd spent years cultivating.

As a seasoned foster parent, she'd seen a lot. What she hadn't encountered firsthand, she'd learned about in foster-adopt classes, or heard secondhand from Imani. Families beset with all manner of ills, where abuse was the norm. The photos attached to those case files were difficult to view. Many of the children stared furtively at the camera, as if they'd like to disappear—as if they'd had no experience of human kindness, and certainly not of love. In others, the children's eyes gleamed with sorrow or hatred, or—most upsetting of all—they looked out with blank, lifeless stares.

Those children seemed cut off from human emotion. Their hearts beat in shadow. They frightened Nova more than the wolf that stalked her dreams.

It was painful to confront the darkest corners of human behavior, but Henry and Bella weren't foster kids she'd heard about secondhand. Bella's hair smelled like freshly mown grass and Henry—obstinate, willful, angry—fell asleep each night curled up like a small animal caught in a storm.

Affection for them made Nova's resolve slip. Listening to Imani speak of abuse they'd suffered would be hard.

Needing to bolster her spirits, Nova thought about her own life after adoption. The joy on their faces when Helen and Finch first met her at Job & Family Services. Her third Christmas as their daughter, when Nova—her belly full of roasted turkey and her arms laden with child-size gardening tools—impulsively climbed onto Finch's lap. The day she broke Helen's favorite vase during a tantrum, and her mother, stepping over the shards of glass, scooped her up and brought the tears to a halt by singing "Over the Rainbow" with gusto—and decidedly off-key. The snippets of memory were gilded with love so pure, they gave her the strength to hear whatever Imani might share.

She gave a short nod. She was ready.

Imani wasted no time. "Jean found Paulina."

"The social worker who interviewed Glory Croy?"

"Turns out, she moved to West Jefferson after she retired. Jean drove out to her home last weekend."

"Does Paulina remember the interview?"

"Oh yes. It's hard to forget a woman who's clearly abused but unwilling to press charges. Especially after the call to social services from Henry's kindergarten teacher. Paulina felt Glory and her children were one of the families she'd failed."

She hadn't, but Nova understood the sentiment. Social workers like Paulina cared about making a difference in people's lives.

"During their conversation, Paulina remembered something important." Imani paused for emphasis, then added, "The Croy family lived in Muncie, Indiana, for several years. They lived in Columbus twice—before and after residing in Muncie. They moved back to Columbus when Henry was five and Bella three."

"Will you reach out to Muncie social services? They might have something."

"Jean has already taken care of it. She's also been in contact with Muncie PD."

Impatient, Nova drummed her fingers on the picnic table. The excitement in Imani's voice indicated they'd found something. Her stomach knotted.

Donning a brave front, she asked, "What did they find?"

"For starters, Muncie social services had several interactions with the Croys. In the first instance, neighbors called in a domestic dispute to the PD. Glory met with a social worker, but it played out like her interaction with Paulina. She refused to sign a complaint. Neighbors called in another domestic dispute about six months later. After the incident, Egan agreed to enroll in family counseling with his wife."

"What about Henry and Bella?"

"They were placed in foster care while their parents received counseling." Imani hesitated. Grimly, she added, "There was a problem with the first home. The foster parents were taking on too many kids. Insisting they weren't overburdened, and you know how few homes are normally available."

"How many kids were living there?"

"Six other foster kids when Bella and Henry arrived. At best the couple was careless. At worst, negligent. They lost their license after the accident." Imani's eyes flashed. "The couple lived in a two-story house . . . there wasn't a mandated safety gate on the stairwell. Bella suffered a fall. No serious injuries, but she spent two days in the hospital."

Heartache surged through Nova too quickly to fend off. She knew the score. Most foster parents were dedicated to the children in their care. A few rotten apples viewed the program as a fast-cash scheme. She reminded herself there *had* been improvements in child welfare. Prior to the 1970s, children routinely languished in state homes with little supervision. There were other horrors. During the Great Depression and earlier, thousands of orphaned or abandoned children were shunted off to farms. They became little more than indentured servants.

She forced herself to ask, "Did Jean uncover anything else?"

"She did, actually. Egan *does* have a criminal record. The year after Bella and Henry were in foster care, he served thirty days in the county lockup."

Nova grimaced. "For battery?"

Imani nodded. "While he was incarcerated, Glory worked with Muncie social services on a plan to leave him. She intended to divorce him, Nova. It took too long, but she finally realized she had to get out."

Pity for Glory Croy surged through her. Living in fear of her husband. The nerve-racking days while forming an escape plan. The desperation she must've felt. Searching for somewhere to raise Henry and Bella in safety.

"Something went wrong," Nova heard herself say. "Glory and the kids moved back to Ohio with Egan. She never went through with the divorce. *Why*, Imani? Egan was in jail. She had the perfect opportunity to get away from him for good. Don't tell me she changed her mind."

"It wasn't her fault." Imani lowered her eyes. "There was supposed to be an opening at a women's shelter at the end of the month. The Muncie team put Glory and kids up at a motel to wait it out."

"The opening fell through?" Most cities lacked the funds for enough shelters. Demand always exceeded supply.

"No, the shelter *did* have room. They only needed a few more days to move the previous family into permanent housing. The problem was on the housing end. Habitat for Humanity ran behind on construction."

Anger flashed through her. "And in the meantime, Egan was released?"

"It didn't take him long to track down Glory and the kids."

Not surprising. Social services would've put her up in a cheap hotel. Checking out the most obvious ones, Egan had probably sweet-talked whomever he'd found at the reception desk. Or he'd waited in the parking lot near dinnertime, when his wife would take the kids out to eat.

"From what I understand, Glory and the kids moved back to Columbus the same day Egan found them," Imani said. "Social services wasn't aware of the situation until she missed an appointment. They found the hotel room cleared out."

Disgust put bile in Nova's throat. "Lucky Egan," she snapped. "Move across state lines and leave your troubles behind. No wonder Geauga PD didn't find any priors. They didn't look out of state. The assumption being the Croys were in Columbus for years before Egan moved the kids here. I'm sure he did everything in his power to leave you with a false impression."

"He did."

"He's scum. A liar, abusive—the man abducted his family. That's kidnapping, right? It's only been a few years—the statute of limitations hasn't run out. Have the PD haul Egan back to Muncie to face charges. Lock him up for good."

"He didn't kidnap his family. To all outward appearances, Glory willingly moved back to Ohio with him."

"That's bullshit and you know it!"

Oddly, the outburst made Imani smile. Rising, she walked around the picnic table to sit beside Nova. She bumped against her, shoulder to shoulder.

"Save your anger." Her eyes brimmed with triumph. "You're missing the big picture. All of this is good news for Bella and Henry. The best news."

The elation in her voice quickly melted Nova's anger. "Are you saying you're ready to make a determination?" The relief she wanted to feel refused to materialize. Bella and Henry deserved a permanent home, but she hated the thought of losing them.

"The news from Muncie is exactly what I needed. Solid proof Egan is an unfit parent."

"You're advising the court to sever his parental rights?"

"After I write up the report. I can't request a court date until I finish. I'll have to run everything past Bruce, of course," she added, referring to the director of J&FS.

"We're probably talking about a court date in July," Nova guessed.

Imani nodded. "In the meantime, are you fine keeping the kids? You might have them into the new school year next fall. I've already checked—Geauga doesn't have any families waiting to adopt a sibling group. I need to look outside the county for the right home."

Nova resisted the pull on her heart. "Whatever it takes," she said. "Don't stop looking until you find the perfect couple."

Chapter 21

Nova

Entering the kitchen, Nova tugged the rubber band from her hair. "Thank God it's Friday," she murmured, dropping into a chair.

She'd beaten the kids home from summer camp by a mere five minutes. When they arrived, they flew past her with barely a hello. Presumably they were depositing the day's prizes or knickknacks in their bedrooms. Yesterday the camp counselors had sent each child home with glow sticks and a pamphlet on playground safety. The day before, Henry and Bella had made her molars sing when they ran into the house blowing on yellow plastic whistles.

Nova pulled off her work boots. Luckily her mother had dropped off a chicken casserole earlier in the day, sparing her from making dinner. After completing the D'Ambrosios' new water feature, she'd crammed in two smaller landscaping jobs to finish out the week. She was looking forward to a few days off. Tomorrow, she planned to take Bella and Henry to Headlands Beach for a day of fun and sun.

Since their conversation earlier in the week, she'd heard nothing from Imani. She didn't know when social services planned to inform Egan he'd lose custody of his children. Until then, the prearranged visitation would continue. The children wouldn't learn of the determination until after social services spoke to their father.

Anxiety followed her to the stove. The waiting game was already beginning to wear on her. Children reacted in unpredictable ways, and the final visit with Egan was sure to bring anger or tears. Or both— Imani would follow the news of their father losing his parental rights with a gentle but truthful description of the difficulties normally encountered while locating a home for school-age siblings. In all likelihood, Henry and Bella would remain in foster care for months, perhaps a year.

Nova withdrew the casserole from the refrigerator. She took comfort in the knowledge the kids *did* have a long-term foster home. No matter how long it took, she resolved to keep them safe and secure until Imani found the right adoptive parents.

Soft footfalls padded into the kitchen. Continuing past, Bella ducked into the mudroom. She pressed her nose to the window.

Nova put the casserole into the oven. "What are you doing?" she asked, joining her.

"Looking."

The child surveyed the yard's bright spaces with intent. On the windowsill, her fingers tapped a nervous rhythm.

"What are you looking for?"

"Nothing."

Right. It seemed best not to press. "Want to go outside to play? Dinner won't be ready for a while."

"Maybe in a little bit."

Nova sidled closer. In a now-familiar habit, Bella, leaning against her, wrapped her arm around Nova's waist.

"How was summer camp?"

"Fun. I made a new friend."

"What's her name?"

Bella's gaze roamed the yard with the thoroughness of a hunting dog waiting to leap. Whatever it was, the object of her obsession wasn't within sight. A missing toy?

"I don't remember her name," she said at length.

"What does she smell like?" Scent was Bella's go-to identifier when a name evaded her.

"Like Fritos. She eats them all the time." A long silence, then: "I finished my Popsicle house. I'll paint it tomorrow."

"What colors?"

"Rainbow colors, of course. Blue, green, purple, and orange." Bella pulled from her observation of the yard long enough to shoot a disapproving glance. "Why don't grown-ups paint their houses like rainbows? It would look nice."

Or kooky. Unless the homeowners are hippies into tie-dye and sixties culture.

"It probably has to do with sun exposure," Nova said. "Dark colors, like purple, fade in the sunlight. Not a great choice when you're painting a house."

"That's too bad."

She disagreed but kept the opinion to herself. "Where's your brother?" Normally he raided the refrigerator within five minutes of arriving home.

"In the bathroom." Bella pressed her face to the window's glass to survey the right-hand side of the yard. "He's bleeding all over the place."

The calmly issued disclosure sent Nova running. Sure enough, she found Henry seated on the bathroom floor with a thin stream of red trickling down his calf. Splotches of blood stained the washcloth he was pressing to the wound.

"What happened?" She knelt down beside him.

Henry stiffened, going rigid from the curves of his bony shoulders to the dirty soles of his bare feet. Moments of closeness were never welcome. He leaned away, the way one did to avoid someone coughing their lungs out in public. The reaction never failed to make Nova feel like the carrier of bubonic plague.

"I fell down when Kelly picked us up at camp. I was running to the car."

She took the washcloth. "You must've been running awfully fast." Grimacing, she studied the nasty scrape on his knee.

"I always run fast. That's the point, stupid. If you're going slow, you're *walking*."

She decided to ignore the verbal jab. "Why didn't you tell Kelly you hurt your knee?" The babysitter kept bandages in her purse.

"It's just a cut." Snatching the washcloth back, Henry dabbed at the wound. He looked peeved by her interference. "It's not like I'm dying or anything."

"Maybe not, but you obviously fell on gravel. There are creepy-looking crumbs in the wound." Rising, Nova shuffled through the medicine cabinet. She found the topical antibiotic and a large bandage. "I have to get them out."

"No way. Just leave them. They'll fall out on their own."

"I can't. You'll get an infection."

"Who cares? I don't want you picking at me."

"Hey, I'm not thrilled by the idea either. There's no choice."

Turning on the tap, she reached for a fresh washcloth. Henry regarded her with the excitement one reserves for the surgeon before going under the knife.

When she knelt back down, his eyes rounded. She plastered on a smile. "How was camp today?" It seemed better to distract him. "Make any new friends?"

"What's the point?"

"Of making friends? Gee, I don't know. Because it's fun?"

"We'll go back to Pa soon. He doesn't like Chardon much. We'll probably move somewhere else."

"You might stay here," she said carefully. "Nothing's been decided. At least not yet."

"Pa says different. He always gets his way." Letting the subject go, Henry peered at his bloody knee. "Will this hurt?"

"A little."

"How much is 'a little'?"

"More than none at all."

Despite his tough-guy stance, he looked away. "I wish you'd be more precise."

Nice word choice. Plainly he'd eavesdropped on her phone call last night with a potential client. *No, Mr. Conrad. I can't give you a precise cost until I've walked the property.* Evidence he was copying her language gave Nova an unexpected boost.

"This won't feel good, but it'll be over before you know it," she said, closing down the debate. "Ready?"

"No."

"Here goes nothing." She pressed the damp washcloth to the wound.

"Ouch."

"Just don't look."

"Ouch. *Ouch!*"

Working quickly, she patted the wet cloth across the wound. Satisfied when the last bits of gravel came free, she gently dabbed on the ointment. She was pressing the bandage into place when she spotted another cut. A drop of blood from Henry's elbow plopped onto the floor. He'd gone down hard, running for the babysitter's car.

"Oh." He surveyed the cut. "I didn't see that one."

"Yeah, well, Kelly will find out soon enough." Nova grunted. "The back seat of her car probably looks like a slasher movie. Word to the wise—grown-ups *want* to know when you're bleeding. Next time, say something."

"Okay." Henry's eyes roamed the ceiling as he grimaced. "What's a slasher movie? Sounds cool."

"Never mind. Lift your arm higher. There are more bits of gravel."

"Ouch!"

"Almost done." Finishing up, she affixed the bandage.

Without thinking, she pressed a kiss to Henry's forehead. The first affection she'd ever bestowed, a reward for behaving during minor wound cleanup. An impulse Nova might have thwarted with more thorough consideration.

What happened next floored her. Henry's mouth bloomed into a smile of glittering intensity, his sunny relief showing off specks of food stuck in his teeth. She was considering yet another quick convo on the importance of flossing when, ditching the smile, he came to his feet.

The phone rang.

"I'll get it," he said, amazing her once again. He never offered to help without negotiating payment first.

At a jaunty clip, he left the bathroom.

But all good things come to an end, and Nova entered the kitchen to find he'd donned one of his surlier expressions. Henry paced in a tight circle, tangling himself up in the phone's cord.

He thrust out the receiver. "It's a guy."

"Who?"

"How should I know?"

Because common courtesy dictates that one asks the caller for his name. It wasn't a battle worth fighting.

She turned away. "Hello?"

"Nova, hi. It's Jonathon. I hope I'm not interrupting dinner."

"You're not."

"Good. I wanted to let you know we're just about finished building the gazebo. Can you bring your team back next week? You pick the day."

"Monday works." There was no problem rescheduling the smaller jobs lined up.

"Great. Oh, when you order the hardscaping materials, let me know when they'll be dropped off. Some of the men are doing finish work in the new main bedroom. We still have equipment on the grounds, but I'll have them—"

"Which men?" she asked, cutting him off.

Jonathon hesitated, clearly taken aback by the question. "Bud Gaines and Neal Toth."

Not Egan. "Great," she said with an audible sigh of relief. "That's perfect."

"I've already moved the rest of the crew to the new site. The guy who was hassling you was in the first group I sent to Burton. I wouldn't have assigned him to the finishing crew without being there to keep an eye on him."

"Thanks."

"You're welcome. Like I was saying, Bud and Neal will move all their equipment from the backyard. You'll have plenty of room to stow your supplies, and the hardscaping materials once the shipment arrives. If you need help hauling stuff around, ask the guys to pitch in. Oh, and if you need anything once you get started, feel free to call. I'll stop by on Monday to see how you're doing, but I'm not sure about my schedule later in the week . . ."

The rest barely registered. The husky timbre of Jonathon's voice threatened to wash her mind clean of thought. *Snap out of it.* From her desk in the corner of the kitchen, Nova scrambled for a notepad, dropped it, then dropped a pen too. She chased the pen across the floor. It was jolting, the prospect of seeing Jonathon again—soon, it turned out. Sooner that she'd expected. Heat flashed through her cheeks.

Calm down. Seeing him isn't the end of the world.

Hanging up, she felt downright feverish.

Henry broke his self-imposed rule of staying ten feet back. He blocked her path to the sink.

"Who was that guy?" he demanded.

"Why do you want to know?"

"Because your face is red." Henry smirked. "You've got it bad for him."

Nova started to object, reconsidered. *I do have it bad. And I have exactly forty-eight hours to get my act together.*

Lousy odds, those.

Dodging the remark, she pulled a quarter from her pocket. "Do me a favor and drop the subject," she said, handing it over. "It's your turn to set the table."

Chapter 22

BELLA

From the living room window, Bella studied the street with a prickly sense of danger. The bees in her tummy warned it wasn't safe.

On the drive home from camp, she'd kept watch out the back window of the babysitter's car as the truck behind them wove in and out of traffic, never getting too close. Henry, slumped down in the seat beside her, entertained himself by poking at his bloody knee. Kenny Rogers crooned from the radio; behind the wheel, Kelly sang along.

A block away from Nova's house, the truck disappeared. Had Pa gone away? He did sometimes, after speeding by the house, leaving behind only tiny puffs of gray smoke from the truck's exhaust, which Bella watched vanish with her stomach tighter than a rubber band.

Go away.

But she wasn't sure it was safe. Needing to check the backyard, she edged past Henry. He thumped the last plate on the table, then stomped off to the living room. The TV came on, the cartoon reverberating through the house with a host of silly noises, booms and bangs, and high-pitched screaming from a mouse or a roadrunner. At the desk in the corner, Nova seemed deaf to the noise as she pecked on a calculator. Her pencil scratched numbers across a pad.

The kitchen smelled cheesy and warm. Bella considered peeking in the oven to see what Nova's mama had made for them, but a funny taste in her mouth prodded her into the mudroom instead. She reached for the doorknob, the brass cold to the touch. Quiet as a mouse, she went outside.

She'd barely crossed the patio when she caught the reek of cigarette smoke. Covering her nose, she sprinted toward the gate, scooping up a big stone without breaking stride. She wedged it underneath. Frantically she looked around. There were two bigger stones in the nearest flower bed. She pushed them beneath the gate, too, to hold it shut.

Keeping low, she followed the fence to the back of the yard. The odor of smoke grew stronger. The houses on either side of Nova's looked empty, the curtains drawn. Where was Pa hiding? The only way to know for sure meant facing her fear of heights. The bees in Bella's tummy whirled in angry circles as she placed her foot on the lowest rung of Henry's rope ladder. She climbed up the oak tree with her teeth chattering, grabbing hold of the limb where Henry normally sat.

On the other side of the fence, Pa locked eyes on her.

The fright of seeing him just inches away nearly toppled her to the ground. The tree's rough bark hurt her hands as she clung tighter.

Pa grinned like he'd been waiting for her. "You're a sneaky one, Bella. Just like your mother before she went and got herself killed. Don't think you can get anything past me." He took a drag off his cigarette. "Where's Nova?"

Fear for Nova sent chills racing across Bella's skin. She didn't want Pa anywhere near her. Loyalty to Nova battled the terror sweeping through her if she didn't reply.

"She's in the kitchen," she finally got out.

"You don't like her, do you?"

"No, sir."

"Keep it that way. The babysitter . . . does she always wait for Nova to get home before dropping you off?"

Looking away, Bella strained to hold on to the tree. She shut her mouth tight.

"What are you, deaf? Answer me! Does the babysitter ever leave you alone at the house?"

Bella shook her head, angering the bees in her tummy.

"Damn. With it being summer and all, I'd hoped . . . never mind." *Peering over the fence, Pa studied the toys strewn about. He didn't look happy because there were so many. "How late does Nova let you play in the yard?"*

"Until it gets dark."

"That'll work." He glanced over his shoulder, his eyes narrowing when they lit back on her face. "Stop looking for my truck when Nova or that fat babysitter drives you around. What are you, a detective? Get me noticed, and you'll catch hell. You understand, girl?"

"Yes, sir."

The sun dipped below the rooftops. A dog barked somewhere nearby. The tree limb dug into Bella's slippery palms and she hung on with both arms, ignoring the pain, her pulse thump, thump, thumping through her whole body. She wanted to climb down, but she didn't dare. Not until Pa excused her.

He tossed down his cigarette. "We're leaving soon. You, me, and Henry." He gave the sun his back to study her fully. "Maybe we'll go to Kentucky. Or farther south, to the beaches in the Carolinas or Georgia. I'm sick of Ohio. Do you like palm trees?"

"Yes, sir."

"Nothing better than a palm tree and an umbrella drink. You might be sitting under one sooner than you expect. Now, get back in the house. And keep your mouth shut."

Chapter 23

NOVA

The lake glimmered in the humid air of Headlands Beach.

Nova zigzagged through the patchwork of colorful towels and lounging sunbathers, looking for a spot to set down their things. She clasped Bella's hand, conscious of the child's every step as she tripped forward in the oversize sun hat. She'd refused the child-size hat purchased earlier in the week, and Nova's old standby drooped past her shoulders like an umbrella shielding her from sunburn and a clear view of the crowded beach. Henry brought up the rear. The two inflated swim tubes coiled through his arms bounced against his hips each time he craned his neck to survey boys splashing in the surf. Couples waded into the shimmery waters and small children, seated at various spots on the beach, lofted sand over their shoulders in the perennial quest to dig their way to China.

Three teenage girls shouted to friends down the beach. When they rolled up their towels and hurried off, Nova grabbed their spot.

"Let's get our stuff unpacked." She dropped the heavy canvas bag she'd been carrying and began rooting around inside.

Henry surveyed the boisterous crowds. "Do you come here a lot?"

"As much as I'm able. We'll come back sometime with Imani and Maya. Maybe before the month's out."

"This place is great."

"It's not the ocean, but there's no place better on a hot day." Nova pulled three towels from the canvas bag. She unrolled them on the sand. "Lake Erie is the shallowest of the Great Lakes. It warms up fast in the spring. You can jump in if you want—but don't go in past your waist. If you want to go in deeper, I'll go with you."

"It's okay. I'll wait until you're ready."

"Sounds good. We'll all go in together."

Bella stepped onto a towel and sat cross-legged, inhaling deeply. "Everything smells like sugar and butter."

"It's the coconut from all the suntan lotion. Speaking of which, you need to put some on. You too, Henry. I don't want either of you to burn."

"I like the smell." Bella dug the tube of suntan lotion from the bag and squeezed a blob on her wrist. "It's yummy!"

Henry dropped down beside her. "Let me see."

"Wait your turn. I'm not done yet."

"You're taking forever."

"No, I'm not."

He snatched the lotion away. "Time's up."

"Don't use all of it! I want more."

Ignoring his sister, he squeezed lotion down his arm. "Cool. This smells better than sugar cookies."

"It does!" Bella agreed, beaming at him. "It's the best smell in the whole world."

They went on like this for a startling moment, sniffing and slathering the lotion on with the focus of scientists. As if a common lubricant to protect one from sun damage were an extraordinary find. Standing over them, Nova was baffled and amused by their friendly chatter.

The first in days. A miracle really. They'd rarely ceased hostilities since their mysterious falling-out in May.

Then she fell upon the reason for their excitement.

"Hold on," she sputtered. "Is this the first time you've gone swimming?"

Henry looked up with mild contempt. "What do you think?"

"Seriously? You never swam when you lived in Columbus?" There were countless public pools in every metropolitan area in Ohio. "No one ever took you?"

Bella sniffed her coconutty arm, exhaled with delight. "Mama couldn't swim." She tucked the precious lotion beneath her hip. "She would've taken us if she'd known how."

"Mama knew how to swim," Henry objected. "Pa just didn't let her."

Nova frowned. "Why not?"

"He made us stay home, mostly. Except on school days. We didn't go out much on weekends. Pa didn't like people nosing around in his business."

Nova inhaled a sharp breath. *Egan didn't want anyone to see the bruises on his wife and kids if they visited a public pool.* She dismissed the thought before it lit her anger.

She tossed a swim tube that Henry neatly caught. "There's no time like the present." She picked up the second one and steered it over Bella's head. "C'mon. I'll teach you the basics."

They spent the next hour paddling around the crowded lake. Swimming didn't come naturally for either child, and Nova repeated instructions for long minutes, to keep their legs rigid to produce a scissoring motion, and their bellies flat on the inflated tubes. A fear of drowning was understandable if you'd never been in water deeper than a bathtub, and she admired their perseverance as they splashed and foundered. At last, they began swimming with ease, their eyes bright with determination as they watched other children stream past like dolphins. When they tired of the lesson, they sloshed out of the water like young conquerors.

Henry flopped down onto a beach towel. "That was great." Rolling onto his side, he snatched the suntan lotion and squeezed out a fragrant handful. "Can we go back in soon?"

"Do you have any cramps?" Nova asked, sitting down beside him.

"My legs hurt. It's no big deal."

"The rule is twenty minutes out of the water if your muscles are tight. Then you can go back in."

"Can I play in the surf?" He finished rubbing lotion on his torso.

"Turn around, first." She plucked the lotion from his fist. "Let me get your back."

"Why can't I do it myself?"

"You can't reach every spot that'll burn. Do you want to go to sleep tonight redder than a tomato? It won't feel good, I promise you."

"Okay, okay. Man, you're pushy. Just hurry up."

"Relax. I'm almost done."

A shadow fell over them. A boy with a shock of black hair stood before them. He looked about Henry's age.

He held out a football. "Wanna play?" he asked Henry.

A normal query on a summer day. Henry's response, however, was far from guaranteed. He'd managed to finish the school year without forming one solid friendship; he'd made no effort to meet any of the kids in the neighborhood, while Bella now regularly played hopscotch with the other girls on the street. Nova still nurtured the hope that Henry would come out of his shell, but when he eyed the boy with suspicion, she held her breath.

While he weighed the offer, Bella offered the boy a brilliant smile. "Can you throw a ball real good?" she asked him.

"Not really," he admitted.

"Are you bad?" she pressed.

When he rubbed the back of his hand across his lips, clearly embarrassed, Henry surged to his feet. "C'mon," he said. "Let's play."

At the surf's edge, they tossed the football back and forth, missing as many catches as they landed. Neither boy possessed much in the way of natural athleticism, but it didn't matter. They were having fun.

Watching them, Bella cradled the suntan lotion with a devotion normally reserved for the treasure box she'd left at the house.

She nodded with satisfaction. "That's one." Her voice gained a hint of maturity when she added, "Took him long enough."

Nova smiled. "At least he's made a friend. Better late than never."

"*I* have twenty-seven friends now."

"You're amazing. Keep it up, and you'll be voted prom queen in high school."

"What's a prom queen?"

"A girl who dresses up like a princess for a special dance at school." Nova lay down on the beach towel. "It's a big honor if you're picked."

"If she's dressed like a princess, why call her a queen?"

"Tradition, I guess."

From the corner of her eye, she noticed Charlotte Holly wending her way toward them with a blue pail swinging at her side. Sitting up, Nova waved. The metal beads on the hem of Charlotte's white coverup jingled pleasingly when she came to a halt.

"I see you've already met Aiden." She pointed to the boy playing with Henry. "Too bad we didn't coordinate our trips to the beach. He's been lonely since we got here. We have to leave soon—my fiancé wants to spend some time with Aiden before driving him back to his mother's."

"I didn't know you have a stepson." It occurred to Nova that she knew very little about Jonathon's sister, other than that she'd wed soon. "Stepson-to-be," she added, catching the error.

"I should get your advice." The consummate extrovert, Charlotte sat down beside her. "I need it desperately."

Nova glanced at her quizzically. "My advice about what?"

"Children! I knew absolutely zip about kids before getting involved with Brent. You learn fast when you agree to marry a man with a ten-year-old."

"Oh, I'm no expert."

Amusement flashed in Charlotte's eyes. "You know more than I do. I'm not even sure Aiden likes me. He goes overboard with polite responses, but most of the time he's quiet. Keeps to himself when I'm around. Going to the beach together was Brent's idea. He suggested I take Aiden to break the ice." Letting the subject go, she regarded Bella, who was listening to the exchange with her lips pursed with interest. "You're awfully pretty. What's your name?"

"Bella Croy."

"It's nice to meet you, Bella Croy. I'm Charlotte Holly." She held out the pail of toys. "Would you like these? I bought all sorts of stuff for Aiden to dig in the sand. He wasn't interested. To tell the truth, I may have insulted him. Some of the toys are totally *not* the right choice for a boy his age." For proof, she pushed a plastic trowel aside and withdrew two dolls from the pail. Barbie and Ken, both dressed in swimsuits.

Bella's mouth fell open. "I can keep *everything*?"

"It's all yours."

The suntan lotion immediately lost its most-favored status. Tossing it aside, Bella scooped up the dolls and put them back in the pail. "Can I go play, Nova?" Unable to contain her excitement, she hopped up and down. "I'll stay where you can see me."

Nova waved her off. "Have fun, sweetie."

Bella stationed herself fairly close to the boys. Not too close—with each pass, the football gained speed, encouraging the boys to move farther apart. Nova chuckled as Bella dumped everything from the pail, then proceeded to kiss each toy in turn before getting to work. Soon wet clumps of sand were flying through the air.

Charlotte pulled off her sandals. "She's precious." She dug her toes into the sand. "I don't know how you do it. Honestly, it would kill me."

"What would?"

"Being a foster mother. Taking kids in, then letting them go."

"It's worth it, helping them through a rough patch in their lives."

"What happened to their parents?"

"They only have their father, Egan."

"There's no Mrs. Croy?" Hesitating, Charlotte lifted her shoulders to her ears. "Sorry. *Not* my business. They seem like sweet kids. I'm merely curious."

"It's all right." She explained about Glory's death, adding, "Their father hasn't treated them well. It's a safe bet he'll lose custody sometime this summer."

"Do the kids know?"

"Not yet."

"What happens then?"

"They'll stay with me until their social worker finds an adoptive home. Hopefully they'll be placed in Geauga County so I can stay in touch." Nova's heart fell. She knew the odds weren't in her favor. "At the moment, there aren't any couples here waiting for a sibling group." Catching the quaver in her voice, she inhaled a breath. "Enough about me. You must be excited about your wedding. September is just a few months away."

Charlotte beamed, clearly pleased with the conversation's turn. "The clock is ticking. If I can get Aiden to warm up, it'll be smooth sailing. Not that a divorced man doesn't come with baggage. I started dating Brent right out of college, but it took him four years to pop the question. Totally understandable if you'd ever met his ex-wife. She keeps him in a perpetual state of emotional guilt. Which is crazy since *she* divorced him. Threw him over for her tennis instructor. I swear, her piece of beefcake is a year younger than me. Twenty-five, tops."

Which meant Charlotte was twenty-six. *Two years younger than me and twice as confident.*

Nova didn't go in for jealousy—she didn't see the point—but she'd gladly accept a helping of Charlotte's self-assurance. Enough to keep the self-doubt at bay.

"Jonathon's a lot like my fiancé," Charlotte revealed suddenly, as if they'd been discussing her older brother all along. As if, Nova realized, he were the reason she'd struck up a conversation in the first place. "Some men . . . they come out of a bad marriage wounded in more ways than they know. Brent's ex and Lisbeth are made from the same mold."

"Lisbeth . . . Jonathon's ex?"

Nodding, Charlotte absently drew swirls in the sand. "At least Brent's ex was faithful until the beefcake came along. Ten years of semi-happy marriage. Never great but not torture. Lisbeth was unfaithful right from the start. Within months of the honeymoon—with a friend of Jonathon's."

They were crossing a boundary, delving into secrets Nova had no right to hear. She searched for a diplomatic way to shut down the conversation. Her throat tightened when Charlotte stopped doodling in the sand and looked up.

"I don't know why my brother put up with it," she said with fierceness. "He never should've married Lisbeth in the first place. Living with an unfaithful wife stole his dignity, piece by piece. Jonathon hasn't been on a date since. It's been four years."

The sun was too bright. It hurt Nova's eyes. She wondered suddenly if Jonathon had shot her down because he was afraid of getting hurt again. Of trusting any woman.

"Charlotte, we shouldn't talk about your brother. It's not right. He's a private guy."

"You *do* need to understand."

"Why?"

The question lifted Charlotte's lips with amusement, but her gaze remained sober. "Because he's crazy about you. I thought you knew. He's not great at hiding his feelings."

The comment left Nova dazed. Charlotte was confirming her initial belief—Jonathon was drawn to her—yet he'd turned down the offer to meet for dinner or drinks. *Now I'm not sure what to believe.* One of her mother's pithy expressions crashed into her thoughts. *You could've knocked me over with a feather.* She'd never fully understood the colorful adage Helen used when confronted with a surprising or shocking event. Now it made perfect sense.

"Obviously you don't remember," Charlotte added. "It was a long time ago, that night when he saw you." She pointed down the sand.

"At a bar over there. I don't remember the name of the place. You came in with a friend."

"Imani," she said, recalling their conversation about that night.

"Jonathon wanted to ask you to dance."

"He didn't."

"Lisbeth stopped him. She walked in with a bunch of her friends. Took one look at my brother and zeroed in. He couldn't get rid of her. Anyway . . . I guess I'm asking a favor."

"Which is?"

"Don't give up on him. It'll help if you give him some encouragement." They both got to their feet, and Charlotte brushed her knuckles across Nova's hand. "You like him too. Don't deny it. You're blushing."

Nova continued to blush after Charlotte went to fetch Aiden. After they left, she took Bella and Henry back into the water. When they tired of swimming, she collected up their things and ushered them back to the truck.

She was still riding the emotional waves when they arrived home. Surfing between elation and disbelief. She unloaded the truck in a hazy stupor.

"Henry, take the beach towels." She heaped them into his waiting arms. "Put them in the laundry hamper. I'll wash them tonight."

"Sure."

Water ran off the toys and inflated tubes crammed inside the hatchback. "While you're at it, unlock the mudroom door," she called to him. "I'll bring everything else out back to dry on the picnic table."

"Okay."

Bella took possession of the pail brimming with toys. "Can't my stuff dry in the kitchen?" She followed Nova around the side of the house.

"You'll trail water everywhere. Let's put the pail and the digging toys out back. You can take Barbie and Ken inside."

Withdrawing Barbie from the pail, Bella kissed the doll. "You'll like my bedroom," she whispered. "It's nice."

Chuckling, Nova pushed unsuccessfully at the garden gate. She pushed again and the gate creaked in protest. When it refused to open, an expression of consternation overtook Bella's features.

Frowning, Nova lowered to her knees. "Something's stuck." She peered underneath but couldn't identify the problem.

"I'll open it from the other side," Bella offered.

Nova got to her feet. "Don't bother. The gate's hinges are rusty. I need to oil them." A job for another day, she mused. "Just give me a sec. I'll get it open."

She pushed harder. When the gate refused to budge, she put her entire weight into it, ramming hard against the wood. The planks cried out in complaint.

With a crack, they gave way.

The gate flew open, tumbling Nova through hands first, the toys flying from her grasp and sailing over her head. She crashed to the ground.

Heaving herself into a sitting position, she groaned. The three middle planks were broken in half, leaving a gaping hole in the bottom portion of the gate. It would take the neighborhood's racoons no time at all to find their way into the backyard. Less time afterward to nibble through the flowers putting out a colorful array of tasty blooms.

Wincing, Nova felt something hard beneath her. A rock, bigger than her fist. Three other rocks of similar size also lay on the grass.

"I'm afraid to ask." Brow arching, she regarded Bella. "Have you been stuffing rocks under the gate? Or do I need to have a sit-down with Henry?"

"I don't know." Bella hid the Barbie doll behind her back. Given her magical way of viewing the world, it seemed she didn't want the doll to witness her tattling on her brother.

Letting her off the hook, Nova started toward the garage. "Go inside and tell Henry to find the Tabasco in the fridge." Nothing repelled wildlife faster than the scent of hot sauce. It was the simplest means to ward off raccoons if they wandered into the backyard. "Tell him to look for a red bottle and *not* to open it. Tabasco is very hot. Bring it to me."

Glad for the reprieve, Bella dashed off. Nova searched for odd bits of lumber and a hammer in the garage. There was no choice but to douse the flowers with Tabasco in case a makeshift repair of the gate didn't hold. Her sudden irritation—and an hour's worth of unwanted work on a Saturday afternoon—managed to shake off her fog of confusion over Charlotte's disclosure.

She nailed the new lumber over the jagged hole in the gate. The kids were arguing when she went inside, battling over what to watch on TV. Bella dropped a glass while setting the table for dinner, shattering it across the floor. Henry tracked sand from the living room to his bedroom, then clogged the vacuum cleaner when Nova ordered him to clean up the mess.

A day meant for relaxing had gone terribly awry. Frustration simmered inside Nova. She climbed into bed with her skin still itchy with sand. She'd spent so much time repairing the vacuum, she'd forgotten to jump into a shower.

When sleep finally claimed her, she dreamed of the wolf.

Chapter 24

Nova

With frustration Nova studied the garden gate. The series of wooden planks nailed into place yesterday were badly misaligned. Several nails stuck out of the boards, pulled loose by the summer humidity. Would the gate fall apart before she hired a handyman to rebuild it? From the looks of her subpar job, she didn't feel optimistic.

A few paces behind her, Bella rocked from foot to foot. She'd stuck Barbie in the can of nails hugged to her waist, and the doll rocked with her every movement. When Nova had inquired about Ken's whereabouts, her contrite helper had informed her that he'd decided to sleep in.

This morning Bella had confessed to putting rocks beneath the gate without giving a reason for doing so. Unlike the teenagers Nova had fostered in the past—who were content to hole up in one of her guest bedrooms when not out with friends—she was learning fast how much wear and tear younger kids put on a house. Last night, after clogging the vacuum with sand, Henry had flushed a washcloth down the toilet. No pipes burst, and he'd tried to pin the blame on his sister. It didn't take Nova long to deduce the real culprit.

At least Bella had come clean about *her* crime.

Nova glanced at her. "Well, here goes nothing."

"What are you going to do?"

"See if the repair holds."

Bella covered Barbie's eyes.

Nova kicked the gate. The two bottom slats promptly sprang free.

"Try something bigger." Bella pulled a long box nail from the can. "How 'bout this one?"

"It's too big. The gate is practically ancient—the older boards will splinter. Hand me some finishing nails."

"What do they look like?"

"Smaller and not as thick." Repositioning the upper plank, Nova reached for the hammer. Beside her, Bella fished out a handful of gold nails better suited for hanging pictures. "What the heck. Let's give them a try."

She was nailing the board into place when Henry appeared on the patio. "It's the guy calling again," he said.

Guy? What guy?

"Work with me, Henry. Did you get a name? If not, go back inside and ask."

"It's Jonathon Holly." Henry crossed his arms. "Should I say you're busy?"

"No! Tell him I'll be right there."

Sprinting into the house, Nova wondered if some issue was putting the landscaping on hold. A real headache since she'd pushed back her other clients to the end of June.

She snatched the phone from Henry. "Jonathon, hello," she said, relieved when the boy marched out of the kitchen. "How are you?"

"Not so great."

An odd response and she frowned. "What's up?"

"Listen, I hate to bother you on the weekend. I wouldn't if this weren't important. Can you stop by my house this afternoon?"

"Let's talk now. I'm not busy." She reached for a notepad. "Has Charlotte made changes to the landscaping? Tell me what she wants, and I'll call my supplier."

"This isn't about the job."

"It's not?"

"Nova, it's a private matter. It's best for everyone concerned if we meet in person."

Guessing the topic, she winced. *He knows I ran into his sister at the beach. He's upset because Charlotte mistakenly believes he's interested in me.*

Embarrassment surged through her. "Jonathon, there's nothing to discuss," she stammered. "You know what Charlotte is like. There's no stopping her once she's fixed on an agenda. I didn't believe half of what she told me. I had *no* idea she's been trying to fix us up."

Horrified by the outburst, Nova clamped her mouth shut. *My diplomacy is worse than my ability to fix a gate.* On the other end Jonathon had gone mute, allowing the awkward moment to lengthen.

She rushed forward again. "Your sister totally took me off guard," she said, needing to defend herself. "I would've set her straight if I hadn't been floored. Do us both a favor—tell her she's totally misread the situation. If it'll make the going easier, you have my permission to say I asked you out weeks ago and you shot me down. That should put an end to it."

Silence.

From the doorway, Henry snickered. She spun around.

"You have the hots for . . . *your boss*?" Henry grabbed his throat and faked gagging. "Sick."

She covered the phone's mouthpiece. "Go!" She pointed toward the hallway like a traffic cop.

Henry stomped off.

The wall clock loudly ticked off the seconds as the silence on the other end continued. It went on for so long, Nova gave the phone a shake. Hope surged with the prospect that Jonathon had hung up after realizing the error of demanding a face-to-face. Charlotte's meddling was *not* her problem.

Hang up, hang up, hang up. She'd give a month's worth of paychecks to be spared further humiliation.

"Nova? You still there?"

"I'm here." *Sinking into the floor, wishing I'd kept my mouth shut.*

"This doesn't concern anything you discussed with my sister."

"It doesn't?"

A long pause, then a note of tenderness crept into Jonathon's voice. "There's something my mother wants to discuss with you. She's pretty upset. Worried about you, in fact."

"Why is Denise worried about me?"

"She won't go into it. Not until she speaks to you directly. Whatever she needs to cover, I have a feeling it won't be easy for either of you." Jonathon hesitated. "Can you get someone to watch the kids? If you prefer, we can drive over to your place."

Her embarrassment sank beneath a new, stronger emotion. Something elemental. Fear, she realized. It scattered ice through her blood.

"Your place is fine," she rapped out. "I'm taking the kids to my parents' house this afternoon for Sunday dinner. I'll skip the meal and drive over. They won't mind babysitting."

"How's three o'clock?"

"I'll see you then."

She took Bella and Henry to her parents' house an hour early. She felt nervous and edgy about the impending conversation, begging off with an excuse about meeting with Jonathon to discuss last-minute changes to the gazebo's landscaping plans. The excuse barely registered: Helen and Finch had shopped for the kids, purchasing enough toys for Christmas. Spreading the loot out on the living room carpet, they watched with delight as the kids tore through the packages. They barely noticed when Nova slipped out of the house.

Jonathon lived in a pricey area of South Russell. On large parcels of land, stately Colonials and brick Tudor mansions peeked out from behind fluttering stands of trees. Following his directions, Nova discovered his sleek A-frame house tucked beside a horse farm. Two white JH Builders vans were parked before the garage, and she pulled into a spot behind them. A glittering thread of the Chagrin River looped through the property's steep backyard.

Apparently Jonathon had been watching for her arrival. He strode out of the house in faded jeans and a Cavaliers T-shirt. He was unshaven, his dark-brown hair slightly unkempt, as if he'd repeatedly dragged his hand through the thick locks. Tension fanned out from the corners of his eyes.

"Thanks for coming," he said, holding the door open.

She stepped inside with her anxiety ratcheting higher. "Can you give me a hint why I'm here? The suspense is killing me."

"I wish I could. Something happened at dinner last night. Charlotte mentioned seeing you at the beach, then she brought up your foster kids and Egan Croy . . . for some reason, it upset my mother."

"Denise didn't explain?"

"She was pretty tight-lipped until Charlotte left. After she'd gone, my mother asked to see you today. She had that urgent tone."

Nova let it go, despite a momentary qualm.

She paused in the foyer. To her right, a U-shaped couch dominated the living room, with a square granite coffee table in the center. A triangular wall of glass framed the front yard. Before it, a collection of parlor palms and fiddle-leaf fig trees soaked up the afternoon light.

When she peered toward the kitchen, Jonathon said, "My mother hasn't arrived yet. She's running late."

Nova wondered if Denise was having second thoughts about setting up the meeting. Even more curious: Why had Charlotte's mention of the Croy family upset her? None of it made sense.

"When do you expect her?"

"In about twenty minutes."

She wandered over to the plants, glad for a diversion from her worried thoughts. Each looked well tended, the leaves glossy and thick.

"You have a green thumb." She glanced at him approvingly. "I never would've guessed."

"Don't give me all the credit. Sometimes my mother stops by to help with the watering. I suppose I get the knack from her. She loves to garden."

"Your house is beautiful."

"Thanks." Jonathon nodded toward the stairwell. "Upstairs is a work in progress. I've nearly finished laying the tile in the guest bath. It took a lot longer than expected. In fairness, I don't have loads of free time to spend on home projects."

"You're laying the tile yourself? Jonathon, you must have thirty trades on the payroll. Delegate the job."

"Finishing the house is a labor of love. A way to decompress."

"It's a *big* house," she noted, rejoining him in the foyer. "What's the point of owning a building company if you don't put your employees to use?"

"I only bring in help with the jobs too difficult to handle alone."

He led her down a hallway that opened up into a kitchen boasting a large center island and miles of counter space. Brass pots hung near the six-burner stove. Did Jonathon like to cook? She wondered if it was another thing they had in common.

"How long have you been tackling all of this solo?" she asked him.

"Too long." He smiled ruefully. "If it takes years to complete, so what? I'm not disturbing anyone if I take a sledgehammer to a wall after dinner. Which *did* happen last winter. I framed in one of the extra bedrooms, then decided the configuration was off. So I got to work fixing the problem."

The remark struck her as sad. Did he often work on the house late at night? It seemed a lonely way to spend his free time.

She ran her fingertips across the granite countertop. "Do you enjoy living alone?"

"Not really. Do you?"

"It doesn't happen often. There are never enough foster homes here. Most of the time, I keep my file active at Job & Family Services."

"Right." He eyed her, a summing look, and she sensed a question hovering on his lips. Looking away, he reached for a drink of amber liquid he'd left on the counter.

Ice tinkled against the glass as he took a sip. "Would you like wine, or something stronger?"

"What are you having?"

"Whiskey. Do you want one?"

"Sounds good," she said, aware his solicitous behavior signaled a difficult conversation ahead.

Yet Jonathon continued to stall after pouring the drink. Handing it off, he retreated to the french doors framing the green vista outside. A large redwood deck seemed to float in midair, suspended above the treetops and the sharp drop to the river's edge. Beneath the curtain of leaves, three ducks paddled around in the waters far below.

Nova took a generous sip of her drink. The whiskey burned going down her throat. She welcomed the sensation as Jonathon kept his own counsel, the lines on the sides of his mouth deepening. Was he waiting for the drink to dampen her senses before launching into a difficult conversation?

Emptying her glass, Nova picked up the bottle. She poured two more fingers of whiskey.

From over his shoulder, Jonathon nodded with approval. She held up the bottle. *Need a refill?*

He shook his head.

Approaching, he asked, "Can we clear the air before my mother arrives?"

"Let's not, okay?" There was no reason to rehash her embarrassing attempt to ask him out, or reveal what Charlotte had told her at the beach. "I'd rather put it all behind me."

"Well, I can't. Will you please listen?"

"Jonathon, drop it. It doesn't matter."

"It *does* matter, and I need to get this out. I'll feel better if I do."

"And I'll feel worse. Let's just move on."

"Nova, stop talking. I'm saying my piece whether you like it or not." He neared with a mix of amusement and consternation stoking his features. "My sister has a one-track mind, especially when it comes to my private life. Charlotte is relentless. She's been pushing me to ask you out like it's her reason for living. And I'm talking about lobbying me on a daily basis."

"I'm sorry she's been pushing you into something you don't want." Despite her desire to drop the subject, curiosity tugged at Nova. "How long has Charlotte been doing that?"

"Since my divorce." He glanced at the clock. "We can't go into it right now—my mother will be here any minute. But I do owe you an apology."

"For what?"

"Fumbling my response when you asked me out. I shouldn't have turned you down."

"Then why did you?"

The hint of injured pride rimming her query seemed to please him. He stepped too close, invading her space. "You totally threw me, Nova. I never saw it coming. In my defense, you don't act like the sort of woman who's comfortable making the first move."

"Because I'm not."

"I didn't think so. You tend to keep to yourself. Between foster kids and running Green Harmony, it's a safe bet dating isn't high on your agenda."

"Not lately. I'm too busy." She wished he'd step away. He was too close, the ragged timbre of his voice lighting tiny fires beneath her skin. "Are we done now?"

"Almost." Jonathon's amusement faded. His eyes were soft as he studied her. "I suppose Charlotte told you the thing."

"What thing?"

"That night at the bar, when I first saw you . . . what I said about my ideal woman."

Nova's breath caught. *Is he implying I'm his ideal?* She looked up at him with confusion and a sudden, sweeping exhilaration she prayed her expression didn't betray.

"What *did* my sister tell you at the beach?"

"Nothing important."

The evasion made him grin. "Right." Turning away, he plunked ice into his glass, then grabbed the bottle of whiskey. "I'm sorry if I've made you uncomfortable."

"You haven't." Needing to lighten the mood, she forced a smile. "I'm glad we cleared the air."

"We've made a start."

"There's more?"

Jonathon nodded, although he chose not to elaborate. Instead, he said, "Let's wait in the living room."

Her anxiety returning, Nova took a seat on the far end of a couch meant to seat twenty. She noticed a coaster on the end table and set her whiskey down. She had no intention of letting too much alcohol make her fuzzy. Intuition warned she needed to be alert for whatever Denise had to say.

On the opposite side of the coffee table, Jonathon nursed his whiskey while organizing his thoughts. His thumb tapped absently against the side of his glass. With his free hand, he pressed the bridge of his nose, apparently settling on a way to proceed.

At length, he looked up. "I didn't know you were adopted."

"Denise told you," she guessed.

"It came up last night at dinner."

"My mother took care of your father the same year as my adoption. She must've told Denise about her plans."

"In 1960. You were . . . ?"

"Six years old."

Jonathon set his drink aside. "What do you know about your real parents?"

The way that question was posed never failed to irritate. *Real parents*, as if Helen and Finch weren't the genuine article. As if they were somehow less, a poor replacement for the people who'd brought Nova into the world only to abuse her.

"Helen and Finch raised me. They *are* my real parents. I prefer not to think about the people who came before them." Catching his gaze, she frowned. "Why did Denise bring up my adoption? If she's concerned about the Croy family, I don't see why it's important."

"I'm not sure it is. She may have just mentioned it in passing."

"Before or after Charlotte told her I'm caring for Egan Croy's children?" For reasons Nova couldn't decipher, the timing felt significant.

"I don't recall. After, I think." Jonathon scraped a hand through his hair. "When my mother left the table, she *did* seem concerned about Bella and Henry. I assume this has something to do with them." He exhaled a frustrated breath. "I didn't get much sleep last night, trying to work it all out."

She wondered if Denise meant to offer proof that Egan was an unfit parent. It seemed the simplest explanation. Or was her concern somehow related to Dale Croy? He *had* worked at the mill during the 1950s. Had he done something bad while employed by the Hollys? If he was Egan's father—meaning he was Henry and Bella's grandfather—perhaps he still lived nearby, and Denise wanted to warn Nova to steer clear of him.

She was still trying to work it out when Jonathon spoke again.

"You were awfully young when you were adopted." Compassion warmed his features. "Did you spend much time in foster care?"

"Just a few days, with a couple who took in emergency placements. I was one of the fortunate few."

"How so?"

"My parents had the foresight to jump through all the hoops for a foster-adopt license before they began searching for a daughter. My mother even hired a private social worker to complete the home study to speed up the process. When I entered the system, they were able to take me in quickly as a foster child while they completed the adoption paperwork."

"You *were* fortunate." Jonathon studied her closely. "Do you remember anything about your first parents?"

"Only that they didn't love me." For proof, she rolled up the sleeve of her blouse to reveal the puckering webwork of scars hidden above her wrist. When Jonathon blanched, clearly appalled, she added, "The burns are probably from cigarettes. My biological parents were older, with substance abuse or mental health issues. I don't know the specifics. I've never asked."

"You aren't curious?"

"My parents don't often talk about my early life, which is great since I don't like thinking about it. All I've taken from those years is a bad nightmare about a wolf I still can't shake off."

The remark lifted Jonathon's brows. Emotion darted through his eyes, sharpening his gaze. Sharpening the tension raining down between them.

It seemed an effort to keep his voice steady. "You have nightmares about a wolf?" he asked, clearly taken aback.

Something in his tone sent a chill down her spine. "Crazy, right?" she said, trying to make light of it. He looked worried now, his mouth drawn in a grim line. "Adults aren't supposed to have dreams that scare them half to death. It usually only happens to kids."

"Do you have them often?"

"A couple of times a year. More often when I'm under stress."

"What do you dream?"

It occurred to her that she didn't mind broaching a subject rarely shared with anyone. Her mother, Imani—lately, she didn't even tell them when the wolf stalked her dreams. The reason for Jonathon's interest was unclear, but his expression telegraphed the desire to offer support if the conversation proved overwhelming. She felt safe discussing a taboo subject.

"The wolf is bigger than a Great Dane," she explained. "It corners me in a seedy mobile home like the one my biological parents owned— or so I've always assumed. I'm young in the dream. Too young to protect myself." Her heart thumped when his jaw tensed. "I've been having the nightmare for as long as I can remember. Does it matter?"

Jonathon scraped the hair from his brow. "Now it makes sense. My mother's behavior last night, your nightmare—" He cut off abruptly. Then he muttered an oath. "I wish it didn't."

The remark jolted her. *Why does it make sense?*

She decided suddenly that she didn't want to know. Feared knowing. Did the nightmare provide him with unexpected confirmation of something his mother had alluded to? If it unlocked the door to secrets Denise felt compelled to share, Nova realized she wasn't prepared to hear them. Steeling herself, she closed her eyes. Fought the impulse to surge to her feet and leave immediately.

Her eyes sprang open when the cushion beside her lowered beneath Jonathon's considerable weight. He was a tall man, solidly built. Yet he'd moved with the stealth of a great cat.

"Should I call someone?" He rested his hand on her knee. "Whatever my mother has to say, you don't have to hear it alone. If you need someone else present, just say the word. We'll wait until they get here." His mouth tightened. "I don't want you upset."

"I'm already upset."

"I can see that."

"I'm okay."

"Not even close." He smoothed a calming hand down her hair. "I didn't think this through. It was my idea to have the three of us meet at my house. My mother is so upset, I wanted to sit in on the conversation to give her moral support. I didn't stop to consider . . ." He left the remark unfinished, his voice drifting into an uneasy silence. Then he asked, "Should we call Helen?"

"I don't want *her* upset."

"If you'd rather put this off until another—"

"No. If this concerns Bella and Henry"—*or their grandfather*—"I need to hear what Denise has to say."

"You're sure?"

A buzzing started in her ears. "I'm staying, Jonathon. I'll be all right."

The doorbell rang.

Chapter 25

Nova

Jonathon disappeared into the foyer. The door opened, and a burst of air rushed into the living room, tingling across Nova's skin, making her suddenly lightheaded. She listened to the short, stilted exchange between mother and son.

They came into view, appearing at the threshold to the living room. Denise's gaze briefly alighted on Nova before flitting away. Her skin looked patchy, her eyes dull. Like her son, she looked like she hadn't slept well last night.

At last, she tipped her head in greeting. "Thank you for coming." Denise entered the room, her gait stiff. "I'm sure you're wondering what this is all about."

Nova came to her feet. "I am," she admitted.

"I regret keeping you in suspense. I'm not even sure where to begin. There's so much I need to tell you."

She appraised Denise's all-weather mocs and casual attire—faded canvas pants and a loose-fitting shirt with grass stains peppering the sleeves. She'd dressed for an outing, not an afternoon stuck indoors.

"Why don't we take a walk?" Nova asked. "The weather's perfect."

The suggestion melted some of the tension around Denise's eyes. "You don't mind?"

"Not at all. I could use the fresh air."

Jonathon caught her gaze. The look of gratitude he telegraphed helped allay her nerves.

"Is it all right if Jonathon tags along?" Nova realized her need for his steadying presence equaled his mother's. "Unless you'd rather speak to me alone."

Relief crested on Denise's face. "Oh, I'd much prefer he join us."

"We're close to the South Chagrin Reservation of the Metropark," Jonathon said, holding open the door. "There's a trail we can pick up behind my neighbor's farm."

They followed the white fencing of the horse farm next door, spotting two fillies grazing near the long rectangular barn. Farther off, a tractor growled across a large swath of land, kicking up clouds of dust. The sound receded when they reached the back of the property, where the fierce sunlight gave way to the cooling shade of a hemlock forest. A wide path led upward, toward sandstone ledges fanned out above the Chagrin River.

Nova waited for Denise to organize her thoughts. It didn't take long.

"Last night at dinner, Charlotte mentioned Egan Croy. I had no idea he's one of the men on my son's crew, or that the children you're fostering are his." Denise glanced briefly at the river below. "Egan grew up here."

The confirmation sent a chill through Nova. "In Geauga County?"

"Outside Chardon. His parents owned several acres. Enough land to raise chickens and grow much of their own food. Egan's mother suffered from an illness, something debilitating that kept her at home. Or so people said. With the Croy family, information was always scarce. From my understanding, Egan's younger sister cared for the mother. The girl rarely came into Chardon. I don't remember her name. Wild-eyed, skittish—she'd grocery shop at odd hours and didn't attend school."

"How old was she?"

"Egan was seventeen when I first met him . . . his sister must've been two or three years younger. People said she was simple-minded, which might explain why she didn't attend school. I had my doubts. After I met their father—Dale Croy—I came to believe he kept her out of school." Distaste filtered across Denise's features. "Free labor, to manage the property while he was at work. No one at the high school would've debated the point with him. The rare times I spotted his daughter at Dee's Grocer, she appeared competent, if disheveled."

Bands of sunlight dappled the path leading them higher into the forest. On the opposite side of the river, a skittish doe foraged in the undergrowth. Slowing her pace, Nova recalled everything Imani had gleaned about Dale Croy when she'd visited the library.

"Egan's father worked at the mill." With growing unease, she explained what Imani had learned from Chardon's reference librarian. Summing up, she added, "The dates fit, and we thought he might be Egan's father."

"I'm sorry your hunch was correct."

"Is he still alive?"

"Thankfully, no." Denise lifted her shoulders, then let them fall with a sense of resignation. "Dale Croy was a thoroughly unlikable man. Large, muscular, with arms like sides of beef. He practically dwarfed his son—he never stopped taunting Egan, who wasn't small by any means."

"We learned he had a reputation for getting into bar fights."

"Dale never drank on the job, but if someone looked at him the wrong way, they regretted it. Everyone at the mill stayed out of his way."

Jonathon, silent until now, looked up with surprise. "Why was he kept on at the mill? Dad didn't have much patience for troublemakers."

"Believe me, your father wanted to let him go. He couldn't, in good conscience."

"Why not?"

"Dale came to work for us in 1947. The country had been through so much, and no one put a man out of work who'd served in the war. It was our duty to help GIs get back on their feet." Denise glanced at the canopy of leaves growing thick above them as they climbed higher into the forest. "No one would've approached Dale directly about it, but rumor was that he'd been a POW in one of the Japanese camps. I assume it explained his brutality. It certainly explained why everyone stayed out of his way."

Brutality. Nova had read enough case studies to understand how easily men passed down the habit to their sons. Egan had visited the same lessons in cruelty on his own children. Which made it impossible for her to feel sympathy for the young man he'd once been—it would take Bella and Henry years to heal from his mistreatment.

"Dale was in charge of maintenance at the mill," Denise was saying. "He truly had a gift. There wasn't a machine he couldn't take apart and reassemble within the hour. Egan worked as his assistant. Part-time, during his last year of high school. After he graduated, he put in much longer hours, six days a week."

Nova instinctively reached for Denise's arm, to help her navigate a sharp bend in the trail. "How did the arrangement work out?" she asked.

"Not well." Denise studied the shadows darkening in charcoal hues as they approached a ledge overlooking the river. "Dale enjoyed disciplining his son. Criticizing the tiniest mistake. Teasing him in front of the other employees. Mrs. Croy packed hearty lunches for them, but he made Egan wait until he'd finished eating. Then he'd toss over half a sandwich, the way you'd throw scraps to a dog. When my husband learned about it, he asked our restaurant's chef to make Egan's lunch every day. Dinner, too, if he put in a double shift. Egan had the sense to duck out when Dale was busy with some repair. His father would've been livid if he'd discovered his son was taking charity."

"Tough life for a teenager," Jonathon put in.

"It would've been easier if Egan had been a good mechanic. Unfortunately, he didn't inherit his father's talent."

Jonathon came to a standstill. "He's a decent carpenter." Looking astonished by his ready defense, he backpedaled quickly. "I don't like him, but he's good at his trade."

197

"I wish we'd known when he came to work at the mill. Oliver had lots of connections. We could've found Egan work as a carpenter's apprentice. Anything to get him away from his father. The way Dale rode him . . . it was awful to witness."

"Sounds like enough to scar most kids." There was no missing the censure in Jonathon's voice. "Dad should've put a stop to it."

"I know."

"Why didn't he intervene? Try to reason with Dale?"

Denise raised her palms with a sigh. "Don't judge your father too harshly. We saw the same outcome with workers after the Korean Conflict and Vietnam. Some of those soldiers never put their lives back together." To Nova, she said, "My husband never stopped hoping Dale would moderate his behavior. Or that Egan would quit the mill and find employment elsewhere."

"But Egan stayed, and Dale never got his act together," she guessed.

"In the end, it didn't matter. We all learned that Egan was made of tougher stuff."

Denise set her mouth in a grim line. Dredging up those years plainly took a toll. Large slabs of sandstone surrounded them like cards splayed out in a deck, and she lowered herself onto the nearest one. A change overtook the air, a tension stretching the moment taut. She patted the stone, encouraging Nova to join her—an unwanted invitation. They'd reached the heart of the story.

Anxiety plucked at Nova's skin. She came forward with the moisture evaporating from her lips. Once she was seated, Denise went on.

"Egan came to work one day with a black eye and badly scraped knuckles. Everyone knew he'd begun fighting back. It went downhill from there."

Nova's brows lifted. "He'd started taking on his father?"

"With a vengeance. Most weeks, he'd show up at the mill with bruises or cuts on his face. We never saw a scratch on Dale. I can't imagine what it was like when they got home at night. After suffering through his father's daily taunts, Egan had reached the breaking point.

There wouldn't have been anyone to stop them when the fights broke out."

Nova winced. *Not the unfortunate Mrs. Croy and her daughter.*

Two women, caught in the cross fire. Defenseless, with no means to broker a truce between father and son. Anger surged through her.

Denise stared unseeing at the forest. "The day Egan came to work with a black eye, he arrived well before his father. He must've hitchhiked to the mill. There was quite a bit of time before his shift began. He took the opportunity to go to the restaurant's kitchen for ice to take care of his swollen eye." In her lap, she bunched her fists. "That was the day he met Rosie."

Her voice caught on the name. *Rosie.* For reasons Nova couldn't identify, the pain rimming the word struck her like an electric shock. She flinched.

The reaction didn't go unnoticed: Jonathon sank down beside her. Taking her hand, he wound their fingers together. Nova hung on tight, thankful for his support.

"Rosie O'Haver was a year younger than Egan," Denise said in a voice so oddly calm, it seemed she'd entered a trance. "Like Egan, she came from a troubled home. Rosie's parents never married. Uneducated, working odd jobs, both with drinking problems—they were in their forties when they met. I doubt they planned on having a child, and Rosie learned to fend for herself. It still astonishes me how they produced that beautiful, engaging child. And such an apt name. Like a rose blooming in a wasteland."

"She worked in the kitchen?" Nova heard herself say.

"As an assistant to the junior chef. Started right after she turned sixteen. There wasn't a task the chef assigned that she didn't master quickly. I'd heard Rosie was looking for work, and asked my husband to hire her."

"She fell in love with Egan?"

"He bowled her right over. They became inseparable."

Denise seemed to rise from her trance. She noticed a stone at her feet and, scooping it up, lobbed it into the river far below. Anguish marked the gesture, as if she wished to fling away the memory of that love affair.

A spasm racked her face. "Rosie was barely seventeen when Egan got her pregnant. She was afraid to tell her parents. Terrified of how they'd react."

"But she told you," Nova whispered, and Jonathon's hold on her fingers tightened.

Denise nodded. "Right away. We'd grown close by then."

"She knew she could trust you."

"I was the only adult she *could* trust. I wanted so badly to help her."

Nova was about to pose another question when a jangly sensation invaded her limbs. She'd assumed Egan's past connection to Holly's Mill related to her fostering of Bella and Henry, that Denise meant to stress how unfit he was to regain custody. But this wasn't about the children, at least not directly. Something alarming hid within the story.

Taking over, Jonathon regarded his mother. "What about Dale?" he asked. "I doubt he was happy about the pregnancy."

"He was furious. They moved in with Rosie's parents for a few months. Not for long."

"So you got involved."

Frowning, she glanced at him. "Your father didn't approve. An out-of-wedlock pregnancy between two of his employees . . . he wanted them fired."

Jonathon grunted. "*How* did you get involved?"

A hush fell between them. Denise searched his face, as if ferreting out clues. Searching for a response she didn't find. "You don't remember," she decided.

"Remember what?"

"I thought Rosie had made such a strong impression on you. An unforgettable one." She appraised him with sad eyes. "Jonathon, she adored you. Rosie never skipped an opportunity to take you outside to play. She loved tucking you in at bedtime whenever your father and I worked late at the mill. Granted, it *was* a long time ago. You were only four years old when she lived with us."

Nova felt his fingers loosen around hers. He stared at his mother, flabbergasted.

"I don't remember her. I'm sorry."

"Don't be. I suppose it's for the best. You'd also recall the terrible arguments I had with your father."

"You argued about Rosie?"

"I wanted to keep her with us. At least until she was old enough to raise her child on her own. When she gave birth at Trinity Hospital, I *did* convince her not to list Egan on the birth certificate. Why should she? They weren't married. And he'd become too much like his father—combative, rough. He didn't treat her well. He cared even less for the baby."

"But he stuck around."

The remark seemed to drift past Denise, caught fully in the reverie now. Consumed by it. Nova slipped her hand free of Jonathon's and began rubbing her arms to ward off the chill putting goose bumps on her skin. When he draped an arm around her, she leaned against him, too unnerved to hear the rest without the comfort he offered.

"Egan believed he owned Rosie," Denise said. "His first possession, this beautiful girl with long red hair and green eyes. A girl too decent to survive Dale Croy's son. I meant to keep her out of his reach. As if my powers of persuasion were a match for young love. It wasn't long before Egan convinced her to move away. He'd found a job in Dayton."

Nova's anxious mind latched on to the description—*long red hair and green eyes*. The description fit her too neatly. It fit her perfectly. As if Denise were describing her, and not a girl she'd known in the past. For a long, bitter moment, she resisted the truth rising in her mind.

When it broke through, bewilderment seized her.

She's implying Rosie was my mother.

The knowledge struck like a fist. Pushing back on the obvious conclusion, Nova grappled for an explanation other than the one pressing down on her.

Denise exhaled a long, shaky breath. "Rosie died six years later." Willing herself on, she brushed away the tears collecting on her lashes. "We'd lost touch by then. I continued to write, but she stopped responding after the third year."

Nova was too stunned to reply. Too shocked to put form to the denial raging inside her.

Jonathon took up the gauntlet. "You didn't hear anything more until Helen came to help with Dad," he said with conviction. "I'm right, aren't I? But you didn't tell her." He muttered an oath. "Why didn't you tell her you'd known Rosie? She deserved to know."

"She did."

"But you kept silent. For the love of—why didn't you tell her?"

Denise's expression crumpled. "I've never been sure . . . was it a blessing or a curse when Helen came to us during your father's last months? It can't be coincidence. It must be fate."

Nova found her voice. "My mother told you about Rosie's death?"

"And how little else she'd learned from the case study. Maybe it was my punishment, hearing the details from Helen. I added insult to injury by withholding everything I knew."

"Who does that?" Nova couldn't stop herself from piling on. "You had no right to keep my mother in the dark."

"I don't expect you to forgive me, Nova. I'm a coward. I didn't stand up to my husband when we were in a position to help Rosie. Oh, I fought him. We had terrible rows. I didn't fight hard enough." Denise's shoulders curved inward with the weight of her shame. "Rosie overheard those arguments—Oliver wanted her shipped off to one of those halfway houses for unwed mothers. Why wouldn't she choose to leave with Egan instead?"

Something inside Nova snapped. Anger pulled her to her feet.

She faced off before Denise. "None of this makes sense," she sputtered. "My biological parents weren't teenagers."

"They were, dear."

"You're wrong! They were an older couple, two people unfit to raise a child—alcoholics, or dealing with mental health issues. My parents didn't invent a story about my early childhood. Why would they? They would've told me the truth."

Denise reached for her, but she stepped out of reach. "I'm sorry. I don't know the reason. You'll have to ask them."

"Egan Croy is *not* my father."

"He is, Nova. It's a lot to take in."

Laughter burst from her throat, which didn't make sense because she felt like crying. "You've got your facts wrong. It was almost thirty years ago—you're remembering the wrong guy."

She wasn't aware of Jonathon standing beside her until he clasped her wrist. A tender gesture, to draw her away from the precipice, and the river churning beneath them. Until he'd touched her, she hadn't realized she'd stepped too close.

She wheeled her attention to him.

"The facts aren't wrong," he said quietly. "Your nightmare, everything my mother has told us . . . it all fits. Egan Croy *is* your father. I wish it weren't true."

"What makes you so sure?"

"There's a tattoo on his arm."

She felt the blood drain from her face. "Of a wolf?"

"Yeah. The tat's four, five inches long. Hard to miss when Egan rolls up his shirtsleeves."

Her expression went slack. As did her mind for one brutal moment.

Then she pivoted away. "Great. Just great. The carpenter who was baiting me in May—*he's* my biological father? The same guy whose children I'm currently fostering? I share a father with Bella and Henry?" She landed her furious gaze back on Jonathon. "He's got a tattoo of a wolf?"

"He does, Nova."

Another piece fell into place, dousing some of her ire. Egan's tat, the nightmares about a wolf—it *did* fit too neatly.

Revulsion gripped her, but only for a moment. Her thoughts leaped back to an afternoon in May.

Alarmed, she turned to Denise. "I've never asked my parents . . . now I wish I had. When I was born, what did Rosie . . . ?" She swallowed down her dread.

"What did she name you?"

"Was it Nora?"

A whisper of a smile traced Denise's mouth. "That's right. Rosie named you for her grandmother in Dublin."

Nora.

Startled, Nova caught her breath.

Chapter 26

Nova

Homemade soup was the perfect antidote to the day's upsetting events. Lifting the spoon to her lips, Nova began to relax for the first time in hours.

Denise had said her farewells thirty minutes ago, climbing into her car with a brief wave and a look of apology for the stunning news she'd dropped in Nova's lap. After she left, Jonathon offered to make dinner. Nova begged off. She was traipsing around the living room in search of her purse when he popped a bowl into the microwave. The soothing aroma of chicken mingled with rosemary and thyme had lured her back to the kitchen.

"Did you really make this from scratch?" She captured the last bits of carrot, orzo, and chicken swimming in the rich golden broth. "It must've taken hours to prepare."

"About fifteen minutes, actually. Once the prep is done, the ingredients go into the Crock-Pot to simmer. Nothing's easier."

"I've never used a Crock-Pot."

"It's a real time-saver. You should get one."

She made a mental note to check them out at Kmart. "Do you make soup often?"

Jonathon struggled to suppress a smile. "I know what you're thinking—my freezer must be filled with the stuff. Too much food for a single guy to finish on his own."

She eyed the tureen on the counter. "It *is* a lot of food." They'd barely made a dent.

"The leftovers never go to waste. Soup, stew, chili—if I pull together something on the weekend, I take the leftovers to work on Monday."

"Your staff must love that."

"Yeah, it sure beats fast food. My secretary lets everyone know if I've brought lunch in."

There was something charming about a big, strapping man preparing nutritious meals for his employees. "How do you decide who gets a home-cooked meal?" Nova asked. "There can't be enough to go around."

"We used to do 'first come, first served.' Talk about a disaster."

"I'm visualizing a stampede to the lunchroom."

"With the same guys pushing their way to the front of the line every time. A real morale killer for the men who never got back to the office in time." Jonathon's mouth curved wryly. "Now everyone takes turns. My secretary keeps a list."

She noticed the row of cookbooks perched on a shelf near the stove. They appeared dog-eared from use. One particularly fat tome wore a dark smear of sauce on the spine.

"When did you learn to cook?" She finished the last bite of the crusty french bread he'd paired with the meal.

"When I was twelve."

She did a quick calculation. "The year your father was diagnosed with cancer?"

"That's right." Jonathon slowly swirled the wine in his glass, sipped. "It was a hard time for all of us, especially Charlotte. Our cook pulled double duty preparing meals while keeping the house running. I don't know how Annie did it. She even tried to keep Charlotte entertained, but most of the time, my sister was stuck playing alone in her bedroom."

"Annie taught you to cook?"

"Whenever she had a spare moment. I wanted to learn a few recipes that would appeal to Charlotte." He smiled, adding, "Chicken soup is one of Annie's specialties. Charlotte constantly had an upset stomach—soup usually appealed. I'd make a game out of getting her to eat. Promise to read an extra story at bedtime, or hang out in her bedroom doing my homework while she played with her dolls. Whatever worked."

"Sounds like a tall order for a boy."

"Charlotte needed me. There was no one else to pick up the slack." Jonathon set his napkin aside. A trace of sorrow whispered across his face. "School days were the hardest. Charlotte hated when I left in the morning. I'd get home later, and she'd be waiting in the foyer with half of her toys arranged on the floor like an occupying army."

"Ready to take you hostage?"

Jonathon chuckled. "You know what it's like with little kids. Big mistake to disappoint them. Especially if they've been counting down the minutes until they'll see you again."

His voice carried a blend of stoicism and pride for having met his duty well. His expression became vulnerable, filling Nova with sudden yearning. She wanted to drape her arms around his shoulders and breathe him in, to hear every story he kept in his heart until she knew them all.

"My sister had to have been lonely. Charlotte didn't understand why Mom didn't have time for her. She saw Dad even less. He was too weak, losing weight by the day . . . barely recognizable. It didn't take long for me to figure out that I needed to quit sports and my other after-school activities."

"You became her caregiver." *At twelve. When you were just a kid yourself.*

"I didn't mind. It was the least I could do."

She imagined the boy he'd been—a lanky kid reading classics like *Bambi* and *Cinderella* to his four-year-old sister. Skipping the social life adolescents craved to sift through cookbooks. Jonathon seemed unaware of how big of a sacrifice he'd made.

Nova caught herself smiling. "Well, that about does it." She set her napkin aside. "I can check off another item from the list."

"What list?"

"Of all the things we have in common." She tipped her head to the side, warmed by the soft light in his eyes. "Complementary jobs, cooking, plants, and now kids. You stood in as Charlotte's guardian when Denise couldn't. You gave her a sense of safety. Which makes you—"

"A foster parent, more or less?"

When she nodded, his eyes gained a sudden intensity that made her breathless. She couldn't look away.

"This list of yours . . . how many boxes do I need to tick off before asking you out? Don't make me wait too long, Nova. I'd like to start dating you. See where it leads."

The hoarsely issued remark moved her heart into her throat. "I'd like that too."

"Good." Pushing back his chair, Jonathon rose with an air of confidence. He picked up the bottle of sauvignon blanc. "Want a refill? I'm having another glass."

"Thanks."

"Let's talk in the living room. For starters, explain how you knew your birth name before my mother told you," he said, finally addressing the elephant in the room. Since returning to the house, he'd avoided mentioning Denise or her revelations. "It makes sense your parents chose something similar. You weren't a baby. They didn't want to confuse you."

She followed him out of the kitchen. "Hearing the name isn't what surprised me."

"What did?"

She paused before the living room's wall of glass. Outside, shadows rippled beneath the trees. In the center of the lawn, a bluebird shot out of a white fir, arcing toward the clouds as if powered by the sheer joy of living. By contrast, Nova felt burdened, overwhelmed.

She sat beside Jonathon on the couch. He waited for her to collect her thoughts.

"Bella knows my birth name," she said at length. "One day before summer break, she came in from school and began calling me Nora. Insisting it was my name, even after I told her to stop joking around. Like she'd known all along and had decided to let me in on the secret. The next day, nothing. Like she'd forgotten all about it."

Jonathon's face registered disbelief. "You didn't press her for an explanation?"

"I wrote it off to weird childhood behavior. Bella *is* a dreamy kid. She believes magic is a reliable force of nature and kisses the flowers in my yard to let them know they're loved. Plus, the spelling is close. Nova, Nora—just one letter difference. Which made me wonder if she'd invented a game and got upset because I didn't follow the rules."

"Could it be a coincidence?"

"That's the obvious explanation, but it doesn't fit. She had a major tantrum when I didn't play along. Stomping around the kitchen, banging down plates while setting the table—totally out of character for a normally cheerful kid. First time I'd seen her upset in a major way."

"Because she *did* know your original name."

"She was adamant. So, yeah, that makes sense."

"She didn't have a clue you'd never heard it before."

"It never occurred to me to ask my parents if they'd changed my name. I'm sure they tried to tell me, but I did everything possible to avoid those conversations."

"For argument's sake, let's say Bella *does* know your birth name. How did she find out?"

"Great question. I have a feeling the answer is inside an old candy tin. When the kids first came to live with me, she carried it around constantly. Bella calls it her treasure. She keeps her best magic inside, whatever that means. She's never let me see the contents."

"Could she have one of my mother's letters?" Jonathon asked. "Denise stayed in touch with Rosie after she left Geauga County with Egan. I'm sure she wrote a few times each year. They didn't break off contact until Rosie stopped writing back."

Absently Nova tapped her fingers against her wineglass. Was it possible Bella had seen one of Denise's affectionately penned missives? It seemed nearly inconceivable for letters from the 1950s to survive nearly thirty years.

She looked up sharply. "Does Denise use print or cursive?"

"Cursive, definitely. She considers it bad form to dash off a printed note for anything but a grocery list."

"Then Bella doesn't have a letter. Her reading skills are above average for a first grader, but there's no way she's muddled through whole paragraphs of cursive. She *has* seen the alphabet—her class began practicing it this year."

Jonathon stubbornly held to the theory. "Like you said, she's smart. She may have picked up more than you realize."

"I doubt she's memorized all the letters."

"She wouldn't have to. It's enough if she deciphered *Nora* in between other words she didn't understand."

"I don't know, Jonathon. That feels like a stretch."

Mulling it over, he took a sip of his wine. "What about an old photograph? Everyone jots notes on them. Bella could've found one of you with *Nora* written on the back. Even if the name were in cursive, she'd be able to decipher it."

Goose bumps rose on Nova's flesh. The first time Bella had noticed her birthmark, she'd been really excited. The heart-shaped mark *was* distinctive. If it was visible in a childhood photo of her, the odds increased considerably that Bella would recognize her.

The theory made sense, but she wasn't sure it mattered. "What are the odds there *are* any photos? We're talking decades ago." Frustrated, she sank her head against the cushions. "Egan wouldn't hold on to them. Even if he *did* have one, he'd never show it to Bella. According to the kids, he's like a pit bull when it comes to his privacy."

"That doesn't rule out Bella having an old snapshot of you." Brow furrowing, Jonathon set his wineglass on the coffee table. "Egan may have photos he's forgotten about, stuffed in an old shoebox or in a drawer. Bella could've been playing when she happened across them—"

"And decided to snoop around in his stuff?"

"Assuming he wasn't around to stop her."

"It's possible," she conceded.

She wished suddenly that Denise had never shared her awful secrets. The truth was too complicated, too painful.

With dismay Nova sent her gaze across the room, as if seeking out a solution to an unsolvable problem. "I can't decide what's thrown me more—learning that Egan Croy is my father or that Bella and Henry are my little sister and brother. The latter, I suppose. I'm providing foster care for two kids who happen to be my siblings. Half siblings," she added, correcting herself, as if the distinction made any difference.

It didn't. They were her blood, her family. The option didn't exist of pretending the fact hadn't changed everything.

"What am I supposed to do now?" She heaved out a sigh. "I can't tell the kids we're related, and I won't know what to say if Bella *has* worked everything out and approaches me. I don't want her hurt."

"You don't have to do anything right away." Jonathon slung a comforting arm across her shoulder. "This is all coming at you too fast. Give yourself time to regroup."

Time. A fleeting luxury. She needed to regroup immediately. Figure out next steps before Imani located the right parents for Bella and Henry. Once an adoption was set in motion, the opportunity to intervene vanished—assuming she wanted to throw her hat into the ring. A life-altering decision she was only just beginning to consider.

She scrubbed her palms across her face. "I'm not even sure how to tell Imani. She'll be shocked when she learns she's placed kids with me who just happen to be my siblings. I mean, what are the odds? I'm still having trouble believing it."

"She won't blame you for circumstances beyond your control."

"That's true. We've been friends for just about forever, and she'll understand that I've been totally in the dark. Anyway, she seems ready to sever Egan's legal rights. Petition the judge, put everything in motion. She's already begun searching for adoptive parents. Am I supposed to waltz into her office and throw a monkey wrench into her plans?"

"You're not helpless, Nova. What *do* you want?"

"Not to lose the kids," she said, with heat. She felt dreadful even considering the possibility. "It's wrong to walk away from family. How am I supposed to live with myself if I do?"

Jonathon brushed a lock of hair from her brow. "Sounds like you've come to a decision."

"I haven't." She didn't possess the skill set to make a snap decision. To forge ahead with confidence that she'd make the right choice.

"You're sure?"

"Jonathon, I'm not an ideal candidate. Not even close."

He attempted a serious expression, but his eyes danced. "Aren't you setting the bar too high?"

"No! I'm not ready to become a parent. How am I supposed to pull it off? With Green Harmony and full-time work and practically nothing in my savings account?"

"People raise kids on a shoestring every day."

"With nine months to prepare. Which isn't much, but it's better than nothing. I'll have ten minutes to pull my financial house together," she added, grasping at hyperbole to drive the point home. "This is one hurdle I can't jump."

"Talk to social services. They'll help you work something out."

Doubt rolled through her, impossible to suppress. "They won't," she shot back. "The adoption rules are stringent, especially for sibs. An applicant must demonstrate solvency before social services will consider the request. One look at my bank statements, and they'll laugh me out of the room. There are kids running lemonade stands in better financial shape than me."

More hyperbole, and a grin toyed with Jonathon's mouth. "Guess I'll take optimism off my list," he murmured, caressing her cheek. "You don't have any."

"Not today."

"What about on other days?"

"You'll have to wait and see," she said, trembling when his fingers rested at the base of her neck. "Unless you'd rather bail out."

"On you? No way. You're too much fun. Especially when your heart does a number on your head. You've got melodrama down to a science."

"Ha-ha."

"I'll front you the money." His eyes, suddenly earnest, did battle with the amusement on his face. There was no telling which emotion would gain the upper hand. "Whatever you need. We'll find a way to make this work."

The ridiculous offer tickled her. It barreled right through her pessimism, tossing it aside like an obstacle in her path. She felt freer suddenly, lighter. A relief after carrying the day's heavy secrets.

"What are your thoughts on an installment loan?" she joked. "Small payments from now until doomsday?"

"Keep it up, Nova." The grin broke loose, spreading across his features. "You're on your way to hosting a one-woman pity party. All you're missing is the funny hat."

"I have one in my purse."

Jonathon gave an elaborate sigh. "Leave it there. How much cash are we talking?"

"I need thousands. No. More. Raising two kids is a major investment. What are your thoughts on a six-figure loan?" Enjoying herself, she began ticking off expenses. "Braces, activities, a second family car—no self-respecting kid rides the bus during the last year of high school. Wait. I'll need two more cars. Henry will insist on taking his wheels to college." She flashed a mischievous glance. "What if they both set their hearts on the Ivy League?"

"Fine," Jonathon tossed back. He leaned tantalizingly close. "Let's make the loan zero interest. Pay me back . . . whenever. Or never," he added, dipping his face into her hair. "Never works for me."

He dragged his mouth across the soft skin of her temple. The press of his lips shivered pleasure down her spine. Then, spoiling the mood, she laughed.

"You *are* a pushover, Jonathon." Mirth caught her so quickly, more laughter erupted from her throat. "Anyone ever tell you?"

"Not lately," he murmured, snaking his arm around her waist and leaning in for a kiss.

Giggling, she scooted out of reach. "I don't need a handout, but thanks. You're sweet to offer."

"Let me know if you change your mind."

"I won't, but you're still sweet." She drained her glass, then handed it over. "Can we open another bottle?" Hesitating, she glanced out the window at the shadows deepening to charcoal on the lawn. "Unless I've overstayed my—"

"I'm glad you're here, Nova. I don't want you to go."

At the far end of the couch, a phone sat on the end table. "I'll call my parents, ask if they mind keeping Bella and Henry a little longer. They bought so many toys, the kids won't notice I'm not there. I need some time to process everything."

It was a relief when her mother agreed, buying into the falsehood that Nova was still at the Holly estate discussing plans for the gazebo's landscaping. When Jonathon returned with two fresh glasses of wine, she was hanging up.

He handed her a glass. "Everything fine with your parents?"

"They were thrilled about keeping the kids longer. They'll save me the trip and drop Bella and Henry off at seven thirty."

A comfortable hush enveloped the room. For long minutes they sipped their drinks, cuddling together with their feet propped on the coffee table. Nova felt her thoughts unspool into a blissful calm, thanks to Jonathon's reassuring company and the southern rock beat of 38 Special's "Caught Up in You" playing in the background. Her attention drifted across the room, finally picking out the sound speakers artfully set into the walls near the fireplace. When had Jonathon turned on music? She wasn't sure.

With a sigh, she drew her legs up, curling into the couch like a lazy cat. Nova wondered if the wine had loosened her inhibitions, or if the shock of everything she'd learned had pushed her outside her comfort zone. She rested her cheek against his shoulder and let her fingers trace across his jean-clad thigh. She heard his breath hitch. She didn't have much experience with men, or know the best way to flirt, but the effect she worked on him was a heady discovery.

It gave her the confidence to say, "Will you clear something up for me?"

"Fire away."

"What *did* you think Charlotte told me at the beach?"

He captured her gaze. "It doesn't matter now."

"Why not?"

A vein throbbed in Jonathon's neck as he searched her eyes. "Because you're here. That's all that matters."

He lifted her onto his lap. Cupping her face, he kissed her and promptly lost control, his hands moving from her neck to her breasts to her hips. She responded in kind, giving herself up to a passion unlike any she'd known before. Jonathon kissed her like a lover. He kissed her like a man familiar with every secret pleasure of her body.

When they drew apart, they were both panting. He looked dizzy, triumphant.

She leaned close, shivering her breath across his skin. "We're going too fast," she whispered.

"Only if you think so."

"I like you, Jonathon." Nervous laughter escaped her throat. "A lot. But I'm not . . ."

"We'll slow down."

"We should."

"Can I call you this week?"

"Call every day if you want. I'd like that."

"Then I will."

She smiled. "If you're not too busy, drop by while I'm landscaping the gazebo." She nipped at his ear. "I'd like that too."

In response, he kissed her again. When they came up for air, Nova eased herself to her feet. She didn't trust herself to stay any longer. If she did, *she'd* be the one suggesting they go upstairs.

"You're leaving?"

Gathering up her shoes and her purse, she walked to the foyer. "I should go home and sort myself out before the kids get back. There's a lot to think about." She hesitated. "It'll also give me a chance to look inside Bella's treasure."

He joined her at the door. "If you need anything, let me know."

On tiptoe, she kissed his cheek. "I will."

A growing nervousness accompanied her on the drive home. What secrets lay inside Bella's old candy tin? Entering the living room, she assessed the jungle of plants surrounding the picture window, steeling herself to solve a new mystery.

At some point in early June, Bella had moved her treasure from her room; Nova had discovered the new hiding place while watering the plants. Respect for a little girl's privacy had stopped her from riffling through the contents. Children, like adults, deserved to keep their secrets until they were ready to share them. There certainly hadn't been any urgency to look inside. Nova wasn't yet aware Egan Croy was her father; she didn't understand why the heart-shaped birthmark beneath her ear held such fascination for Bella.

Now, with Denise's revelations drumming through her thoughts, she couldn't avoid the growing conviction that the tin—a child's most cherished possession—held proof from her own past.

In medieval times, mapmakers inscribed a phrase on unknown regions of the world: *Here Be Dragons.* What danger hid inside Bella's treasure? Were the contents too painful to view?

Dragons. Nova feared wolves more.

Her stomach clenching, she dragged the fig tree out of the way. The maidenhair fern sat on a mahogany stand near the picture window. Coasting her palm across the plant's feathery leaves, she recalled that strange afternoon with Bella.

"Stop it, okay? You know my name. It's Nova."

"It should be Nora."

Dispelling the memory, she removed the fern from its glossy throne. Anxiety lifted the hairs on the back of her neck.

She tugged Bella's treasure free.

Chapter 27

NOVA

Taking a seat on the couch, Nova willed her pulse to slow. She cradled the candy tin, which was surprisingly light for an object of such weighty importance, her fingers moving across the rough bumps of rust marring its surface, as if testing her resolve to open it.

With her heart knocking around her rib cage, she worked the lid off.

The contents charted a little girl's life. An empty bottle of Coty perfume lay on top, the glass yellowish and clouded. Many drugstores carried the inexpensive brand. Nova wondered if the fragrance had been a favorite of the late Glory Croy.

When she picked up the bottle, the stopper fell out. The faint, overly sweet notes were nearly obscured by the bright, green scent of the object underneath, a bushy twig from a pine tree. The stem wore a coat of festive red paint; a coil of gardening wire looped around the base. A Christmas ornament made by Bella last year, before her mother's death? Sadness washed through Nova.

The two keepsakes floated upon a raft of Bella's artwork—crude drawings of her family done in crayon and homemade cards for birthdays and holidays clumsily fashioned with construction paper. A Mother's Day card was particularly touching. Hearts drawn in a rainbow of colors surrounded stick figures of Glory and Bella holding hands.

Beneath the hearts: *I luv U Mama* in bold red crayon.

Leafing through the artwork, Nova found other treasures. A cheap woman's necklace, the thin chain greenish and dull. A brown feather, the barbs frayed from too much handling. A four-leaf clover ironed between stiff pieces of waxed paper.

At the bottom of the tin: an object wrapped in pink tissue. Nova lifted it out.

Like the feather, the tissue was worn from too much handling. Clearly the item hidden inside was one of Bella's most cherished things. Nova traced the stiff edges. A photograph?

A lump formed in her throat. How could a simple photo protect a child from life's brutal heartache and disappointments? Too many losses and frightening events had scarred Bella's young life. Nova's fingers shook as she traced the edges of the packet, her pulse drumming unevenly with the awareness that the precious object in her hand—the key to Bella's deepest yearnings—might serve to unlock the door to her own past.

Time slowed as she unfolded the tissue.

The photograph inside lay face down. It looked old, the edges of the heavy paper softly rounded. No wonder Bella thought it carried magic—her birth date flowed across the top in attractive, feminine cursive: *March 28.* The year, however, wasn't correct.

March 28, 1959.

Nova's gaze fell to the note underneath. Her stomach did a hard flip.

Me and Nora at Sil's house.

She reread the words with her breath catching in her throat. In 1959, she'd been five years old. *Me and Nora.* She knew instantly the pretty cursive belonged to Rosie. It was tangible, real, an undeniable link to the mother she'd erased from her memories.

1959.

Nova was destined to become a ward of the state one short year later. She'd never glimpsed an image of herself so young. The photograph of a frightened girl, taken by social services after she came into custody, provided the only glimpse of her early life.

After the adoption, nearly a year passed before her parents submitted her to the rigors of a professionally shot family portrait. She'd tentatively begun to trust them by then, and agreed to sit for the portrait. Nova remembered the day well. Helen, ever pragmatic, laid out three dresses and two play outfits for her to choose from. Nova, unused to fine things, selected the most casual outfit in the lot—brown corduroy pants and a cotton jersey top.

Steadying herself, she turned the photograph over.

A sensation like falling overtook her as she studied the image of Rosie, her oval eyes crinkling with laughter, her cheekbones high and well defined above a full, expressive mouth. Most photos in the 1950s were still in black and white, and this one was no exception, but Nova was certain Rosie's long, flowing hair was the exact same shade of red as her own.

She'd expected a resemblance, but they could easily pass as twins.

On her lap, Rosie held her young daughter. Nora's arms were flung around her mother's neck, her face partially obscured. The heart-shaped birthmark beneath her right ear was clearly visible.

Transfixed by the image, Nova absently traced the blemish on her own neck. A tear rolled down her cheek. She brushed it away, her heart rebelling against the proof that once she'd been Rosie's child—not Helen's.

Outside, a light tap on a car's horn. A door slammed shut on the vehicle, and the children's voices neared the house.

Scrambling, Nova shoved the tin beneath the couch. She placed the fern back on its pedestal and pushed the fig tree back into place. How long had she been studying the photograph? A quick glance at the clock confirmed it was nearly eight o'clock.

Henry burst through the front door, his arms laden with bags. "Your parents had to take off—they're late for bowling." Diving to the floor, he shook out the toys and promptly began rooting through them.

"Look at all the stuff they gave me!" He showed her a green Matchbox car.

With effort, Nova composed her features. "Looks like you hit the lottery." The tears were still too close to the surface, but she managed a smile.

"They got me *six* cars and a Speedtrack. There's other stuff too!"

"That's great, Henry."

Bella swished into the room wearing a costume gown of satiny purple. A crown listed toward her ear. "I'm a princess!" Righting the crown, she twirled for Nova. "I also got a new baby doll. She has brown hair just like me. And look—Helen got me *two* games. I can play them with Maya."

"She'll like that a lot."

"I got a basketball *and* a game," Henry said, not to be outdone. He held up the board game, Trouble. "Can we play right now?"

"It's nearly bedtime, kiddo. Let's play tomorrow."

"But it's early! Can I at least watch TV?"

"Not tonight."

With her heel, Nova nudged the candy tin deeper beneath the couch. The last thing she needed was for the children to discover she'd riffled through the contents. Bella's feelings would be hurt, and Henry would tease her if she cried.

"Big kids don't go to bed this early," Henry complained. "Especially not in the summer."

"Why don't you set up your new racetrack in your bedroom?" Nova suggested. "You can play with your Matchbox cars until nine o'clock."

The children showed off the rest of their new toys as she gently herded them toward the bedrooms. In their excitement, they didn't notice the sadness pooling around her.

Seeing the photograph of herself lovingly seated in Rosie's lap had uprooted something essential inside Nova, leaving her floundering to make sense of *who* she was. She'd grown accustomed to the holes in her life: when she cut a first tooth, said her first word, or started to walk. Those memories had died alongside her biological mother, and filling in the missing pieces threatened to carry Rosie from the realm of the theoretical and make her real.

Worthy of entry into Nova's burdened heart.

By the time the kids finally went to sleep, it was after ten o'clock. Nova took a long shower to ease the tension from her muscles, replaying the day's events as the water pounded her back. Donning a robe, she went into the kitchen and made a cup of chamomile tea. Nursing the cup, she considered calling her parents. On bowling nights, they usually returned home by eleven o'clock.

It was a relief when they didn't pick up. Denise's revelations would upset them. Besides, Nova decided it was best to get herself into a better frame of mind before approaching them. She couldn't shake the anger bleeding through her thoughts as she made another cup of tea. Helen and Finch couldn't have known about Egan—he wasn't listed on her birth certificate—but why hadn't they told her the truth about Rosie? Why allow her to believe a false story? It seemed cruel, a betrayal. Which made it all the more imperative to sort herself out before telling them everything she'd learned.

Past midnight, confusion led her back into the living room. Sliding the candy tin out from beneath the couch, she carefully sorted through Bella's treasures to ensure there weren't other photos of Rosie stuck between the reams of artwork. Confusion and dread warred inside her. She was glad when she found none, then disappointed. Her eyes were hot with tears when she lifted out the photo of them together, studying it for long minutes.

From the hallway, the shuffling of feet. Henry cleared his throat.

Startled, Nova looked up. He padded into the room, his cheeks rosy and his hair tousled from sleep. There was no telling how long he'd been watching her.

He peered over her shoulder. "Are you the little girl in the picture? Bella thinks so."

"I am." She quickly wrapped the photo in the tissue.

He watched intently as she returned it to the tin. "The chick was one of Pa's girlfriends. He's had lots of girlfriends."

"You've seen the photo before?"

"Sure. Mama found it last year. She told us Pa liked some other lady a long time ago. Were you her daughter?"

"I was."

"How long did she date Pa?"

The more critical fact—that they were both Egan's children—plainly hadn't occurred to Henry. Given his father's penchant for chasing women, he assumed Egan had dated Rosie sometime after she'd given birth to her daughter.

"I'm not sure how long they were together," she said, glad to avoid a complicated subject.

"Bella says the picture is magic."

"Because her birthday is on the back?"

Henry nodded. "Stupid, right? She makes wishes on it. Like it's a magic wand or something."

"What does she wish for?"

He shrugged. "Don't ask me. She keeps her wishes to herself."

"Did your mother give her the photo?"

"No way. Pa would've been mad. Mama found it one day in the bottom of a drawer when she was cleaning. Sometimes after Pa left for work, she'd look at the photo with Bella. They always put it away when they were done. Pa doesn't like anyone messing around with his stuff."

"Then how *did* Bella get it?"

Plainly a thorny question, for Henry began swinging his legs, the agitated burst of energy lengthening the silence between them. She let the moment wind out, glad for a chance to settle her emotions. When his legs finally came to rest, she took a gander at his feet and his hands. His toes, like his fingernails, were in desperate need of a trim.

"I guess I'm asking the wrong question," she said, breaking the silence. "You don't want to talk about it."

"It's no big deal." He sank his head against the cushions to stare at the ceiling. "Pa was angry after Mama got herself killed."

"She didn't *get* herself killed. It was a traffic accident."

Henry smirked. "Pa only cared that she'd stuck him with me and Bella to raise." His tone was depressingly matter-of-fact as he continued. "After she died, he threw all her stuff away, like he couldn't stand to look at it anymore. I knew to get out of his way. So I took off for my bedroom. Stayed there while he cussed and drank booze and started throwing stuff around. You don't cross Pa when he's angry."

The description pained Nova more than the photograph.

"When you took off for your room, why didn't you take Bella with you?"

"She wouldn't go. She followed Pa around the house saving whatever she could."

Bella's astonishing act of bravery clicked the rest into place. "There aren't any family photos in her treasure box. Not one of you or Bella with your mother. She couldn't save them?"

"There's none of us? You're sure?"

"There aren't. I'm sorry."

Henry took the disappointment in stride. "I guess Pa threw them all out," he said. "Bella *was* happy she'd rescued the photo of the lady."

Along with Glory's perfume bottle and necklace, and the Christmas ornament. Given his description of that day, it was a miracle anything had escaped Egan's wrath. Anger flashed through her as she imagined Bella darting through the house, risking punishment to save a few precious items, tokens to keep her memories of Glory alive.

Nova pushed the bitter emotion aside. Anger wouldn't erase the trauma the children had experienced.

"It's way past your bedtime, Henry." Rising, she decided to return Bella's treasure to its hiding place after he left. "Do you want me to tuck you in?"

"No, thanks." He padded across the room, hesitated. He gave her a long glance. "Aren't you going to put it back?"

"After you leave."

He rolled his eyes. "Suit yourself."

Chapter 28

Nova

Henry reached around Nova to pick up a plastic mermaid on the bathtub's rim. "You've been in there forever, Bella." He tossed the toy into the tub, sloshing the bubbly water and drawing a yelp from his sister. "When are you getting out? It's my turn in the bathroom."

"You'll get your turn," Nova told him.

Bella yawned. "The water's still warm."

"You're falling asleep in there!"

Nova pointed to the door. "Henry, she's almost finished. Go ahead and watch TV for a little while longer. I'll call you when we're done."

"I'm ready to brush my teeth *now*. Can't a guy have any privacy?"

The complaint was new. Lately Henry required ample time in the bathroom, locking himself inside for long minutes. Cupboards banged open and shut, the water ran at full blast and—incredibly—Henry sang to himself in a fairly decent tenor while performing his nightly ministrations. He offered no explanation for his sudden interest in personal hygiene. He still belched at dinner and farted in public. He brooded in his room and rarely smiled. Yet he'd begun scrubbing his face and combing his hair each morning before heading off to summer camp. His teeth gleamed from dutiful brushing.

Nova shooed him toward the door. "Patience is a virtue, mister. Do me a favor and grow some while you're watching TV."

"Yeah? And what am I supposed to do about this?" He angrily spread his arms wide to encompass the room. "Bella poured stinky perfume everywhere. It's my bathroom too."

"What's the big deal? It smells nice in here."

"Guys don't like flowers."

"Some guys do."

"Not the ones my age."

"Then they don't know what they're missing." Last week, her mother had picked up the inexpensive perfume for ultrafeminine Bella. "Breathing it in won't kill you."

"What if it gets on me? I'll smell like a girl."

Bella, content in the tub, swished the water to form new bubbles. "You smell like mud," she informed him. "Take a bath when I'm done. You can use the bubbly stuff Helen gave me."

"Thanks, but no thanks. Then I *will* be a girl. The guys at summer camp will make fun of me."

"It'll make the girls happy if you smell nice." Leaning close to Nova's ear, Bella dropped her voice. "Henry likes a girl at camp."

Nova grinned with surprise. "He does?"

"Her hair smells like popcorn. She smiles at him all the time."

The disclosure nipped at Henry's anger. He joggled from one foot to the other, at a loss for a snarky reply. *Since when does he have a summer crush?*

He turned on his heel, slamming the door on his way out.

The washcloth, still dry and lying on the tub's rim, provided a carpet for the various toys placed on top. Nova flicked the toys off. They plunked to the bottom of the tub, making Bella laugh.

"About Henry and Popcorn." Nova dunked the washcloth into the warm water, then washed behind Bella's ears. "How long has this been going on?"

"Oh, I don't know." Bella rubbed her eyes.

"A week?"

"Longer." From the water she fished out the plastic crown Helen had given her on Sunday and placed it on her head. "Henry's in love. He makes googly eyes at Popcorn. All. The. Time. When the camp ladies made ice cream cones today, he gave his to Popcorn. His face was happy the whole time he watched her eat *both* cones."

"Wow. That *is* something. Especially since your brother has a serious ice cream obsession."

"He likes Popcorn more than chocolate chip."

"What's she like?"

"She's in Henry's grade but she's a beanpole. A lot taller than him. She snorts like a pig when he tells her jokes." Bella demonstrated her rendition of a pig's snort, making them both laugh. After they calmed down, she added, "Popcorn is never mean to little kids like me. She's nice all the time."

"I like her already."

"Me too."

"I'm glad."

Bella studied her with childish sincerity. "Nova, can I ask you something?"

"Sure."

"Can we go shopping next month for new school clothes? Some of the girls at camp said their mamas take them shopping in July."

"I don't see why not."

Social services provided a small stipend for clothing; Nova was tucking away cash to buy the kids a few extras. If they were still with her come August, she didn't want them starting the new school year with skimpy wardrobes.

Please let them still be with me. Contrary to what Jonathon believed, she held out no hope that social services would consider her request to adopt the children if she were foolish enough to fill out an application. She didn't have the financial resources to raise them, and she knew it was best not to pursue the option. After everything the kids had been through, they needed a stable, secure homelife with two parents capable of providing for their every need. Still, Nova secretly hoped the search for the right parents would stretch out for months. Much as she wanted to see the kids happily ensconced in a new life, it became harder each day to contemplate losing them.

Dismissing the thought, she asked, "What should we buy for school?"

"Lots of dresses. Some pants and pretty shirts too." Bella plucked off the crown. "Can I get new shoes?"

"Of course. We'll get your brother outfitted too."

"When can we get a Christmas tree? Do we have to wait until it gets cold? Can I help decorate?"

The questions pierced Nova like a blade. A proper response escaped her.

Bella captured a yawn and swallowed it down. "What do *you* want for Christmas? Before Mama went to heaven, she loved the presents I made for her. I'll draw a picture for you or make something with the Play-Doh Helen gave me." She chortled with little-girl excitement. "I'll make something pretty, okay?"

"Sure," Nova agreed.

Her eyes stung. *I won't have the kids at Christmas.* Imani was sure to make their adoption a top priority. They'd be happily living with a married couple who'd cherish and protect them. Would they allow her to visit Bella and Henry? She wanted to remain a part of their lives.

She glanced at the clock. "Ready to get out?"

"Do I have to? The water's still warm."

She'd expected the response. Tomorrow after camp, Egan was scheduled for a supervised visit with the kids at Job & Family Services. Imani was still wrapping up paperwork for an impending adoption, so Tim Kenner would oversee the visitation. The night before each visit, Bella used every delay tactic in her arsenal to keep from going to bed. As if putting off sleep could stop the next day's approach.

"Five minutes, no more. You've been in the bath long enough." Nova swirled her fingers across Bella's wet cheek, drawing a giggle. "It's almost bedtime, kiddo."

When she finally got out and dressed in frilly pajamas—another present from Nova's parents—Henry immediately commandeered the bathroom, snapping the door shut and banging about. In a break with recent tradition, no singing resounded inside the tiled room. The faucet, however, ran long enough for Nova to wonder if he'd empty the hot water tank.

Bella kissed her Barbie doll and other random toys good night before jumping into bed. Nova raced through a reading of *Cinderella*. Bella dozed off as she reached the last page.

Henry stomped down the hallway, his hair slicked back and his face pink from scrubbing. His nails were still overlong, with half-moons of grit underneath. A small inconvenience when compared to the bigger, positive changes in his personal hygiene.

Nova drew back the blankets, then stepped away. She knew better than to offer a good night kiss.

"All set?" she asked when he climbed in.

"Yeah."

She turned off the light. "Good night, Henry." She began closing the door.

"Nova?" He sat up in bed.

She leaned against the doorjamb as he collected his thoughts. The boy heaved out a breath. Looked away.

Finally, he drew his embarrassed gaze back to her. "I have to ask you something important."

A first, and she tamed her expression to hide her surprise. "Go ahead."

"How does a guy know if a girl likes him?"

"There are lots of ways," she said, pleased by his desire to seek her advice. She recalled her first school crushes when she'd been about his age. "She likes talking to you, right?" A safe query since Bella's account of Popcorn described an extroverted girl.

"All the time."

"Do you catch her staring at you?"

Henry drummed his fingers on the blanket. He looked older then, a boy happy to exit the little-kid years and greet the next stage of life.

"Yeah. She does that too."

"I'd say the feeling is mutual."

"I didn't say I like her," he volleyed back, his expression closing.

"You do, though," she pointed out. "Why else bring it up?"

Caught in an obvious lie, he rolled his shoulders as if preparing to vault from the bed to outrun his affection for the girl. A grin broke across his face.

Reading his thoughts proved easy: *Adults are tricky. You never know when they'll outsmart you.*

"So . . . what should I do next?" he asked.

"Get to know her better. What's her favorite color, does she play sports, does she have any hobbies—the sky's the limit. It'll make her happy if you show an interest in the things she finds important. Girls like that a lot."

"Okay." He turned off the lamp. "Thanks."

"Anytime." Nova started to walk off, stopped. She ducked her head back into the room. "Oh, and Henry?"

"Yeah?"

"Don't belch in front of her. No farting either."

"Why not? The guys at camp think it's funny. They do it too."

"Most girls don't like it. Just saying."

"All right."

In the living room, a rerun of *Three's Company* flickered on the TV. Did Henry now enjoy sitcoms? Plainly his tastes were maturing. Since the onset of summer, Luke Skywalker and his other action figures had been gathering dust in the back of his closet. Outside of Henry's favorite foods and the vegetables he despised, most of his preferences remained unvoiced. Sadness pierced her. There wouldn't be enough time left together to discover his personality in full.

Her spirits rebounded when Jonathon called, something he now did nightly. After they chatted about her progress on the gazebo's landscaping, he said, "Let me take you out for dinner on Friday. I'll wine and dine you on a proper date."

"I can't. All my potential babysitters have other plans." She'd checked in hopes they *could* go out. Her parents were meeting friends for dinner, Imani planned to work late, and Kelly's sister was in town visiting. "Maybe the following weekend."

"What about Saturday? Not for wining and dining. There's a carnival in Burton. Games, rides—we'll take Bella and Henry. Make a day of it."

In the past, she'd avoided dating whenever foster kids were staying with her. Not that she could imagine any of her past suitors suggesting she bring them along.

The past is no guide. This is different. They were ignoring the normal rules, falling for each other fast. Was it too soon to introduce him to the kids? Bella would accept the news that Nova was dating without fanfare, perhaps even with excitement. Henry, on the other hand, would make it his life's mission to give Jonathon a hard time.

"Let me think about it."

"What's there to think about? It's a carnival. The kids will have a blast."

"Bella, for sure. Henry . . . he's not ready for prime time. He'll pretend to throw up when he meets you. Or he'll fart the minute we pile into your car. It'll sound like a pop gun, and you'll wish you had a gas mask." Nova cringed. "Trust me on this. Henry's got disgusting behavior down to a science."

"Little-boy antics—I can handle it. I was one." Jonathon chuckled. "I'll use all my persuasion to get on his good side. So, we're going?"

She couldn't stop the smile tugging at her lips. "Do you always get your way?"

"Usually."

"It takes some getting used to."

"Am I pushing too hard? I *would* like to see you this weekend, and meet the kids."

"You're not pushing too hard. Your resolve is sexy. It makes me even more attracted to you." The smile overtook her mouth. "Should I have kept that to myself?" she asked. "I'm not trying to shock you."

"I like knowing where I stand with you, Nova."

A rap sounded at the door.

"I've got to go," she said.

They hung up, and she went to see who it was. She wasn't expecting anyone at this late hour.

Opening the door, Nova blinked, then did a second take. Her mouth fell open.

Chapter 29

NOVA

On the front porch, her mother glared.

Tufts of her sensibly cut hair stuck out in all directions. Worry lines framed Helen's eyes. Chocolate flecks dotted the front of her beautifully starched white blouse.

Why bother to iron a blouse if you were going to tear through a box of chocolates? Nova's brows lifted. Her mother's former career as a nurse gave her an abiding respect for the dangers of too many sweets in one's diet. From the looks of it, she'd binged on a jumbo box of Whitman's.

Helen shot a look of dark warning. "Aren't you going to invite me in?"

"Sorry." Nova swept the door wide. "What are you doing here? It's ten o'clock." Bedtime, in Helen's universe.

"In case you haven't noticed, today is Wednesday. I'm out of patience, sweetheart. *That's* why I'm here." Her mother radiated pure annoyance. "I'm aware of your penchant for avoiding difficult subjects. Whenever you have trouble processing your emotions, your first instinct is to push away the people who love you most. Enough is enough. When were you planning to tell me and your father about your conversation with Denise Holly last Sunday? We're your parents, Nova. We can't give you emotional support if you shut us out."

The chance to reply never came. Helen marched past to the kitchen.

Cupboard doors thumped open and banged shut. An apple leaped from the fruit bowl and tumbled to the floor as if fleeing the woman searching frantically for a missing item.

Nova crept into the room. "Need help?"

"I'll find it myself."

More chocolate? Valium? "Mom, you're in a serious frenzy. Totally a new look for you."

"Don't you dare crack jokes. I'm not in the mood."

"Obviously."

With a wheezing expulsion of air, Helen eased down onto her knees. "Where do you hide Finch's Scotch?" She thrust her head into the cupboard beneath the sink. A can of oven cleaner clunked out, rolling past Nova's ankles to disappear beneath the table. "I know you keep a bottle for your father. Where is it? That man. Agreeing to give up the hard stuff, then hiding his stash at our daughter's house. If you'd known each other during Prohibition, you could've made bathtub gin together."

In her father's defense, Nova also stashed chocolate for her mother to nibble whenever TV news segments on puppy mills or sappy commercials featuring babies tested her normally sturdy emotions. Best not to mention that at the moment.

Nova took down two glasses. "The Scotch is in the back corner, on the left." She rarely drank on weeknights; her mother never did. *Unusual visits called for strange remedies.* "Want to talk outside?"

"Yes. The night air will calm me down. Are the children asleep?"

"Great question, Mom. Keep banging around like a crazed toddler and they won't be."

"They're children. If you fed them a proper dinner, they'll sleep like the dead." Brandishing the Scotch, Helen wheezed herself back to full height. She jabbed a finger toward the door. "Get moving. We're not hashing this out in here."

Stars winked in the heavens. Clouds of fireflies danced above the yard's recently watered flower beds. The murmur of voices drifted from a nearby property.

Nova sat down at the picnic table. Henry's bedroom lay at the back of the house. A quick glance confirmed the drapes were shut. Hopefully her mother's arrival hadn't wakened him.

Helen splashed liquor into the glasses.

"When did Denise call you?" Nova asked.

"Monday afternoon. She wanted to apologize for any distress she'd caused my family, and for withholding the information about your birth parents." Helen paced across the small patio. "I still can't get over the coincidence, taking care of Oliver Holly during the same months we were preparing to adopt you. And Denise knew all along about your biological parents. I *am* angry with her—I trusted her with every detail I'd been told by your social worker. Why didn't she fill in the missing blanks?"

"She had her reasons. It doesn't matter now."

"From where I'm standing, it feels like a betrayal."

Nova regarded her with disbelief. "*You* feel betrayed? How do you think I feel? You let me buy into a fiction about my birth parents. You lied to me. Who does that? You should've told me the truth from the get-go!"

The rebuke brought her mother to a standstill. "Oh, I don't believe this. You're blaming *me?*"

"If the shoe fits."

"Be fair, Nova. I've lost track of how many times I tried to correct that ridiculous story your father told you and Imani when you were in elementary school."

"But you didn't."

"Oh, really? How often did I attempt to broach the subject? I didn't have all the details, but I *did* try to share what I knew."

"You should've tried harder."

"Oh, please. You refused to listen. You did everything in your power to avoid the difficult conversations. You never gave me the chance to set the record straight. Not once."

Nova tested the claim against her memories. Was she treating her mother unfairly? Had she bailed every time Helen brought up the past? A sinking feeling invaded her bones.

It wasn't enough to stop her defense. "Don't put this on me. I was the kid, you were the adult. You had a responsibility to set the record straight."

"Take responsibility, sweetheart. I did my best. Every time I tried to strike up a discussion about Rosie, you shut me out. Remember your freshman year of high school?"

"Not really."

Helen crossed her arms with frustration. "It was October," she rasped out. "After I made yet another attempt to discuss her, you spent a week sleeping at Imani's house. You hid out to avoid me. The longest sleepover on record—I'll bet her parents assumed you were moving in."

Uneasy beneath her mother's injured pride, Nova flicked a leaf from the picnic table, watched it spin to the ground, its gentle movement retrieving the forgotten memory.

We were raking leaves. Now she viewed that day through the lens of maturity.

The Sunday before the weeklong sleepover, her father was out of town on business. Her older brother, Peter, enjoying his first year at Ohio State, rarely came home. While Nova and her mother raked leaves in the yard, Helen attempted to broach the subject of Rosie.

Guilt took a swipe at her. No wonder her mother had waited until they were out in the crisp autumn air before touching on the difficult subject. She'd been aware Nova had felt safest when surrounded by nature. That the breeze whispering through the trees and scent of freshly mown grass centered her like nothing else.

"I was scared," she admitted. She looked off at the fireflies blinking above the lawn, growing thick in clusters of light. "You know what happened every time you brought up my early life."

"You'd have nightmares about the wolf?"

She nodded.

"Here's the problem with the past, Nova. We choose *what* we recall. We throw away the memories that don't fit our current viewpoint." Her mother paused for emphasis. Assured of Nova's attention, she added, "You did *not* dream of the wolf every time I brought up the past. You only want to believe you did. Those dreams were a crutch."

The observation furrowed her brows. Did she use the nightmare to avoid filling in the blanks about her early life? As a barrier to protect her emotions?

"Maybe," she conceded.

"Do you remember what I used to tell you?"

"That the human mind is a marvelous instrument, and I'll stop having the nightmares once I resolve my fear of the past."

"But you haven't resolved the past. Now you must face your demons, whether you're ready or not." Despite her irritation, Helen managed to layer her voice with affection. "We choose what we take from our history, child. What lessons, what habits. Never underestimate the power of intention. *Who* do you intend to emulate—the unfortunate people who brought you into the world, or the parents who raised you?"

"You and Dad." Nova swallowed around the lump in her throat. "Obviously."

"Are you convinced you've succeeded?"

No. Because I haven't.

Self-doubt guided her choices. She second-guessed every decision she made, questioned every motive before it rose, fully formed, from her heart. She retreated from the brightest moments life had to offer because she believed she was undeserving. She didn't even trust her feelings toward Jonathon.

Nova pushed the glass of Scotch away. Her most formative years were riddled with neglect. With abuse. The damage she carried was knit to the bone, part and parcel of her personality, her sense of self. It guided her mistrusting heart.

Helen sat down beside her. "You aren't your biological parents," she said firmly. "You're one of a kind, unique in your own right—you aren't destined to repeat their mistakes. Rosie O'Haver wasn't perfect. There's no telling what might have come of her life under better circumstances. Be grateful for the gifts she gave you—your gorgeous red hair and beautiful green eyes."

"I know." Nova explained about the photograph kept in Bella's tin. "Guess I don't have to wonder about where my looks came from anymore."

Helen took the news in stride. "I guess you don't." She picked up her glass, took a thoughtful sip. Getting back on track, she said, "With regard to Egan Croy, I'll grant it's harder to view him as anything but reprehensible."

"He's a monster."

"Denise mentioned he's quite good at carpentry. You've always been handy."

"With plants, not carpentry. Subject closed." Nova felt her eyes water. "Let's move on."

"What do you think we're doing? We're having a conversation that's long overdue."

"Would you get to the point?"

"I'm trying!"

Helen took an anxious swipe at her hair. Catching herself, she placed her hands on the table. But her ill-concealed agitation started her rubbing the skin around her large, arthritic knuckles, making angry red patches beside the bluish veins. A familiar habit, one she used to resist touching Nova before she was ready to accept physical comfort. Recognition jolted Nova. She used a similar strategy with Henry, rarely getting too close, keeping her distance from his battered heart—never providing the comfort he desperately needed because the psychic scars leave such a child too raw to accept love from well-meaning adults. The uncanny similarities in her emotional state and Henry's blurred Nova's vision as her mother spoke again.

"It all comes down to acceptance," Helen said. "Do the hard work to make your life better. You've been standing in place for too long. You'll move forward once you allow yourself to *see* your birth parents as real people—to accept their good qualities alongside the bad. You'll learn to accept yourself in return. I pity Rosie for the chances she never received." Hesitating, she released a shuddering breath. "It's certainly more difficult to forgive Egan. From what Denise described, he's become his father. An abusive man without the conscience to recognize his failings."

"I can't forgive him, Mom. Not after what he's done to Henry and Bella—what he's done to me."

"Forgiveness is about freeing *yourself*. Let go of the hate, Nova. It's the most destructive emotion there is."

"I can't. I—"

Anger caught her, taking her voice. It burned through her like a mighty blaze.

Helen barred further debate by steering Nova's head to her shoulder. And what a large, solid shoulder it was. An inheritance from her Swedish ancestors, big-boned and well muscled, capable of hefting large sacks and small children. The sea swell of pain threatened to drown Nova as she sank against her mother, the dam breaking on her sorrow, the tears streaming down her face. Helen rained down kisses and murmured soothing words until Nova had thoroughly soaked her mother's chocolate-stained blouse with the wealth of her tears.

When at last she reined herself in, sniffling and gulping for air, her mother gave a nod of satisfaction.

"I'm proud of you, sweetheart. I know how hard it is for you to let your feelings out."

"I hate when I fall to pieces."

"You shouldn't. You're stronger than you think. Look at what you've accomplished in two short months with Henry and Bella. You've already broken the chain of abuse. You've given those children a safe place to heal after all they've endured. What do you plan to do about them?"

For once, Nova pushed her reservations aside. "I love them. Not like a big sister, even though that's what I am. There's nothing I want more than to make them mine." A new wave of tears threatened to swamp her, but she steadied her voice. "I can't even tell them we're related. What's the point? They'll be adopted, and I'll never get the chance. They'll never know—"

"That you belong together?"

More tears crowded her eyes, her nose, her heart. "What *should* I do?"

"You're asking my opinion?"

"Yes!"

"Adopt them." Helen clinked her glass against Nova's untouched drink.

Nova regarded her with disbelief. "I'm not qualified."

"You've already proven you can handle the kids. Look how well they're doing."

"I'm not married. Social services might consider a single adult for one child, but not two. I've never heard of anyone in my position adopting a sib group."

"That doesn't mean it's never happened. Once Egan is out of the picture, you *are* the children's closest relative. I'd say you're more than qualified." Helen took a small sip of Scotch, then set her glass aside. "Your father and I will help. On-call babysitters. Advisers for the new parent. Whatever you need."

"Mom, I can't afford to keep them. They deserve better than to live on a shoestring."

"I agree, which is why Finch and I will contribute. We'll help you support the kids for as long as needed." When she began to protest, Helen waved her off, adding, "Henry and Bella are your family, Nova— which means they're our family too. Mine and Finch's and Peter's. We're all financially comfortable. We won't let you fail."

The offer was incredibly generous. *It's what families do. They look out for each other.* Gratitude swept through her.

"You really think I can handle single parenting?" She rubbed her runny nose. "I don't want to lose the kids."

"Stop doubting yourself, sweetheart. You're perfectly capable. Speak to Imani. Tell her your intentions."

"She won't be on board with the idea."

"Convince her to reconsider. Point out how you've established a loving relationship with Henry and Bella. Social services prefers to place children with family members whenever possible."

Hope crested in Nova. "You think I can sway her?"

"Of course I do." Helen clapped her hands down on the picnic table, ending the debate. "Anything else?"

"One thing."

"Go ahead."

"Dad invented the story about my birth parents. Why bother? It would've been easier to tell me the truth."

"Well, he couldn't have told you about Egan because he wasn't mentioned in your case study. The bit about a middle-aged couple . . . your father is a softie. You'd never asked about your background, and it took him by surprise when Imani began riddling him with questions. Finch went with his first impulse."

"A fib about a couple similar in age to you?"

"He just wasn't thinking." Helen shook her head with bemusement. "If you must know the truth, your father preferred his little fabrication. It's hard for him to accept the difficulties you endured with teenage parents."

"Then I'm not the only one struggling with acceptance."

"No, you're not. Finch struggles with it too. So did I, for a long time. I finally got over it." Helen sighed. "Good parents want an assurance their child is safe, protected. Those feelings are just as strong when you adopt."

"You weren't my parents at the beginning. There's nothing you could've done."

"Logically, that's true." Helen patted Nova's breastbone. "It feels differently in here."

They went into the kitchen. Helen set their glasses in the sink.

"Have you seen Imani?" she asked.

"Not lately. Why?"

"I called her after I spoke with Denise."

"You told her?"

"She's your closest friend. I assumed you'd already done so."

Nova frowned. Keeping Imani out of the loop wasn't her best move. Especially with news relating to children she'd placed in Nova's care. Was she furious? Hurt? Nova resolved to catch up with her tomorrow and offer a heartfelt apology.

A decision she quickly shared with her mother.

Helen nodded with satisfaction. "My work here is done."

Nova walked her out. "Thanks, Mom. For everything."

Chapter 30

Nova

Nova glanced up the mountain of stairs leading into the courthouse.

She checked her watch again: ten thirty. She couldn't afford to wait much longer. Bear and Leroy were completing the gazebo's landscaping; she'd promised to return quickly. Once they finished, they needed her to plot out the pathway to the Hollys' patio before they installed the slate pavers.

Above her, people streamed in and out of the courthouse's heavy walnut doors. Nova paced below, wondering if she'd erred in showing up unannounced. According to the bailiff, the civil proceeding before Imani's adoption hearing—a divorce—had taken longer than expected.

At last, Imani stepped outside, her briefcase swinging at her side and a sheaf of papers in her fist. She came down the steps at a rapid pace while skimming the pages.

And nearly careened into Nova.

"What are you doing here?" she demanded.

"I owe you an apology."

"Save it. I'm busy right now."

When she began marching past, Nova caught her by the arm. "I'm an idiot," she blurted. "I should've called you Sunday night, when I got back from Jonathon's house."

"Damn right you should've."

"I know!"

Irritation narrowed Imani's gaze. "Then why didn't you call?"

"I was thrown by everything Denise told me. It was a lot to take in. I needed to sort myself out."

"You needed four days to sort yourself out? It's Thursday, Nova. You know, it really hurts when you shut me out. I thought you'd outgrown the habit."

"Save the speech. My mother's already done the honors. In fact, she helped me come to a decision, one I'd like to discuss with you." She hesitated. "I *am* sorry. I'm totally a dope."

Incredibly, Imani reined herself in. "Stop putting yourself down— you're not a dope." She offered the barest glimmer of a smile. "Thank you for apologizing."

Her reaction gave Nova the courage to plunge ahead. "Can we talk? It's important."

"I need to get back to the office. I'm swamped."

"C'mon. Spare ten minutes for your closest friend."

Imani sighed. "All right." She scanned the center green. "Let's find somewhere to sit."

They chose a sun-splashed picnic table near the south end of the green. Imani set her briefcase on top. "It must've been a shock, learning Egan Croy is your biological father," she said. Sympathy glossed her features as she regarded Nova fully.

"That's putting it mildly."

"He's now working at the new development in Burton?"

"We're not in contact, if that's what you're asking. I hope I never run into him again." Considering, she took a seat. "Maybe Jonathon will fire him. Or he'll quit."

"Whether or not Egan remains at JH Builders is immaterial." Unlocking her briefcase, Imani placed the sheaf of papers inside. She remained standing, a clear indication of her concern. "What if he stays in Geauga County?"

"Why would he? Once he loses custody, he'll move away. There's no reason for him to stay."

"You're making a bad assumption. Even if he's no longer employed by Jonathon, he may find another job nearby. You can't control where he decides to live."

The conversation wasn't going the way she'd expected, and Nova fought to remain calm. "You're right, Imani—I can't stop Egan from staying here if he chooses to do so. But it doesn't alter my decision." Anxiety spilled through her, but she managed to plow forward. "I want to adopt Bella and Henry."

Imani stared at her.

"They *are* my siblings." When Imani still didn't respond, Nova spiked her voice with false cheer. "It's great news, right? I never expected to learn the missing bits of my family history—I never wanted to. Finding out they're my sibs makes the rest easier to bear."

"You haven't told them, have you?"

"Of course not. It's too soon. I don't want to confuse them."

"Good. They have enough to deal with right now."

The reply put her on the defensive. As did Imani's professional tone, veering toward brittle. Was she implying Nova should *never* tell them?

Imani bowed her head briefly before lifting her gaze. "Judge Cassidy has ruled on the case," she said. "She's severing Egan's parental rights."

"When will—"

"We'll notify Egan next week."

"That fast."

Imani frowned. Then she rushed forward quickly, saying, "I'm confident I've found the perfect couple to adopt the kids. They live in Cincinnati and have a twelve-year-old daughter. First in her class at school, wants to be a dentist when she grows up. They adopted her when she was Bella's age."

The news jolted Nova. "They want a sibling group?"

"Preferably a boy and a girl, or two boys since they already have a daughter. School-age kids—unlike most couples, they aren't even remotely interesting in adopting an infant. They understand how diffi-cult it is to place older sibs."

"You've spoken to them about Bella and Henry?"

"You know I haven't. I can't make a formal inquiry until we notify Egan, and the adoption file is drawn up." A furrow of distress appeared between Imani's brows. "I *have* spoken to the couple's social worker, and she believes they'll want the kids. The husband is a professor at Xavier, the wife, a marketing exec. And moving the kids to the other end of the state is the best solution, in case Egan *does* stay here."

"Stop putting out feelers. Henry and Bella should stay with me." Nova came to her feet, a dizzying wave spilling through her. "I can do this. I want to raise them." Alarmed when Imani didn't relent, she faced off before her. "You're looking at me like I'm crazy. Out of line to even consider this. Say something!"

"What do you want me to say?"

"You won't help me?" She'd anticipated some resistance, but not this.

Imani's voice sharpened. "What about Egan?"

"Forget about him! I want to adopt the kids. I *will* adopt them." Anger coursed through Nova. "I expect your help."

A terrible silence fell between them. They locked stubborn gazes, leaving Nova searching for the right words to sway Imani. When she realized they didn't exist, that her closest friend refused to consider the request, her heart hollowed out. She might, in fact, lose Bella and Henry.

Her expression crumpled.

Imani pivoted away. She paused by the sidewalk encasing the center green to survey the shops around Chardon Square. A busy morning awash in sunshine, the pedestrians thick and the scent of coffee wafting from the diner at the corner of the square.

When she returned, she blurted, "Letting the kids go may be the hardest thing you ever do. Especially now that you know they're your little brother and sister. But I'm a social worker, Nova. It's my job to put their needs first. Before everything else. Before my loyalty to my closest friend, who may be making a snap decision, or any reservations I have about your ability to pull off full-time parenting."

"I'm not making a snap decision!"

"Maybe you're not. But it doesn't change anything. In my judgment, they're better off living as far away from their father as I can place them. With a married couple experienced in adopting older kids."

"No! They're better off with me."

A tiny growl burst from Imani's throat. "Don't you think I *want* to agree with you? I can't, not when factoring in their father. Egan Croy is manipulative and way too charming when he wants to be. He's completely lacking the self-awareness to even consider if his children are better served in an adoptive home." Imani's voice shook when she added, "I've with a case like this one before. With instances of serious abuse, once the state steps in, most adults voluntarily surrender their parental rights. It's heartbreaking and depressing and no one comes out in the end without lots of pain and suffering, least of all the children. But those parents know they can't cut it. They're willing to put their children's needs first. Egan's different. He won't let Bella and Henry go easily."

"You don't know that."

"Oh, yes I do. I'd be lousy at my job if I didn't trust my gut. If they stay in Geauga County, he'll find malicious ways to interject himself into their lives. I'm sure of it. He won't stop."

A chill raced down Nova's spine. *She's right. Egan will be relentless. He'll make their lives hell.*

Resisting the possibility, she shook her head. "It won't happen," she said, grasping at her fading confidence. "Stalking is a crime. The police will stop him."

"Don't be naive. Lots of abusive men evade the police. It's pathetically common. Did the police stop Egan when he forced Glory and the kids to leave Indiana? Did they stop the abuse we both know occurred when the Croys lived in Columbus? It's sheer luck the case ever reached my desk. If a neighbor hadn't notified us that Bella and Henry were being left unsupervised, they'd still be living with their father."

Nova sensed a chasm growing in their friendship. A demarcation line she hadn't known existed. A pang of hurt sliced through her, sure and swift, cutting her to the bone. If she pursued adoption, she'd go it alone. Without the support of her closest friend. Without her counsel and encouragement. When had she ever made a life-altering decision without Imani on her side?

Never.

Stepping into the breach, she leveled her stony gaze. "I don't care about the past, or your concerns. I'm formally notifying you of my intentions. When can I begin the adoption paperwork?"

"After Egan appears in court." Imani sighed. "I won't attach my recommendation to your request."

"You'll push for the couple in Cincinnati?"

"I'm sorry, Nova." Imani picked up her briefcase. "I don't have a choice."

Chapter 31

BELLA

Bella followed Henry into the building and immediately pinched her nose shut. The man complaining at the reception desk smelled funny. The lady behind the desk, her thick eyeglasses foggy and her brows jumping to hide beneath her snowy-white hair, opened and closed her mouth while the man talked over her. She looked like a fish out of the water, gasping for air.

Bella wished Nova were here. She knew how to make grown-ups behave and would settle the angry man down in a flash. Once, when they were in line at the grocery store, a grumpy man was screaming at the skinny boy working the cash register. Nova stepped right in. She gave the man a talking-to that shut him right up.

In the center of the lobby, young Mr. Tim fiddled with the lapels of his blazer as the man began shouting. When he spotted them, he rushed forward and took Bella by the hand. He pulled her forward so quickly, she nearly tripped.

Trotting beside them, Henry glanced back. "Is that guy drunk? He sure smells like it."

Mr. Tim cleared his throat. "Don't worry about it. Mrs. Cooper will call security if he gets out of line."

"Good luck with that. Your security guy is in the parking lot."

"He is?"

Henry grinned. "He was lighting up a smoke when the babysitter dropped us off."

"Great. Just great," Tim muttered. He pasted on a nervous smile. "C'mon, kids. Your father is waiting."

They were rounding the corner to start down the corridor when the angry man leaned over the desk. The lady wheeled her chair back. The look on her face put bees in Bella's tummy.

Henry laughed. "He's really pissed." He savored a last peek before entering the corridor. "What's his problem, Tim?"

"I don't know."

"You're a guy. Shouldn't you deal with it?"

Tim ignored the question as they neared the playroom where grown-ups met with their kids. The shouting rose in pitch. A lady with frizzy brown hair darted out of an office, her eyes narrowing on Tim and her mouth tipping into a frown. The heels of her fancy shoes clacked loudly as she raced past.

Tim let go of Bella's hand. "Stay here." He sprinted toward the lobby.

The moment he was gone, Pa strolled out of the playroom. He looked amused by the scary commotion.

"Think there'll be a fight?" Henry asked him.

"Maybe." He motioned for them to follow him inside. "Might be fun to watch."

Henry's eyes brightened. "Can we?"

"Better not." He gave Bella a cursory glance. "What's your problem? You scared of a drunk?"

She was scared of Pa, but she knew better than to admit it. He'd start teasing her, and Henry would join in.

She stayed rooted in the doorway to the playroom. "Mr. Tim told us to wait outside. We're not supposed to be in here."

"To hell with his rules. I'm here, you're here—what's the problem? I have a right to visit with my own kids. If you don't want to see me, go play with the baby dolls." Pa nodded toward the back of the room. "There are some real ugly ones. I'll bet they came from Goodwill."

"You heard him, Bella." Henry puffed out his chest. *"Get moving."*

Bella made herself scarce, darting to the back of the room. Someone had added a sad heap of dolls in a plastic bin to the playroom's toys. Pulling them out one by one, she pretended to play, stroking their hair and rubbing the dirty marks off their plastic arms. She propped them up against the bookshelf in a nice row, the way Nova organized the toys in their bedrooms whenever they were tossed all over the place. The sun threw bands of gold through the window behind a table just the right size for little kids. She pretended Nova was right outside beside Mama's ghost, watching out for her.

With her back to Henry and Pa, it was hard to catch all their conversation. She finally latched on to Henry's voice, rising with excitement.

"See there? She's the kid with your other lady."

"Nova Doubeck is Rosie's daughter? Are you sure about this?"

"It's true, Pa. Nova told me herself."

Pa muttered a cussword.

"Look here. I fixed the name on the back."

"How'd you get this, boy?"

"Bella had it in her treasure box. I took it from her."

Bella spun around, the doll in her hands plunking to the floor. They were looking at her magic picture.

Pa shot a dark look toward the corridor. *"What the hell? The authorities took Nora away. Now they're scheming to let her raise you and Bella? This is bullshit."* He threw down the photo.

The bees started buzzing in Bella's tummy, but she chased them away. Something flashed through her like white lightning. She suddenly wasn't scared.

Racing across the room, she snatched up the picture. Pa swore again, his arm shooting out to catch her, but her feet didn't fail her. She flew out the door and back down the corridor without breaking stride. Most of the rooms she ran past were empty, the lights turned off. In the last one before the lobby, she spotted a lady in a blue dress barking into a phone.

The lobby was nearly empty. She skidded to a halt behind Mr. Tim and the frizzy-haired lady. Together, they were holding the angry, thrashing *man against the wall. The older lady cowered behind the reception desk, blubbering like a baby.*

Bella tugged on the back of Tim's jacket. "I want to go home now."

Tim pressed his arm firmly against the man's shoulder. When his wild eyes found her, his face went white as snow.

"Oh, Jesus." He landed his attention on the receptionist. "Milly, stop crying. Get security. He's somewhere in the parking lot."

It didn't take long for the security guard to bring order. He shoved the angry man into a chair and stood over him until the wail of sirens announced the arrival of the police. Henry appeared in the lobby, and Bella huddled against the wall beside him to wait for Nova to pick them up.

Pa loped past, his expression fiery. He wasn't happy about the visit being cut short.

He stalked out. The lobby's glass door shuddered, then banged shut. Bella scooted farther away from her brother.

She made her voice into a tiny, stinging hiss. "You're bad, Henry," she told him. "I don't like you anymore."

She expected a mean reply. Hard words meant to hurt her. But Henry's face creased. He looked worn out, like an old man.

"I didn't have a choice." He bumped his head against the wall four, five, six times. "Pa will get us back. It's better to stay on his good side."

The way his shoulders slumped forward reminded her of a butterfly dying, its pretty wings curving inward before growing still. Bella wasn't sure why, for the first time in her life, Henry's reaction gave her the upper hand. She only knew that it did.

"Pa won't get us back," she insisted, her voice growing stronger. "We're going to stay with Nova. She'll be our new mama."

"Why don't you grow up already? Your magic picture won't make it come true."

"It already has. Nova loves us." She scooted closer, forcing him look at her. "Don't you love her? She's been good to us. Like a mama is supposed to be."

Henry didn't reply. He started blinking fast, and she knew he meant to ward off his tears.

"Nova will stop Pa," she said. "You'll see. Imani will help her."

Sadness lowered Henry's voice to a whisper. "They'll lose, Bella. Pa always wins. You'd know that if you remembered Indiana. He made us come back to Ohio with Mama. He made us all pay when she tried to run away."

Indiana. The word never failed to make her bones weak.

No, she didn't remember. Not even tiny wisps of memory of how Mama tried to run, or what Pa did when he found them. Mama used to say that angels protected little girls by erasing things it was best for them not to remember. Indiana. Henry was older; he carried more stories of that scary place than all the special things she kept in her treasure box, the sweet, sure keepsakes that protected her from danger. The stories he told made Bella sick with fear. It was the first time he'd mentioned Indiana since they'd found a new home with Nova.

Was Henry right? Would Pa win them back?

At the reception desk, handcuffs clicked into place. A policeman walked the man out.

Chapter 32

Nova

"Fair warning," Nova said. "If Henry's behavior doesn't improve, we're bailing on the carnival. It's embarrassing how he's treating you."

"Give him time." Jonathon draped his arm around her waist, drawing her closer. "He'll warm up."

"He's practically ignoring you."

"You worry too much."

"Sometimes."

Jonathon chuckled. "Well, stop. We aren't leaving—the kids are having fun. Why spoil it? I can handle a nine-year-old giving me a hard time."

He appeared supremely unaffected by the chilly reception he'd received from Henry, the stony glances and the curt remarks. Bella, on the other hand, had warmed to him immediately. In between dashing to game booths at the Burton carnival, she'd hugged him repeatedly—an endearing sight, given her small stature and Jonathon's height.

Children jostled for position before the bucket toss booth. Bella and Henry were among them, flinging tennis balls with abandon in pursuit of the stuffed animals on display for winners.

With the kids suitably occupied, Jonathon stole a kiss. "If you're curious, Henry isn't completely ignoring me." A smile spread slowly across his face. "When you and Bella went to get cotton candy, he broke radio silence. In fact, he interrogated me."

"About what?"

"Whether or not we're getting laid. His words, not mine. And if we *are* getting laid, where do we do it?"

Nova stared at him, mortified. "No way."

"Oh yeah. You have to give the kid credit. He's awfully confident for a boy his age."

Not confident. Obnoxious. "You didn't let him drag you into a discussion of sex, did you? I have *no* idea how much Henry understands."

Jonathon studied her with amusement. "Give me a break. I'm fast on the uptake. He's nine—so I asked *him* what it means to get laid. He informed me it's about grown-ups lying down together where no one can see them. The details about sex never entered the picture. I'll bet he picked up the phrase at school."

Or from his father.

She nearly mentioned how troubled the children seemed since their short visit with Egan on Thursday. Filling the house with moody silences. Slamming doors and barely eating. But if she gave Jonathon a recap, it would be tempting to tell him about her decision to fill out the adoption paperwork. Which would inevitably lead to a description of Imani's thoroughly negative reaction to the plan. They hadn't spoken since their standoff outside the courthouse.

Taking the kids to the carnival wasn't exactly a date, but they were enjoying themselves. She didn't want to dampen the mood.

At the booth, Bella lobbed a final ball. Like all her other throws, it bounced off the rim of a pail without sinking. With a frown, she pivoted away from the booth to rejoin them.

"I didn't win *anything*." She puffed up her cheeks with frustration. "I can't throw good. Nobody throws bad like me."

"Want to try the goldfish toss?" Nova suggested. Mostly toddlers and their parents were playing the game. Winning was easy.

"I don't want a goldfish. I really want the pink bear. Do you see it?"

The stuffed animal hung at the back of the booth. A major prize, nearly Bella's size, with neon-pink fur. No wonder she wanted it.

Jonathon led them back to the booth. "All ten balls must land in green buckets to win," he said, scanning the rules. He regarded Nova. "Want me to give it a go?"

Naturally the green buckets were much smaller than the blue and yellow ones. Precious few of the kids playing the game were sinking balls in them. Like the bear, they were positioned at the back of the booth.

Nova rolled her shoulders. "I'll do it."

"You will?"

The disbelief in his voice made her laugh. "Men aren't the only ones with good aim, Jonathon. You've never seen me pitch."

Admiration lit his features. "Hey, prove me wrong if you can."

"Watch and learn."

Bella, quiet until now, looked up at her. "I believe in you, Nova." Closing her eyes, she began making small circles in the center of her chest.

"What are you doing, sweetie?"

"Wishing hard." On a sigh, Bella opened her eyes. "I want the pink bear more than anything."

"Then I'll do my best to get it for you."

Nova rarely made promises too difficult to keep. She felt confident about this one. On countless occasions, she'd thrown baseballs and footballs around with her older brother, Peter. They'd shot baskets on summer afternoons until he, demoralized, stopped asking her to play. She possessed near perfect aim.

Henry, down to his last three balls, materialized beside her. "Forget it, Nova. Girls can't throw good. Let me try."

"Back off, Henry. I need to focus."

"You're wasting your money."

"No, *you* are the one draining the till. Unless you break the losing streak and score with your last three balls."

"If I lose, will you give me five bucks?" He made it sound like the deal of the century. "I'll have better luck at another game."

She'd already given him more cash than warranted. The subtle bribery wasn't improving his disposition.

"I'll give you one dollar." She went into a windup. "Now, let me concentrate."

The moment he stepped back, she lobbed six balls into green buckets in quick succession. A twitter rose among the children lined up before the booth. The next three balls plunked in, and Bella started jumping up and down. When the last ball scored, Jonathon let out a low whistle.

Henry regarded her with disgust. "Beginner's luck," he muttered.

"Don't you *ever* have anything nice to say?"

"No." He stuck out his hand. "Let me try the balloon and dart game."

She dropped coins onto his palm. "Please stay where I can see you." He ran off. The stout man working the booth approached. She pointed to the pink bear. "That one, please."

Bella took the stuffed animal and hugged it tight. "My wish came true!"

"Nova's killer aim had something to do with it," Jonathon put in. "We should send her to the majors."

"Not this year." Nova laughed. "Between the kids and Green Harmony, my schedule is full."

Bella kissed the bear's black nose. "Thank you so much!"

"My pleasure, sweetie."

"What should I name her?" She held the bear at arm's length. "I know! I'll call her Pansy."

Jonathon said, "You sure picked a name fast. You don't need to think about it?"

"Pansy is Bella's middle name," Nova told him.

"Ah. It all makes sense now."

"Bella, why not call her Princess Pansy?" She knew the name would appeal. "You can take turns wearing your play jewelry."

"But not my crown."

"Why can't you share?"

"Pansy should have one of her own." Bella gave a look of supreme authority. "She's a *princess*, remember? She'd like one with blue jewels and sparkly stuff all over it. Like glitter, or teeny-tiny jewels that aren't blue—purple, maybe. Will you buy it for her? There's a booth with play jewelry by the hamburger stand."

Jonathon lowered a hand to the top of Bella's head. "You walked right into the trap," he told Nova.

She flashed him a grin before returning her attention to the earnest child. "No promises, sweetie. The carnival has tapped out my extra cash for the month." When Bella toed the ground, clearly disappointed, she added, "Here's an idea. Tonight, we'll count up the allowance money you haven't already spent. You might have enough to buy Princess Pansy's crown without my help."

"What if I don't?"

"I'll make up the difference next month."

"You promise?"

She crossed her heart.

Bella nodded with satisfaction. "I love you, Nova."

"I love you, too, silly girl."

Bella tipped her head to the side, her expression suddenly serious. "Can I ask you something important?"

About buying more toys? The answer is no.

"Go ahead."

"Do I have to call you Nova? I don't want to anymore." Bella leaned against her to offer a winning smile. "Can I call you *Mama* now? You *are* my new mama, aren't you? I've been wishing hard to make it come true."

Above the child's head, she exchanged a glance with Jonathon. He brushed a palm across Bella's hair before fleetingly resting his hand on Nova's wrist.

His eyes telegraphed a message: *You can handle this.*

"I'll keep an eye on Henry," he said. He joined the crowd flowing toward the balloon and dart booth.

A bench freed up near the picnic area. Taking it, Nova waited as Bella fussed with the newly anointed Princess Pansy, hoisting the stuffed animal onto the bench and straightening its crinkly yellow bow. The expectancy on her face made finding the right words difficult. How to soften the disappointment sure to come?

Nova opened her arms. Scrambling onto her lap, Bella leaned close.

"Don't be scared." She patted Nova's cheek. "I asked Mama if it's all right for you to take her place. She wasn't sure when me and Henry first came to live with you. She wanted to watch you for a while. To see if you're nice to little kids."

"And now?"

"She thinks it's a *very* good idea."

A child seeking permission from a beloved parent gone from this world: the prospect was touching and bittersweet. From Bella's vantage point, Glory wasn't gone. She'd merely gone somewhere else, a place beyond the everyday world.

"Do you talk to Glory in your dreams?" Nova guessed.

"Oh yes. We talk all the time. She wants you to be my new mama."

"I want that, too, sweetheart."

"Then can I stop calling you Nova?"

"It's not a good idea." It pained her to refrain from adding, *At least not yet.* "You know how this works—I'm your foster mother. We can't break the rules."

"But the rules are stupid. Why can't you be my forever mama?"

"Maybe I can be, at some point in the future." Nova pulled in a breath as she chose her next words with care. "Remember what I told you about the judge? She'll decide soon where you and Henry should live permanently. We have to wait for her to make a decision."

"I don't want to go back to Pa."

"I know you don't." *And you won't.*

The children weren't yet aware of Judge Cassidy's decision to terminate Egan's parental rights. Next week, after social services informed him, they'd learn of the decision. Imani would bring in a child psychologist to assist during the conversation.

Bella pinned her with a look of entreaty. "Will you tell the judge you want to be my mama?"

"I will. I'll do my best, but I can't make any guarantees. The final decision isn't mine."

Bella accepted this with a sigh. "Okay." Some of her confidence returned when she hopped off Nova's lap. "I'll ask Mama to help make wishes, so the judge gives me to you. And Henry too. He also wants you to be his mama. He's just too scared to admit it."

Nova had her doubts about where Henry preferred to live permanently, but she kept the opinion to herself. At the game booth, Jonathon was demonstrating the proper way to hold a dart. Henry listened intently before making his next throw. The man operating the booth handed over a water gun—plainly the lesson had paid off.

"Ready?" She helped Bella hoist the stuffed bear from the bench.

They'd started off when Bella looked up at her. "Do *you* remember Indiana?"

The question took Nova off guard, pulling her to a stop. A chill raced down her spine. Bella had been only three years old when Egan found them in the Muncie hotel room and forced Glory and the kids to return with him to Columbus. A traumatic incident, one Bella couldn't possibly remember.

But Henry might.

Nova was struggling to find the proper response when Bella spoke again.

"After you become my mama, let's never go to Indiana." A shadow crossed her eyes. "It's a bad place."

Chapter 33

Nova

"I don't want to go home." From inside the pavilion, Henry stuck his palm out into the rain. A few stray drops plopped onto his hand. "You see? It's letting up. Lots of people are taking off—I'll have more chances to win at other games."

Nova studied the sky. The rain *was* letting up. At the outset of the sudden downpour, half of the people at the fair had darted to their cars. There were no long lines at any of the booths, where mostly teenagers were braving the weather to play the games. Henry, on a high after learning how to throw a dart, would gladly join them.

Jonathon transferred the stuffed bear to his opposite hip. "It's fine with me if we stay." He'd promised to guard it with his life after Bella had tired of carrying it. "There's probably more rain on the way, but it'll hold off for a while."

Bella pointed toward a booth across from the pavilion. "*I* want to stay." All variety of play jewelry hung from the rafters. "I don't see any crowns, but maybe I can win a necklace for Princess Pansy. She'd like one."

Well, that settles it. Nova looked to Jonathon. "Mind if we split up? I'll see if Bella can win a necklace for Pansy."

"Let's meet at the burger stand in thirty minutes." Jonathon glanced at his watch. "It's getting close to dinnertime. No arguments—I'm buying."

"Okay."

They stayed past dinnertime, until the crowds dwindled. The sun dipped low in the sky. With fewer people vying for prizes, many of the booth's operators made winning easier. No doubt they preferred handing the toys out rather than packing them up later that night.

It was past eight o'clock when they climbed into Jonathon's Audi. Bella promptly dozed off. Beside her on the back seat, Henry sorted through his new toys.

Bella's head lolled against Jonathon's shoulder when he carried her into the house. Laying her on the couch, he cast a sideways glance. At his feet, Henry spilled out the contents of the largest bag.

"Don't go through your sister's stuff." Jonathon plucked up the mini prism she'd won at the last booth and tossed it to Nova. "Do you know which is which?"

"Sort of." Henry put a yellow pinwheel on the couch near his sister's feet. "All the girly stuff belongs to Bella."

Nova walked Jonathon back to his car. Overhead, the clouds were again darkening. A blast of wind rustled through the trees before suddenly dying out.

"Thanks for taking us," she said. "We had a great time." Embarrassment lifted her shoulders. "I'm sorry Henry wasn't more pleasant."

"Don't worry about it. He'll warm up to me eventually."

The remark sent something good swirling through her. Jonathon made no secret of his desire to stay in her life—and he believed the children would too. His optimism gave her hope.

He asked, "Do you and the kids have plans tomorrow?"

"Other than dealing with laundry?" She'd been putting off the chore. "Nope, we don't."

"Want to catch a movie? *E. T. the Extra-Terrestrial* is playing in Mentor. I've heard it's good, and it's definitely kid-friendly."

She was touched by the offer. "That would be great."

He gave her a quick kiss. "I'll call you in the morning with show times."

She waved when he drove off, returning to the house with a bounce in her step.

The buoyant emotion instantly fled. Bella, now awake, wailed loudly.

"Where's my princess?" She scrambled off the couch. "She's not here!"

Nova stifled a groan. She'd meant to retrieve the stuffed animal from the Audi's trunk when she'd walked Jonathon out.

"Calm down, sweetie. Jonathon will bring her over tomorrow." She explained about seeing a movie the following day, which did nothing to halt the tears. "He won't forget. He'll keep Princess Pansy safe tonight."

"Make him come back! I need my princess."

"I can't. Jonathon lives twenty minutes away. By the time he makes the round trip, you'll be asleep."

She scooped Bella into her arms, desperate for a solution to lift her spirits. She was astonished when Henry supplied it.

He held up a packet of sparklers. "Bella, look. Want to see how they work? They make tiny stars when you light them. It's magic."

The word *magic* halted the tears.

Squirming out of Nova's arms, Bella approached her brother. "Show me how," she commanded, swallowing down a hiccup.

"We'll light them together," Nova said. "One sparkler each. Afterward, you'll both get ready for bed. It's been a long day."

She found a box of matches in the kitchen. Dropping it into her palm, she prayed the rain would hold off for a few more minutes. If they were caught in another downpour before Bella's curiosity was sated, she'd cry a new river of tears.

Flicking on the patio lights, Nova led them outside. Shadows rippled beneath the trees. The wind gusted across the backyard. Once it died down, she lit the first sparkler and handed it to Henry. Darting off, he waved it around, the glittery sparkles following behind.

Bella wiped the last of the tears from her cheeks. "Make one for me."

"Patience, kiddo." A stronger gust of wind snuffed out the flame. Nova struck another match, relieved when the sparkler sizzled to life. "Here you go."

The kids raced into the yard's shadows, yelping and laughing, releasing trails of silver into the air. A raindrop plopped onto Nova's head. Holding her breath, she studied the sky. They didn't have long before the next downpour arrived. The kids, having reached the back of the yard, ran toward her whooping with delight.

Later, Nova would realize that Bella heard the sound first, the faint creaking of wood. Before she did, smiling on the patio, or Henry. A noise easy to miss—an announcement of danger.

Skidding to a halt, Bella dropped the sparkler. Her attention landed on the garden gate. A shudder passed through her small body as she released a frightened gasp. Confused, Nova started toward her.

She'd barely taken a step when the gate crashed open, cracking wood and spinning boards across the grass. Egan came through at full force, nearly stumbling to the ground.

Regaining his balance, he looked to the children. "Get over here. Now." When Nova moved toward him, he shot her a dangerous glance, stopping her in her tracks. "Come any closer, and you'll wish you hadn't. You got that?"

The threat drained the blood from her head. Egan wasn't much taller than her, but he was all muscle. Wiry and strong.

"You're not taking the kids." She risked another step forward. "Leave. Now. I'm calling the police."

His hands curled into fists. "Try it, and I'll make you pay. Stay where you are."

The impasse put a deadly silence between them. Bella's plaintive cry broke it.

"Don't hurt her! Don't, Pa!"

Dread gripped Nova when Bella ran toward him. She couldn't protect both children. Not with one of them standing within arm's reach of their menacing father.

"Good girl." He stabbed his icy regard on Henry. "Get over here, boy. We're leaving."

At the command, Henry flinched. Fear trembled down his body. Dropping the sparkler, he swung his gaze to Nova.

"Did you hear me, boy? Get moving!"

Henry's eyes were wide and black with terror as he began walking, incredibly, toward her. He stepped behind her, his thin frame pressing tight against the shield of her back.

The dangerous impasse slowed time to a crawl. Yet Nova's mind sped up. She calculated the odds of pushing Henry toward the house before his father could react. Would he know to lock himself inside? Egan would surely give chase. Which meant she must stop him.

Her frantic gaze latched on to the shovel propped in the shadows near the back door. The prospect of using mortal force nearly made her black out. *There's no choice. If I have to take on Egan to save the children, I will.*

The decision charged adrenaline through her blood, clearing her vision. Bella was the wild card. Did she have the sense to run out the gate, to a neighbor's house? If the situation were reversed, Henry would know to seek help. He'd bang on doors until someone answered. His sister was younger.

Terror washed through Nova. *Oh, God, please don't let her run to me. I can't fight off Egan and protect her at the same time.*

The thought had barely cleared her brain when a growl erupted near the gate. Jonathon launched himself through, tackling Egan to the ground.

Their fists flying, the men rolled across the grass. Jonathon was younger, stronger, and he caught Egan with a right hook across the jaw that momentarily stunned him. But Egan was a street fighter—he'd learned well at Dale's knee—and he struggled out from beneath Jonathon. Lightning fast, he rose. A split second before Jonathon hauled himself up.

Whirling around, Egan spotted a board torn loose from the shattered gate. He grabbed it up.

Nova screamed. "Jonathon—look out!"

The warning came too late. The board hit the side of his head with a terrifying crack of sound. Arms flailing, Jonathon careened backward. He lay motionless.

Like Nova, Egan swiftly calculated the odds. Scooping up Bella, he ran out the damaged gate. Henry darted out from behind her back, to follow them, but Nova latched on to his shoulder to stop him.

She fell to her knees. "Jonathon, can you hear me?" Her stomach twisted at the sight of blood oozing from his scalp. "Please—wake up!"

Groaning, he opened bleary eyes. She felt a moment's relief.

It died quickly. Out front, an engine roared to life. The sound brought Nova to her feet.

Bella.

"Henry—call 911!" She sprinted toward the gate. "Tell them a man is injured and a child has been abducted."

Jonathon struggled up onto his elbows. "Nova, wait!"

Ignoring the command, she raced around the side of the house. Tires burned rubber as Egan threw his truck in reverse. It sped down the darkened street. Nova grappled for her keys, her hands clammy with sweat, and dropped them. She scooped them up and leaped into the Ramcharger.

She was firing up the engine when the storm arrived in a fury, sending rain down in sheets. Lightning streaked the sky.

The windshield wipers thumped against the glass, fighting against the rain that made it nearly impossible to see. Nova's heart lurched as she spotted Egan's truck making a wide, dangerous turn out of the residential area. Her pulse beat in her throat as she sped up.

He's heading for Route 44.

A mile down the road, lights illuminated the entrance ramp to the interstate. Allow him to reach it, and he'd get away.

Her teeth chattering, Nova drove through a stop sign. The truck shuddered as she swerved onto the slick pavement of Route 44. The only car on the road was an old Ford Pinto traveling well below the speed limit. She flew past, suddenly aware that she didn't have a plan on how to rescue Bella. Ram the truck from behind? Force Egan from the road? What if the accident left Bella injured? She feverishly prayed the frightened child was huddled on the floor of his truck in relative safety.

Please, Lord. Don't let anything happen to Bella.

Up ahead, Egan was gaining ground. Through the heavy rain, she spotted the truck zooming past the sign for the interstate. She never saw the green Chevy Caprice pulling onto the road in front of her.

A horn blared.

She clipped the Chevy's bumper. The impact spun her vehicle sideways. Slamming on the brakes, she came to a jerky stop on the berm.

A furious blond jumped out of the car. "Don't you look where you're going? You nearly killed me!"

Beneath the lights to the interstate, Egan's truck disappeared down the ramp.

Chapter 34

NOVA

"Is this one better?" Henry asked.

From the leafy shade of Dee McDooney's oak tree, he lifted a plug of periwinkle for Nova's inspection. Chunks of the thick ground cover surrounded him. At Dee's bidding, Leroy and Bear had lifted the periwinkle from a bed at the back of her cheery Arts and Crafts–style home first thing this morning. Like many of Green Harmony's recent clients, the retired schoolteacher had devised an additional landscaping project sure to keep a traumatized child busy.

During the last month, Nova had sat through interviews with the local PD and the FBI as they searched for clues to Egan's whereabouts. Imani, who'd apologized repeatedly for their falling-out that day in Chardon Square, accompanied her each time to encourage her not to lose hope. Nova had stopped reading the *Plain Dealer*, after finding Bella's photo splashed across the front page. She avoided the nightly local and national news with their depressing updates on the Ohio girl kidnapped by her father.

With the news traveling far and wide, people she hardly knew stopped her in the grocery store to offer encouragement. Notes from Chardon residents she'd never met appeared in her mailbox. Toys for Henry were left on the front porch, with sweet cards penned by children from Longfellow Elementary. Last week, when they'd visited the library together in search of adventure books to keep his mind occupied, a librarian had taken them both into her arms and promptly burst into tears.

Having so many people rooting for you *was* a blessing. But it didn't keep the worry at bay. Too often, Nova roamed the house past midnight, unable to sleep. On the nights when Henry joined her, they sat together in gloomy silence drinking cups of hot chocolate.

Nova stepped on the shovel to leave it standing in the bed. She sauntered over.

Crouching before Henry, she surveyed his handiwork. Three heavily leaved stems of periwinkle were wound together by the longest stem. Too loosely—the plug of ground cover would fall apart before Leroy replanted it in the new bed he was preparing.

"Pull the stems together tighter so the plug doesn't fall apart." To demonstrate, she rewound the longest stem around the others, tucking in the end. "Don't worry about breaking the stems. They're stronger than you think."

"Like you," Henry murmured. With a bashful glance, he pared back the remark. "You do all right . . . for a girl."

"You're doing all right too."

The compliment—like his need to rarely let her out of his sight—was new. During the first week after Egan took Bella, they'd both wandered the house in a fugue of despair. Hardly eating, rarely sleeping. Jonathon, who'd thankfully suffered only a minor concussion, came over daily; sometimes Denise and Charlotte accompanied him. Often they found Nova's parents or Imani cooking meals in the kitchen or straightening the house while Henry stayed in his bedroom and Nova floated from room to room, mired in grief.

On the following Monday, Nova decided to return to work. She wasn't doing Henry any favors, allowing them both to sink into depression. The normalcy of a daily routine wouldn't lessen the sorrow—a balm didn't exist to soften the pain of losing a child. Keeping active would, however, stop them from worrying about Bella morning, noon, and night.

Henry refused to return to summer camp. The decision was understandable, and Nova gave him two options: stay with a babysitter, or tag along while she worked.

He'd quickly chosen the latter.

Dee McDooney stepped out her front door. The large silver tray she held caught glints of the July sunlight.

"Henry, are you hungry?" Dee had spread a crisp doily across the tray, as if for a holiday meal. On top of the linen, a variety of sandwiches were neatly cut on the diagonal beside a mound of carrot sticks and rounds of cucumber. Cinnamon-scented oatmeal cookies surrounded the tasty offerings. "It's almost lunchtime. You must be famished."

"I'm okay." Henry shrugged, his attention fixed on the periwinkle in his hands. "I'm not really hungry."

"Nonsense. You're a growing boy. You need a hearty lunch. Which do you prefer—roast beef and cheddar or chicken salad? I made them both, just for you. I baked the cookies yesterday, but they're still fresh."

He lowered his head, a subtle dismissal. Nova lifted her palms in apology.

"Thanks for going to the trouble," she said. "It's kind of you. Maybe he'll want something later."

Dee ran an assessing gaze down Nova. "From the looks of it, you've both been skipping meals. How much weight have you lost?"

"I didn't realize I'd lost any."

"Well, you have. Too much, in fact. Stand sideways, and you'll practically disappear."

Nova plucked at her shirt. Was she losing weight? She ran a thumb beneath the waistline of her jeans. They *did* feel loose. They were practically swimming around her waist. Henry wasn't faring any better: the fullness he'd gained on his face during May was melting away. Why hadn't she noticed?

Dee harrumphed with mild disapproval. Prior to retirement, she'd taught junior high social studies to half the residents in Chardon—Nova, Imani, and Bear included. She wasn't easily put off.

"Bear!" she shouted. "Get over here."

The command made Bear jump. Throwing down his shovel, he jogged over.

She thrust the tray into his hands. "Nova, sit down with Henry. You'll have lunch together." From her pocket, she plucked out two napkins. "Roast beef? Chicken salad? No one cares which? Fine—roast beef it is."

Dee produced more napkins, which she filled with carrot sticks, cucumbers, and four oatmeal cookies. Nova murmured her thanks when the food was lowered into her palms.

Bear gazed longingly at the tray. "Can I have the rest?"

It was enough food for an army—or a hungry young man just shy of 230 pounds.

"No." Dee patted his arm. "You'll share the rest with Leroy. But first, come inside. I'd like you to carry out glasses of milk to Nova and Henry."

"Can I have milk too?"

"Yes, yes. There's enough for everyone."

They walked off. In tandem, Nova and Henry picked up half a sandwich from their napkins.

Henry eyed the roast beef with mild interest. "Why is everyone . . . I don't remember the word."

"Coddling us?"

"That's it."

"Well, they know we're hurting. They're just trying to help."

"It doesn't make me feel any better."

Me either. "Maybe it will, in time."

Tearing off a chunk of crust, Henry tossed it to the ground. "When will we get Bella back?"

Nova's heart jumped painfully. *When will we*, not *will we get Bella back*. A tiny display of hope, a glimmer. Enough for her to grab hold of. Which she did, as she pressed a hand against her breastbone.

Henry set the sandwich aside. "Are you okay? You look funny all of a sudden."

The remark hardly registered. What *did* make an impact: he'd been about to eat. Concern over her welfare had derailed the action.

Children weren't supposed to keep watch over the adults they cared about. Nor awaken to the sound of hoarse sobbing, or wander the house until daybreak. They *were* supposed to drain the hot water tank when holed up in the bathroom, grooming to impress a summer crush. A boy like Henry should relish poop jokes even though his awful-smelling farts put family members off their food. Soon enough, life promised to stuff his head full of algebra, thoughts of sex, and team sports—the sports hopefully keeping his mind off the sex. He should climb trees for the sheer thrill of testing his young, strong body, and with no desire to take aim at the squirrels. He should laugh more often than he cried.

I want to be his mother. I should act like it.

The smile Nova donned actually felt nice. Her first in weeks. It nearly faded when guilt nudged her battered heart. With all the activity surrounding Bella's disappearance, she'd put off an important conversation with Henry for too long. She resolved to stop stalling, and talk to him once they finished the job.

"I'm good." She bit into her sandwich with relish. "Not bad. This is one tasty roast beef." Bear returned and handed them each a glass of milk. After he walked away, Nova nodded at Henry's lap. "How's yours, kiddo?"

Henry picked up his sandwich, took a small bite. "Not bad."

"Jeez, I love Dee. She put mayo on mine. I'll bet it's homemade."

"What's the difference from the store-bought kind?" Henry took another bite. His eyes lit up. "Wait. I can tell the difference. Creamier."

"Good, eh?"

"Yeah."

In short order, they finished off the rest of the food. Sated, Henry sank back against the tree trunk. He let loose a roaring belch. A real charmer.

Bear and Leroy, seated on the front steps with the silver tray between them, both laughed.

The approval lit Henry's eyes with delight. "Want to hear another?" he asked.

Chapter 35

NOVA

During the afternoon, they landscaped Dee's front beds while sampling more treats: Rice Krispies squares at two o'clock, and bags of peanuts not long before the last rhododendron was planted, mulched, and watered. Dee insisted on adding a generous tip to Green Harmony's fee. Once she returned inside the house, Nova let Bear and Leroy split the extra cash.

"My parents are coming over," she told Henry on the drive home. "My dad is grilling steaks tonight."

Henry peeled his dirty T-shirt up his chest. "Why can't we skip dinner like we usually do?" He studied his slightly rounded belly.

She steered the truck onto Cherry Street. "Because it's not healthy." They'd fallen into a bad habit of throwing out most of the food lovingly prepared for them. "We aren't doing your sister any favors by not taking care of ourselves. We need to be strong for when she gets back."

"Where do you think she is now?"

The question haunted Nova daily. "I don't know." The FBI had expanded the search nationwide, but they'd received no good leads. "Maybe we'll hear something soon. We have to stay positive, right?"

She'd meant to strike a cheery note, but Henry caught the strain in her voice. Turning away, he absently blew on the passenger-side window. He drew squiggly lines through the foggy glass.

"It's my fault, Nova." A sob broke from his throat. "I helped Pa take Bella."

They neared a drugstore as he started to cry, and Nova pulled into the parking lot. Henry still didn't welcome much in the way of physical affection, and so she waited until he mustered the courage to look at her.

"You're not responsible. Egan is a grown man," she told him, skipping the phrase *your father*. He wasn't Henry's father—not anymore. "Don't you remember what I told you? The police found he'd closed his bank accounts the day *before* he took Bella. Egan had planned the whole thing. If you hadn't come to me when he broke into the backyard, he would've taken you too. I'm grateful he didn't."

"You don't understand. I gave him a Green Harmony brochure. Right after we started living with you. And I showed him Bella's magic picture. He was really angry when he found out it was you. Like you were plotting to take us from him all along."

The confession startled her. Egan *had* known she was fostering his kids—but not from Bear. He'd learned of the arrangement from Henry. With a warped sort of logic, Egan had presumed Rosie's daughter was scheming to take the kids away. *His* daughter, although he'd clearly felt no connection to Nova.

Which suited her fine. She doubted she'd ever fully accept her blood tie to Egan Croy.

"Henry, listen to me. A child is never responsible for a grown-up's actions. You did what you had to do to survive. You were scared of Egan."

"I'm still scared of him."

"I know." *Me too. I'm scared he'll hurt Bella.* Dismissing the thought, Nova forced herself back on track. "When you first came to live with me, you constantly talked about how you worried about catching hell from Egan. I'm sure you were scared he'd come at any moment to take you away. You didn't trust me, or Imani, or anyone else to keep you safe."

"I didn't."

Emotion rolled through her, too quickly to suppress. "I understand the reasons, Henry." Tears dampened her eyes, but she brushed them away. "You remembered what happened in Indiana. When social services put you, Bella, and Glory in the hotel room in Muncie. You had good reason to fear what Egan might do this time."

Henry blinked, drew back. "You know about Indiana?"

"Oh, sweetheart. I know lots of things about your family history. We'll talk about it someday. Whenever you're ready."

Henry swallowed. With a nod, he lowered his eyes.

Imani had suggested scheduling visits with a child psychologist to help him process the trauma he'd endured. And he plainly carried too much guilt. When Nova had broached the subject last week, he'd immediately shut her down. She'd try again soon to sway him.

For now, there was a more important issue to discuss. Reaching across the car seat, she rested her hand on his shoulder.

When his eyes lifted, she said, "Since we're baring our souls . . . there's something I have to tell you too. I shouldn't have waited this long to bring it up."

He sighed. "What's that?"

"It's about Bella's magic picture."

"The one of you and Pa's girlfriend?"

"She wasn't just his girlfriend, Henry. They had a child together . . . me."

"You were their kid?" His features went slack.

"That's right. I'm Egan's firstborn," she supplied, unsure if Henry understood the implication. He looked shell-shocked. "Do you get it? Egan Croy has three children." Nerves made her grin suddenly. "That we know of."

"Three kids."

"Right."

"You're my sister?"

"Technically your half sister, but it's all the same. We're sibs. You, me, and Bella."

"Does Bella know?"

"I'll tell her when she gets home. Scratch that. Let's tell her together. We'll make it a celebration."

Henry rubbed his eyes. Too overcome for words, he turned away and looked out the window. His shoulders began to heave with the soft, little sobs he tried to swallow down.

"Henry, sweetheart . . . it's okay."

Scooting closer, she rested her hand on his back. She noticed the hair growing past his ears. When had she last taken him to the salon for a trim? She had no idea.

Nova flicked at the strands. "You need a haircut, buddy."

"Do not," he croaked.

"Fine. You don't. When we get home, I'll braid it for you."

From over his shoulder, he attempted a smile. "Like I'd let you."

Swiveling around, he buried his face against her shoulder.

Chapter 36

Bella

The days blurred one into the next.

Curled against the passenger-side door, Bella dragged her eyes open to look out the window. The darkened highway flew by, the empty miles lit briefly as they passed a small town. Pa avoided big cities, and he only drove at night.

Bella dared a glance at him. Behind the wheel, he sipped the large coffee he'd bought in a place called Branson. She guessed a lot of hours had passed since then; the coffee smelled bitter and cold. After he put it down, he smoothed his palm across his new beard and mustache. He stared at the road like it was his enemy.

Last week, in a place called Bigelow, they'd spent the night in a musty motel, where Pa used a smelly liquid to turn his hair black. She hardly recognized him at all.

Bella hardly recognized herself either. The day after Pa took her from Nova, he'd cut her hair short and made her wear overalls that were too big. "You're Ben now," he'd told her. She'd bitten at her lips until she'd tasted blood to stop herself from arguing with him.

He noticed she was awake.

She asked, "Which one is this?"

"Tennessee."

Silently, Bella added the name to her list. Kentucky, Illinois, Missouri, Tennessee. She searched her drowsy thoughts for the place with the funny name. At last, she dredged it up. Arkansas.

"Are we staying in the Tennessee place?"

"Only to crash for the day. There are lots of state parks."

Which meant they'd sleep in the truck. They'd wash up as best they could in a public restroom. Lately, they only stayed in motels every now and then. On campgrounds, Bella refused to enter the men's room. Pa always went inside the one for ladies and girls first, to check that the place was empty. Then he'd wait outside while she used the toilet and washed up. He didn't trust her at all. He knew she wanted to run back to Nova more than anything in the world.

Find me, Nova. I'm your baby girl now. Look for me real hard.

She dared another glance. "Where are we going next?"

"Georgia. There are lots of places I can work. Small towns and such. Places where people mind their own business."

Pa only worked for cash, and they never stayed anywhere for more than a day. He'd find carpentry jobs or help paint a barn or lug bags of feed. If nothing turned up, they drove the dusty streets until he found a diner with a pretty waitress inside. He'd flirt with her while paying the bill, then swipe the tip jar when she walked away.

"I'd like to see the ocean." Pa slowed down to peer at a sign flying past. "Never been to one. There's a beach in Savannah. Want to see the ocean, Ben?"

Ben. Bella hated the boy name. She imagined setting loose the bees in her tummy until they stung Pa a thousand times.

"There's a lake in Ohio," she said. "I've seen it. There's a beach and everything."

The remark put anger all over his face. "What did I tell you? Forget about Ohio."

"I miss Henry." She knew better than to mention how much she missed Nova.

"Forget about him. He's gone now." Pa gripped the steering wheel. "Shut up and go back to sleep. You're getting on my nerves."

Obeying, Bella closed her eyes and pretended to sleep. Nova, please find me. Please, please, please, Mama.

Rubbing small circles across her chest, she drew up a few special memories. Splashing in the tub's bubbly water while Nova washed her hair. Opening the presents Helen and Finch had bought for her and Henry. Climbing onto Nova's lap and holding on tight. Bella didn't have the magic picture anymore, but she knew it didn't matter—she could make her own magic if she breathed enough hope into her thoughts and wished with all her might.

Beneath her slowly moving fingers, she felt her heart beat, thump, thump, thump, a sweet music sure to carry her wish all the way home.

Chapter 37

NOVA

Inside the house, Jonathon and Imani bustled around the kitchen. Like everyone else in Nova's immediate circle, they now let themselves in. Jonathon had gone with Helen to a hardware store weeks ago to make duplicate keys.

"Who's hungry?" Jonathon tossed a handful of red peppers into the sizzling pan.

"Not me." Henry clomped mud across the floor, noticed the trail, and tugged off his tennis shoes.

Nova, who'd had the sense to leave her muddy boots outside, went to the stove. "Smells yummy," she said, after Jonathon gave her a kiss. "Do you mind if we hold off dinner? We hit calorie overload on the job. Most of my clients are still plying us with food."

"How long do you need?"

"Ten years," Henry said. He poked at his belly. "I'm ready to burst."

When he finished cataloging everything he'd consumed today, Imani nodded toward the cheesecake on the counter. "FYI, I spent half of my day off making the best cheesecake of my life."

"That's not saying much," Nova teased. "You're a lousy cook."

"Not today. I threw out the first two attempts. This is the third, and it's fabulous." She pointed to the small indentation where someone had scooped out a sample. "Hubby didn't grade my effort on a curve. Uri assured me it's perfect."

Imani's husband *was* a first-rate cook.

Nova sampled the dessert. "Wow. This *is* good. I'll have some now."

Jonathon tossed cashews into the pan, frowned. "I thought you hit calorie overload on the job."

"There's always room for cheesecake."

"What about dinner? FYI, *I'm* starving."

"Then eat. We'll keep you company. Me, Henry, and Imani's fabulous cheesecake." Nova served herself a generous slice.

Imani picked up her purse. "Well, I'm going." She hesitated. "Do you need anything before I leave?"

"Yes," Nova said between mouthfuls. "I need you to stop doing my laundry. You're doing a great job, but I'll take it from here. Who knew you ironed sheets?"

"I like to iron. I know . . . weird. I find it calming. You should try it."

"No, thanks. I wasn't even aware I owned an iron."

"You didn't. I bought one for you."

Imani had also replaced Nova's discount bath gel with a luxurious brand and dropped too much cash on flowers, which she placed weekly in each bedroom—including Bella's—and on the kitchen table. As if the cheery blooms would dull the grief permeating the house.

They didn't, but Nova appreciated the gesture. "Anyway, you have enough to juggle without loading on my chores." She'd been relying too heavily on her best friend. On everyone, in fact. "I'll take care of the laundry from here on out."

"Are you sure?" Imani said with ill-concealed relief.

"I'm sure." Nova hugged her. "I love you."

"I love you too."

"See you soon, Henry." From the doorway, Imani smiled at him. "The offer stands. Anytime you want to come over to play with Maya, just let me know. I'll pick you up or Uri will. You don't have to spend every waking minute watching Nova dig in the dirt."

"I like helping her . . . but thanks for the offer." Henry drummed nervous fingers on the table. "Can you wait a sec?"

Something in his tone alerted them all to the seriousness of the query. Jonathon slid the pan from the burner. Nova lowered her cheese-cake to the counter.

Retracing her steps, Imani said, "Sure. What do you need?"

Henry went to the desk in the corner of the kitchen and slid out the large, official-looking envelope. Nova stifled a gasp. Since when had the kid been snooping around in her stuff? She'd tucked the envelope beneath Green Harmony's payroll register to ensure he didn't see it. Imani had brought the packet over weeks ago.

Naturally Henry—a stealthy child—had riffled through the contents.

Returning to the table, he shook open the envelope. The adoption paperwork dropped out. The eighteen single-spaced pages requested everything from Nova's current medical history to the amount of money in her checking and savings accounts, down to the penny.

Henry thumped his fingers on the questionnaire's first page. "When can we start filling this out? I mean, does it matter when we do?"

"It's up to you." Imani took a seat beside him. "Nova wants to adopt you. She's been waiting to discuss this because she wasn't sure if you're ready to talk about it. With everything going on with Bella, she thought it best to wait. Are you okay if she starts the process?"

At the counter, Jonathon gave Nova a pointed look. Grinning, he nudged her toward the table. *Get over there.*

She floated to the table. Weightless, expectant—she sat down on Henry's other side.

"It's your call," she told him. "No pressure. If you want to wait, we wait. If you want to get started, let's go for it."

"What about Bella?"

"What do you mean?"

"I'm the only kid listed." He picked up the document stating he was now a ward of the state. "There's nothing here about Bella."

"I'll also adopt her once she's found."

The reassurance took some of the strain from his features. "What happens to my name?"

"You'll become Henry Doubeck," she said with mounting eagerness. "You'll be my son."

"Even though you're my sister?" When Imani's and Jonathon's mouths dropped open, Henry's features gained a surprising maturity. "Get it together," he told them, chuckling. "What's the big deal? Nova told me yesterday."

Imani glanced at her. "Took you long enough. As far as I'm concerned, you should've let him in on the big secret weeks ago."

"You're telling me," Henry groused. But only mildly: he looked to Nova with pleasure. "She's my half sister. That's how it works. We have the same dad."

Overwhelmed, Nova smiled.

But Henry's mesmerizing thought experiment wasn't finished. He exchanged a thoroughly masculine glance with Jonathon, who was wisely keeping his distance, leaning against the counter with his arms and his ankles crossed, and with the faintest hint of amusement on his features.

"What happens," he asked Jonathon, "if you marry Nova someday? Do I have to change my name again?"

The dreaded *have to*. Nova sank back in her chair.

Jonathon didn't miss a beat.

"Well, sport, if I get down on bended knee someday and Nova accepts, there's an option we can all consider. What are your thoughts on hyphenating our last names?"

"What's that?"

"We all become Doubeck-Holly. You, me, Nova, and Bella."

Mulling this over, Henry crossed his legs. He rubbed his chin. It was a fine imitation of an adult post until his lower lip wobbled.

Taking a deep breath, he planted his gaze back on Jonathon. "Before then—I mean, even if that *never* happens—will you help us find Bella? You've got lots of money, right? People say the Hollys are rich." He cast a look so rife with desperation, it carved a fissure in Jonathon's composure, rendering his eyes damp. "You can hire a private detective to help with the search like they do on TV. Those guys always find the missing person. You can even hire two."

"I've hired five, son. One each in Indiana, Kentucky, West Virginia, and Pennsylvania. The last one is here, in Ohio. If the authorities don't find your sister, they will."

"Good."

A hush descended. After a moment, Nova came to her feet. From her desk she fetched a pen.

When she returned to Henry's side, she gave him a brief hug. It was stiff, awkward; despite the spontaneous affection they'd shared in the car yesterday, Henry was back to his old tricks. He seemed unsure of how to respond to her second attempt at conveying her love.

In time, he'd learn.

Nova reached for the adoption paperwork. "Let's get started," she said.

Chapter 38

BELLA

Bella held up the swimsuit for Pa's inspection.

She'd found it at the back of the store, on a table with a sign reading **SALE ITEMS**. *Yellow goldfish swam across the bright-pink fabric. There were tiny blue starfish, too, floating in pretty curves across the one-piece swimsuit.*

Pa smiled at the lady behind the cash register with the big spangly earrings. He'd already bought himself swim trunks and a new T-shirt, and had been happy to flirt while Bella looked around. The lady nodded when he murmured an apology. He nudged Bella toward the back of the store.

"What are you, stupid all of a sudden?" he whispered. He dug through the sale table, selecting a boy's T-shirt and shorts. "You'll wear this to the beach. And don't talk to anyone while we're there." He thrust a tin pail and a digging claw into her arms. "You can build sandcastles or something until I come get you."

Bella did as she was told, finding a spot among the many children playing near the surf. Waves crashed before her, a heavy, unrelenting noise. She ached all over inside, and she knew her heart was breaking. Did a heart break in two? Or did it crumble, bit by bit, like the lumpy piles of sand she arranged before the ocean carried them away?

She didn't want to cry—tears only made Pa mad—so she pretended Nova sat on a beach towel nearby, keeping an eye on her like a good mama.

Henry was farther down near the surf, tossing a ball with the boy who'd come to Headlands Beach that day. Any minute now, Nova would tire of sunbathing and come over. They'd build a sandcastle together.

There were lots of curvy ladies on the beach, flung out on their towels and smelling like coconut. Pa roamed through them. He reminded Bella of the wolf painted on his arm—he was looking for something tasty. He hadn't been out having fun since they'd left Ohio, and now he'd bought a beer at a stand near one of the hotels. Swigging it down, he paused before a lady suntanning alone. She was older than his usual dates, and tanned darker than a biscuit left in the oven too long.

They talked and laughed and drank beers Pa fetched from the stand while the sun bit at Bella's skin. Many of the families with little kids were already gone, leaving mostly teenagers running around or sitting together in big groups. A few surfers still rode the waves; farther out on the blue-gray waters, a sailboat drifted past.

Bella's tummy growled. Her mouth felt like sandpaper. She'd finished the Coke hours ago, along with the burger Pa had bought for her. Closing her eyes, she imagined scooting out her chair in Nova's kitchen and sitting down on the cool wood to wait for dinner to come out of the oven.

At last, Pa helped roll up the lady's beach towel. Like a real gentleman, he picked up her canvas bag and helped her steer it over her shoulder. Savannah was written on the side of the bag in swirly green letters.

As they approached, Bella caught snatches of their conversation.

"My place is close," the lady said. "Ten minutes from here."

"Want me to drive?"

She gave a twittering laugh. "You'll have to, honey. I walked to the beach. Might be best if we save our energy."

They were trading silly glances when Pa drew her to a stop. "Caroline, I'd like you to meet my son, Ben. He'll be no trouble at all. Ben, say hello to Caroline."

"Hello."

The lady made a sourpuss face. "You sure don't look like a boy. Aren't you a girl?"

Bella shrugged.

"You got a babysitter for the kid?" she asked Pa. "She's not coming with us."

When the lady dropped a hand to her hip, Pa looked like he'd forgotten how to use plain English. His jaw worked, but nothing came out of his mouth.

The lady spit out a laugh.

"Better luck next time," she said, walking away.

Chapter 39

NOVA

Monday morning. It was time to get up.

No, thanks. Nova buried her face in the pillow. Today they were starting a job in Chesterland, a big install for a new home. *Give the work to someone else.* She toyed with the idea of pulling the covers over her head and sleeping until next weekend. Or later. *I'll get up when the authorities bring Bella home.*

A long, weary exhale—not hers—broke the silence. She sat up.

Seated on the opposite side of the bed, Henry twirled the wheels of the Matchbox car in his fist. Throwing off the blanket, she swung her feet to the floor. Sunlight painted the floor in golden hues.

She walked around the foot of the bed and sat down beside Henry. "How long have you been waiting for me to get up?"

"Oh, forever."

"That long?"

"You snore, Nova. Like a grizzly bear or something."

"I do not."

"You sure do. And I mean *loud.*"

Nova regarded her newly painted toes. "Blame Denise's spa day. I've never slept so hard." Yesterday Jonathon's mother had insisted on taking her out for an afternoon of relaxation. She'd also received a trim of her long tresses and the first massage of her life. "I don't even remember falling asleep last night."

"I'm glad you had fun."

"Did you have fun yesterday riding go-karts?" After Jonathon dropped him off last night, he'd been moody and quiet. He'd promptly gone to bed. "Me and Imani used to ride them in high school. There was a place in Mentor back then."

"It was okay," Henry told her, and he sounded blue. Another hard day ahead—for both of them. "I'm glad we're not going to work."

"*I* have to go—you're off the hook. Want me to call Imani? You can spend the day hanging out with Maya. Or I'll call my parents. They won't mind if you hang out there."

"No can do." Henry got to his feet. "The surprise will be here any minute."

"What surprise?"

The doorbell rang.

Pulling on a robe, Nova went to answer it. Leroy stood on the front porch; at the back of his truck, parked in the drive, Bear heaved out a four-foot Japanese maple.

"What's going on?" She watched Bear disappear around the side of the house.

"You're taking the week off," Leroy told her. "Helen's orders. Or Denise's. They're both so bossy, I can't remember who decided you need the whole week." Wiping his brow, he gestured vaguely toward the back of the house. "We've moved all the plant stock, along with bags of mulch and bedding soil. It'll keep you busy."

"Guess again. We're supposed to be at the job in Chesterland soon."

"Bear and I will take care of it."

"Without me?"

Leroy grinned. "You've taught us well, Nova. We can handle the job. If we run into problems, you're a phone call away."

She was touched by the offer. Then stunned when they went into the backyard together. Shrubs and flats of periwinkle shared space on top of the picnic table. Aside from the Japanese maple Bear was placing carefully on the patio, she spied two lilac bushes, a flowering butterfly bush, six boxwood shrubs, and more pots of herbs than she could count. Everything, it seemed, on her wish list.

Which Helen knew, since Nova had often talked about how she'd finish landscaping her property once she'd saved enough cash for the project.

"Who paid for all of this?" she asked no one in particular.

Bear leaned against the picnic table. "Group effort," he said. "Your parents and Mrs. Holly pitched in. Jonathon paid the lion's share."

It was an incredibly generous gift. *Exactly what I need.*

Savoring the joy flowing through her, Nova pressed a hand to her heart. She knew the emotion would soon fade. The sadness was sure to come roaring back, like it did countless times every day. Did it matter? At least she'd spend the week toiling beside Henry, transforming the property with all the plant stock she'd dreamed about buying someday.

She couldn't wait to get started.

Leroy glanced at his watch. "We'd better get going."

"You're sure you'll be okay at the Chesterland job?"

"We've got this, Nova. We'll call if we run into problems."

Bear gave her the thumbs-up. "Don't work too hard. You've got all week."

"I'll pace myself," she promised, giving them each a hug. "Thanks for the holding down the fort while I goof off. You guys are the best."

After she ate a quick breakfast with Henry, they donned their grungiest clothes. Back outside, she did a quick inventory of the plants. "Should we start in the front or the back, Henry? Makes no difference to me."

He pointed at the Japanese maple. "Let's plant the tree first. It's bigger than everything else. Might as well get the worst job out of the way."

Nova handed over a shovel. "Front yard it is."

They worked all day, stopping only for meals and quick rest breaks. All the weeks accompanying her on jobs were putting muscles on

Henry's arms and legs. From the looks of it, he'd also grown another inch since early summer. With all the worry over Bella, she'd hardly noticed.

When they surrendered for the day, exhausted and pleased with how much they'd tackled, they each showered before she made burgers and fries. She called her parents and Denise, thanking them for the gift. Nova saved the call to Jonathon for last. They didn't talk long—Henry found an action flick on TV, which they watched until midnight.

Nova fell into a deep, dreamless sleep. Near dawn, the telephone's shrill ringing jogged her awake.

Groggy, she snatched up the receiver. "Hello?"

"Is this Nova Doubeck?" A gravelly woman's voice.

"Speaking."

Silence bloomed on the other end. The woman coughed.

Nova turned on the lamp. "Who is this?" The clock read five fifteen in the very early a.m.

"Erin Lopez."

"Who?"

"I'm Egan's sister."

The announcement brought Nova to full wakefulness. "How do I know this isn't a crank call?" A cruel one, she decided. She was about to hang up when the woman put a challenge in her voice.

"You want proof? Ask me something."

"What was your father's name?"

"Dale," the woman supplied without hesitation.

"Where did he—"

"At Holly's Mill, as a mechanic. He worked there when your boyfriend's parents ran the place." A long silence, then the woman added, "I know who you are, Nova. I read about Bella in the papers. More than a month ago . . . there was an article with a picture of you. I knew right away you're Rosie's child, and my brother's. I've been meaning to call, but I wasn't sure if I should. If you'd want to hear from me."

The reasonable explanation lowered Nova's guard. No, she wouldn't have taken kindly to a call from one of Egan's relatives. *She's my relative too—my aunt.* She felt dizzy beneath the discovery.

She scraped the hair from her brow. "Why are you calling now?"

"You'll be wanting to come right over." Erin rasped out her address. "I've got something that belongs to you."

Chapter 40

Nova

Not something. Some*one*.

In record time, Nova and Henry pulled on their clothes. They sprinted from the house and jumped into the truck. Backing out of the driveway, Nova barely missed swiping the mailbox.

Henry surveyed the darkened street. "Lights!" he barked.

Nova turned them on. "Right." She sped up.

"How far away is Hambden?"

"Not far. Twenty minutes." From her pocket she pulled out the address she'd jotted down.

The truck swerved, pinging off the curb.

"Watch where you're going!" Henry gripped the passenger-side armrest. "Want me to drive?"

"You don't know how."

"Get it together or I'll learn. And I mean fast."

Nova eased off the accelerator, slowing down to an acceptable speed. She made herself breathe.

She regretted hanging up on Erin Lopez while she was bumbling through an explanation in her gravelly voice. Something about a late-night trip. Meeting at a rest stop on the highway. An argument with the brother she hadn't seen since the funeral. *Their mother's funeral? Or their father's?* Nova couldn't recall as she crossed Chardon Square with her thoughts careening one into the next.

Bella is safe.

The house in Hambden Township lay deep at the end of a bumpy, unlit driveway. Overgrown limbs on vine-covered trees scraped the sides of the truck. The faded white dwelling, in desperate need of fresh paint, seemed the perfect home for a hermit. Dandelions flourished in what must've once been the lawn. A few shingles were missing from the roof.

Erin appeared on the front stoop. She lifted a hesitant palm in greeting. She wore baggy jeans and a boxy, mannish shirt. She looked older than a woman in her midforties, with streaks of white in her cropped, dark-brown hair.

Nova climbed out of her truck. She slid a glance to Henry, his expression now wary as he hurried to her side. He avoided looking at Erin.

She's his aunt . . . does he recognize her? On the phone, before Nova had rudely hung up, she'd gathered enough to surmise there was no love lost between Erin and Egan. Had the children never met her, then?

"Mrs. Lopez?" Lightheaded, she climbed the steps with Henry trailing close behind.

"Call me Erin, please." She caught Nova peeking over her shoulder and into the house. "It's just me," she added. "I lost my husband in '67—Vietnam."

Stepping aside, she allowed them to enter. A faded couch and a radio perched on an old crate took up most of the space in the tiny living room. No TV—*but then, a hermit wouldn't have one.* On a side table, Nova spied an arrangement of photographs and a mason jar filled with musk roses. The flowers' rich, spicy fragrance seemed out of place in the dreary house.

She peered toward the kitchen. "Where's Bella?" She yearned to see her.

"Still asleep." Erin gestured toward the hallway. "Did her best to stay awake the whole drive back. We were outside Medina when she conked out."

Henry frowned. "Is she all right?"

"She's fine. Out like a light in my bedroom."

"I didn't catch everything you told me on the phone," Nova admitted. "Where did you pick her up?"

"A rest stop in Florence, Kentucky. Egan wouldn't cross the Ohio state line." Erin rubbed her bloodshot eyes. "I don't mind telling you, making a ten-hour round trip sure wore me out."

She *did* look exhausted. "You just got back?" Nova studied her with concern.

"A few minutes before I called you. Figured you'd want to get Bella right away."

"Thank you."

Erin regarded her for a long moment. The lines around her mouth deepened. Henry moved off, to study the photographs, and she appeared grateful for the chance to speak with Nova privately.

She lowered her voice. "Me and Egan . . . we don't talk much. Hardly ever. Never did get along. Glory called sometimes, to see how I'm doing. Mostly she'd get in touch when my brother wasn't around." Pausing, Erin pressed a palm to her forehead. Her eyes skated away. "I sure didn't expect to hear from him out of the blue, demanding I come get Bella."

"Did you know he'd . . ." Nova's voice broke, halting the words *kidnapped her.*

"Like I tried to tell you on the phone, I'd seen the articles in the *Plain Dealer.* I knew the authorities were looking for Egan weeks ago, and that the kids had been in foster care again. It happened once before, you know. But I didn't read those articles too close. I thought everything had settled down, and the kids were back with Glory—but Egan was fighting with her again. That he'd gone and done something stupid by driving off with their youngest to get her upset. Mean like a snake, my brother. No different than our father, may he rot in hell. I figured Egan would tell me to take Bella home, to Columbus—and he did just that, lying straight through his teeth."

"You got Bella, thinking you were going to Columbus?" It occurred to her that Erin hadn't known about Glory's death.

"She's a smart one, our Bella. She didn't make a peep until we drove off. Then she filled me in on the real deal. The story she told . . . why, it rattled me." Erin's shoulders twitched, but she managed to ward off the grief when she added, "I didn't know we'd lost Glory. I sure didn't know my fool of a brother was still in trouble with the police."

Wrapping up, Erin flexed her fingers. She folded her arms. Strong emotion seemed a nuisance she didn't sanction, and she arranged her features into a scowl. A woman who'd known too much heartache, who knew how to bury the pain deep. It was, Nova realized, something they had in common.

Yet underneath her gruff disposition, Erin hid a strong heart.

In the bedroom, she'd tucked a quilt around the sleeping child. Bella was curled up on her side, her right hand splayed out on the pillow, where a whimsical pattern of bluebirds and daisies cavorted across the pillowcase. On the nightstand, the fresh sprigs of lavender in a porcelain vase sent their calming, woodsy scent across the room.

There was also a glass of milk, still cold, with rivulets of condensation running down the glass. On a plate, carrot sticks were chopped thin, just the way Bella liked them. Her favorite fruit—red grapes—filled a small bowl.

Approaching, Nova cried out. Bella's soft, wispy hair was chopped short. She looked noticeably thinner, her face badly sunburned. Her nails were bitten to the quick. Sinking down on the mattress, Nova pulled back the quilt. On a sob, she scanned the boy's T-shirt and shorts Bella wore. Egan, in his cruelty, had attempted to erase all evidence of the frilly, feminine girl who would soon become Nova's daughter.

The legal hoops hardly mattered. *She's already my daughter.*

An awareness that made the tears increase until she was gasping out great big sobs.

"Nova?" Bella opened drowsy eyes. "Is that you?"

"Yes, sweetheart. Mama's here."

297

"I'm not dreaming?"

"No, you're not. You're safe, I promise." Nova cradled her close. "I'll never let anyone hurt you again."

"I can call you Mama now?"

Nova covered her face with kisses. "Yes." She planted more love on Bella's pink, tender scalp, where the scissors had cut too close. "Yes, yes, yes."

"I was scared."

"Me too, baby girl."

Bella clung to her neck. "I made lots of wishes for you to find me. Did you hear them?"

"Of course I did. I made lots of wishes too. So did Henry and my parents and everyone else. And now you're here, thanks to Erin. She's pretty amazing." She glanced at their aunt, hovering near the base of the bed. "She's the best. We owe her a lot."

"Can she come over for dinner? We'll make her something tasty."

The comment—unexpected, hopeful—signaled a return to normalcy. The dark days were over.

"Absolutely," Nova promised. "We'll make her something really great."

"Can she come over tonight? Erin's real nice. She sang funny songs for me on the way home."

"Sure. If she's not too busy . . . ?"

Erin's back stiffened as her eyes softened. She clasped her hands tightly. "I'd like that," she said. "I'd like that very much."

Hopping down from Nova's lap, Bella raced to her aunt. The loss stung Nova, but only for a moment. Bella, with a child's instinctive comprehension, knew that love wasn't a finite commodity. It multiplied, growing ever stronger as you welcomed more people into your heart.

Bella flung her arms around Erin's waist. "What do you like to eat? Mama has all sorts of good recipes. She'll make anything you want. Just name it!"

Mama. Nova dragged her arm across her leaky eyes.

Blank faced, Henry stood in the doorway. He was clearly unsure of the reception he'd receive from his younger sister. Looking from one child to the other, Nova felt her heart lurch. It seemed the ordeal had increased the age difference between them. While the first hints of puberty were filling Henry out, Bella appeared thinner, younger—more like a six-year-old than a girl past her seventh birthday.

But the air of hesitancy surrounding Henry wasn't shared by his sister. When she stopped yammering to Erin about the best dishes in Nova's repertoire—all of which, she hoped, Erin would like—she noticed her brother.

"Henry!" She flew into his arms. Laughing, he scooped her up. When he set her down, she exclaimed, "I missed you so much!"

"I missed you, too, Bella—a lot."

They went into the living room together, hand in hand. They were still talking nonstop when Nova took Erin aside.

"May I use the phone? I need to call the police and my boyfriend."

"Of course." Erin led her into the kitchen.

Call Jonathon first.

One of the detectives he'd hired worked out of Lexington. During the last months, the PI had blanketed small towns across Kentucky with photos of Egan and Bella.

Egan was in Florence just a few hours ago. Maybe he hasn't left the state. At long last, there was a chance he'd be apprehended.

Nova picked up the phone and dialed.

Chapter 41

November 1982

The couple, dressed for dinner out on this chilly Saturday night, dashed through the pelting snow. The man swiped a layer of white from his hair as he reached for the beveled glass door of the restaurant at Holly's Mill. The door rattled. It was bolted shut. Frowning, the woman noticed the elegantly hand-lettered sign taped to the glass.

CLOSED UNTIL TOMORROW FOR A PRIVATE EVENT.

"That's five," Nova murmured.

Jonathon handed her a glass of champagne. "Stop counting. They'll find somewhere else to eat."

"I feel bad. Charlotte didn't need to close the entire restaurant. We could've used the back dining room. Or held the festivities at my parents' house. They offered."

Grinning, Jonathon nudged the glass toward her lips. "Drink. And stop worrying. Nothing gives my sister more pleasure than throwing a party. She missed her calling. She should've been an event planner." He nodded with satisfaction when Nova took a sip of the bubbly. "Besides, everyone's having a great time."

It was true, Nova realized, surveying the crowd. Her parents, Denise, and two couples she didn't know were chatting before the restaurant's gold leather banquettes. At a table near the wall of glass at the far end of the restaurant, Imani and her husband, Uri, several court clerks, and the Honorable Judge Tammy Cassidy nibbled appetizers while overlooking the historic mill and the meandering waters of the Chagrin River. Bear had arrived with a giggly brunette he couldn't stop staring at; Charlotte and a group of her girlfriends were encouraging Henry to try the chilled shrimp. Bella darted from table to table, demonstrating how nicely she twirled in her charming rose-pink taffeta dress.

Above the mile-long granite bar, where two liveried bartenders served drinks, a banner congratulated the newest members of Nova's family, Bella and Henry Doubeck.

The Hollys had spared no expense for the party. Although Nova estimated she knew less than 50 percent of the guests, it was heartwarming that so many people wished to celebrate the adoption finalization with her and the kids.

Their lives, however, weren't back to normal. Bella often wet the bed. She played with Maya and other friends in her bedroom—newly wallpapered with cheery posies—but insisted on sleeping with Nova. Some nights she awoke from bad dreams about her kidnapping, frantic. At times, after rocking her back to sleep, Nova would close her eyes, exhausted, only to dream of the wolf.

Even with the speed bumps, they were all making progress. Bella loved school, and continued tallying up a bevy of new friends. After an incredibly lucrative year with Green Harmony, Nova had tucked away enough cash to remain a stay-at-home mom until spring. And Henry—growing taller, moody some days but more often sunny—was deep into his first schoolboy crush. Nancy, the girl from summer camp that Bella had called Popcorn, was in his fourth-grade class.

Egan Croy was in a medium-security prison in Marion. He'd pleaded guilty to the crime of kidnapping, a first-degree felony. He was serving a twenty-year sentence.

"Your aunt is trying to get your attention," Jonathon said, drawing Nova from the reverie. He took her hand. "Let's not leave her standing alone."

"I thought Erin was with Henry." She'd arrived just a few minutes ago.

"She was, until Charlotte and her friends carted him off." Jonathon chuckled. "Most kids don't like shrimp. Too weird looking. If your son takes the dare and tries one, Charlotte will push escargot on him next. No way will the kid like snails."

My son. The reference tickled Nova all the way to her toes.

Erin stood beside one of the leather banquettes looking, for all the world, like a wallflower. Clearly her experience with large parties was limited. She wore a dated cotton dress that swam on her slender frame. Her coat was still draped across her arm. To allow her to make a fast exit?

Nova smiled. *Not on my watch.*

"Don't tell me you're leaving." She took Erin's coat and handed it to Jonathon. He walked off to hang it up. "We were just about to sit down and eat. The buffet is in the back room, over there. Let's fill plates and eat together."

"Oh, I don't know." Erin cast nervous eyes across the crowd. "I've only stopped by for a minute."

"No. Please—stay and eat with us. We'll find a quiet corner. You'll enjoy yourself."

"You sure have a lot of friends."

"Actually, I don't. Half of the guests were invited by Jonathon's sister. She's a real social butterfly. I'm more an introvert."

The remark pleased Erin. "Me too." She brushed gentle fingers across Nova's wrist. "Must run in the family."

"I guess it does."

"Well, I've never been to a party this fancy." Erin offered Jonathon a smile as he rejoined them. "I'm nervous."

"Try this." He'd wisely stopped at the bar on his way back. He handed her the tall crystal flute. "It's champagne. It's good."

Erin took a sip. "Not bad."

They found an empty table in the corner, near the wall of glass.

"Why don't I fill plates?" Jonathon looked from Nova to her aunt. "Any preferences?"

Nova smiled. "Surprise us."

Once he left, Erin began fishing around in the pocket of her roomy dress. Nova made a mental note to take her shopping soon. The outfit looked three sizes too big.

A fat white envelope appeared on the table.

Erin pushed it forward. "I thought you and the kids might want these. I scoured high and low, finding them all. With tonight's celebration and all, it seemed like a good time to give them to you."

Breathless, Nova reached for the envelope. She hesitated. There were photos inside.

"Of Glory and the kids," Erin supplied, "and some of me and Rosie. Those took the longest to find." Her voice grew rough with emotion. "You look just like her, Nova. That first day when we met—when you came to my door to get Bella—I nearly passed out."

"I'm sorry I gave you a shock."

"Don't be." Erin sighed. "But it *was* like seeing my big sister risen from the grave. That's what she was like to me, before she moved away with Egan. I wish they'd stuck around . . . I was looking forward to meeting the baby."

She lowered her hand on top of Nova's. Drew in a breath.

"Well, I'm glad I finally did," she added. "You're a good woman. Rosie was too."

Nova heard herself ask, "What was she like?"

"She was funny as hell. The jokes she'd tell made me laugh so hard, I thought I'd pee. She loved McIntosh apples. Her favorite fruit."

Nova dabbed at her eyes. *Mine too.*

Henry, standing nearby, handed the plate of shrimp back to Charlotte before approaching.

He pulled out a chair. "What are you guys talking about?" He noticed the envelope. "What's that?"

"Photos," Erin said. "You probably don't remember the visit—you and Bella were little. It was the only time you came to my house."

"Hey, Bella!" Henry motioned to his sister, who was twirling before a table of Jonathon's employees.

After skipping over, she wiggled onto Nova's lap. "What are we doing?" she asked.

Henry spilled out the photos. They scattered across the table, color pics of Glory and Erin with the kids seated between them, others of Henry and Bella plowing through bowls of spaghetti and running through the overgrown grass before Erin's house. Bella was a toddler and Henry around age four. The kids sorted through the photos eagerly while Erin described the visit from long ago.

In the middle of the trove, an old black-and-white photo peeked out. Nova slid it closer.

She felt Jonathon's hand settle on her shoulder. "Is that Rosie?" he asked.

"With Erin."

"My God. She's just as beautiful as you." Dazzled, Jonathon set the plates aside and sat down beside her. "I wish it were a color photo."

"They were pretty rare in the fifties." Nova traced the smiling faces of two young women hugging each other. "It's strange, knowing I look so much like someone I've never met." She glanced across the room at her parents, her love for them buoying her as she added, "I wish I'd known Rosie. I have a feeling I would've liked her a lot."

Chuckling, Erin shook her head. "Don't look so sad. You would've loved her—she acted a lot like you. No nonsense, but sweet as sugar on the inside. That landscaping company of yours, Green Harmony? Well, you can thank Rosie. She had a green thumb like nobody's business."

Joy embraced Nova. "She did?" It was followed by a deeper emotion as the young woman she'd never known took her rightful place inside Nova's heart.

Welcome, Rosie.

Bella, sifting through the photos, found a close-up of Glory. With a sigh, she gave it a kiss.

"Mama?" She flapped the photo before Nova. "Can we hang this one up when we get home?"

Nova gave her a watery smile. "We'll hang them all up," she promised.

BOOK CLUB QUESTIONS

1. Early in the story, the reader learns that Nova relies on the family photographs hanging in her house to center herself after dreaming about the wolf. Young Bella also finds comfort in a photograph she keeps—her "magic picture." Many of us would agree that photographs are strongly tied to our memories.

   Do you believe the sense of sight provides our strongest link to past memories? Why or why not? How do our other senses evoke memory? For example, does a particular taste or scent recall past events in your life?

2. In chapter 1, the woman living across the street from the Croy family notifies the PD that Bella and Henry are home without adult supervision. Her intervention sets the plot in motion. How do other secondary characters influence the course of events?

3. Nova has resisted learning the details of her early life prior to adoption. She believes the foundational bricks of identity weren't gifted to everyone and wonders, "If you didn't know where your life began—*who* you were, from the very beginning—how could you understand anything about yourself?"

Do you agree with Nova? How do we give children the foundational bricks of identity? Discuss.

4. In chapter 6, Imani reveals her belief that people are capable of change, even when those around them have given up hope.

   Do you agree with her? Is someone more apt to change if the stakes are high, as they are when a parent is at risk of losing custody of a child? What other influences might compel someone to embark on much-needed change?

5. When Imani first learns of Nova's desire to adopt Bella and Henry, she resists the idea in favor of seeking out a more established couple to take in the children. Was Imani wrong to put her duties as a social worker before her friendship with Nova? Why or why not?

6. Children familiar with the foster-adopt system are more likely to consider adopting or providing foster care when they reach adulthood. What do you think accounts for this decision?

If your book club would like to discuss *A Heart Like Home* with the author, please contact her at christine@christinenolfi.com with BOOK CLUB in the subject line. Christine is able to schedule online meetings through Zoom, Skype, or Facebook.

Acknowledgments

The publishing journey is demanding, and I'm grateful to work with so many tireless, dedicated professionals: my agent and trusted friend Pamela Harty of the Knight Agency, Lake Union editorial director Danielle Marshall, the great staff in Author Relations, my incredible developmental editor Krista Stroever, production managers Jen Bentham and Angela Elson, copyeditor Sarah Engel, proofreader Kellie Osborne, and cover designer Amanda Kain. Special thanks to Lake Union editor Erin Adair-Hodges, for her invaluable insights as she patiently read the drafts that would become *A Heart Like Home*.

For helping my books reach a wider audience, many thanks to Crystal Patriarche and the fantastic team at BookSparks; Suzanne Weinstein Leopold and the fun reviewers at Suzy Approved Book Tours; Pulpwood Queen Kathy Murphy; and the many generous book bloggers, reviewers, and bookstagrammers who have sent my publishing career aloft.

And to Barry, for reading every review throughout the years and believing even when I entertained doubts. I love you, always.

About the Author

Photo © 2016 Melissa Miley

Christine Nolfi is the bestselling author of *A Brighter Flame*, a She Reads best book club pick; *The Passing Storm*, which *Publishers Weekly* called "tautly plotted, expertly characterized, and genuinely riveting"; *The Road She Left Behind*, a top book club pick by *Working Mother* and *Parade* magazines; the award-winning Sweet Lake Series: *Sweet Lake*, *The Comfort of Secrets*, and *The Season of Silver Linings*; and other titles. Originally from Ohio, Christine now resides in South Carolina with her husband. For more information, visit christinenolfi.com.